PRAISE FOR *SWEET WATER*

"An unsparing account of 'rich people problems' that goes on forever, like all the best nightmares."

—*Kirkus Reviews*

"[A] nail-biting psychological thriller . . . Reinard knows how to keep readers turning the pages."

—*Publishers Weekly*

"*Sweet Water* is electrically suspenseful, impossible to put down until the last gut punch of a killer ending."

—Luanne Rice, *New York Times* bestselling author

"A remarkable tale of family loyalties and lies set in a fresh new world. Fans of *Defending Jacob*—both the book and the television show—will relish this sinister story of the lengths two parents will go to in order to protect their child."

—J.T. Ellison, *New York Times* bestselling author

"Reinard's domestic thriller *Sweet Water*, a story about betrayal, murder, and dark family secrets, held me riveted as one woman's search for the truth threatens everyone she loves."

—T.R. Ragan, *New York Times* and Amazon Charts bestselling author of the Sawyer Brooks series

"Hypnotic and absorbing, a compulsive page-turner to the very end."

—Minka Kent, *Wall Street Journal* bestselling author

INTO
THE
SOUND

ALSO BY CARA REINARD

INTO THE SOUND

CARA REINARD

THOMAS & MERCER

Published by Thomas & Mercer, Seattle

www.apub.com

Amazon, the Amazon logo, and Thomas & Mercer are trademarks of Amazon.com, Inc., or its affiliates.

ISBN-13: 9781542029742
ISBN-10: 1542029740

Cover design by Laywan Kwan

Printed in the United States of America

This book is dedicated to my father.

The most dangerous of all falsehoods is a slightly distorted truth.

—*Georg Christoph Lichtenberg*

1

HOLLY

She straightened the emergency supplies she'd picked up at the store, adding them to the storm kit—four gallons of distilled water, about a dozen flashlights, batteries in all shapes and sizes, candles, matches, canned goods, one battery-powered NOAA Weather Radio, and of course, the bottle of vodka she stashed under the sink behind the floor cleaner.

There was no way Holly would survive a storm stuck in the house with her husband and two children without it. Mark rarely tolerated her drinking because of her family history, but if the power went out, his nerves would force him to focus on other things besides the slip of clear she'd sneak into her coffee cup.

"Did you make sure they aren't the matches you got last time?" Mark asked. "Those snapped in half as soon as I tried to strike them." Her husband paced the laminate floors made to look like wood. Holly secretly wished their house would flood just a touch from the storm. Not so much that the rainwater reached the stairs, just the floors, so she could buy new—real—hardwood.

"Yes, they're Penleys. The long ones. We only had leftover matches from a restaurant last time, and I think they'd gotten wet." Holly took the new box of matches and slid off the cardboard top so Mark could see the contents. His eyes ignited with the promise of all the fires he could light for days with those matches. Just one more boy in the house she had to placate.

Yes, Otto, you can participate in the Speedway Demolition Derby at sixteen if you're still interested. Fast cars and destruction can all be yours in six short years . . .

Tyler was the easiest one. At seven years old, staying up an extra half hour past bedtime was a thrill.

"A wet matchbook to fight Sandy. That was our first mistake." Mark frowned at the mention of the monster storm that had taken out much of Long Island several years earlier. After reading an article about flooding and electrical shocks, he'd made them unplug everything that wasn't necessary for survival. Fortunately, their town hadn't been decimated like Long Beach. Sayville was a coastal town, but their house was inland. "You know they're calling this one another superstorm."

Mark began the ritualistic process of clicking on and off each flashlight to make sure it still worked.

"Well, at least we're prepared this time." The news made everything sound worse than it was, but it would only give Mark more anxiety if she told him that she'd been following the anticipated surge patterns and they didn't appear to be nearly as large as the last storm's. It was best to say as little as possible when he was in one of his states.

"He only wants to protect your family," her sister said whenever Holly tried to complain about how overbearing Mark could be, and how could Holly *possibly be upset by that*? Vivian's husband was much less attentive, but sometimes Holly thought that was preferable.

An alert sounded on the television with the same warnings that had already been scrolling across the bottom for hours. "Oh, wow," Mark said.

Holly refrained from rolling her eyes and thought about how good that first sip of vodka was going to taste when she could finally drink it. "Did you get dinner? The boys already ate. Grilled chicken and cheesy potatoes?" she offered. Holly moved toward the refrigerator to fix him a plate.

But Mark was standing in the living room, face inches from the TV screen. "No, I don't want to eat now. Let's see what this thing does first. How can you think about food?" he asked.

Logic would have it that he might want to heat up dinner while they still had electricity, but logic didn't live in their house right now.

"Are you still subscribing to that premade-meal company?" Mark asked with his back turned to her. He'd applauded her new meal choices until he'd learned they were someone else's ideas.

"Yes." She rinsed a plate and put it in the dishwasher.

He grumbled, "Because going to the store is such a struggle, we have to pay someone to do it for us?"

"You want healthy meals during the week, that comes at a price."

Before she'd subscribed to the service, Mark had complained about the occasional fast-food runs she'd make after the boys' activities. Holly was beginning to think he just didn't like anything that made her life easier. He had the false impression that she had nothing but free time just because she no longer worked as a journalist. But Holly had never intended her maternity leave to last forever. She was ready to reenter the workforce now that both kids were in school—and this meal-prep service was a first step toward that goal.

"It's funny," Mark said darkly. "My coworkers' wives produce healthy meals without a service."

Holly yanked on the faucet, turning it off, but she held her tongue. It wasn't worth the fight. "Look at all the closures on the TV already," she deflected. The boys charged down the stairs in a tandem of light-saber fervor.

"Take that." Tyler jabbed at his brother's side with the glowing plastic sword. Otto didn't strike back. He only pointed at the TV screen. "No school!" he cheered. "Look."

Holly glimpsed at the chyron again to see that all the area schools had already been canceled. Great. The boys started flying around the house like wild monkeys, hanging off the stairwell railings, making awful sounds.

"Quiet," Mark barked. He reached for the remote to turn up the volume and glared at Holly as if it were her job to silence the children.

"Boys." She tried to shush them, even though she hated how she'd grown up and had always encouraged her sons to express themselves freely. She and Vivian had been raised by psychology professors, and heightened emotions were best expressed in the confines of their writing assignments. Verbal exacerbations were highly discouraged, reserved for emergencies.

Holly could hear her phone vibrating on the kitchen counter. She turned and saw her sister's name flash across the screen. Vivian worked at the library in town, and Holly wondered if she was calling to warn her to stay off the roads. She glanced through the windows, where the wind whipped the trees like streamers in a jet wave. The rain blasted the panes of glass, splatting sideways in the harsh torrent.

Holly answered. "Viv?"

She thought she heard water on the other side—a rushing sound—but then she realized it was her sister, breathing heavily into the phone. "Vivian, what's wrong?"

Mark turned his head her way, a questioning look on his face.

"You have to come get me." Vivian's voice sounded battered, breathless, like she'd been running. Her older sister was always so put together, the definition of the quiet, poised librarian. Maybe the storm had already gotten worse than she knew.

"Where are you?" Holly asked. She'd ask the *why* later.

"Bay Shore."

"What?" That was nowhere near the library. Holly plugged one of her ears, but either the connection was bad or Vivian was standing in a downpour. Holly held her breath to drown out her beating heart.

There was more muffled noise, the sound of her sister trying to speak to her above the noise of the storm. "Come get me, Holly. Bay Shore Marina. I'll explain later. If you make it here in time . . ." There were more rushing sounds.

"Otto. *Stop* and close your mouth," Holly hissed. Her son halted his celebratory school-cancelation dance, mid–Fortnite Floss, and Mark looked at Holly like she was positively terrible. She never talked to her sons like that, but something was wrong with her sister, and she needed to focus. "Bay Shore Marina? In this storm? Vivian, call the cops."

"I had to get away. No police." She sounded desperate. "Holly, please come get me; I need to talk." Vivian gasped. "There's somebody coming—"

The line went dead. "Hello?" Holly's body prickled with chills. She hit "Redial," but the call went straight to voice mail.

She shoved her phone into her pocket. What mess had Vivian gotten herself into that she couldn't call her husband or the police? It didn't make sense, and it was out of character for her sister, an ordered human. Holly grabbed her coat.

"You're not going anywhere." Mark's voice was firm. Anyone else might chalk it up to husbandly concern, but Holly heard the threat threaded in his voice. *You will not go anywhere.*

"Vivian needs me. She's in trouble," Holly said.

"So call the police," Mark said, scowling.

The boys had remained frozen in place from her last outburst, waiting to see what would happen next. Mark stalked from the living room to the kitchen. He picked up her purse off the island. "You can't go out in this storm."

Her car keys were inside the purse. She imagined trying to pry it from his six-foot-three frame without success. Her sister's heavy breathing and her words—*"there's somebody coming"*—were frightening. She didn't have time to delay. "Vivian wouldn't ask me to come unless she had no other choice."

Mark's sneer indicated he wasn't going to let her go.

In that moment, Holly thought two things: she needed to get to her sister. And she needed to show her boys that men couldn't order women around and hold their belongings hostage.

Without thinking twice, Holly grabbed the keys to Mark's SUV off the kitchen island and sprinted for the door.

"Don't you dare!" She could hear his dress shoes smacking the laminate floors, running after her, but she was faster. By the time he made it onto the porch, she was already in his vehicle. She heard him scream something that ended in the words *wasting gas*. She quickly eyeballed the gas gauge—full—then she stuck the SUV in reverse and floored it.

She got it now. After Sandy had hit, there was no gas available for two weeks. People missed work, and it was complete madness. Mark had tried to prevent her from leaving during a superstorm not because he was worried about losing her or about Vivian's well-being but because he was concerned about preserving the gas in their Yukon.

"Asshole," she whispered.

Holly looked behind her and saw Mark still standing on the porch. Someone had to watch the kids, and there was a storm. He'd stay put.

Water was heavy on the road, causing the Yukon to skid. Bay Shore was across town, closer to where she and Vivian had grown up. When they were teens, they used to take the Bay Shore ferry on summer jaunts to Fire Island, just the two of them, a brief reprieve from their life under their parents' observation. It always felt like a time of magic—the short boat ride across the bay to the island, where people walked barefoot everywhere, not just the beach. No cars allowed, no behavioral patterns for their parents to research, just the horseshoe crabs Holly and Vivian chased along the thirty-or-so-mile stretch of skinny sand. Vivian never wanted to leave at the end of the day.

What the hell was Vivian doing out there? It made Holly sick inside that her sister had called her in distress from this familiar spot. The mix of nostalgia and fright felt like a scab being picked off an old wound.

All along the road, cars were pulled over with their hazard lights on, and Holly was glad she'd stolen her husband's big-ass SUV for this voyage, because it was powering through, whereas her minivan might've lost traction. She could hear the storm sirens going off, see the waves cresting the docks as she approached the marina. She shouldn't be out there, but fear for Vivian kept her going.

The parking lot at the marina was an empty paved square surrounded by a raging sea, a postage stamp of cement trying to hold down a beast. Holly noticed a car that had been parked with its lights on, but it left in a hurry as she approached. Holly squinted through the night, which had turned from an aging bruise, black and slate blue, to a wicked gray swirl. The white swells of the waves slipped over the wood and flooded the dock.

And then—Vivian's car. It was parked as close as possible to the water, so close it looked like it might float away. The ferry was docked there, bobbing wildly.

Holly parked, grabbed the heavy-duty flashlight Mark kept in his SUV, got out of the car, and ran. Her tennis shoes squished with all the water on the wooden dock, rain blasting her face. As she approached Vivian's car, a wave leaped over the rail, icy inlet water pushing its way down her hooded sweatshirt, knocking her onto her knees. Her flashlight slipped out of her hand. She immediately found it, the only light in a spray of misty hell.

"Oh my God." She was in a crouching position, shining her light on the car. She wouldn't dare direct it at the ocean, where the lashing of the autumn storm tides threatened to take her down again.

Holly fought to steady herself as she stood. She had to hurry. The storm was picking up speed and she was afraid she'd be swept away.

She wiped the water out of her eyes and shone the flashlight along Vivian's car.

"Vivian!" she called, but her voice was swallowed by the wind, a squeak in the middle of Mother Nature's mighty howl. Holly's curls

whipped around her head, blinding her. She had to hold them back as she approached the vehicle. A piece of random debris hit her knuckle, drawing blood.

"Ouch," she yelled, but her voice was snuffed out again.

When Holly made it to Vivian's little black Mercedes, she gripped the handle, further splintering the skin on her finger. She yanked on it, and the door clicked open. "Vivian?"

The interior light popped on, but there was no one inside the car. Holly checked the back seat—nothing.

"There's somebody coming—"

Vivian had told Holly to hurry, that someone was after her, but Holly was too late.

"No." Maybe someone else had picked her up. Perhaps the person screeching out of the parking lot had offered to give Vivian a ride. But then why hadn't she called Holly to tell her? Maybe Vivian hadn't noticed Mark's SUV pull in.

As Holly turned around to fight her way back to her car, she saw a glint of something near the tire of Vivian's Mercedes. She reached into the frigid water that was pooling at the wheel, shining the flashlight on the metal with her other hand.

It was a piece of jewelry—a broken tennis bracelet.

Vivian's broken tennis bracelet.

2

When she'd barged into the Sayville police station to report her sister missing, they hadn't even given Holly a towel. They'd placed her in a room and told her to sit on a plastic chair, where she shivered and wrung out the curls in her hair.

Before arriving, she'd sat in the SUV for several minutes, alternating between dialing Vivian's cell phone, which went straight to voice mail, and watching her screen in the hopes her sister would call. As the storm continued to surge, she'd decided she couldn't wait any longer to get away from the water, so she'd driven here. While she was driving, Holly had called her brother-in-law's landline and his cell as well as Mark's, but no one answered, so she'd left messages. At least Mark would know she hadn't died.

But what about her sister? Had she?

Died?

A horrible noise left Holly's mouth.

She fingered the simple diamond bracelet in her pocket, letting the settings rub over her fingertips. She wasn't sure it was Vivian's, but her sister had a few statement pieces she wore often, and her diamond tennis bracelet was one of them. Had she lost it in a struggle? How else could it have broken?

Holly drew in a deep breath, hoping the police could make sense of this. Maybe they'd already found Vivian. Maybe she'd had to abandon her car because there was too much water. Perhaps she'd managed to walk back to town or get a ride home already. But deep down, Holly didn't think so.

Vivian hadn't called her husband when she was in trouble. It made Holly suspicious that something strange was going on here. That coupled with the broken bracelet and the fear in her sister's voice. And how close Vivian's car was to the raging water. It terrified her.

Every inch of that empty car sank into her cold bones with the realization that Vivian was gone. It wasn't the first time she'd slipped away.

Gone.

Vivian was gone, and Holly couldn't find her, and it was all Holly's fault.

When they were kids, Green Acres Mall was a special treat, with its Gimbels, Sears, and JCPenney. Mother and Father made nice salaries as university professors, but they always talked in terms of *needs* and *wants*, and who needed more than a couple of pairs of jeans and shoes? *Nobody* was the right answer to that question. Always.

Their parents were shopping for a new washing machine at Sears, and the girls were bored.

"Wanna play hide-and-seek?" Holly asked.

Vivian rolled her eyes so high, they got lost in her hair. Mom wouldn't let her get a perm, so she'd cut her bangs herself and had teased them to high heaven. "Baby games. I wish we had enough money for the arcade."

They were both out of money and would rather poke their eyes out with the Pixy Stix they'd bought at the candy store than stand beside their parents and wait for someone to talk to them about clunky washers. Father would haggle. Mother would bicker. The salesperson would get frustrated.

"Come on, one game?" Holly asked.

Vivian popped the Hubba Bubba bubble she'd blown out all the way to the tip of her nose. It stuck all over her face. They both laughed as she picked it off her cheeks. "Fine. But here are the rules: you cannot go inside a store, you're not allowed on the second floor of the mall, no bathrooms, no food court. And I'll count first."

"Yes!" Holly said.

Vivian counted, and Holly ran around the perimeter until she found a coin-operated carousel. One of the horses was toting a carriage, and she squeezed her body inside it so her top half didn't show.

Holly made it through the whole ride concealed, but when it stopped, she had to get off to let the next rider on. She popped her head over the side of the carriage, trying to remain unseen. She'd always been self-conscious about her wild, springy hair, a giveaway in itself, although in the age of the perm, hers was "in" and a source of envy for her sister.

"Got you. Good one!" Vivian shouted from the opposite side of the circular carousel. A nosy parent who'd been eyeing Holly when she'd gotten on the ride seemed satisfied an older sibling was there. Vivian gave off the air of someone older than eleven, while Holly usually produced the opposite effect, especially lost in a fit of giggles as Vivian dragged her away—a typical eight-year-old.

"Darn it," Holly said, although she was proud she'd remained hidden for the length of the ride, maybe her longest stretch ever where Vivian couldn't find her. "Your turn." She pinched her sister.

"Ow," Vivian said, rubbing her arm. "I don't want to play your baby game."

Holly pouted. "You promised."

"No, I promised to find you," she said.

"No, you promised to play! Just once?" Holly asked.

"You know that if I really wanted to, I could hide and you'd never find me." Vivian's voice was daring. She blew out a new bubble of gum.

"Nope. I'll find you," Holly said confidently. "Just don't cheat."

Vivian looked down at her. Those were fighting words. "Please."

Their mother made them write in journals at least once a week and would often ask them questions about their experiences, usually personal and sometimes invasive, whatever her latest psychology research required. Then she'd compare their answers. Vivian and Holly despised these exercises. Vivian called them mind benders, because her questions were never straightforward—*if you found a dollar in the park, would you return it or leave it be?* Holly would read into the question and have secondary questions—like if they were in the middle of the park, who could they return it to? If they left it there, wouldn't it blow away or get destroyed?

But they weren't allowed to ask secondary questions. The most important rule of all was that there could be no cheating, and they could not share answers. Cheating, their mother proclaimed, was not only cheating in the exercise but cheating themselves. Only individuals who weren't capable of figuring out a problem on their own had to rely on others, and *"We're better than that. Foresters aren't lazy; they're workers,"* she'd said.

So, in other words, only the stupid and lazy cheated.

"Put your hands over your eyes and count off," Vivian said.

Holly did, and when she got to ten, she opened her eyes, and Vivian was gone. The volume of people in the mall had seemed to double. She could still see the simple blue lettering of the neon Sears sign where her parents were, but it was blurry. Everything was. The mob of people ogling her as she stood there all alone made her uneasy.

She wished she hadn't suggested this game. She and Vivian were supposed to stay together. Holly searched the whole first floor for her sister, including the bathrooms and the food court in case Vivian had forgotten they weren't supposed to hide there, but she was nowhere to be found. Holly could feel the shoppers watching her as they walked by. She was more nervous than she'd ever been in her life. She'd never been alone this long before.

She stared at her plastic wristwatch. She didn't have time for the second floor or the department stores, because she had to meet their parents now, and Mother and Father were always punctual.

When Holly arrived at the pretzel stand across from Sears, Mother's onyx eyebrows were pulled together in an angry V. She'd passed her sleek hair on to Vivian, and Holly thought it gave her sister a dark edge. She knew her mother had inherited her coloring—pale like a porcelain doll except for her inky hair—from her own mother, but not because they ever visited Grandma and Grandpa.

"I don't like to go upstate," was all Mother had ever said about going home. She didn't like to talk about her family, and Father's parents were deceased. It made Holly wonder about a lot of things.

"Where is your sister?" Mother asked, tapping one of the flat patent leather shoes she often wore to teach her students. Mother hated shopping. It was a waste of time that she could've used to read something, learn more. Objects didn't have a pulse and didn't hold her interest.

"I don't know," Holly confessed. "We were playing hide-and-seek, and I never found her."

Their father, who very seldom showed alarm, turned to their mother. "I told you we shouldn't have let them go off on their own!"

Mother straightened up, turned to him, and said nothing until he shut his trap. "Have you gathered all the information first, Henry? Ask yourself if there's truly a reason at this point to A. raise your voice to me, or B. react in a way that may elicit fear or disagreement."

Her father ran his hand through his own dark hair. Holly bit her lower lip because she knew this would be a bad one if Father disagreed with her. The problem with having two psychology professors for parents was that they both had interesting theories on how things worked, but if they disagreed, they clashed like thunder and lightning.

"I suppose we don't have all the information," Father said, "but I'd say the fact that our daughter is missing is enough reason for fear."

Mother shot daggers at him with her eyes again. "Vivian is not *missing*. There are to be no missing children signs put up next to Piercing Pagoda, Henry."

She turned her attention back to Holly. "Do you think your sister could still be hiding? And aren't you a little old to be playing that game?"

Holly shrugged, clenching her bag of candy in her hand. It had gotten sweaty from running around. "She could be. We had rules."

"Make-believe rules or real ones?" Before she'd taken their Barbies away, it had irked Mother that Holly liked to make up imaginary games instead of playing intellectual ones like Scrabble. *"Exercising your vocabulary through play heightens both your creativity and your intelligence."*

"Real ones," she insisted, aiming to please.

"What were the rules? These are the important questions. The ones we should've asked first before we decided to panic." That jab was thrown at her father, Holly understood, even at that age.

Holly outlined the rules for her. "And you looked in all those places?" she asked.

"Yes. And even some of the other ones too."

"Why would you waste your time looking in places that weren't outlined in the rules?"

Just then, Vivian hurried through the front door of the mall with a boy who looked to be around twelve or thirteen. She had a teddy bear and an ICEE in her hands. When Vivian saw them standing around waiting for her, she quickly said goodbye to her new friend and ran over. "Sorry I'm late. I was at the arcade."

"The arcade?" Holly was furious.

Vivian looked right at her. "We never made any rules about hiding outside of the mall, so I went across the street, and that nice boy gave me a few extra coins, and I won this." She held up the bear. "And a free drink." She held it up too.

"But . . . I looked everywhere for you." Holly was so mad, she thought she might cry. "No fair!" She wasn't sure if she was angrier that Vivian had broken their rules or that she'd gotten to go to the arcade without her. The teddy bear had on a dress, and Holly had never seen one like it, and she wanted a chance to win one too. "You said we had to stay on the first floor!" Holly yelled.

"No, I didn't. I said *you* couldn't go on the second floor." Vivian smiled.

Holly wailed, "That's no fair! You—"

"Left the mall," their mother said.

"But I—"

"Enough," Mother said. "Vivian, you broke our rules by leaving the mall, and you broke your own rules by circumventing the ones that you set. We're going home. Then we're going to discuss what hide-and-seek really means and talk about the fact that omitting exclusion criteria doesn't make it a fair game."

Their parents never punished them physically, but sometimes Holly thought she would've preferred a quick swat on the bum to listening to her mother lecture.

It didn't stop on the car ride home. "You placed yourself and your sister in danger," Father said.

But Mother didn't seem concerned with that part. "Your actions are stereotypical boundary stretching, industry versus inferiority, showing a greater need for independence, defiance."

"I know what I did was wrong," Vivian said. She'd say anything to make her stop.

Holly stared at her hands. When their mother talked like this, she felt naked, like their mother was stripping away parts of them that shouldn't be allowed to be seen. Holly wished her parents would just have these sorts of conversations when she and Vivian weren't around. She wasn't ready to hear them yet.

"Of course you know, Vivian! You knew when you were doing it that it was wrong. It's part of your metacognitive skill development. But what you didn't understand is that you endangered your sister by leaving her alone."

There it is. Thank you very much. Holly had been scared to death by all the strange eyes on her as she paraded the mall alone, but she dared not bring it up.

"The consequences of your actions aren't something you're aware of yet, which is why you need to listen to us. While you are well on your way to developing these skill sets, your sister is behind."

"Hey!" Holly said, but as she protested, she was brushing the hair of her My Little Pony.

"Well, Holly, let's talk about you. What's your game of choice here? Hide-and-seek? That's a game toddlers like to play. You're four to five years past the appropriate age for that game."

"Cynthia, don't you think that's a little rough—"

"No, Henry, I don't."

Holly shrank in her seat as her parents debated whether her problem was her infantile state or her egocentric behavior that led her to falsely assume that others saw things the same way she did. Mother claimed that children who engage in hide-and-seek actually want to be found. It was why toddlers played the game, because they knew their parents would eventually come for them. But that wasn't true in Holly's case. She'd been truly disappointed when Vivian had found her.

Holly threw her My Little Pony on the floor and began to cry.

Vivian turned slowly to her little sister and whispered, "You're not a baby. I shouldn't have left you." Then she handed her the teddy bear she'd just won. "Here, you can have it."

Where are you, Vivian?

"Come out, come out, wherever you are," Holly rasped shakily as she waited for the cops to come in the room. She closed her eyes and saw the blurry Sears sign. The memory was always distorted, like she was looking in a two-way mirror, but the fear it brought with it was very real. Holly had been alone and afraid without her big sister. No one would ever understand what they'd endured as kids and how much she needed Vivian in her life because of it.

Finally, a woman in a navy-blue raincoat and gray slacks walked into the room. She sat down and flicked the wet out of her own hair, which took about two seconds because it was nearly shaven to her head. "Hello, Mrs. Boswell. I'm Detective Nadia Pryzewski. You can call me Detective Nadia if you'd like. You want to tell me why you were out in this weather?"

"My sister called me. The car." Holly could barely speak, still in shock. "Did you call her husband? Clay?" Holly had tried several times to no avail.

"We located him, but he doesn't know where your sister is."

The door opened again, and a tall, lanky man entered the room. "Detective Linden Rigby." He offered his hand, and Holly shook it, slightly dismayed.

She recognized him from her brief stint in journalism—years ago, the time when she'd first learned not to blindly trust all cops. She couldn't remember if Detective Rigby was directly responsible for the poor handling of a case she'd reported on where a local teenage girl had gone missing, but she was certain he'd been in the precinct at the time. That was enough to instill doubt in her now. That whole case had been a sham.

"I apologize. I'm soaked through." Her hair was probably a frizzy mess, and she couldn't look sane to them right now between her garbled speech and her appearance.

He wiped his hand on his jeans. "That's okay."

"Did you find my sister?" she asked.

"No. But I have to ask why you didn't call us first before driving in that storm looking for her. Did you know there was a storm brewing? You had to have seen the warnings."

"I did, but Vivian asked me not to call the police. I'm not sure why, but I thought it was just trouble from the storm. Now I'm concerned. I saw a car pull out as I was pulling into the lot."

"Did you get a look at the car?" Nadia asked.

"No, not really. It was dark. They were driving fast, though. And she said there was somebody coming."

The cops exchanged a brief look, and Holly felt the weight of that glance. Did they think the other party meant bad news where Vivian was concerned? Until she'd said the words out loud, she'd hoped that maybe the person was another motorist out in the storm stopping to help Vivian, but the longer it was since she'd heard from her sister, the more her gut instinct told her otherwise.

"Do you have any idea who that might be?" Rigby asked.

"No, and then the line went dead."

"And you didn't think to call the police after that?" Nadia asked.

Holly opened her mouth to reply, then closed it. "Look, I'm here now because I'm worried. Do you have any idea where my sister is? I found this beside her car." Holly pulled out the bracelet and set it on the table. The diamonds glimmered in the light, and Holly could clearly see the broken clasp now. She pictured someone pulling on her sister's arm, yanking her out of the car, the bracelet getting broken in the process.

"Are you sure it's Vivian's?" Rigby asked.

"I'm not sure, but she had one just like it. Do you want to take it for evidence?"

"No, we're not investigating a crime scene. It's an abandoned car. You can keep your sister's bracelet." He said this as if it should bring her comfort. It didn't.

"How do you suppose this happened?" she asked, flicking the clasp, then grabbing the bracelet back and shoving her hands in her pockets.

"Jewelry breaks." Rigby shrugged.

"It's fourteen-karat gold," Holly said.

"It happens. Maybe she slipped and banged it," Nadia said.

Holly thought her comment was interesting, considering she didn't have a lick of jewelry on—no wedding ring, not even a pair of studs in her ears.

"Mrs. Boswell." Rigby held her gaze. "Was anything off in the weeks prior to your sister calling you? How was her mental state? Did she seem distressed at all? Anyone bothering her?"

Holly thought back. She hadn't talked to her sister much at all in the last week, but that wasn't odd. They led such different lives, they sometimes went a month without speaking. They were close because of what they had experienced together as children, not because they had a lot in common. Vivian had always been more guarded—suppressed, as their mother had said.

Maybe that's because Mother had once locked Vivian in a closet after she'd lied about sneaking out with a boy. She was thirteen years old. Holly had padded the covers for her after she'd gone out the window. She'd tried to help her, but it hadn't worked.

Oppositional defiant disorder will not occur in my house. You had no problem squeezing out of something the size of a box to leave this house, so you should have no problem spending the night in something just like it!

Solitary confinement could suppress the hell out of any teenager, Holly imagined. Vivian had freaked out in there, pounding on the walls, howling in a manner that still made going to haunted houses an impossibility for Holly. She'd learned a lot from her big sister, most of all what mistakes not to repeat. In their two-woman army, Vivian had been the frontline infantry. Her big sister had always taken the brunt of the force for Holly.

"She seemed fine last week when I talked to her," Holly said.

"Any disagreements with anyone?" Rigby asked.

The word *disagreement* rang a bell. "Yes. Maybe a week or two back? But it was just with the neighbors. Something about the gate between their properties being unlatched and one of them being in her backyard watching her through the window. But I think it was settled. Nothing major."

Rigby looked at his notebook. "The Carringtons?" he asked.

"Yes." Holly looked at him in surprise. "Why?"

"They reported a disturbance at their home a week ago," Rigby said. "They claimed that your sister was harassing them and that she was mentally unsound. The officer who responded to the call noted that the Carringtons had used the word"—he cleared his throat—"*crazy*."

Holly felt hot under her wet collar. She gritted her teeth. That word was personally offensive. She and Vivian had fought to keep their sanity after being raised in their parents' nuthouse. "That's not true." Holly had met the Carringtons only a few times while visiting her sister, and they were straitlaced, if pretentious. Peter was an oral surgeon with a personality as dry as sunbaked clay, and his wife didn't seem to have enough wit to cause harm. "Vivian told me she thought one of them had unlatched the gate. She went to talk to them about it, and Eve started a fight, and Vivian didn't understand why. They're friends." Or at least they had been up until that point.

"When we called your brother-in-law, he said there was absolutely no reason for Vivian to drive to Bay Shore Marina, especially in the storm," Nadia said. "Why would she do that? Any problems at home? Any reason she couldn't stand to return there? She drove to a spot where her life could've possibly been compromised."

"Not that I'm aware," she said, although she knew that Vivian and Clay's marriage was far from perfect. She thought again of the beautiful diamond bracelet Clay had bought for her. Holly's instincts told her that it hadn't broken by accident.

Even so, she didn't feel comfortable dishing on her sister's dirty laundry. It wasn't so soiled that she suspected Clay of having anything to do with her sister's distress tonight or her actual disappearance—yet. But that's not what Holly thought the cops were insinuating here. "Are you suggesting she wanted to cause self-harm? Because we don't do that."

"Who's we?" Rigby asked.

"The people in my family." These officers didn't understand how they'd been raised. Suicide was unconscionable, a preposterous conclusion to this story.

"Well, there was no note left behind in the car." Nadia was nodding in her favor, but it felt like a kick in the stomach. They were really contemplating that Vivian had killed herself. Vivian would never take her own life.

"Is there a search team? Can I join them?"

Nadia and Rigby exchanged a dubious look. Rigby shifted his long body in the chair. "Standard protocol is to wait until someone is unable to be located for forty-eight hours. At that point, the unreachable party is considered missing."

"But the storm. This must be a special circumstance. No one can survive on foot in this." Holly motioned to the wall, even though there was no window to the outside world. It was so quiet in the room, she wasn't even sure if it was still raining.

"I understand your concern," Nadia said in a way that made Holly unsure that was true. "But the aftermath of the storm makes an effective search even more difficult, and there's no sign of present danger. We have to follow protocol. There're possible scenarios that you may not be considering."

"Like what?"

"You said yourself that you saw a car leaving the marina and that you don't think your sister intended self-harm. Perhaps her cell phone went dead, and that's why her call to you was cut off. She could've gotten into a car with someone who was also without a phone or had a dead cell."

"So you expect me to believe that two people forgot their car chargers on the same day or that someone who operates a car doesn't own a cell phone?" Holly didn't want to be a smart-ass, but she knew from being a former journalist that asking good questions was the only way to gain ground with law enforcement.

Nadia looked at her, peeved. "Maybe your sister simply doesn't have your phone number memorized. Mrs. Boswell, we're going to ask you to go home. We'll be in touch in the morning. A search team will be sent out once we've verified she's actually missing. That's how we handle things when the party is over eighteen. You'd be surprised how many people come back on their own after a marital spat or misunderstanding."

Holly stared at them, speechless, because they didn't know her sister.

Vivian wasn't playing hide-and-seek. She was gone.

3

CLAY

When the detectives pulled into the driveway, Clayton Eddy knew why they were there. He'd been waiting an hour or more, ever since they'd told him Vivian's car had been found abandoned at Bay Shore Marina, of all places.

Stay put for now and try to remain calm, they'd said, as if that were an option. *We'll be there soon.*

He'd tried his wife's phone with no luck, and the library didn't have a clue where she was because she'd called in sick that afternoon. Peculiar, since Vivian had been fine that morning and hadn't said anything about feeling ill. He'd tried to track her phone using their cell provider's app, but it showed no signal. It was either turned off or the battery had gone dead.

It gave him a horrible feeling that Vivian was in danger and that something much more insidious than a cold had been plaguing her. The police had phoned earlier to see if he'd heard from Vivian, but now that the storm had died down, they were making a house visit. They claimed it would be quicker to talk to him in person. While Clay appreciated efficiency, he knew the truth.

They were checking him out. The quicker they could pin him down, the better, but he had a solid alibi for tonight and no reason to harm his wife. This scenario with her abandoned car was frightening, especially in this storm.

They'd purchased a house in the nicest neighborhood in Sayville, close to the water so Vivian could walk to Great South Bay. Having grown up on Fairfield Beach in Connecticut, Clay didn't care for the nuisances that came with sand or the mystery of what lay beneath the murky ocean water. But he lived near the sea for Vivian.

They lived far closer to the Sayville ferry, no reason to drive to Bay Shore. There was no explanation for why Vivian should've been there tonight.

Damn it, Vivian, where are you? The last thing he needed was the police on his back when he was in the midst of one of the most important trials of his career. If Vivian didn't return home soon, he knew they'd start digging for clues in his backyard. And if they started digging, he was afraid of what they'd find.

Through the blinds Clay could see the police cruiser pulling up his driveway. His phone buzzed with a text message as he walked toward the door.

Vivian? No. It was Holly. Her sister.

His sister-in-law had already left him a dozen messages, and he didn't have the patience to call her back.

Well, where is she? Where is she? Holly would screech into the phone until his ears bled. She'd expect him to explain everything and comfort her, and he just couldn't. Not right now. Sometimes he wondered how the two women were related. Vivian's temper simmered slowly, while Holly's hovered at a rolling boil.

His heart was pounding against his tonsils when he opened the door without waiting for the knock. "Detectives."

Rigby showed him his badge, as if it were necessary.

"Please come in, Linden," he said, opening his door wide. "Detective." He acknowledged the younger female cop. She must be new. They walked into his house, and it seemed so empty without Vivian; their heavy footsteps made him uneasy.

"Clayton Eddy." He stuck out his hand for the female detective to shake.

"I know who you are," she said, too gruffly. "You're the one defending that creep, the doctor trading sex for pills."

"Wow. Forget due process." He lowered his hand, offended. She was a man-hater; he knew the type.

"Detective Nadia," she announced. He tried to swallow, but his throat was too dry. Worse, his eye had begun to twitch, and he couldn't make it stop. He should be better under pressure, but this was a new kind of stress, much different from courtroom stress.

"We've towed your wife's car to impound. We'll let you know when it's ready to be released," Rigby said.

"All right." Clay didn't like how that sounded. They were definitely doing a thorough sweep if they were keeping Vivian's car overnight. They'd find his DNA all over it, and even though that was typical, he still didn't like it.

"Has the coast guard . . ." What he wanted to ask and where his mind traveled were two different things. He didn't want to imagine Vivian's body floating facedown in the bay, her lovely dark hair strung out in waves, but he couldn't control it. Or the thought that she could've drifted off to sea with the wicked wave patterns. "Has the coast guard found anything?" he finally managed.

"No, they haven't, but they've been patrolling hard with the storm, and we told them about your wife's case, so they've made an extra effort to do rounds in that area."

Clay nodded, satisfied. Normally, they'd wait until there was more proof of threat to spend taxpayer money on a search, but the storm was working in his favor.

"Where were you tonight, Mr. Eddy?" Rigby asked.

They'd walked into the living room, and Clay was uncomfortable with how Nadia was pacing in front of the mantel. Anyone would think she was just looking at pictures, but Clay knew better. He was the husband, and in this situation, he was their prime suspect until Vivian turned up. She was hunting for clues.

"I was with a client in Farmingdale," he said.

Rigby wrote down the name of the town. "Can they confirm you were there?"

"Of course." Clay took out his phone. "Would you like me to call them?"

There was zero incentive for Bellini's guys to say anything negative about him, especially right now. When he defended one of them, he defended all of them. For the members, it's just the way the club worked. This time his client was a surgeon who'd gotten in trouble for inappropriately prescribing opioids, but Clay was going to prove that the women who were suing him were just looking for an easy payday.

"Or I can give you their names instead." Clay handed Rigby a paper out of his wallet, where he'd written down the contact numbers and addresses of all the men he'd been with that evening.

Nadia bared her large teeth; they didn't go well with her boyish haircut, too close to the scalp. "Well, you thought of everything before we came, didn't you? Even got your references sheet together."

That's because I'm an attorney, and I understand how these things work. "Listen, I'm just trying to help find Vivian. I'm smart enough to know I'm your first suspect. So I'm just giving you the evidence you need to take me off your list so you can find out what happened to her."

Rigby's head jerked up. "We don't know anything happened to her. Right now we're just investigating an abandoned vehicle."

Clay exhaled harshly, realizing his misstep. He shouldn't have referred to himself as a suspect; there'd been no crime committed here. But they didn't know Vivian. She didn't do things like this.

"Do you think someone hurt her?" Nadia picked up a framed picture of Vivian and him from a vacation they'd taken to Montauk with the neighbors.

"I don't know. Her sister left me a message that said someone was at the marina with Vivian, and now she's gone." He had to blink, because just saying it out loud made him queasy. "I don't know who that could've possibly been." Vivian had left for work this morning like it was any other day. What had happened between then and now that led her *there*?

"Mrs. Boswell told us the same thing. It's interesting that Vivian called her sister when she was in trouble instead of you," Rigby said.

Clay's chest burned with uneasiness, because he hadn't liked that fact either. "Yes. I'm not sure why that is."

"Normally, if a woman were in trouble and she didn't feel the cops could help, she'd call her husband first, wouldn't you think?" Nadia asked. And for as much as she'd razzed him about having a prerecorded script, he could've sworn these two had practiced this routine in the car.

"Why would you say that? Have you spent a lot of time in trouble?" he said.

Her expression soured. "Watch yourself, Counselor. If your wife didn't feel she could call you, wouldn't that mean she couldn't trust you to save her from whatever she was running from?"

This was beyond awful. His wife was gone, and they were beating him up even though he had a solid alibi. Not to mention it was disrespectful after all the early years he'd put in at the DA's office before going private. He couldn't pass up the salary hike. "I'd say it meant she knew I was with clients and that I sometimes turn off my phone in that case. If she was in a hurry, which it sounded like she was, she might've called her sister because she always keeps her phone on."

Rigby bit the inside of his cheek, considering this. "Okay."

"Who are the people in this photograph?" Nadia walked over, picture in hand, but he didn't need her to show it to him; he knew the one.

"Our neighbors. Peter and Eve."

"I thought so. The station has a call logged from Eve Carrington about your wife."

Clay shook his head. "She dropped the complaint. Silly fight." Eve had morphed into something ugly over that spat, and Clay didn't know if it was menopause or what, but he hoped she'd stay on her side of the fence from now on.

"Silly fight, and your wife goes missing the next week. Maybe you should elaborate. Your sister-in-law, Mrs. Boswell, mentioned something about a gate that was unlatched. Someone watching your wife from your backyard?" Nadia asked.

Damn it, Holly. Leave it to that big mouth to crack open a can of worms that didn't need to be opened.

"Vivian hadn't been feeling well. She thought . . ." He had a hard time painting his wife this way, because it wasn't her fault, the way she'd grown up. Her parents had made her paranoid, done things to her to make her doubt her own thoughts and realities. He'd been trying to earn her allegiance for years, but it was a lost cause. Especially the last few years. "She was fine most of the time, but she'd been having issues lately. Her imagination may have gotten away from her."

Nadia gaped at Clay like he was positively stupid again, and much like the first time, he felt like it.

"So you're saying she imagined someone was there?" Rigby asked.

Clay cleared his throat. "I think so."

"Uh-huh," Nadia said. "And when you checked the gate between the two yards, the one that separated yours and the Carringtons', did you find it unlatched?"

"Well, yes."

"Then, that doesn't sound like your wife was imagining anything. She accused the neighbor of being in your yard because she saw someone there and thought it was a Carrington."

"That's possible," Clay said. He'd made Vivian feel bad about it at the time. Both Clay and Eve had thrown around the word *crazy*, and if he were honest, he'd been scared they were right and that she'd imagined the whole thing. But the more unsettling consideration was that if someone really was there and it wasn't a Carrington, Vivian had every right to be fearful. He needed to quash this investigation before the detectives started looking too closely at his business.

"People don't generally see phantoms. Unless they have a mental issue. Like schizophrenia," Nadia said.

"Right." Clay thought of Vivian's poetry. He'd hidden it from the cops in his desk drawer to protect her, and now he was wondering if he should show them. She'd always written, but her latest poems . . . there'd obviously been a decline in her thoughts, a downward slide toward something darker. But Nadia and Rigby didn't need to know that. It wouldn't help them find her.

He wished he would've noticed her sadness sooner, before he'd gone through her things an hour ago. Lately, he'd been working all the time—while she'd been suffering. Even if he'd been home more, he couldn't have helped when he didn't know what was wrong. She'd stopped talking to him about her problems long ago.

"Mr. Eddy, did you hear me?" Nadia asked.

"Yes," he said, but he'd blanked out between the thoughts of the spiraling words in Vivian's little book and the uncontrolled images of his wife floating in the water. He didn't want to imagine her body, pale and lifeless, bobbing on the surface of the ocean inlet, because he knew when a body filled with water, it caused the gut to burst and gases to be released. But his mind took him there anyway.

"Has your wife been diagnosed with a mental disorder?" Nadia repeated.

He rubbed his eyes. "No." *But she should have,* he wanted to say.

"Mr. Eddy, is your eye bothering you? You keep touching it," Nadia said. And she was looking at *everything*.

"It's just a bit of a twitch," he admitted.

Rigby shot him a sympathetic look.

Nadia was gripping the picture frame so hard, he thought she might slice her palm. "I can see how you'd be stressed. Who are the children in this photo? Yours?"

"No, they're the Carringtons' daughters."

"So no children?" she asked.

"We couldn't have any," he revealed, like he always did when people asked this dreadful question, which felt like an intrusion but was somehow acceptable to ask anyway. He'd wanted children to fill their big house, but it couldn't happen for them. "It was hard on Vivian," he said, because it was such a big part of her sorrow. And his, but it didn't seem to matter when men couldn't be fathers, only when women couldn't be mothers.

Rigby had taken a seat on the couch. "Excuse me for being direct here, but it sounds as though your wife suffered from depression and possibly hallucinations, and you're trying to hide that. This doesn't bode well."

Clay nodded because he was doing an awful job of relaying the right information to help them find his wife. He'd never imagined it would be so hard from this side of the examination table, even though he'd been a criminal defense attorney for years.

"We need to know what's going on here. Was your wife sick?" Rigby asked.

Clay had known Detective Linden Rigby a long time, and he felt like he could trust him. He just wished Nadia were somewhere else, because he didn't trust her.

He couldn't bring himself to show them the journal containing her dismal poems. He was worried Vivian's enigmatic verses might allude to something terrible about him, and he also didn't need to expose her in that way to tell them what was evidently clear. "Yes, she was sick. My wife was sick."

4

Holly stood outside the newly renovated Sayville Library, located on tree-lined Greene Avenue, its parking lot connected to the local college where her parents used to teach. The library was within walking distance of Great South Bay, a mile from Vivian's twentieth-century colonial on Handsome Avenue.

Handsome Avenue.

Holly sucked in a breath at the name.

Vivian had never felt comfortable giving out her home address because she thought it sounded silly, but she most certainly enjoyed the compliments from her guests after they'd arrived, marveling at the fine postwar details, like the half-circle flags hanging from the houses that practically marched down the streets in red, white, and blue—a common trimming of the Victorian-style homes on the block. Vivian lived on a street that ran parallel to the library and the bay. She could walk to work and the water.

So why did she drive to Bay Shore Marina? And who was there?

Holly had been so jealous of Vivian's house, her humble career, one she seemed to love, her stress-free life. She was well taken care of, married to a man who worked hard although was not often at home to torture her like Holly's husband, Mark—who she'd had to beg for permission just to leave the house again today, *after the stunt you pulled last night.*

Forget the fact that her sister had been missing now for fourteen hours. Holly's sophisticated older sister, who she'd imagined had this quiet, yet envious life. They'd had the same parents, came from the same genes, yet Holly was the only one who stashed bottles of alcohol in the laundry room. Vivian didn't seem to struggle—not in that way, anyhow.

Holly sighed, grateful she'd been able to manage a sip—okay, a few sips—from one of those bottles before coming here. She never should've quit her job as a journalist for the *Suffolk County News*. Maybe then she wouldn't drink. But her job hadn't paid enough to cover the day care.

Or so Mark had told her. It might have covered it, but with his career as a project manager for a nuclear-energy company, it just *didn't make sense* for her to keep her job. Mark's mother hadn't worked when he was a child, and Mark just assumed that's what would happen in their home.

He knew she'd enjoyed having a career, but she'd convinced herself he was right. After all, as her mother had not so politely informed her, long before she'd gone to work at the paper, her writing could use some *work*. The words didn't flow naturally for Holly the way they had for the other three in their family, on paper or from her mouth.

The kids had no school today, so Holly'd had to wait until midmorning, when Mark's mother could drive to their house to babysit. Mark had harped on her the whole way out the door for asking his elderly mother to drive, considering the possible destruction of the storm—*the traffic lights could be out* and *she's getting her cataract surgery in less than a month*. But Sue's eyes were good enough to drive *today*, and Vivian had been missing since *yesterday*.

Mark was a spoiled only child, and he just didn't get what this felt like. Losing a sibling was like losing a limb, especially after all she and Vivian had seen and heard together. There was no one else on earth who understood Holly like her sister. She couldn't just go about her day and *"let the cops do their jobs,"* as Mark had insisted. He kept saying, *"Relax, Vivian will turn up."*

"She'll turn up, how?" Holly had asked, but he was already out the door. It was as if Vivian's disappearance were nothing more than an inconvenience to their daily lives.

Holly leaned on a tree as her breath quickened with ugly thoughts of what *Vivian will turn up* could mean. Sure, Vivian could turn up—dead.

Before Holly had left the house, she'd tried calling her sister's husband one more time, but he hadn't answered. Clay had gained a bit of a reputation representing some shady characters in court. When Holly had asked Vivian about the rumors that Clay was *connected*, Vivian blew her off, saying that his present client was a well-respected physician and that the patients suing him were just after the defendant's money.

Holly took the bracelet still in her coat pocket and raked it over her fingers as she stood at the crux of Vivian's life now, her place of work, where she'd dedicated the last fifteen years of her life, hoping to find some answers. Vivian loved her job more than anything else, perhaps even her husband. Maybe someone in there knew something. Although Vivian was never one to confide in others.

She'd been *suppressed* long ago.

Holly stepped inside the library and took in the rows of dusty shelves, the light streaming through the abundant windows, the rounded, modernized front desk that made the space look like an actual office, a smattering of students from the local college engrossed in a study group.

It was like the storm hadn't even happened last night.

But it had. And Holly had lost her sister in it.

Emotions seemed to shimmy down from the windows and bounce along the flat white walls. This was Vivian's place. Her mother's favorite venue to work when she'd taught at the college. It didn't seem right being there without them.

Holly moved toward the front desk. There was a children's area across from it with life-size building blocks stacked on either side.

Where were the cops? Shouldn't they be here asking questions?

She hadn't been impressed with them last night. Rigby and Nadia had basically told her they'd only launch a search party after there was probable cause to believe Vivian was in danger. The more she'd thought about it, the madder she'd become. Everyone knew the first forty-eight hours were crucial in a disappearance. The police were just going to forfeit the most pivotal window to see if the missing person would turn up on her own? Vivian wasn't a stray dog who had lost her way home; she was a human being, a wife, a sister.

Then again, Holly shouldn't be surprised. Ever since she'd seen Rigby last night, she'd been thinking about the worst police scandal she'd ever witnessed, and that had been a missing persons case too. Several years ago, a young woman named Delilah Ramirez had disappeared. There had been gang-related violence in the area, and devil horns—the infamous MS-13's signature symbol—found spray-painted on the park bench where Delilah had last been seen.

The detective Holly'd interviewed had confirmed they suspected a gang abduction. Holly was a part of the crime beat at the time, and it'd been the largest story she'd reported on before having Otto.

But Delilah was found forty-eight hours later in a New Jersey suburb. She'd run off with her boyfriend, and Holly later learned the police had used her reporting as an excuse to bring in one of the gang members on an unrelated charge. The cops had known Delilah's boyfriend had been unaccounted for, and they suspected she was likely with him, but the detective hadn't told Holly that.

It had made her story look unethical. Holly wasn't only pissed that her journalistic credibility had been compromised; she was upset to be the first one to publish a story that had likely caused the Ramirez family undue stress.

Detective Rigby wasn't the cop who'd lied to her, but Holly had a vague memory of him being involved with the case. So she didn't trust him. But she hoped she could trust Detective Nadia.

At the front desk of the library, a young twentysomething girl with thick tortoiseshell frames was helping a patron. A little boy squeezed in front of the woman to slip his book into the return slot.

"I'm sorry," the mother apologized to Holly, reaching around her to grab at his shoulder. "That's rude, Landon; she was in front of us."

The little boy stared up at Holly fearfully, and she was sure it was due to her appearance. Her eyes were swollen from crying, and her hair, which was never tame to begin with, was hanging out of her ponytail in matted springs. Vivian used to help brush through it after baths when Holly was younger, because their mother didn't have the patience or fortitude to tackle the knots, especially with the frequent alcoholism-induced tremor in her hands.

"It's fine," Holly said to the boy's mother. "I have two little guys." She smiled at the boy, probably around four years old, but the effort felt herculean. She hadn't slept a wink last night, the shadows from the tree limbs outside her bedroom window mimicking the imagined arms that had stolen Vivian away in the storm.

The mother nodded and smiled politely, but there was something in the way she looked at Holly, a suspicion, that made Holly cup her mouth and discreetly smell her breath once the two moved toward the children's area. Could they smell the alcohol on her?

She turned to make sure the mother wasn't still watching her. The children's area was directly across from the curved front desk, where Vivian would have spent her days working. Holly wondered if the recent renovation was a new source of torture for her sister.

Vivian had gotten her English degree from Harvard but never acquired her teaching certificate like she'd planned. She'd gotten her

MLIS instead. Holly thought it was because her sister had been unable to conceive a child of her own, and it was too painful to be around them all day. She'd never outright told Holly that was the reason, but after Vivian's two miscarriages, she'd stopped trying—both to have children and further her career.

Alone with my books, worlds to explore, she'd say. Vivian had always been a bit of a solitary creature and hadn't seemed to mind. But now Holly wondered if it was all a ruse, and if she'd used the library to hide from the world because she couldn't have the life she really wanted. Drowning herself in fantasy so she didn't have to face reality.

"Can I help you?" someone asked.

Holly's head snapped up, and she looked at the pretty girl behind the front desk again. "I'm Holly, Vivian's sister." Her voice came out scratchy and strained.

"Oh . . ." The girl's face broke into sympathy. "I'm sorry. I didn't work with her long, but we all loved Vivian here. I heard they found her car."

Holly nodded, confirming the town gossip.

"Let me get Jane."

Loved? Are people already talking about Vivian in the past tense?

Everyone did love Vivian, though. She had a calming smile that could coax warmth into a saber-tooth tiger.

Holly was confused for a moment when the girl returned with an older woman. Holly almost had to rub her worn eyes twice. Jane Rothman had been head librarian when she and Vivian were younger. She still had the same perfect crop of white hair and sturdy glasses. Dressed in one of her fashionable outfits, she strolled over with her tall gait. She opened her arms, and Holly fell into her embrace.

"Oh, dear. I'm so sorry, Holly. They haven't found her yet, then?"

"No." Holly took a couple of deep breaths in and out, the familiar scent of Chanel No. 5 filling her nose. It transported her back in time.

Holly pulled her cheek away from Jane's royal-blue silk scarf, embarrassed. "I'm sorry," Holly apologized.

"Don't be," Jane whispered. "They called me to fill in until they find Vivian. I still help out here and there. Keeps me busy, with Hank gone." She smiled, still beautiful for an eightysomething-year-old widow. Holly shouldn't be surprised. Jane had always brought cut-up fruit and veggies to the library. She'd offered her snacks to the girls most days and told them to drink lots of water and stay out of the sun when they were younger.

It'd sounded preachy back then, but Holly could see now that Jane was just trying to bestow upon them a healthier lifestyle than their parents, who drank and smoked themselves into an early grave before their sixtieth birthdays.

"Were the police here?" Holly asked Jane.

"No, but there was a person who phoned the library last night to verify that Vivian had called in sick. Abby took the call." Jane motioned to the girl at the front. "We were fortunate the electricity didn't go out during the storm."

"What time did Viv's shift start?" Holly asked.

"It was one to eight. It's considered the night shift." Jane winked.

"Hmm." Holly hadn't received Vivian's call until around dinnertime. After six. If she were really ill, she wouldn't have been gallivanting around town in a storm. What had she been up to?

"Did the police want to know anything else?" Holly asked.

"No, it was just a confirmation call that she'd called in sick. Do you want to talk to Abby?" Jane asked.

Vivian hadn't been sick. She'd been in trouble. Holly looked at Abby again, nose deep in a book. "Sure," she said.

Jane motioned for her to follow, and they walked over to the front desk. "Abby, Holly would like a word." Jane's voice was so authoritative, it would be hard to resist her. "I'll leave you to it," she whispered before sauntering away.

Abby glanced up, biting her lip. She looked like she'd rather shrink beneath the countertop. Holly guessed she was a shy, introverted grad student who'd just wanted an easy job where she could study at the same time she worked. Her boss going missing in the interim was likely not part of the plan.

"I don't mean to bother you," Holly said. "But I'm curious to know if my sister was acting strangely or if she said anything odd in the weeks before she went missing? I'm sure the cops will ask you the same question," she added for good measure. Maybe Abby would see this as a form of practice for the real show.

"No . . . not that I'm aware. Although I've only been here a couple months. Vivian was a hard worker, and then sometimes at the end of the night she would go online and chat." Abby pointed to the computers.

"Chat? Are you sure?" Holly asked. *Who would Vivian be chatting with at the library?* She and Clay had a home office the size of Holly's living room.

"I'm not sure." Abby's cheeks went pink. "But she'd smile a lot when she was over there, and I thought I saw a chat box once when I walked by. I assumed she was talking to someone. Maybe it had something to do with the librarians' conference coming up."

Vivian was smiling. Holly didn't know why she found that statement odd. "Librarians' conference?"

"The ALA," Jane said. "They meet every January. It's when the librarians get together to talk about the new books that will be coming out the following year."

"Already?" Holly asked. School had just started.

"Books are slated a year in advance so the librarians can plan for them."

Holly nodded. She did recall that her sister went away every year sometime after Christmas. She was probably just planning for her trip and chatting with some other librarians she'd met over the years. But

Vivian wasn't an overly expressive person, and Holly couldn't imagine her sitting at the computer, openly smiling. The mental image felt off.

"Where did she sit?" Holly asked before she could think twice, her old journalism skills coming back in a flash.

Abby looked at Jane. "Go show her. I'll handle the desk," Jane said.

Abby led her to the area the college had always referred to as "the stacks." "She always sat there." She pointed to the last computer in a row of three.

It made sense that Vivian would choose the seat farthest away, by the window, for privacy. Holly had the sudden urge to sit there. "Thank you," she said.

Abby logged her in and then took the hint that Holly wanted to be alone. "I'll be at the front if you need anything else." She scurried off, a little wisp of a thing, but she could move fast.

Holly immediately clicked on the public computer's browser history. There were a ton of searches but nothing she could immediately link to Vivian or the ALA. Mark was right. Maybe she should've just stayed at home. She was probably more useful there than running around town retracing Vivian's footsteps. But she'd missed her sister at the pier, and now she needed to do something to find her. She'd already failed her once.

Holly blew out a long breath. It tickled her forehead, and another curl escaped.

The number forty-eight kept pulsing in her brain. Every second, every minute Vivian wasn't found added to another hour that would all but guarantee her death. *Think.*

Holly used to be quick. When she worked at the paper, she used to be able to solve crimes before the headlines were announced. She often figured out the mystery preemptively when she watched *48 Hours.*

If Vivian had been chatting from the library, it was because she didn't want Clay to see her doing it from home, which meant she wanted to do it in secret. If she wanted to keep her chat sessions private, she'd want to do it from a site that couldn't be easily pulled back up on something as simple as a library browser window.

It would have to be a website she could log on to that wouldn't raise a red flag. There were a ton of searches on the library computer listed for Google, which was almost laughable, because—it's Google. But it also made Holly think of her sister's email address.

Her password-protected email.

Vivian used a Gmail account, the same one she'd had since she married Clay. Her email address had the number twenty-four in it, the age she was when she got married.

Holly pulled up the sign-in page and typed in Vivian's username. She thought she'd be sitting there for hours trying to guess Vivian's password, but to her joy and dismay, it logged in for her, password saved. Vivian had checked the "Remember My Password" button on the library computer.

Her sister should have been more careful, but as smart as Vivian was, she was a little sheltered when it came to security stuff—*Clay will fix it; Clay will pay for it.* It's how Vivian excused his frequent absences, explaining he took care of her in other ways. She'd mentioned several times that Clay was aiming to make partner, and the only way to do that was to take high-profile cases, which required loads of his time.

The police could follow the same tracks Holly had and log in just as easily from this computer, and something about that made Holly extremely uneasy, as did the mention of Vivian's smiley chat-room sessions. Holly had found Vivian's bracelet because she'd been at the scene first.

Logging into her account felt very much the same, like she'd discovered something important. The cops had just let her keep the bracelet. Holly would be more careful with what she handed over to them in the future.

Something was off here, though. It was likely that Vivian might chat a few nights about the ALA conference, but how much time did she need to devote to her library friends?

Who were you talking to, Vivian?

Once Vivian's email loaded, Holly breezed through it quickly and didn't see anything of interest. There were a dozen or more store discount messages. No emails from Clay, but Holly didn't think that was odd. Mark rarely emailed her. It wasn't nearly immediate enough. Mark's preferred form of communication was to text incessantly until she responded.

Holly saw an icon for Hangouts, Google's messaging app, on the sidebar. She took in a deep breath and clicked on it. The name associated with Vivian's account popped up and almost knocked Holly off her wooden chair.

SassyVivi38

Huh?

There was nothing sassy about Vivian. She was a refined lover of classic literature and poetry. She had a Walt Whitman quote plastered in her foyer that read, KEEP YOUR FACE ALWAYS TOWARD THE SUNSHINE AND SHADOWS WILL FALL BEHIND YOU. She was elegant and brainy and quiet and punctual, none of which touched the word *sassy*.

There'd been a time when they were teenagers when Vivian had tested her boundaries, but she'd gotten burned. Torched, really, and all to protect her little sister. Holly cringed at the memory. Vivian couldn't be testing those boundaries again at thirty-eight years old.

Midlife crisis?

That's the other thing that bothered Holly.

Vivian had used her current age in her screen name—and if that were the case, she had to have created the screen name in the last six months. It was September now, and Vivian was a March baby. Pisces. Generous. Amiable. Likable.

Holly couldn't imagine she'd greet her librarian friends as SassyVivi38. So who had she been chatting with? Holly had a sick feeling in her empty stomach.

She saw a section for "Archived Hangouts" and clicked on it. There were a ton of dates that registered beneath it, all with the same chat partner—TomKat45.

Holly put her hand over her mouth and then immediately removed it, fearing she was being watched by Jane or Abby.

The chat times had increased in duration and frequency over the last three months. First, they occurred every few weeks and then most weeks. Who was this man Vivian was chatting with, most recently every Thursday? Could he be the one who had followed her to Bay Shore Marina—some online predator?

Holly clicked on a chat dated last week and read a line.

SassyVivi38: I bought brand-new shimmery lip gloss. You'd like it. And a leather jacket too.

Holly rocked in her chair. *What?*

She remembered commenting on Viv's new moto jacket—not totally out of the norm for her, because she was always super trendy, but the jacket was a little on the sassy side, now that Holly thought about it. As was the extra layer of mascara she had on to go along with it. Had Vivian dressed up to chat with this man? Sounded like some sort of weird librarian kink.

No, Holly didn't believe it. Vivian couldn't be having an affair.

These messages were just a harmless cry for attention, since Vivian hadn't been getting any at home. If the police weren't searching hard for Vivian now, this could only make it worse. They'd assume she'd just run off with this guy, but Holly knew if Vivian had gone somewhere, it hadn't been willingly. Holly hadn't come to the library to cover Vivian's tracks, but she needed to protect her sister until she could figure out what she was into. Vivian would do the same for her.

Think, Holly.

She needed a record of these Hangouts chats, but she wouldn't be able to log in to the account from home because she didn't have the password. It was only saved here at the library. But she also didn't want the police to have access to the chat logs either—not just yet.

Holly couldn't simply download the files and email them to herself, because there would be an electronic trail, one the police could trace to her email account.

She selected the five most recent Hangouts chat sessions and began printing the conversation logs. The library was near empty, and Jane and Abby had left Holly alone, so she had no witnesses.

Holly walked over to the printer and began taking each paper as it came off hot.

Hot off the press. Nostalgia washed over her as she remembered her old job, when newspapers were still relevant and fake news didn't exist. Since she'd left her position, she felt like everything about her old self had become extinct. Mark was all too quick to remind her that no one read papers anymore, and fighting to become an online journalist was a rat race Holly didn't care to enter. But her old cylinders were firing now, and she couldn't stop herself.

She'd intended to print all the logs in a few batches, but as she grabbed the last page from the printer, she saw the detectives she'd spoken to the night before enter through the front door of the library.

Oh, shit.

She could not let them find Vivian's flirty conversations. Her sister would be deemed a cheating wife who'd run off. They wouldn't believe she was in trouble, and they wouldn't move mountains to find her.

Without thinking twice, she hurried back to the computer, quickly unchecked the "Save Password" button, and logged out of Vivian's Gmail account so strangers, including the cops, couldn't access her account from the library.

By doing so, she'd also locked herself out for good, but she had to protect her sister, and those Hangouts sessions looked bad. Holly wouldn't let the media demonize Vivian. Only TomKat45—who may very well be her sister's kidnapper—had a copy.

She thought she heard the approaching footsteps of the officers as they padded along the new carpet. Holly folded the printouts and hid them in the middle of her day planner, which she stashed in her purse. She got up from the computer.

"Ms. Boswell," Rigby greeted her.

Holly inhaled sharply. "Hello, there." She held her breath and let it escape slowly through her nostrils, afraid the detectives might smell the liquor on her if she didn't.

"Is that the computer your sister always works on?" he asked.

Holly could feel her face heating up. "Yes." Her mouth salivated. Stress made her want a drink, and as horrible as she felt, she still craved it.

"Did you find anything interesting?" he asked. Holly could tell Detective Rigby was disappointed she'd beaten him to the computer. By the way their eyeballs drifted to and from her midsection, the cops seemed to be focusing on Holly's hand clutching her purse.

"No." She coughed, quickly covering her mouth. "The browser history is just student inquiries. I searched through them all."

Nadia looked at her as if she didn't believe her. "Are you running out?"

"I have to get my sons; they're at the sitter's. No school today. Any new leads?" Holly asked.

"Not yet. But the disagreement between Vivian and Eve Carrington, are you sure it was just over the property gate and suspicions they were in her yard?" Rigby looked down at his notes. There was more there.

"I think so." Vivian had called her, upset over her argument with Eve, but then told her not to worry about it.

"According to her husband, your sister seemed to be having some troubles at home before she drove to Bay Shore. Anything you can think of that might've been on her mind?"

You can't be trusted, her mind pinged. Behind the real story, the police were always trying to sell the news a different one, an angle that would please the public and make the cops appear like the unsung heroes.

"No. She didn't mention anything." What had Clay told them? And how much did he even know about his wife's activity lately? Vivian seemed perfectly fine in her chats, happy even. But it wasn't like Holly could tell Rigby and Nadia that her sister's happiness stemmed from conversing with a man who wasn't her husband.

"Okay, well, let us know if you think of anything. I don't want to keep you, but if you don't mind, we're going to take a look at the computer," Rigby said.

Holly glanced over at it, hoping she'd done everything correctly when she'd logged out of Vivian's account. She hadn't had time to double-check.

"Sure. It's all yours," she said, but as she left, she was worried that she'd made a mistake logging out of Vivian's account. And the questions they'd asked bothered her. They didn't seem interested in whether Clay and Vivian had been arguing or if Clay might know anything about where his wife was. They seemed focused on Vivian's emotional state.

Holly couldn't allow their investigation to teeter toward suicide. The truth was, nothing had been wrong with Vivian before she'd gone missing. They were both mentally sound women now. Nothing from this life could shake them after what they'd endured in their childhood.

Suicide wasn't an option. It never had been.

5

"What did we learn from Mrs. Burgess's death?" Mother asked as they drove back from the funeral home.

Mrs. Burgess, their neighbor, hadn't lived right next door but down the road on the opposite side of the street. She was an old, feeble woman who'd resided with many cats until her weekly caretaker discovered that she'd swallowed a bottle of her prescription medication. They'd closed the casket at the funeral, forever transforming Holly's perception of death. Their mother had informed them that by the time they'd found Mrs. Burgess, her starving cats had stayed alive by eating her remains, and Mrs. Burgess wasn't presentable for public viewing.

It'd rocked Holly's world that the body was so bad inside the casket that it had to be closed. She hadn't heard of such an awful thing before, and at ten years old, she didn't need to. Holly didn't understand why they'd even gone to the funeral.

"Life is not a game we take ourselves out of voluntarily, girls. It is a privilege to be here, and breathe this air, and study and learn and live this life."

Holly's stomach turned when she realized their mother was using Mrs. Burgess's death as a teaching opportunity.

"By taking yourself out of the running, you're doing much more than cheating the game of life. You're failing so impossibly at existing that there can be no greater shame. We aren't quitters. No one should be *that* much of a quitter." She said this as if she were angry at Mrs. Burgess for killing herself.

Holly hadn't even known you could kill yourself with your own medicine up until that point. She sometimes took aspirin for headaches, and now she wouldn't.

"Is that an egocentric way to look at things?" Vivian had asked. "Perhaps Mrs. Burgess was very sad and didn't see life the same way you do. What if every day living all alone didn't feel like a gift to her? Maybe she'd learned all she wanted to by her age," Vivian argued.

Holly tensed in the back seat of the car as her sister challenged her mother using her own words. Vivian had disagreed a few times with their mother's theories, and Holly had thought Mother would become enraged, but sometimes it seemed she liked the banter.

"There are circumstances that drag people down, for sure. You just can't let yourself be one of those people. You're stronger than that. You're a Forester," she'd said with pride. Mother and Father had been published in multiple medical journals, their names renowned. Holly was certain it had given Dr. Cynthia Forester an extra boost of confidence she didn't need.

Forget the days she couldn't make it to class because she'd been *"celebrating her academic victories"* the day before. Mother talked about people being dragged down but never acknowledged her own shortcomings. It was like her faults didn't count, the cracks in her facade invisible, although she was eager to point out everyone else's, like poor old Mrs. Burgess's.

"Got it," Vivian said, although she'd rolled her eyes at Holly.

"What about the cats? What happened to them?" Holly asked. She wondered who would take care of them now.

Their mother clucked. "That's all you have to ask of this scenario? They put those mangy cats down. They'd eaten human flesh."

Holly was so sorry she'd asked. Vivian stuck out her tongue.

When they returned home, Holly thought the horror of their day was over, until Mother grabbed their journals. "Sit." She pointed at the kitchen table. If they didn't write it down, it was like it didn't happen. "It doesn't seem as if the importance of life or death has really resonated today."

"It has, Mother. Please," Vivian begged.

"Cynthia, maybe you should let them sit and watch TV. That was a lot on them. The way that poor woman went." Now Father was the one sticking out his tongue.

"This will just be a short exercise."

Father walked away, mumbling something under his breath. There was no sense arguing with her.

Holly wanted to crawl under the table and hide. Forever. It was bad enough experiencing the funeral and learning about Mrs. Burgess's death firsthand, but journaling about it meant they would have to dive deeper into the topic. The only things deeper than a grave were the tiny worms that wiggled beneath the casket like the ones in *Tales from the Crypt*, a scary show Holly liked to stay up late and watch with Vivian. She didn't think she could take any more scary today.

"You'll notice there weren't many people at the funeral. If Mrs. Burgess would've had a life worth living, there would've been more people there. You live a life worth living by filling it with mentally stimulating individuals and life accomplishments, not things that tarnish and filthy animals that turn on you when they're hungry."

Holly started crying. Those cats. She just couldn't.

"Wipe your face, Holly. After all, you're alive. No reason to be woeful," Mother said.

How could she say that? Poor Mrs. Burgess. Poor cats. They'd been hungry. What did she expect them to do for food? They'd just killed them? There must've been at least ten in that house.

Holly had her head down, but she could hear her mother's low heels clomp closer to where they were sitting at the table. Mother had little tassels on her shoes that shook as she walked. "The assignment is to write my obituary."

Holly popped up her head. "What is that?"

Mother breathed heavily, clearly agitated that she had to explain. "It's what the newspaper will say about me after I'm dead. It can be short. Mother of two, wife, and my accomplishments. You'll see that if you have even one discernible paragraph, that makes for a life worth living. Here is a sample obituary." She pulled a newspaper clipping out of the drawer and placed it on the table.

Vivian gawked at her. "You have an example ready to go?"

"Of course," she answered.

It was then that Holly knew this entire day had been one giant experiment. If Mother had *an example* ready to go, she'd gotten a brainstorm when she'd heard of Mrs. Burgess passing and had used it as an opportunity to clinically examine death—through them. Mother was a clinical researcher in a large study being conducted by the *Michigan Family Review* on children's concepts of death. Holly had seen the odd terminology beneath the trial's title: *Irreversibility. Nonfunctionality. Causality.*

The only thing Holly remembered from glancing at the papers was something on irreversibility because it sounded like an interesting word. She'd read: *Younger children are more likely than older children to view death as temporary or reversible. Some young children see death as similar to sleep.*

But Holly was old enough to understand that Mrs. Burgess was gone forever and that what had happened to her in that house was not changeable. She didn't need to do a journaling exercise to prove otherwise.

"Cynthia, that's enough," their father called from his office. "Tomorrow." His voice echoed off the french doors as they closed shut. He was done for the day, in retreat. Holly wished she could join him.

Mother acted like she didn't hear him and set their journals down in front of them on the kitchen table.

There was a clock on the wall in the shape of a black cat. It ticked furiously, the eyes moving when it reached the new hour. Holly always imagined it was timing her when they sat down at the table to do their journal exercises. Now all she could think of when she stared at it was the cats.

The cats. The cats. The cats.

Vivian put her hand on her sister's shoulder. "Holly. It's okay."

Holly sniffed up some more tears and started writing a personalized replica of what was on the newspaper clipping just to get it over with.

Cynthia Forester, loving mother of Vivian and Holly Forester, who passed away peacefully in her home . . .

But Mother stopped her midway, which was rare. "Dear, you have to date it and give me an age of death."

Holly peeped up at her through teary lashes. Mother didn't understand that when she made them dissect life's most tenuous moments, it rattled her insides. Vivian had soldiered on and was almost done, but Holly could barely stomach the cats, and now her mother wanted them to move on to the subject of *her* death.

"I don't want to give you a date and age of death." If she did, it was like she was wishing for it to happen. Like an episode of *Tales from the Crypt.*

"Just date it, Holly. My God," Vivian said under her breath.

"Fine." She wanted to get it over with. Holly dated the journal, adding forty years to the present one, a random number. She shut her eyes, trying not to think of those cats. The only problem was, when she closed her eyes, it wasn't the cats she imagined but her mother—in a casket.

It would be a week or so later when Holly saw the feline scampering along the bushes beside Mrs. Burgess's house, which had already been put up for sale. It was rumored that when the cleaning crew had gone in to fumigate the house, one of the cats that'd been hiding had escaped. Holly knew this had to be the one, because it was so skinny, she had almost mistaken it for a weasel or some other rodent.

She felt bad for the cat, trapped in that house for so many days all alone without food. Holly started feeding it cans of tuna, pieces of leftover chicken, and warmed milk. She'd place the food out near their garage and told no one about him, not even Vivian.

When she petted the cat, she tried not to think that it'd been one of the ones that'd feasted on her neighbor. She convinced herself that this cat was so thin, it'd nearly starved itself instead. Over the weeks, the cat filled out and became more affectionate, and Holly named him Boots; he was all black except for his white paws.

"What do you have there?" Mother asked on the day she caught her with the cat.

The sun was shining in three streaks across Mother's face, a bright fall day, but Holly couldn't read her expression. Boots was nuzzling against Holly's hand to see what she'd brought him to eat, his tail dragging a maple leaf along with it. She was crouching on the ground. "Oh, it's just a stray."

Mother smirked. "Sure that isn't the runaway from Burgesses'? The one that ate human flesh?" Mother crossed her arms across the argyle pattern on her sweater. She'd come back from the university a little early. "You can't keep it. It's diseased."

"He's fine. He's a nice cat. He was wasting away when I found him, so he wasn't one of the bad cats," Holly defended, her own arms strapped across the chest of her white private-school button-down. The cat darted away.

"Ha! Holly, cats are filthy. They're all bad. Especially that one." Mother felt animals were *"dirty and pestilent, companions for the lonely and bored."*

Holly looked over her shoulder to find Boots, but he was long gone into the hedges. Her exposed kneecaps still tingled from where he'd brushed against her legs. He was not *bad*.

"Come inside," Mother demanded.

"You promise you'll leave him alone?" Holly asked.

Mother gave her a stern look that made her shut her mouth in a hurry.

Holly grabbed Boots's dishes so he wouldn't make the mistake of coming back to finish the rest of what she'd left for him. Holly was afraid of what might happen to him if he did.

But Boots never came back.

Holly had asked her parents about him and they'd said they didn't have time to be bothered with a stray cat, and especially *that* one. Holly had cried into her pillow nearly every night afterward for a long time. Her sister had tried to console her, but Vivian couldn't really sympathize with Holly because she'd never known about the cat or seen Holly with it. No one understood her despair, how she was only trying to save Boots, the way she wished someone would save her—save both of them.

Vivian had been discovered missing from the house just a few weeks before. She'd run off with a boy who she'd claimed had taken her to watch a meteor shower and nothing more, but her parents didn't believe her. Holly wasn't sure she did either, but it sounded like something Vivian would be interested in. Listening to her sister's cries through the walls, locked in her closet, made Holly more aware of what could be done to her if she pressed the issue over the cat.

In the following weeks, Holly noticed her mother watching her closely, the way her gray-blue eyes flicked up and down to appraise her when she walked past the study. Strangely, Mother would also ask about Boots every few days. At first, Holly thought it was out of concern, but then Holly had made the mistake of going into her study to find a pencil for her homework and saw what her mother had been jotting down.

It was a log of dates. Holly counted back on her fingers, and the first date on the page was the same day Mother had discovered Holly with Boots beside the garage. The log, she'd decided, had to be related to the cat.

The top of the notepad had a word and definition scrawled across the top:

Causality: involves an abstract and realistic understanding of the external and internal events that might possibly cause an individual's death.

It hit her harder than any of the previous ways her mother had used them to get ahead at work. Her skin screamed, hot and itchy. She balled up her fists and tried to holler, but no sound escaped. Her chest felt like it would cave in from all the days she'd walked the streets looking for Boots and the nights in the car when her eyes would comb the streets for his little white feet.

Boots hadn't gone missing; Mother had made him go missing for her study.

Did she kill him?

Holly couldn't rule it out, but it'd happened so quickly. Boots was here one day, gone the next, too fast for Mother to find the animal and get rid of it, but Holly shouldn't have underestimated her. Because she hadn't been mothering Holly when she'd asked her all those questions about the cats.

She'd been studying her.

6

TomKat45: Thursday has become my favorite day of the week

SassyVivi38: It's definitely a lift in my week too. It's nice to have met you on here

TomKat45: Totally kismet. It's hard to believe I have to wait until January to see you IRL

SassyVivi38: JUST five more months . . . but I know what you mean. The anticipation is killing me

TomKat45: Is that what the lit girl calls foreplay? I've never wanted to go to Louisville, KY, so badly in my life!

SassyVivi38: Words you thought you'd never say ;) And no . . . dirty mind . . .

TomKat45: Dirty mind? Not guilty. It's hard when you put the thoughts in my head though. Why do you think the conference is there this year?

SassyVivi38: IDK. Phoenix was so beautiful last year. We hiked Camelback. Were you there?

TomKat45: Nope. Are you a hiker?

SassyVivi38: NO. Lol. But I enjoyed the views

TomKat45: That's okay. I prefer being by the water to dusty trails, myself

SassyVivi38: Me too! I love the water. And boats. Preferably yachts ;)

TomKat45: High maintenance, lady. Mine's not a yacht, but it's nice. Just Bodie and me aboard. He keeps me company, but it gets lonesome sometimes with no one to talk to . . . at least not with actual words. Although I have gotten better at decoding his barks

SassyVivi38: Cute. Well, just because a person lives in your house doesn't mean they talk to you

TomKat45: Ouch. It sounds like you're lonelier than I am. At least I have Bodie

SassyVivi38: Possibly. But I think it's something that happens as you get older. Your circle gets smaller until it shrinks so much that all that's left is a line with a few stretch marks

TomKat45: Jeez. And I thought I was having a day

SassyVivi38: I was an English major, remember? Everything I say is more dramatic than it needs to be ;)

TomKat45: No college for me, but I'll tell you one thing. Nothing is sadder than being in a room full of people who make you feel like you're all alone

SassyVivi38: Now you're depressing me. Maybe I do need a dog

TomKat45: You should get one

SassyVivi38: My husband is allergic

TomKat45: Better yet!

SassyVivi38: LOL. I have to get going—the library is closing. And you're being bad. Maybe we can take a hike in Louisville. Even though I hate hiking.

TomKat45: I hear Tioga Falls is lovely. It's near the water just for you. We can always go "off trail" ;)

SassyVivi38: Sounds nice . . .

TomKat45: And why do I only get the crumbs of time you have left at the end of the night, and only once a week? (Did you like that? I tried to use a metaphor, i.e., for my English major)

SassyVivi38: I LOVE crumbs of time. And . . . so I don't get sucked through the screen and never return. Good night, Tom

TomKat45: That doesn't sound so terrible. Because if you're getting sucked through the screen, it means you're headed my way . . . Good night, Viv xo

Holly sank back against the headrest in her minivan and closed her eyes, scrunching the library printouts of her sister's chat session in her hands. "You've got to be kidding me." She pinched the space between the bridge of her nose and her eyes. Her lingering headache from no sleep had taken full residence in her forehead, spreading up and across her T-zone.

This was a nightmare.

She wanted to keep reading the other four most recent Hangouts sessions she'd printed, but it all felt like such an intrusion. It was like Holly was listening in on someone else's private conversation, their chat sessions, so intimate. She hated to admit she'd enjoyed reading their back-and-forth flirting. It made her think Tom and Vivian might actually make a nice couple—IRL—and that was disturbing.

Holly enjoyed Tom's jokes, his play on words, his sad truths. And Holly understood her sister's need to speak to him; she felt strangely jealous of their connection, one she hadn't shared with Mark in a long while. But Holly also saw the imminent danger in their conversation, like the innuendos in Tom's seemingly innocent words and phrases like *kismet*. He was telling Vivian he thought they were meant to be, and that was scary after just a few months of interaction, if that's all it'd been. Tom was clearly obsessed with her sister. And maybe she was just as taken with him. Vivian had said the anticipation was *killing* her. Did she really want to see him that badly?

"Thursday has become my favorite day" was also suspect to Holly. As eager for attention as Vivian might have been, Holly had the sinking feeling that Tom was worse off. He kept telling Vivian she was lonelier than he was, but Holly thought he was projecting his own emptiness onto her. Vivian had a husband and extended family, and it seemed all Tom had was his dog. Loneliness might cause a man to do desperate things. Had he been desperate enough to kidnap her sister?

She didn't like mentions of going *"off trail"* either or how her sister had said, *"sounds nice."* They were plotting to have a physical affair. An online one clearly already existed.

Maybe this was the way dating worked these days. Holly wouldn't know, but it still didn't sit right with her.

She thought about Clay and the fact that he hadn't returned her messages. The detectives had clearly spoken with him, but they'd walked away with the impression that whatever troubles existed in their marriage, Vivian's mental state was responsible for them.

Holly still didn't buy that. After reading her sister's chat with Tom, she had two plausible suspects.

Either Tom had become so intrigued with Vivian and so eager to meet her that he'd decided he couldn't wait until the conference and snatched her away in the night. Or Clay had found the chats and had become enraged that she was having an online affair.

Could Clay really have hurt her over it, though? He seemed too measured for that.

One thing was for sure: someone had scared Vivian last night. If it was her husband, Vivian would've certainly recognized him. She hadn't seemed to know who was on her tail—at least not that she could tell Holly over the phone.

Tom could be just a friend, another librarian, but this internet creeper reminded Holly of the ones she'd seen on TV. Her mind flashed to all the missing-women cases she'd watched on *Dateline*. Ever since she'd left her job, crime-investigation shows and podcasts were Holly's crime beat outlet, the gorier the details the better. It was her little bit of grit in an otherwise mundane existence.

Mark hated to watch the shows with her, and Holly was constantly pausing and muting the TV when the kids came down in the middle of the night for a snack, because she couldn't let them see the horrors of the world. Unlike her parents, she was content to keep her children in their innocent bubbles as long as possible.

Nonetheless, what she'd absorbed from her stint in journalism and those crime series was that it was important to question everything, even the things presented as facts. Holly just never thought she'd have to use that knowledge to find her own sister.

One question almost always popped up in the cases where a victim had been lured into a relationship online: How could they be so stupid?

Vivian was not an unintelligent woman, not by a long stretch. She'd gotten into Harvard and graduated with honors from their English department. She'd pursued a master's in library science.

She didn't have to take up with this man, but she had, a logical decision in her mind.

The only clue Holly had picked up outside the chat messages themselves was that Vivian and Tom always seemed to chat on Thursdays. Holly regretted having locked herself out of Vivian's account permanently. Who was the stupid one now?

It was possible the police had already hacked into her account and retrieved the chats, and that brought her no comfort either. Part of her didn't want to offer the information to the detectives, and the other half thought she should drive straight to the police station and serve up the information on a platter. But she was worried that it could incriminate her sister. Also, it wasn't like she had this guy's full name. There were a gazillion Toms in the world, and maybe that wasn't even his real first name. Perhaps the police could quickly trace his screen name, though.

No. She thought of Delilah's case again. Her gut was telling her not to take this to the police just yet. Not until she was finished reading.

Between the pull in her belly and the hot spikes of pain behind her eyes, she was losing it. "Ah." She placed her thumb and forefinger over the bridge of her nose again and grabbed the skin there, hoping to relieve pressure. As much as her head hurt, she also had a need for a drink—all this stress. She needed a clear head to figure out the best course of action here.

The headlines about the respected wife of a high-powered attorney going missing sounded much better than those of an estranged cheating spouse. **Missing wife of defense attorney linked with an online lover.**

Longtime small-town librarian vanishes off pier in the middle of a thunderstorm would pique the interest of the public, warrant a search party, garner sympathy. Do-gooders might even offer a reward.

No, revealing this information right now was not to Vivian's benefit.

Holly grabbed her cell phone for a moment, wondering if she should call Mark and ask him if they could offer a reward for anyone who knew anything about Vivian's disappearance. Then she remembered who she was talking about. Offering a reward meant opening up their pocketbook, and Mark was not a fan of that. She noticed missed texts from him and one missed call.

Mark (15 minutes ago): **Are you home yet? My mother wants to know if she'll be able to make water aerobics**

Mark (5 minutes ago): **Why aren't you answering my texts? You aren't trying to meddle in the police investigation, are you?**

Mark (1 minute ago): **Call me**

1 missed call

Ugh. She couldn't take it. Not today. *Sue's fucking water aerobics? Meddling in Vivian's investigation? Is he for real?* Her sister was missing.

Holly had never seriously considered leaving Mark and had never even been tempted to have an affair. She wondered how Vivian could be so foolish as to fall into this online trap, but at the same time, she understood it. There was something Tom had said that had made her reflect on her own marriage.

"Nothing is sadder than being in a room full of people who make you feel like you're all alone." The words caught in her throat, the hurt Vivian felt all too familiar.

Holly's boys loved her, but she often felt alone when she and Mark were in the same room, like he loved her only as much as she could contribute to their family, her worth measured in chores and meals and completed homework assignments. She no longer felt connected to him in the way a wife should feel connected to her husband. She often made excuses that when the kids were older, they'd sort themselves out—but was that a mistake?

Vivian's dire situation was making Holly aware of the faults in her own marriage. But how severe were the faults in Vivian's?

When Holly pulled onto Handsome Avenue, she saw the barrage of cameramen and press vehicles outside her sister's house. She had to park on the opposite side of the street. Holly's headache practically blinded her. *Not now,* she told her oncoming migraine.

The news about Vivian was apparently out there. Holly's heart palpitated for a moment.

She checked her watch in panic. She thought of the cat clock on her mother's kitchen wall counting her down to forty-eight hours. The flutters in her chest rose. She could use another drink.

Every hour brought them nearer to the point where Holly knew from working the beat that a missing person was usually presumed dead if they hadn't been found. It had been nearly twenty-one hours since Vivian's panicked call.

Holly sat in her van for a moment, debating about trying to go inside. But she needed to talk to Clay, and he wasn't returning her messages. She couldn't see much from across the street, so she exited her vehicle and tried to blend in on the sidewalk with the other curious neighbors.

"Lawyer's wife. Missing."

Holly heard the mumbles and came to the horrible realization that her sister's life had become a source of gossip, the kind people talked about in the grocery store, the sort their parents had detested.

Holly was the uncouth member of the family with her pedestrian talk and revealing questions, the one who preferred math over English but had nevertheless gone into the lowbrow profession of crime journalism. One thing she did have in common with her parents even then—she hated gossip, especially gossip about one of her family members.

"I heard she was involved with the neighbor."

Holly turned her head to see the source of that preposterous rumor and locked eyes with a little old lady in a bathrobe. There was no way Vivian was having an affair with Peter Carrington. She'd said he was so vanilla, he made Clay look downright kinetic. Holly had to smile for a moment at the memory of her sister's choice of words.

As she did, she caught sight of an older man who was in complete contrast to the elderly lady: well-dressed in slacks and a brown sweater, plaid scarf draped around his neck, walking a dog—a German shepherd mix, perhaps. It made Holly wonder what breed TomKat's Bodie was, and she was mad at herself for taking an interest in Vivian's possible abductor.

Holly was startled to realize she actually knew the older man, though. It was his distinctive mop of wavy hair and swagger as he walked that sparked her memory. That and the plaid scarf. He had been a professor at the same university where her parents had taught.

Holly couldn't remember his name, but she recognized his face, and she knew that he'd at one time been a trusted member of the faculty who partook in the campus happy hours their parents sometimes attended. He'd been in their house once or twice for a nightcap in the nineties, when Holly was a child.

And now it was all coming back to her—more gossip, ironically. He'd pulled some sort of wild stunt and abandoned his whole family and career with no warning. Now, that was a town rumor even her parents spoke of. Eventually, he was discovered holed up on an island in the Caribbean. He'd lost his position at the university, his family, his reputation. Holly couldn't recall the exact details, but she had faint memories of her mother being worried when he was missing and their father not caring one bit. Holly was surprised the professor had come back and still resided in this town . . . and likely somewhere nearby, if he was out for a walk.

A cop car pulled up next, lights whirring red and blue. The LEDs sliced through Holly's temple.

"Disperse. We're going to need everyone off the sidewalk. Please return to your homes."

The cops were kicking everyone out. Another cop car pulled up beside Clay's driveway, and Holly immediately recognized who it was— Nadia. Holly was fearful they'd found out about her secret printouts.

She held her hand over her head, still swimming in pain. "Ugh." She placed her fingers over her eyes like a blindfold. It was time to get home and lock herself in a dark room.

"Excuse me?" a gruff voice said.

Holly peeked through her fingers to find the old professor there. *What does he want?*

"Yes. I'm sorry; I'm having a bad headache," she said.

"I noticed." He held something out for her. It was a small amber bottle with a white lid. The professor had a leather messenger bag strung around his body where he must've pulled the pills from.

Is he giving me drugs? Her mind spiraled to Mrs. Burgess and her closed casket. Holly still had an aversion to pills because of that day. She knew logically that there were good pills and bad pills, ones that were necessary to cure certain infections and ease pain, but she avoided them whenever possible. "Oh . . . no thank you."

"It's ginger," he said with a strong Long Island accent, the *r* getting lost on his tongue. Their parents had taught them to enunciate perfectly, which meant they didn't sound like true New Yorkers. Mother had been from a cow town upstate, Father a Long Island lifer, but he'd converted his dialect for her.

"Ginger?" she asked.

"Cures headaches. Trust me. Just take one tab." He took her hand and closed her fist around the bottle.

The professor's dog rubbed against her leg, and she was surprised how friendly he was for looking so fierce. Holly had a strange feeling the old man was much the same. She normally wouldn't do such a thing, take pills from a man off the street, but this was a person her mother had trusted at one time, a friend of the family. Not that he likely recognized her. Holly didn't think he'd try to harm her, though.

Plus, she was desperate to make the pain go away. She examined the tiny white label on the bottle, and all it said was: *Ginger, pure extract, 750 mg.*

The police made their announcement again. Half the street had cleared out, but the news cameramen and the lady in the bathrobe were holding strong.

"Better get going before they bring out the dogs." The old man looked at his pup. "Come on, Harley."

"Thanks again."

He winked at her and trotted away. Holly opened her car door and collapsed in the seat, her temples throbbing. Sometimes her headaches were related to alcohol, and other times they were brought on by stress. She wasn't sure which had caused this one, but she was betting it was a stress migraine, and those were the worst.

She glanced at her phone—five more texts and two more calls from Mark.

She couldn't call him for help.

If she was ill, contacting Mark would make for less of a fight later about how long she'd been away from home, but she didn't want to make excuses for taking the time to look for her missing sister. She needed to take a stand for Vivian and herself.

But . . . the pain. She'd waited too long to drive home.

Holly texted her brother-in-law again. Maybe Clay would open his front door to her so they could actually talk about Vivian. His car was in the driveway, but she didn't know if she had the strength to bypass the police and face him uninvited.

Holly: Clay, I'm nearby. I want to talk to you about Vivian. Can I stop?

She practiced rhythmic breathing to quiet the zinging in her temporal lobe.

Desperate, Holly cracked open the mysterious bottle. It reminded her of something she might find in an old-school apothecary. The capsules looked more like rabbit pellets than pills.

She sniffed the contents. The odor singed her nostrils. *Whoa.* If that wasn't ginger, she didn't know what was. On the beat, she'd reported on men slipping drugs into women's drinks, but this man had a prescription with his name printed on the bottle—Archibald Steiner. That's right; Holly remembered the name from the university now—Professor Steiner. The substance inside appeared to be exactly what he said it was.

Holly took another whiff. It smelled like the sliced ginger that appeared on the side of her favorite Japanese dish at Koi Sushi. Her reporter brain told her these pills had to in fact be ginger.

Holly took a pill and swallowed it down with the remains of a bottle of water in her car. The cop lights continued to flash, but no one approached her van and asked her to move it.

She checked her phone, but she knew Clay hadn't responded. Why was he avoiding her?

Holly closed her eyes, and the most miraculous thing started to happen. Little by little, the pain that had invaded her T-zone started to dissipate, like tiny fingers slipping over her head in ease. The ginger was doing the trick—and fast.

Freaking miracle.

Thirty-five years of life and no one had told her ginger worked for migraines.

With the windows rolled down, Holly heard another thing from the nosy neighbors on the street before she pulled away.

"It's always the quiet ones. Librarian. Who would've thought she would've gotten mixed up with the neighbor?"

Holly wanted to shout at the woman from her car window to knock off the ludicrous talk, but she stopped herself. It would only make her mother do a double roll in her grave. Mother hated gossip, but she hated public displays over gossip even more.

"Great minds discuss ideas. Average minds discuss events. Small minds discuss people."

They were words Professor Cynthia Forester uttered every chance she got.

Had Vivian talked to anyone else about Peter Carrington, though? The rumor of an affair between them had to have come from somewhere.

Another of Mother's favorite lines by the philosopher and poet Kahlil Gibran came to mind. *"If you reveal your secrets to the wind, you should not blame the wind for revealing them to the trees."*

Mother often talked in quotes and theories. Vivian had adopted that idiosyncrasy, whereas Holly hated it, preferring a much more direct approach to communication. She wished she could say she was more like her father, but he used quotes and proverbs, too, just more sparingly.

It made Holly question whether the insinuations about Vivian and Peter could possibly be true. Was Peter's screen name TomKat? There was all that talk in Tom's Hangouts feed about living alone by the water. It didn't jibe. But if Vivian did have something going on with the neighbor and Clay found out about it, that was troublesome. Clay was a man of power, but was he violent?

Every time Holly tried to forget about the Carringtons, they kept sneaking back into the conversation. If Vivian had been seeing Peter in secrecy, it wouldn't be her first offense doing something she shouldn't have with the opposite sex—but it had been a long time since she'd tried. The problems Vivian had now reminded Holly of the ones they'd covered up when they were younger. Vivian liked to play games with people, like the time she'd taken off at the mall and when she'd run off with the boy to see the meteor shower.

Vivian had thought she was clever, dreaming up ways to circumvent their mother's scrutinizing lens. But her bouts of rebellion had come back to bite them both—Holly and Vivian—during the summer Holly considered the worst of their childhood. There were peculiar things about Vivian's most recent behavior—particularly how sneaky and flirtatious she sounded in the Hangouts sessions—that had the same feel as that summer.

And the consequences then had changed them both forever.

7

1997

"Why is she making us journal about this?" Holly asked.

Vivian was dressed in cutoff shorts and a paisley bodysuit, perched at the tongue-and-groove picnic table at the back of their wraparound porch. The table was the kind found at Robert Moses Park, fire-truck red and dinged from use, sturdy, with heavy planks and bench seating.

Their back porch was made for summertime picnics with its large swinging chair and striped maroon-and-white canopy overtop. It hung in the corner where Father liked to read. When Mother would bother him to do things around the house, he'd sometimes escape out there or to the little roped-off garden in the backyard by the shed if he couldn't hide from her on the porch.

"Just answer Mom's questions so we can get to the beach," Vivian said, never one to challenge their parents' journaling questions, even though they'd been doing these mind-bending activities since they could pick up a pencil. Holly had assumed they would eventually stop once they became teens, but no such luck.

"But these questions are—"

"Don't be repressive. Just answer them, Holly." Vivian rolled her eyes, pebble gray and stormy just like their mother's. She even sounded like her, using large psych words like *repressive*. Their father had light eyes, too, but Holly had been stuck with mud brown. She always got the short end of the genetic stick, and her capability for writing these stinking entries was no exception.

Holly watched as her older sister's mechanical pencil flowed swiftly over the lined paper, no shortage of inspiration from the impressive vat in her pretty head. Her mother often told them *"don't get creative; just state the facts"* in regard to the psychoanalytical questions she posed, but Holly was convinced Vivian had an easier time answering the hard ones because she was older, smarter, more like her parents.

Vivian looked up at Holly, annoyed. "Just make something up if you don't have a real answer. It's like you've never done this before." She sighed.

"Easy for you to say," Holly muttered. Everything was frozen—her hands, her brain—it happened when she was nervous. She was also distracted because she knew her sister's offer was on borrowed time.

It was supposed to be hot today, and Vivian had agreed to drive her to the beach. Holly wanted to get there early so she could find a good spot to set down her towel with the other soon-to-be ninth graders, one near the ice-cream stand, where all the other kids from her school hung out. They just had to finish their assignment first. Their mother couldn't let their brains go soft with an entire three months devoid of learning—not using the best muscle God gave them.

Whenever they complained about journaling, their mother would go on about how lucky they were that they didn't have to be stuck in summer camps like the other children of working parents.

Holly envied the hell out of those kids.

What was the point of having a summer break if they were still assigned homework? The questions today weren't even reasonable, let alone appropriate for parents to ask their teenage daughters.

Holly shouldn't have been all that surprised. Their mother had gone off the rails that past Christmas when she'd begun a study dealing with the Freudian consequences of sexuality and parenting. She was working on an article for a new clinical journal, and when Mother had scholarly papers to write, she became obsessed with the research. Holly despised being viewed as her mother's patient, clinically assessed in her own home.

After Christmas dinner and way too many glasses of eggnog, which Holly could only assume was spiked with the clear liquid hidden in the empty cookie tin, Mother had somehow made the analysis that their fireplace was a sexual symbol resembling the female birthing canal. Santa, of course, was the phallic element squeezing himself through the chimney, chubby and red-faced. Why their mother had shared these thoughts with them, Holly would never understand.

Needless to say, Christmas had been forever ruined. Holly had long been over the actual idea of Santa Claus, but to sexualize him destroyed the entire holiday. Even Vivian had regarded her mother's comments with wrinkled-nose disgust, though she was mostly just happy Father let her sip his glass of wine while she listened. Mother never cared if they drank. She claimed they'd experiment less on their own if alcohol wasn't forbidden at home. Father disagreed, although not as strenuously as he should have.

Holly's hairline was growing sweaty, anxiety percolating out of her pores, acting as tiny springboards for her curls. The lined paper was still nearly blank.

"Who did you put?" she whispered to Vivian.

Vivian sighed, already on her last question. "If you don't hurry up, I'm not taking you."

"Well?" she asked.

"You know we can't share answers," Vivian whispered back. She looked past Holly, no doubt through the kitchen window. They couldn't see their mother watching them, but they knew she was there.

Holly peered over her shoulder just to make sure. "Come on. Just this once. Who did you put for the guy you . . ." She could barely read the question aloud: "Are most likely to have sexual fantasies about, in real life or on television, and why?"

Ew. Holly knew her childhood wasn't normal. Their parents were respected local college professors. But Holly understood enough about other families to realize hers was far from average.

Vivian stared at her as if she were incompetent, although Holly realized Vivian was scared too. Mother's rules were not to be broken, especially when it came to her research.

"Please?" Holly begged. She didn't want to admit it to Vivian or her mother, but she hadn't had any sexual fantasies. These were the moments in her life when her mother's profession made her wonder if she were the one who wasn't normal. Mother had written the question on the paper clear as day, as if it were assumed that both girls had fantasies of this sort. But Holly hadn't. For the life of her, she couldn't think of any movie stars she'd like to kiss . . . let alone . . .

Gag.

Maybe she *was* repressed. These questions made Holly want to move far, far away and never return. She looked at her sister pleadingly.

Vivian looked back pitifully. "Okay. Rico."

Holly smiled. Rico was the tall, dark, and superhot lifeguard. His station was Field 5 beach, and his abs were so defined they reminded Holly of the bottom of a serrated egg carton. A six-pack.

"Good one." And just like that, Holly's fingers started to write. She'd buy her sister a snow cone or something at the beach for helping her out.

Holly was getting through the assignment, but then she came to a full stop again. "Oh God. What about question number five?"

Vivian rolled her eyes again. "Just write something. If she catches us, she's going to flip. You know she's probably using this for her article." Vivian looked at the kitchen window again.

The assignment was making Holly hotter. Her curly mane, pulled up into a bun on the top of her head, was becoming more unraveled by the moment. The sounds of cars rolling by in every direction made her itch even more to get on the road. But if question two was a showstopper, number five was downright immobilizing.

If you were in a romantic setting with the subject in question two and there were no consequences to be had, emotional or physical, would you engage in sexual activity or abstain?

Holly didn't care that she was cheating.

She was fourteen years old, for the love of God, and these questions made her feel completely icky. Vivian was three years older, and maybe they didn't bother her as much. Vivian was mature for her age, and she read *Cosmo*, and so she knew things. Whereas Holly knew nothing, and her brain was at a standstill.

Vivian wrote her last sentence, then closed her journal, glancing up at her with reproach. "What?" she whisper-screamed.

Holly was sweating profusely, and the crashing, cool waves of Robert Moses beach sounded so good right now. "Number five?"

Vivian sat back and crossed her arms. "Fine. Yes. Engage."

Holly shut her eyes, trying not to think about the defined lines on Rico's belly and her own curvaceous body pressed against them. Puberty had come swiftly for Holly, and even though she had shit for hair, she was rounder than Vivian in every way, including her breasts, which had blossomed into a full D-cup already. She hadn't been ready for the sudden changes, and now their mother was making her write about them.

She felt like she couldn't breathe.

"Engage," Vivian had said.

Holly would engage, too, she decided. This was all a fantasy world anyway.

She finished the assignment as Vivian sat there hemming and hawing.

Mother eventually reemerged on the back porch, none the wiser, and collected their notebooks. It was so brutally sweltering outside, Vivian had decided to both drive Holly and stay at the beach. She even hung out with Holly for a while, a rare occurrence.

It just so happened that Rico was working that day, playing music on his boom box while he sat in his tall white chair, king of the beach.

Once a day, he played Def Leppard's "Pour Some Sugar on Me" and took off his shirt. That day, when he did, Vivian smiled at Holly, and she knew they were both thinking about the assignment, their shared secret.

"He's all that and a bag of chips," Vivian said.

"No doubt." Holly giggled.

They both thought they'd gotten away with sharing answers until they'd arrived home. Mother was waiting, drinking a glass of tomato juice, which they both knew was more than just juice. The whites of her eyes were nearing the shade of the liquid in the glass, her smile as poisonous as the clear stuff rimming the top. The house was a mess, papers spread all over the table, the girls' journals at the center.

"Did you have a nice time at the beach?" she asked. Her voice was raspy and slurred.

"Dad?" Holly called. If Mom found out they'd conspired on their answers, they were dead.

Beyond dead.

They were dead and buried. She'd lock them both in a closet this time. Holly didn't think she'd survive it.

She pushed away the thought, scouring her brain for a resolution. It had only been a few questions. They'd had similar answers in the past, and their mother had been okay with it, making special note of it and adding the similarities to her research.

"He can't save you from the hole you've dug for yourself, dear. I've sent him out to get some milk."

Holly had caught too much sun, and her burned cheeks were flaming with fear. *Save you?* Why would she need to be saved?

There had been a whole gallon of milk in the refrigerator when Holly made cereal that morning. She ran over to the humming appliance. The metal handle felt good on her tender skin. She yanked the door open and pointed to the nearly full container of milk. Fear ratcheted up her spine. Maybe if she could prove Father didn't need to get milk, it would make him reappear.

Mother shrugged, her bony shoulders jutting out of her cardigan. It was nearly ninety degrees outside, but Mother was always cold. Holly imagined it was a side effect of being heartless.

"Look at that. I wanted skim, and there's only whole milk. It seems we've all been a little piggish in this house about what we want."

Holly looked down at her body, because it couldn't be Vivian she was talking about. Her sister had adopted a Courtney Love waifish appearance, skinny, with full, bleached-out bangs and lots of eyeliner. Vivian stood rigid as she watched them, poised on the tiptoes of her Keds. She looked like she was going to sprint away at any moment.

"Piggish and selfish. With my time. And yours. You know what I mean." Mother stared at them with that half-crazed look in her eye. She'd wait there all day until they answered her. Then she'd analyze every word that sprang from their mouths until she shook out the ones she wanted.

"I don't," Vivian said. "Do you, Holly?" Her urgent gaze told Holly to follow her lead.

"N-no idea." Holly's hand still gripped the refrigerator handle. She had the sudden desire to be closer to her sister. They pushed each other's buttons, but Vivian was better at handling their parents than she was.

Mother picked up her work papers and threw them all over the floor. Vivian flinched. "You're trying to screw up my research. Everything I've done for you . . ." Mother inhaled a sharp breath as if it pained her; meanwhile, Holly couldn't think of one single good thing her mother had ever done for them. "You talked to each other while I was on the phone during your assignment. Shared answers," she said with contempt.

Holly instinctively shook her head—*no*. Vivian remained stock-still.

Mother rose from the table, chair screeching beneath her. Both girls jerked back. Their parents had never harmed them, but their mother's mind games could elicit the kind of response that came with a physical beating. When Holly had accidentally spilled spaghetti sauce on one of Mother's clinical papers, she'd made Holly sop it up with her favorite blanket—the one she'd had since she was a baby.

Holly hadn't realized it would ruin the blanket, the red sauce leaving a nasty stain on the thin fibers. Later, they didn't just toss it; they burned the blanket in a barrel in the backyard because Mother didn't want it to soak through the garbage. *Oh well, you were about done with that anyway. It was time.*

The blanket had also been one of the only things she'd ever received from her grandmother. Holly thought that had a lot to do with Mother torching it, because she didn't care to talk about her parents.

Maybe leaving them to their own devices that afternoon had been its own experiment? It was just like their mother to do that. Holly didn't want Vivian taking the fall when it was all her fault. She opened her mouth to confess, but Vivian started defending them again. "Why would you assume we shared answers? What happened? Did we have similar responses?"

Mother snorted and laughed, but it sounded like a stifled "ya."

"That's not unreasonable, Mother. It's happened before. What if we both just had the same opinion?"

Vivian's voice was cool and convincing. Holly could never sound like that under such duress.

"Impossible!"

"It's not. We live together. We're around the same people. The subjects in your study don't come from the exact same environment as we do. It's not fair for you to blame us for having similar answers," Vivian said.

Mother wobbled on unsteady feet. She raised her hand, and Holly gasped. She thought Mother was going to strike Vivian, but she wiped the saliva from her mouth.

"You lie. You're messing with my life's work. You've been given everything. All I ask for in return is honesty." Her voice held bitter accusation.

"We were honest!" Vivian sounded pissed, and Holly applauded her acting ability. They were officially in too deep to confess now.

"Really? *Your sister* is ready for a sexual encounter? Holly still plays with dolls."

"No she doesn't." Vivian crossed her arms.

Holly stiffened by the refrigerator. Her mother had wanted to get rid of her doll collection, but Holly liked her dolls and asked to keep them in her closet. She never played with them anymore, but she didn't want them in some dusty box in the basement or dropped off for donation. "I just didn't want to give them away," Holly protested.

Mother had allowed her to keep them but then later chastised her for it, asking her if the dolls were somehow uncanny, a Freudian analysis that meant they were real to her. She'd asked if Holly had fancied them because they represented a childhood she was still holding on to. The comments felt insulting, and Holly had explained that she just still liked her dolls, and there wasn't any more to it. Just like she'd liked her blanket.

"Of course. So a child who doesn't want to give her dolls away certainly wouldn't be ready to engage in sexual activity. You would never sleep with this Rico." Mother said his name as if it disgusted her, adding an *ugh* to the *c* in his name. "You lied on the research. You lied to me. You copied your sister, who also lied, because I received the records from her last OB-GYN exam, and her hymen is still intact."

"What?" Vivian gasped.

"So that means she hasn't given it away to one of her little boyfriends, and she certainly wouldn't to some punk who works as a lifeguard at the beach. I'd bet my life on it. You wouldn't dare," their mother concluded.

Vivian's mouth dropped open. Holly's cheeks sizzled, embarrassed for her sister. She shouldn't know her sister's virginity status. Not unless Vivian had chosen to share it with her.

The horrible conversation abruptly halted when their father busted through the front door. "A hand, please?" he asked in regard to the groceries.

Holly ran through the foyer and out the front door to grab as many bags as she could from the car. Anything to get away from their mother and the awful confrontation that had erupted in the kitchen. When Holly and her father came back in, Mother was yelling at Vivian to pick up the papers. "Look what you made me do."

Their father nearly knocked over Mother's glass when he set down the grocery bags on the counter. "Really, Cynthia?" He picked up her drink and moved it to the table.

"It's nearly dinnertime," she said defensively.

"Yes. But you look as though you've been drinking since noon." He ripped off some paper towels from the dispenser and dabbed at the mess.

Mother glowered at him. Their father rarely challenged her on her drinking, but she was a special shade of drunk today.

She started patting at his coat pocket. "A little warm for a coat. How many cigarettes did you smoke on the way home from the store? And how many packs did you stuff in your jacket?"

"Not nearly enough," he said.

They continued to argue about who was the more offensive addict, but Holly was just happy the heat was off her and Vivian for the moment.

Holly hated their mother for creating this situation, the impossible questions she'd made them answer, the horrible feelings of inadequacy that came along with them. Making her feel bad just because she wanted to keep her dolls. Defending herself for not wanting to grow up so fast.

But Mother shouldn't have pushed Vivian's buttons the same way.

Vivian should've been pissed, furious, ready to rip a hole through their mother's dark marble eyes, but instead she turned to Holly. In the place of a scowl was an expression of defiance, plain and simple. Vivian had taken their mother's words as a challenge.

I'd bet my life on it. You wouldn't dare.

8

The press had swarmed Clay's house earlier, but as he looked through the blinds, he noticed there weren't as many news trucks this time. He also noticed his damn sister-in-law charging up the drive.

"Shit."

He hadn't called her back yet, because every time he thought about it, she'd text him again, and his anxiety would rise just thinking about what that conversation might sound like. Then he'd set his phone right back down.

Holly wasn't accepting his unresponsiveness any longer, and he couldn't blame her, but he had nothing to offer her.

There went his eyelid again. Clay tried not to focus on the twitch as he watched Holly interact with the law enforcement in front of his property.

She showed an officer her license, and he checked a paper on a clipboard and nodded.

"Damn."

Holly pushed past the officer without thanking him, charged up to the front door, and started pounding. Clay was in for it, and there was nowhere to hide.

He cracked open the door. Holly's angry face was on the other side, pinched pink cheeks, wild brown eyes. She looked like she was ready to take him down.

"Holly, this isn't a good time," he said. "As you can see."

Cameras clacked in the background. "Clay, where the hell is Vivian?"

It was a completely reasonable question, but he had no answers. The news cameras were probably recording their conversation right now.

Clay looked over Holly's shoulder. "Please don't yell."

She looked at him like she was about to fire off a shot next. "I'm going to yell a lot louder if you don't let me in this door and talk to me."

He waved her inside. "Come on."

Holly stepped inside and slammed the door behind her. Clay stood with his arms crossed at his chest and didn't allow her to move off the doormat. He had no intention of letting her stay.

"You haven't returned my calls," she said.

Clay stepped back, giving her a little breathing room. "That's because I don't have anything to report. I don't know where Vivian is, Holly."

"So you just don't call me back? Your own sister-in-law. When you know I'm likely hysterical."

"That's exactly why I didn't call you back," he admitted.

Holly placed her hands on her hips. "That's ridiculous. I need to know what's going on. We could work together."

Work together on what? He didn't know anything. Did she know how annoying she was?

"I've got no news, Holly."

"Let's go search for her, then. What're you doing just sitting here?" She looked at him like he'd been inside knitting a sweater.

"Did you have something useful to add to this conversation? Because if not, I'm going to have to ask you to leave." He just didn't know how to handle her, never had. Vivian had said they weren't allowed to fully express their emotions growing up, and after their parents died, Holly had finally come out of her shell. Well, he wished someone would find a way to show her how to crawl back inside, because he'd married the reserved, rational sister, and he didn't know how to talk to this one.

"What did you tell the police? Do they know anything?" Holly flailed around her arms.

He let out a heated breath, exhausted from the day. "I've been working long hours for my case. I told them that I was with a client when Vivian went missing and that she was having troubles lately."

Holly glared at him as if waiting for him to finish.

"With her mental state," he finished.

"Oh, no. Not that bullshit again!" She went off.

"What do you mean?"

"What really happened with the neighbors? And Vivian didn't just leave her car at Bay Shore Marina and take a dive into the ocean, Clay."

As she said the words, his heart almost stopped beating. That wasn't what he'd been insinuating at all, but it was what he'd been imagining in his head, a premonition of sorts. "Is that what the cops told you happened?"

"Not exactly, but why else are they pushing this narrative about her mental state?"

That was another thing that irked him about Holly. Just because she had worked in journalism for a few years, she thought she was some sort of modern-day Columbo. He didn't think Vivian even noticed how often Holly finished her sentences for her when they were together. They were oddly close for being so vastly different.

"Because it's true. Maybe if you'd talked to me before you went to the cops, we could've discussed that."

"You wouldn't answer your damn phone!" She balled up her fists like she was going to punch him.

"I wonder why I wouldn't answer my phone for *you*." He squeezed his arms tighter, and Holly looked flattened. It usually didn't take much, and he hated to be a brute, but she'd caused problems bringing up Eve and Peter. More than he'd admitted.

"Why did Eve call the police on Vivian? The neighbors on the street said Vivian was having an affair with Peter," Holly said.

Clay chuckled. "That isn't true." The rumor was so twisted, it was one of the reasons Clay would never talk to Eve again. That mess was all her fault. "You can imagine Peter's wife wasn't too happy when Vivian questioned her about her husband being in our backyard, watching her. Eve keeps Peter on a very short leash."

"But . . . they're friends, aren't they? Vivian and Eve?"

"They were," Clay said plainly.

"This doesn't sound like a lapse in mental faculties to me, Clay. It sounds like a simple misunderstanding."

Clay looked away. "Yes, well, I don't think there was anyone watching Vivian. No man in the backyard." If there had been a man, Clay was nervous about who it could be. His case was getting heated. It wouldn't be the first time a family member of a defense attorney had been targeted. "She's read one too many thrillers if you ask me."

"So you think she made it up? For attention?" Holly asked.

He sighed. Holly was asking way too many questions about the neighbors. More than the police. The quicker the Carringtons were eliminated from the scene, the better. They were searching for his wife in the wrong places. "That's not what I said. I believe she did think she saw someone, and that's the problem."

Holly sucked in a giant breath. "Like she was seeing things? That weren't there?"

"Yes. The incident with the Carringtons where she saw something that wasn't there—it wasn't her first. She wasn't well, Holly. I was hesitant, but I told the police that." He remembered the night he had come home and Vivian had insisted someone was walking along their property line smoking a cigarette. She'd said she *saw the orange ember and the smoke swirl away* like she was writing a fictional scene in a bad romance. It was ridiculous, because Eve was a personal trainer and would never in her life smoke. And forget Peter, an oral surgeon. He'd treated oral cancer cases and had teeth that were so white, they almost glowed. He wasn't even a coffee drinker—no way he smoked cigarettes. Clay had dismissed her orange ember as a firefly. It'd been summer when she thought she saw it, the season for them.

Holly laughed. She didn't believe him. She squared her shoulders, tilted her head up so her gaze was eye level with his. "What did you do to her?"

This was why he hadn't called her back. She would blame him, and he didn't have patience for her theatrics. "Nothing. Vivian was a mess, okay? If you want to know the truth. She'd slunk back into her depression, almost as bad as she was right after the miscarriages. She kept this notebook of gloomy poetry. I don't know where it is now," he lied. He was worried there might be things about him in there. Things about both him and the neighbors. He'd need to go through it and confront that issue soon. "She was so secretive lately."

Holly made a wincing face and looked away. It made Clay think she knew something more. "Did she say anything to you about her issues? Before last night?"

Holly shifted her weight. "No, Clay. You know we didn't talk that often. Did you do anything to try to help her if you knew she was struggling?"

"I tried, but she pushed me away. She was fighting things. You had the same parents. You understand her demons. I wish someone would've clued me in on them before I married her."

"What?" Holly sucked in a shocked breath at the last line, and he knew he'd gone too far.

"You need to leave. I'm in court again tomorrow on the Gallo case, and I'm very tired and talking out of turn."

He'd said the wrong thing, bringing up their parents. Holly's face had turned bright red, her curls sticking up on end, making her look like a deranged Medusa. Clay couldn't tell her that she had every right to be suspicious of the neighbors. It would be senseless and career-ending to mention it, especially with his wife currently missing. Besides, the incidents were unrelated. He was concerned with this *man* who'd shown up twice now, though, wondering if someone was trying to send him a message, but he couldn't tell her that either. Holly would make the cops dig into his case, his clients, and that spelled bad news for everyone involved.

"I'm going to ask you one more time. What did you do to my sister, you son of a bitch?"

"Get out of here now!" He grabbed Holly's arm this time, opened the door, and threw her out, press be damned.

9

Those pills were magic. Clearheaded now, Holly had renewed energy to search for Vivian. Especially after her argument with Clay.

He wasn't telling the truth. Clay had turned seven shades of guilty when she'd pressed him about the neighbors—there was something there.

And he'd completely avoided eye contact when he'd brought up Vivian's mental state. He'd fed the police lies to cover something up. Clay may not have been in Bay Shore when Vivian went missing, but that didn't mean he wasn't somehow involved with her disappearance.

And what was that bit about him regretting marrying Vivian because of how they'd grown up? It made Holly livid he'd talk about her that way. And it made Holly wonder how much Vivian had told him about their upbringing.

Holly had revealed very little to Mark about her childhood, not because she was trying to hide it from him but because she didn't care to recall it. She couldn't imagine Vivian would elaborate on their abuses, but maybe she had.

Holly couldn't help but think about Vivian and the one incident that had turned things upside down at home, the last time Vivian had acted out, worn provocative clothing, mixed with men she shouldn't have. Their mother had set the stage for it—*I'd bet my life on it. You wouldn't dare.* And Vivian hadn't backed down.

She'd wanted to prove their mother wrong. But in doing so, Vivian had taken the brunt of the fallout for something Holly had started, and the consequences had been devastating.

Vivian had always looked out for her, and Holly would never forgive herself for not making it to the dock in time to save her.

The van's engine purred as she tried to refocus her energy after her fight with Clay. She could still feel his meaty hands on her arms. He'd grabbed her way too roughly. Holly wondered if he'd handled Vivian that way, too, the mere thought bringing on a rage she hadn't felt since they were kids. She finally checked her phone, more aware than ever how long it'd been since she checked in at home.

Mark: Where are you???

7 missed calls.

Mark: WHERE THE HELL ARE YOU? I'm calling the police if you don't respond in 5 minutes.

Shit.

She didn't want Mark calling the police, but she wasn't ready to go home yet. Holly wanted to read Vivian's other chats with TomKat before she faced the music. She timed herself. Mark wouldn't really call the police. He couldn't possibly be that worried. He just wanted to know where she was. Scare her.

Control her.

Holly had at least ten minutes.

She pulled out the chat sessions from the library, *and . . . go!*

Google Hangouts
August 23

TomKat45: You're so punctual. I appreciate that in my "friends"

SassyVivi38: Well . . . I've got no reason to rush home tonight

TomKat45: That's a shame. I'd be waiting with bells on if I knew you were on the other side of the door. Sorry if I'm being too forward. I know you're married. I've become less tactful as the years have passed instead of the other way around

SassyVivi38: No worries, but your address is a bit far for a drop-in. Says he won't make it home tonight due to the storm. I don't know what to believe. He's mixed up with some bad people at work. Clients I don't trust

TomKat45: I hope no one too bad . . . The storms are hitting here too. I've got my windows boarded up. Say a prayer for me and Bodie and I'll say one for you and yours

SassyVivi38: Oh no, that's right. You're in a much more dangerous location than I am.

TomKat45: They've made whole songs about it, it's so treacherous

SassyVivi38: Your locale is as infamous as you are

TomKat45: For sure. The wind is howling outside. You're the only one to keep my mind sound

SassyVivi38: Well, if you disconnect abruptly, I'll try not to take it personally

TomKat45: I would never leave you on purpose, I can promise that

SassyVivi38: You know what they say about promises made on the internet?

TomKat45: What's that?

SassyVivi38: They're just one click away from being broken ;)

TomKat45: I wouldn't break any promises to you, Viv. I can't wait to see you

As she dialed her husband, Holly was left with an awful quandary of who was the more deceitful human—Clay or Tom. She'd smiled at Vivian's little internet joke, but her first reaction had been to call her sister so she could poke fun at her, only to realize she was gone. She'd never get used to it. Holly remembered the storm she was talking about. It had roiled up the East Coast a few weeks ago. Hurricane season was the only thing she disliked about living on Long Island.

Vivian also knew Tom's address, and what was all that talk about Vivian's marriage? Tom seemed overly familiar with Clay's absences, giving him more opportunity to find a time to snatch Vivian.

Mark finally picked up. "Where in the hell are you?"

"On my way home," she said breezily, as if she'd just spent an extra fifteen minutes at the corner market, even though she was still a wreck from her conversation with Clay.

If that's what you could call it.

Mark made an exasperated noise as if a cat had gotten ahold of his tongue. "B-but where were you? Why didn't you pick up your phone?"

"Looking for Vivian. I stopped at Clay's." Holly began to rub her temple even though it didn't hurt. Not yet anyway. Her headaches were no doubt stress-induced. She needed to find her own ginger pills and stash them in every corner of her house and car. But what she really needed was a stiff drink.

"You were gone forever. I was about to call the cops. Did you at least find her?"

"Did you at least find her?"

She wanted to reach through the phone and throttle him. There had been times in their marriage she'd hid in her laundry room and snuck drinks of vodka because he'd made her unhinged, but this was different. He was so nonchalant about Vivian's disappearance, as if Holly had been out looking for a missing dog all day.

"No, she didn't turn up," she said.

Mark breathed into the phone. "Holly, I realize you're worried about your sister, but you just can't drop the boys on my mother and run the town looking for her. That's what the cops are for. And the cops think . . ."

He sighed again, and she knew what he was going to say: *"The cops think Vivian is dead."*

Dead. Her pulse beat heavily throughout her whole body—heart, throat, arms, legs. There couldn't be a world that existed without Vivian in it.

"I'll be home soon." She ended the call. She'd already given Mark way more minutes than he deserved. Two days ago, she wouldn't have dreamed of hanging up on him.

Poor Vivian, engaging in this online relationship, so bottled up with her own issues that she felt like she couldn't confide in anyone else. Loneliness made her trust a man she'd only ever met on the internet. Holly wondered, if she were in the same situation as Vivian and had connected with a man states or oceans away, would she have done the same thing?

It sounded like one of their mother's journal exercises. *Would you have engaged?*

Holly reasoned that Vivian probably thought nothing serious could happen over a computer screen. It was clear she'd kept their online conversations short. She seemed to maintain a type of control by deciding when the sessions started and ended. It was a control she likely didn't have in her own marriage. She also maintained firmer boundaries, shutting Tom down when he became overly flirtatious. However, it was still a relationship with another man, separate from her husband.

And their mother had cautioned them that an emotional affair was far more dangerous than a physical one. She often reverted back to Carl Jung on the subject, the Swiss psychiatrist most well-known for dream analysis and the fact that he'd had a torrid love affair with one of his patients. Freud had been in opposition of his life choices, but Jung claimed that "the meeting of two personalities is like the contact of two chemical substances: if there is any reaction, both are transformed."

Was it true? Had their connection over the internet been so strong that this man had somehow transformed Vivian? Holly wouldn't know what that was like. This whole situation made her question whether she'd ever had that type of chemistry with her own husband. She'd been young when she met Mark, and he'd been the handsome guy who worked in the same building as she did. Mark had been a project manager at a start-up tech company that had a small office upstairs from the paper.

They'd made *eyes* at each other in the stairwell, but it wasn't until her car was broken into in the parking lot, her stereo and a lifetime of CDs stolen, that things had changed between them. Mark took care of everything, from calling the police to instructing her on how to report the crime to her insurance company.

Holly had been a mess, sniffling and sobbing with her little sedan's guts hanging out over the dashboard, the contents of the wires where the radio used to be spread all over her upholstered seats. Later on, Mark had called to check up on her and asked her out on a date, and she was so thankful, there was no way she could tell him no. He'd shown up with a dozen carnations and his iPod, which he gave her, urging her to join the rest of the world. He said he knew he couldn't replace a lifetime's collection of music, but it was a start.

When she'd mentioned his sweet gesture to Vivian, she'd told Holly to hang on to him, and Holly had agreed.

Mark had come to her rescue, and he seemed to have all the qualities she thought a man should possess, but there definitely hadn't been anything remarkable about their union. When couples mentioned feeling fireworks when they first started dating, Holly always thought their statements were romanticized, the kind of idealistic talk that came from people like her sister who believed in poetry and flowery prose.

Holly's analytical brain couldn't process this nonsense verbiage, but lately she'd begun to believe she was missing out on a greater truth. Vivian's chat log had certainly made Holly feel that way. What if Vivian's reality at home was worse than Holly's? Judging from the interaction she'd just had with Clay, she didn't doubt it. He'd known her sister was suffering, and he'd done nothing to help her. Of course, Vivian would see this man's admiring words as a welcome escape from Clay if that were the case.

She pulled into her driveway with a mix of dread and relief. Mark's angry face was pushed through the blinds.

But she could also see a couple of other faces in that same window, and she knew why she'd never questioned her marital status before. She could never leave her boys, and she could never subject them to the pitfalls of divorce.

Maybe after they graduate, I can separate from Mark.

Holly walked up the driveway, nerves dancing up her spine. She rubbed her temple again and wondered if the ginger the professor took was available on Amazon Prime for next-day delivery for when she ran out of his stash.

Mark was there, holding the door open. She kicked off her shoes, not making eye contact with him.

"Mommy!" Tyler ran up and gave her a hug, which was nothing out of the ordinary, but it felt extraordinary after the day she'd had. She clung to him and let his little arms warm the spots Clay had likely bruised. How could she teach her sons to stay this loving and not turn into testosterone-filled ogres?

When Otto followed suit and gave her a full-throttle little-man hug with the kind of arm strength reserved for video-gaming battles, Holly felt the weight of her absence. Her babies had been worried about her. Maybe there was some validity to Mark's point, and she should've at least texted him back, but he had to understand that when he tried to hold on to her so tightly, it only made her want to slip further away.

It wasn't like Mom to go out for so long and not answer her phone. Aunt Vivian had gone missing, and they probably feared she was next. This house may not have gleamed from crown molding to baseboards like Vivian's, but it sure did shine with love, and Holly was sorry she'd made them worry. "Hey, guys. Sorry I got caught up. Your grandmother texted me that she fed you."

"And it's a good thing for that," Mark barked.

Her husband had given up trying to get her attention and had resorted to stomping into the laundry room. He came out with a fresh load that he abruptly dropped on the floor. Everyone jumped, and Holly was reminded of her most recent memory of her mother, tossing papers all over the floor, and the flutter of fear that went along with it.

He's trying to intimidate me. Don't let him.

She was extra sensitive to his provocations after the day she'd had, the men she'd had to deal with. "Oh, good. We're nearly out of fresh towels. Could you fold them? I'm beat."

Mark's lower lip quivered like a fish, his eyes incensed with rage. "Nooo. These are for you to fold! I threw in the load."

She was already halfway up the steps. "It'll have to wait until tomorrow."

Or never. She was sick of being his servant.

No doubt, Mark's biggest issue with her being gone was that the chores from this week had remained undone, an occurrence that'd maybe happened twice in their marriage due to illness or vacations.

"Boys, come upstairs and get washed up for bed. Tyler, I'll help you with your hair." At seven, Tyler still couldn't manage to get all the shampoo out even though he had a near buzz cut. Holly marched up the stairs without saying another word to Mark.

She was just done with him.

She heard a stampede of small feet race up the stairs behind her. No one wanted to cross Mom or Dad tonight.

"Get down here!" Mark yelled. "I'm not finished talking to you."

The boys looked at her fearfully, especially Otto. "You better go, Mom."

"No, I will not go anywhere with his voice raised. This isn't how you speak to women if you intend for them to respond to you," she informed her sons.

Otto gave her a bared-teeth smile as if to say, *"Yikes."* "Okay, good night, Mom." He darted into the bathroom.

God forbid Mark fold a load of laundry. He acted like she'd just asked him to iron the drapes.

Sometime later, Mark was on his way upstairs, but she could tell by the way the floorboards were creaking that he was taking them slowly. He probably didn't understand how to react to her when she was ignoring him because it had never happened before. Maybe he would figure out what he'd done wrong. Holly was pretending to sleep, but she'd used her cell phone's flashlight app under the sheets to read as much of Vivian's conversations with Tom as she could.

She felt like a little kid with her novel beneath the covers after her mother had called *lights out*.

Google Hangouts
August 30

TomKat45: Did you get the info I sent?

SassyVivi38: I did. Thank you, but it was a little unsettling.

Mark's body was like a Mack truck barreling into the room, headlights blaring as he turned on the overheads. Whatever he'd been thinking about on that last step must've made him angry.

He totally interrupted her reading, and she shoved the printouts into her day planner. Not that he seemed to care what she was reading, because he just looked pissed, and she thought of Clay, how his face had resembled a madman's earlier, and how their expressions appeared very similar right now. Mark had been stewing downstairs all that time, thinking about how to reprimand her. Holly could see that now.

"So this is what you're going to do now? Just whatever you damn please."

Holly didn't respond. It was best not to when he was like this—in a state. She had acted irresponsibly not responding to his communications, worrying the entire household, including her boys, making everyone upset. But he needed to understand this wasn't about him—or them—it was about Vivian and the very little time Holly had left before her sister was presumed officially *gone*.

Dead.

93

Mark walked into the master bath and slammed the door. She heard his electric toothbrush. He'd be a while because he couldn't go a single night without flossing.

Holly needed him to fall asleep quickly tonight or get on with his punishing recap of what she'd done wrong. She'd apologize and admit fault if he'd only hurry up so she could keep on reading. She had to find out what was unsettling to Vivian. Unsettling things led to disappearances.

And she needed to finish these chats *tonight* so she could turn them in to the police tomorrow and help track down this Tom guy. She was in over her head. Now that she'd actually read more, she'd decided Tom was a real threat. He wasn't just a love interest or a fellow librarian Vivian hoped to meet up with at a conference. Holly had weighed the risks and benefits, and it was in Vivian's best interest to turn them in, help the police find this Tom character, even if it trashed her sister's reputation. With no other leads in the case, a tarnished reputation hardly held precedence over her actual life at this point.

Tomorrow was Friday, and the kids had school. Holly had one more day of freedom to investigate while Mark was at work. She'd decided to go to the courtroom first thing in the morning for Clay's trial. He'd been hiding something today and had acted almost blasé about Vivian's disappearance.

Holly guessed she should be a little grateful Mark had been so unnerved over her unreturned messages. As Vivian had often reminded Holly when she complained about her marriage—*"at least he cares."* Holly understood what she meant now after interacting with Clay. There were missing emotions there.

Any other man would put his trial on hold and look for his wife. Not Clay. And as far as she could tell, no one seemed ruffled by this, because he was in the middle of a big case, one that had been blasted all over the news. On the face of it, his client seemed like any other doctor who'd traded opioids for something inappropriate like cash or sexual favors. But that wasn't why the case had garnered so much media attention. Dr. Raymond Gallo was rumored to be *connected*.

Vivian had denied it when Holly asked, but she had to have known the type of men Clay represented. She'd even mentioned in her chats that he was working with some *bad* people. The Bellinis and the Gallos were certainly that. They were among Long Island's most notorious crime families. They'd been arrested over the years on charges that ranged from theft to money laundering to murder. There'd been a case way back when where a Gallo had snitched and disappeared, but Holly couldn't remember the specifics.

The whole thing made her physically ill.

She pulled her comforter closer to quell the chill. Could it all be tied up in a bow together somehow? This trial. These people and Vivian.

The door to the bathroom flung open. "Holly. I am sorry about Vivian. Truly." Mark seemed calmer. Perhaps he'd taken his stress out on his teeth. But Holly guessed that he was starting off soft so he could lay down the hammer with maximum force.

Just get it over with.

"Thank you," she said.

"But your behavior today . . ."

"I know. I know it was wrong not to call or text you back." She shouldn't have to make excuses for looking for her own sister. Holly debated telling Mark about what had happened at Clay's house, but it would only work against her. If she revealed that Clay thought Vivian was mentally unstable, Mark would use that line of thought to try to get her to back off. *"She clearly had some issues. There's nothing more you can do. Let the detectives sort it out."*

It was complete crap, though. Just thinking about it made her so angry. Vivian's neighbors had turned a simple misunderstanding into something else. Vivian may have argued with her neighbor. She may have frantically yelled between yards, asking if Peter had been in hers, but that alone didn't make her crazy. It also didn't mean she'd been sleeping with him. Holly was still curious to know how their fight had morphed into that bizarre accusation.

Mark neared the bed. "Your sister is missing, we don't know why, and you decide that's a good time to leave hour gaps between our messages?"

"I get it. I do. But I was busy looking for Vivian, Mark. This wasn't like any other day, and it would be great if you stopped treating it like one."

"I realize it's not like every other day, which is why it's so important to call your husband back!"

She let him yell. She let him get it all out. Holly clenched her planner tighter, letting the metal rings dig into her fingers.

"I need you to give me a pass today, of all days," Holly said.

Mark rubbed the side of his jaw, a habit that would be natural if he had even a shadow of a beard, but he was always clean-shaven. Why couldn't he let the hair grow out even a little? Did he ever relax? She was more at ease when he wasn't there. It was probably a bad sign.

She had her eyes shut, praying he'd shut his, too, so she could read the rest of the chats.

"What's this?" Mark ripped her planner out of her hands. How foolish she'd been for closing her eyes. When she opened them, he was dangling it above her head.

"Bringing your research to bed with you?"

"Give it back." Holly reached up and tried to snag it.

"Nope." He lifted the planner higher "You need to give it a break. Rest your mind. They'll probably find Vivian by tomorrow. She sounded okay on the phone, right?"

Holly shook her head. Who was he kidding?

"Give that back to me, Mark."

"Tomorrow." He climbed into bed with it in his hands.

She knew he wouldn't give it back, if only because she wanted it. She'd pissed him off by not listening to him, ignoring his messages, and then mouthing off when she got home. She wasn't getting that planner back tonight, and she kicked herself for being so careless.

"Fine. Tomorrow."

Mark rolled on his side, the planner on his bedside table. She'd just wait until he fell asleep. His last words to her were, "Ha, not like there's any solid leads in there anyway."

She put the pillow up to her mouth and screamed.

10

When Holly arrived at the courthouse, she had to park in a restricted area because there were no more spaces, and she didn't have time to find alternate parking. Mark hadn't said a word to her that morning, and he'd waited until the very minute before he left for work to give her the planner back. She didn't have a second to read anything because then she'd be late for Clay's trial, and she desperately wanted to get a spot in the courtroom, knowing it'd be a full house today.

As she hurried, Holly caught a glimpse of Clay being interviewed outside the courtroom, and his appearance derailed her mission for a moment. Not because he looked bad but because he looked so put together.

Holly saw things everyone else didn't.

Like his brilliant red tie beneath his black suit jacket, stiff and bright, as if it were the first time he'd ever worn it. She wondered if he'd had the gall to go shopping for new clothing, now of all times.

A bulging, barely zipped leather briefcase with carefully organized files hung at his side. It was obvious Clay had thought of nothing else in the last twenty-four hours but his client's case, when his focus should've been entirely on his missing wife.

When Holly entered the courtroom, it was packed to the gills. She was worried she would be asked to exit. She needed to survey her brother-in-law, get a read on the client he was representing and anyone else who might be positioned on his side, and see how this case could tie to Vivian. The words from her chat sessions came back to Holly. *"He's mixed up with some bad people at work. Clients I don't trust."*

Clay had definitely been hiding something the last time they spoke. Holly didn't know if it had to do with the case, but it was the only thing Vivian had mentioned in her chats that she thought had been off about Clay, and in Holly's mind, that was a clue.

More people were trying to push through the doors. Holly wanted a good seat, and she knew from experience that this presiding judge sometimes had a tiny area partitioned for the media. How to secure a spot without a badge? Holly saw a couple of women from the press leave the courtroom, and she followed them into the ladies' room.

The two women were reporters from competing publications, and Holly quickly used the restroom and listened to their conversation.

"There's not a chance in hell he's getting off. Three female complaints, and the defendant is tied to that family. They're all guilty as sin."

"I don't know. I'd like to think you're right, but Clay got the last guy off."

"I can't believe he's still working the case with his wife missing," the other one whispered.

Holly exited the stall and washed her hands. The lady talking smack about Clay had her back turned to Holly, her press badge stashed on top of her gargantuan designer bag while she reapplied her lipstick and spoke to her friend, or maybe her foe. Holly couldn't tell.

"I can. He's as shady as his clients."

See, everyone knows you're scum, Clay!

"I heard the Liebler jewelry heist was an inside deal."

"Me too."

Holly had no idea what the Liebler heist was, but she filed away that little tidbit of information, and without thinking twice, she quickly snatched the woman's press badge and threw it in her oversize bag. Then she tossed the paper towel she'd used to dry her hands and ran out the door.

When Holly made it to the public seating area, she dashed to the spot reserved for media. She sat in the corner obstructed by a man operating a news video camera, which was an odd nuisance in the courtroom, but this was Judge Jacobs. He liked press. Holly had her badge strung around her neck but hid the bottom portion that named the publication inside her button-down shirt.

She craned her neck to see if the woman she'd stolen the badge from was anywhere nearby, but Holly couldn't find her in the crowd. Her eyes were drawn to a woman with platinum-blonde hair, a doppelgänger for a young Victoria Gotti, daughter of nefarious mob boss John Gotti. The voluminous sunglasses she wore indoors were what caught Holly's attention.

Then her hair.

Then the way she walked in at the last minute and managed to find a seat in the overcrowded gallery. The sea of people parted to make room for her as if she were *somebody*. Holly had had to steal a press badge from an unsuspecting reporter just to get a good seat, and this woman had managed to slip right in. Maybe she *was* somebody.

Not that Holly was obsessed with crime families.

Nor did she consider it odd that she knew exactly where Victoria Gotti's gated mansion was located in Old Westbury, a miniature version of the White House with its palatial alabaster walls sectioned out in partitions, Greek columns lined up in front like they were strong enough to hold up the world.

When she'd driven by, she could practically hear the walls whispering their sordid secrets. The house had been in foreclosure, but whoever bought the real estate would inherit a house full of ghosts.

Holly was still unsure about the unsolved mystery of the teenage boy who'd hit Victoria's younger brother with a car when they were kids. Her brother had survived, but the driver of the vehicle had been beaten to a bloody pulp, hospitalized, released, and then never seen or heard from again—Jimmy Hoffa–style. Holly had watched a few documentaries on the family in which the incident had been mentioned, and she wondered who had decided to punish the driver for his recklessness.

Holly had already concluded from her research into the Gallos that the man Clay was representing had connections to people who had the same kind of ability to perform cover-up jobs, the kind that could make young boys and wives disappear without a trace. She thought back to the Gallo snitch she'd researched more thoroughly last night. After Mark had confiscated her planner, she'd done a little recon on her phone and had discovered that the man had given up the lot of them in a drug bust gone wrong.

As the bailiff appeared, her attention snapped back to the front of the room, her nerves so heightened from the buzz of the trial that she could feel the sweat tingling on her eyebrows. But only the defendant was seated. Holly watched as Dr. Raymond Gallo's feet pattered beneath the table as he waited. She wondered if being left unmonitored with female patients made him as frenzied. Where was Clay?

Finally, both the prosecution and defense attorneys appeared behind the bench from the door that led to the judge's chambers. Holly could only guess that they'd been speaking to the judge before continuation of the trial. Clay appeared pasty and sweaty, less polished than earlier. Something was wrong.

After the attorneys situated themselves at counsel table, the bailiff spoke. "All rise, the Suffolk County Supreme Court is now in session, the Honorable Judge Gerald Jacobs is presiding." The bailiff read the docket number next, followed by, *"The People of the State of New York versus Raymond Gallo."*

Judge Jacobs said, "You may be seated. The prosecution made a motion for a request for a continuance because the state's lead witness is unavailable."

A continuance? Why? Clay certainly wouldn't be happy if the judge decided to postpone the rest of the trial.

Judge Jacobs cleared his throat. "After careful consideration, that motion is denied."

A ripple of different reactions swept across the courtroom like the wave in a baseball stadium.

Judge Jacobs addressed the prosecution. "If you have no further witnesses, do you rest your case?"

"Yes, Your Honor," he said.

"Is the defense ready?" asked Judge Jacobs.

It was Clay's turn. "Yes, Your Honor." He presented his case, but Holly had a hard time listening to him. Or maybe she was just tuning him out. Clay could argue the plaintiffs weren't on the up-and-up—so what? There was a mountain of evidence against his client. Surely not even he could talk his way out of this one.

After Clay finished presenting his defense, the court gave the weary jurors a break before they heard closing arguments. Upon returning from break, Clay presented his closing argument first, as was customary for the defense to do in New York, and it was much more convincing than Holly would have liked.

Then it was the prosecution's turn to address the jury. "The witness in this case, Aliza Levine, unfortunately could not testify the last time we were all together and she did not have the opportunity to testify today either, because she had that opportunity taken away from her last night." Holly held her breath. Aliza was the pretty PTO mom who Holly was counting on to pummel Clay's case. She'd only recently come forward, her testimony arriving later than the other two witnesses. "Because," the prosecutor announced, "she is dead."

There was a rumble in the room again, and Holly had to blink twice to process the information. *Dead?*

"Her death has been classified as a homicide," he elaborated.

"Objection! Facts not in evidence. Irrelevant. This is completely inappropriate and prejudicial, Your Honor," Clay yelled.

"Sustained. Careful, Counselor," Judge Jacobs warned.

Holly swallowed the spit that had been pooling in her throat. The room seemed to turn on end. She overheard the woman beside her murmur something about the news story of Aliza's death televised the night before. Holly immediately looked behind her to check out the lady from earlier, thinking maybe she was a relative of the deceased, but the Victoria look-alike seemed unfazed by the information.

Holly closed her eyes, sick to her stomach.

Aliza's killer had to be a family member of Raymond Gallo's, part of this scandalous crew Clay was associated with, the same ones he'd represented for years. Holly drew in a deep breath, trying harder than ever to remain hidden behind the cameraman because she was sure her face revealed the absolute horror of her thoughts.

Vivian had been mistaken about Clay in her chats. Clay wasn't just fraternizing with *bad* people. He was mixed up with the Mafia. He *was* one of the bad people.

Holly knew from her research that the other female witnesses were serial complainants and that they'd collected more than $1 million in total from previous lawsuits they'd filed. This was a criminal trial conducted by the state, but the victims could still collect restitution, and Holly was betting they'd file a civil suit against Dr. Raymond Gallo if Clay lost this case.

She didn't care about those women, though.

She cared about Aliza. The one good woman who'd complained about Dr. Gallo.

After closing arguments, Judge Jacobs charged the jury with their duties and gave them instructions on how to weigh the evidence and arguments they were presented. He dismissed them from the courtroom to deliberate and decide the verdict.

Criminal juries were a fickle thing—they could deliberate for mere hours or as long as multiple days. The rule of thumb was that the quicker a jury returned a verdict the better it was for the prosecution. The longer the process lasted the better for the defendant.

No matter, Holly hoped the jury would be back quickly but was prepared for them not to be out for at least a few hours. As she waited, she jotted down notes, but only one word was evidently clear. She wrote guilty and drew a circle around it with her pen until it poked through the other side of the paper. When the jury reentered the courtroom a few hours later, Holly's back hurt from sitting all that time, rigid with the stress that this guy might get off.

Holly observed Clay to try to gauge his confidence level.

What an adrenaline rush it must've been for the ringleaders. When Clay convinced the jurors that his client was innocent and they agreed, he must've felt exalted—God. It probably fed his ego, making him think he could do absolutely anything.

Maybe even murder his wife and get away with it.

The jury foreperson handed a document to the bailiff. A decision had been made, and Holly could barely breathe. The judge read the verdict to himself, then returned it to the bailiff to hand back to the jury foreperson.

Clay and the defendant both stood, hanging on the words to come, Dr. Gallo's freedom in the jury's hands.

Holly gripped her pen with force and ground it into her notepad. Order in the court was called—it was time to deliver the verdict. Judge Jacobs turned to the jury foreperson and asked him if the jury had reached a verdict.

"Yes, Your Honor. In the case of *The People of the State of New York versus Raymond Gallo*, we find the defendant, in a unanimous vote by the jury . . ." The world stopped; Holly ceased breathing.

"*Not* guilty on the charges of unlawfully prescribing controlled substances without a legitimate purpose."

No! What? He got off?

There was an uproar in the courtroom, a ruffle of disagreement drowned out by a few stray claps. The court was adjourned. Holly sat there in shock.

However, the reaction that surprised her the most was that of the blonde woman in the audience. Holly turned her head to observe her. She was weeping beneath her glasses, wiping furiously at her eyes with tissues, shielding her face from the crowd until she could get out of the room. Holly couldn't be positive, but if she had to guess, she'd say those were tears of joy, graced with a seemingly relieved smile, the only one in the entire courtroom.

Holly leaped from her chair and squeezed her way through the crowd to find out why. Anyone rooting for Clay's defendant could be a lead to Vivian's whereabouts. As far as Holly was concerned, associates of Clay's client had killed the lead witness before she could testify against him. Perhaps Clay had hired them to do the same thing to his wife. If he'd wanted Vivian gone for any reason, he knew the right people to make that happen. Holly didn't have a motive yet, but she'd followed her gut so far, and it hadn't led her astray.

Holly kept a good distance from the blonde and hoped she'd enter the ladies' room to clean herself up so Holly could get a better look at her or sneak a peek in her purse at possible identification. Holly had scored big in bathrooms today and patted the press badge still strung around her neck.

But to her surprise, the woman entered a maintenance closet instead, which was clearly marked with a Do Not Enter sign and looked to have a keypad lock. *How did she get in?*

Holly leaned on the chair rail against the wall near the closet, pretending to be eye-deep in her purse as people rushed past, most of whom were disgruntled with the outcome of the trial.

"He probably paid off the judge," Holly heard one man yap.

She looked up. The blonde was still in the maintenance closet. At first Holly thought she'd entered the room by mistake, so frazzled from the trial that she mistook a closet for a bathroom. It happened. But it'd been a few minutes, and she still hadn't come out. Holly was certain no one else had seen the lithe woman shimmy inside, because she was one of the first to leave. Everyone else had been appropriately distracted by the verdict—except for Holly.

Her eyes were on Blondie.

Minutes later, Clay and his client were wrestling their way through the press to an all-purpose conference room. Holly remembered this courthouse from her journalist days, and it hadn't changed a bit. The prosecution sometimes had offices in the courthouses, but the defense attorney had outside offices, so sometimes they used these all-purpose rooms to catch up with clients.

The strange thing about this conference room was that it was right beside the maintenance closet. Something about the proximity of the rooms bothered Holly. She would've homed in on this right away, but she was too busy trying to avoid Clay's line of sight as he walked her way.

"No comment," he kept saying to the press. Holly was probably the last person on his mind. As he passed by her, both Clay and his client pushed their way inside the conference room and closed the door behind them.

Holly hovered in the hallway, watching the door to the maintenance closet, trying to imagine what it might look like on the inside. Was the woman standing there staring at a plethora of paper products? Or was she spying?

If the woman was a journalist trying to get intel through the wall, the tears in the courtroom didn't make much sense. Journalists rarely became emotionally invested in their subjects. Holly knew this from experience.

The hallway was clear, and before she could talk herself out of it, Holly walked over to the maintenance closet and raised her hand to the doorknob. Her nerve endings were burning from her hairline to her knuckles, but she knew if she left that courthouse without knowing what the mysterious woman was up to, it'd be another sleepless night.

Holly lightly knocked on the door to give the woman a minute to put away her tape recorder or cell phone. Holly wasn't totally against the idea of exploiting Clay; she just had a strong desire to get in on the action.

There was no answer when she knocked. Holly's heart beat like the time she'd lied to Mark about an outfit she'd purchased— *"This old thing?"*—and then watched him open the credit card bill.

Holly jiggled the door handle and, to her astonishment, it wasn't locked. The lock was busted or had been unarmed. Her heart beat faster. She needed to do this for Vivian. She took a gigantic breath of courage, opened the door, and stepped inside. She expected to find a woman with a drawn gun on the other side, or perhaps a recording device held up to her face, but instead she found an empty room.

The light was on, but nobody was home.

Without thinking twice, Holly shut the door behind her. Where had the woman gone?

She spun around in the small room, and it didn't take her long to spot it—a loose panel in the wall where a stack of cleaning supplies had been moved aside. *A false door?* She knelt down beside it and could clearly hear voices on the other side.

She drew in a sharp breath. On the other side of the closet wall was the conference room.

"I can't believe you're not honoring your end of the deal, Frankie. You said that if I got your brother off, you'd let me see Giana," Clay argued.

Brother? Who in the world is Frankie? Is she the blonde? And who's Giana?

"We'll be back once everything is settled with your wife. Look, Clay, people are watching you. It's a very bad idea for you to be around us right now. Think about what the cops would say if they found out you were hanging out with your mistress and your estranged daughter while your wife is still missing."

Holly rocked unsteadily, almost falling. She had to put her hand over her mouth not to let out a yelp.

The woman who'd slipped into the closet was Clay's mistress? The sister of the man he'd just defended in the courtroom and the mother of his illegitimate child? Wow. Holly thought back to Clay's beautiful house, everything money could buy. He'd gotten rid of Vivian to make room for a real family, this woman and their child.

And now Holly had an awful feeling that Vivian was truly dead. If Vivian had found out Clay had a mistress, that wouldn't destroy her, but if she'd somehow discovered he had a child, it would be a game ender.

It would make it believable that she might have actually jumped right off the edge of that dock.

Holly felt sick.

"No, I guess that wouldn't be good. You're right, but you're still not honoring your promise, Frankie," Clay argued. "Where're you guys staying? I drove by your mother's place—"

"Don't go near my mother," Frankie warned. "We're at the marina for now; just don't bother my mom. You'll see us again soon enough. Both of us."

Marina?

"When? When can I see Giana again?" Clay asked.

"Once the smoke clears from the trial and Vivian turns up. I think your wife is hiding from you," Frankie said with certainty.

Frankie *thought* Vivian was hiding or she *knew* she was? She'd said it as if she were sure. But how could she be when no one else was?

"How do I contact you?" Clay asked a little too pathetically.

"You don't. I will let you see Giana, but not until things calm down. Not until they find your wife and not until the heat around Ray goes away."

"It's best for everyone," Ray said.

Clay sighed.

"Give it time. She'll show; I'm sure of it. I'll be watching, and I'll come back when the time is right, but we can't be around you right now."

Holly couldn't see through the panel in the wall, but she imagined Clay and Frankie were hugging. She'd never been more confused in her life. Did Clay really not know where Vivian was, or was he putting on a show for this woman so he could reclaim her love and that of his child?

"You should've told me about her a long time ago. Things could've been different," Clay said.

"Stop that. It is what it is now. I wasn't given much of a choice. You know that. I gotta get out of here. The press is going to be all over you."

Holly could hear Frankie's footsteps grow closer to the panel in the wall.

Shit! Holly quickly got on her haunches and tiptoed, then flung the closet door open as gently as possible and catapulted herself out into the hallway, closing the door behind her and turning in an almost dead sprint for the front entrance of the courthouse.

When Holly glanced behind her, for just a second, she caught sight of "the other woman" striding quickly down the hall with large black shades obscuring her face. Only Frankie didn't have long blonde hair but a head full of dark waves instead.

It was the woman from the courtroom nonetheless.

And she'd been wearing a wig.

This woman, Frankie, carved secret holes in courthouse walls and fooled the crowd with a fake disguise all so she could anonymously watch her brother's trial and see her estranged lover. These people Holly was dealing with were extremely dangerous and very resourceful. Well,

Holly was sorry to tell Frankie that all her elaborate efforts were for naught, because right after Holly left the courthouse, she was driving straight to the police station to hand over the chat sessions burning a hole in her planner. And she was going to tell the detectives everything about what she'd just heard.

She had a new lead suspect—Clay. And a new motive—Frankie and Giana. But she hadn't ruled out Tom either. She'd spill the deets there too. Someone was going down for her sister's disappearance—she just didn't know who.

11

Holly knew she shouldn't, but she started reading the Hangouts chat sessions as she drove. She didn't have time to pull over, too distraught from all the dirt she'd just discovered on her brother-in-law in the courtroom closet. She needed to discern who was the more likely culprit here—Tom or Clay or one of Clay's connections.

Google Hangouts
August 30

TomKat45: So now that you have the details, you're all set.

Holly flipped back to make sure she hadn't missed a page. Nope, Vivian might be all set, but Holly sure wasn't.

She'd read the part about Vivian being unsettled and Tom asking if she got the info he'd sent, and then Mark had barged into the room and taken her planner.

Where is it?

Had she left it at home, tangled in a bedsheet? Tom's info sounded important.

Her throat closed at the thought of dropping a page in her rush. It could've happened when she was running around in the courthouse. She might've dropped it in the maintenance closet. Anywhere.

One thing was for sure, though—one of Vivian's pages wasn't accounted for in her stack of papers.

She kept reading. What else could she do?

SassyVivi38: I wouldn't say that. There's more I'm running from than just that

TomKat45: Well, run away to an island, then? I'll assure you it's very settling. Only a good storm can unsettle it

SassyVivi38: Ah . . . you know that's not what I mean. Although, forced to live the island life. You poor baby

TomKat45: Hey . . . it's not all sangria sunsets and rosy beaches

SassyVivi38: LOL. Sounds terrible. I'd just hate to visit you somewhere that sounds so dreadful

TomKat45: You'd love it. I have no doubt after our hike in Kentucky, you'll find your way here. That last storm was a wallop, though. Had damage to my boat

SassyVivi38: Oh no. Sorry to hear that

TomKat45: How did you fare?

SassyVivi38: No damage here

TomKat45: How about damage to your heart?

SassyVivi38: Oof. How did you guess?

TomKat45: Had a feeling from our last conversation

SassyVivi38: Well . . . yes . . . my husband smelled a little too sweet when he came home to be hanging out in the office all night, if you know what I mean

TomKat45: That's awful. I'm sending you another package to a PO Box at your local post office. It will be in your name, number 36.

SassyVivi38: What? Why not my home address?

TomKat45: You'll only get the key for the box sent to your home tomorrow. I don't want him to get his "sweet" hands on the package. It sounds like you have enough problems. I don't want to cause more

SassyVivi38: Right. You don't need to send me presents, though

TomKat45: Someone should be giving you presents ;)

SassyVivi38: You're too much. I do have to go soon. Library is closing

TomKat45: The package should be there by next Wednesday. When do you think you'll pick it up? Before our chat Thursday?

SassyVivi38: I'll go right after work on Wednesday, so I'll have it

"Damn." Vivian did know about the mistress, but she didn't appear to know about the child. Maybe she was planning on using Tom as an escape from her tumultuous marriage. Holly could see how easily it could happen, trusting this stranger. She wanted to believe in Tom because she could no longer believe in Clay.

Mark was an asshole, but at least he was a loyal asshole.

Though some days Holly fantasized that he'd meet someone else so she'd have a strong reason to leave him. When she thought of divorce, she cringed at what their close-knit community would think. Mark would never initiate a separation, so Holly would have to do it, and then she'd be made to look like the monster.

"She's the one who called for a divorce. I wanted to work it out," Mark would say.

Although Mark had never once agreed to marriage counseling, unable to acknowledge there was a problem to begin with.

After years of therapy, Holly had learned she'd picked a husband who was successful and controlling—and selfish and callous—just like her parents. And she was beginning to think Mark was just as damaging.

At first, Mark hadn't been, though.

When her car had been broken into, Holly's first thought was to call her father, but he'd recently passed away. Her therapist had told Holly that Mark had taken care of her the same way her father would have, and that's where their bond had started.

Although Holly's true inner turmoil during that time came from her inability to properly grieve her parents' deaths, because when it came down to it—Holly hated them. She despised her mother for emotionally abusing her, and she resented her father for standing by and letting it happen, but these weren't things she could talk about.

So she'd buried her pain and married Mark instead, and everything was fine for a little while. She'd always had the intention of going back to work after she had her first child. She'd told Mark that even when she was pregnant, feeling her independence dwindling away with each prenatal checkup.

Mark would unnerve her by saying things like, *"You'll change your mind once the baby's here."* He was so sure, which angered her even more because he assumed she couldn't balance both, a baby and a career.

But she hadn't changed her mind after Otto was born, and when she'd explored day cares and they stacked up the costs against her salary, it made for an unending fight. Online journalism was just starting to boom, but Mark never allowed her the time to work. His job was always more important.

It gave Holly so much anxiety that she'd slipped up with her drinking. The monotony of the laundry and the toy sorting and the sleeplessness and the prospect that it might never end sent her over the edge. She'd snuck a drink. And then another. She couldn't remember "the incident," as Mark referred to it, only waking up to the baby crying, Mark next to her.

She'd passed out after her shower, stark naked on the bathroom floor, a toilet bowl full of vomit beside her.

Mark had wrapped her in a towel, nursed her back to health with broth and water and burned bagels and whatever else she'd asked for. Holly had been passed out so long, the subway tile on the floor had left a bruised, checkered pattern on her cheek. Mark had asked her if she wanted to play tic-tac-toe in the mirror on her face, and they'd laughed, but his joke was followed by a stern warning—he'd help her straighten out if she promised never to scare him like that again.

And then Tyler came along, and more monetary figures were stacked next to each other, and she'd given up. Mark had made her become the person he wanted her to be—just like her parents had tried to do with their studies.

Holly had fought long and hard to keep her promise to him. It was the reason she let him act the way he did; she didn't think she deserved better. But lately, she was getting tired of the fight—both with her drinking and with him.

Her phone was blowing up. Even though she was somehow mastering driving and reading at the same time, adding talking on the phone to the list could be fatal, even for a super-multitasker like herself.

It was an unknown number flying across her screen anyway, probably a telemarketer. She had one more chat session to go.

Google Hangouts
September 6

TomKat45: Hi, Vivi! Did you get my package?

SassyVivi38: I did. I was shocked. Really unnecessary, Tom. I don't know what to say. I need to give it back

TomKat45: No, you don't. Listen, it's impossible to do B & C on the list I gave you if you don't have some pocket change. A = travel cash. People are easily tracked with credit cards. Cash can't be traced

SassyVivi38: You're lucky it didn't get snagged in the mail, for that amount. SMH

TomKat45: It's the max allowed to be sent through the postal service, play at your own risk

SassyVivi38: You're a bigger gambler than I am. If I keep it, I'm paying it back

TomKat45: Fair enough. Don't send it back through the mail, though. We're lucky it didn't get stolen the first time around. Let's not take our chances on a second try

SassyVivi38: I'll hang on to it for now, but only because I have much bigger worries

TomKat45: Why? What's going on? You're worrying *me* now

SassyVivi38: Something happened yesterday when I went to pick up your package. I still can't believe it and can barely write it . . .

TomKat45: What is it? You know you can tell me anything. There's no one I can tell anyway out here on my little patch of triangle ;)

SassyVivi38: Right . . . well, when I went to the post office, the key jammed in the lock. I had to get a worker and they had to verify the box was mine and when I showed my identification, turns out there are two PO Boxes addressed to Eddy—my last name. My husband has a box there too

TomKat45: That's strange

SassyVivi38: I didn't think I'd be allowed to open it, but my name was on the account. I thought maybe it was something he'd set up when we'd first married and I'd forgotten about it, so I opened it

TomKat45: And??

SassyVivi38: And it must be *their* PO Box, because I found pictures of the two of them inside. Work definitely isn't the only thing making my husband keep late hours

TomKat45: That's devastating. I'm so sorry. I wanted your PO Box experience to be full of pleasant surprises.

SassyVivi38: Well it wasn't. It even had a date and time for them to meet set for yesterday. It's like they use this box to send messages to each other. Then, when I went home, there was someone in my backyard, I swear it. We're fenced in, and the gate to the neighbors' yard was unhinged. I thought it was my neighbor, and when I went to confront him, he ran away. I yelled, and his wife came out, angry, said it wasn't him. He wasn't home. I was terrified. I wanted to find Clay, confront him, but when I drove to his client's . . . I'll spare you what I saw. It reflected the pictures I found in the box. And the day before, when I was walking home, I could swear someone was following me too.

TomKat45: That's awful. Why were you walking home?

SassyVivi38: The library is walking distance from my house. I walk to work. But I'll drive now.

TomKat45: That's disturbing. I wish I were there to protect you. If you feel like you're unsafe, you need to call someone

SassyVivi38: I tried! When my husband came home, I told him about the gate and feeling as though I was being watched, and he begged me not to call the police. He said the media was watching him, and he didn't need the bad press. Or he didn't want to alarm the people he's representing. He's a lawyer. A defense attorney. I wonder if his thugs were watching me

TomKat45: Did you mention the box? You have proof now

SassyVivi38: I'm not ready to do it yet. But I will

TomKat45: I don't like any of this at all. Please consider my offer

SassyVivi38: I need to figure out a way to wire the money back to you. I can't take it, Tom. And I'm not the perfect wife either. These chinks in our marriage didn't get here by themselves

TomKat45: Don't blame yourself. It makes my heart hurt

SassyVivi38: I have to go, library's closing. Please consider a wire transfer for a return

TomKat45: I'd never abuse your loyalty and take something back that was meant for you. I'm not him

"Wow," Holly said out loud. Tom had laid it on thick in his last line. That was Vivian's final chat conversation before she disappeared. Holly wished she'd printed them all out now from the beginning, but at the same time, she was relieved there wasn't more. She thought she knew enough.

This man had reeled Vivian right in.

And she was easy prey.

Although . . . usually in the television shows Holly watched, the predator finagled money from the prey. Then they'd take off with the goods, never to be heard from again. This was an eerie situation in which the predator was instead sending Vivian money, which led Holly to believe he wanted something entirely different.

But why would Tom send her money if he intended to kidnap her? To earn her trust? Had the man following her seen her take the money from the PO Box, watched her count it in her car, then attempted to rob her? Did Vivian know who was there that day at Bay Shore Marina? She'd specifically said, *"There's somebody coming,"* but had she known who it was and then suddenly felt threatened? And why was she there, at that marina? The same one they'd used years ago to board the ferry for Fire Island.

All these thoughts were like awful currents crashing into Holly, one after another, much like the wind and water that'd nipped at her heels as she'd fought to stay vertical while searching for her sister at the marina. Something about that nostalgic location bothered her, too, because Vivian had almost been lost to that spot years ago. If Holly shut her eyes tight, she could see the traumatizing day, her parents holding each of her hands as she waited for the ferry.

The memory was shadowy; the horrible feelings Holly harbored from the event were very real, though. She could see her parents, but their image was watery too. Her shrink had explained that the mind suppresses things that hurt us. It made sense. It even sounded like something her mother would say.

Vivian had seemed a little freer on Fire Island whenever they visited; it did something special to her. The day Vivian had threatened not to come home had reminded Holly of the day in the mall when she'd tested their parents the first time.

Father had panicked, and Mother had admonished him, practically dragging him away down the pier. Holly could still recall how their typically wonderful summer day had been ruined by Vivian's display and the horror on Father's face as his sandal caught on a slat in the wooden dock. He tripped and had almost fallen when he turned around to look for Vivian. The other passengers heading to the ferry were staring.

"Hurry or we'll miss it," Mother urged. "Bye, Vivian." She waved.

"Mom, what're you doing?" Holly had asked, a shopping bag weighing down her hand. They'd purchased colored sand in a bottle, and Holly had Vivian's in her bag. She wanted to give it to her, but Mother dragged her along, too, and wouldn't let her go to her sister.

Holly caught a glimpse of Vivian wandering around near the entrance of the dock, in the far distance. Mother said she'd refused to come with them, but Vivian looked lost to Holly. It made her afraid for her sister—that she wouldn't make it home, that she'd never see her again.

"She'll come. Don't worry," Mother had said, never looking behind her. Never doubting herself. "She'll come, Henry. *Walk*," she yelled.

"What if she doesn't, Cynthia?" he asked.

"Don't doubt me," she said quietly but firmly. "Boundary stretching, industry versus inferiority. She's not ready to leave us. They never really will be."

Mother looked right at Holly when she said it—the baby. It made Holly grip her plastic bag tighter. She had no idea how ready Holly was to leave her. How a part of her wished she were with her sister right then so they could have their own island adventure. They could open a shaved-ice stand, live off the land like the natives they'd learned about on their tour. Their business sign would say, No Shoes, No Cars—No Problem.

"She came back to us at the mall, Cynthia, but she's older now, a teenager. She might not try to find us this time," their father argued, his steps growing slower.

Vivian appeared to be spinning around in a circle, her hand shielding her eyes. *Is she looking for us?* Holly couldn't take it anymore. She wiggled her sweaty hands out of her mother's and father's grips and turned around. She was going to retrieve Vivian herself. Her sister wanted someone who cared enough to come for her. But when Holly turned, she saw Vivian running to them instead. "Stop! She's coming."

Her parents whipped around. The ferry was near ready to chuff away.

They all made it aboard—even Vivian. She was fast and caught up and flung herself at their father's side.

"You were going to leave me," she said to him. She wouldn't look at Mother. "You too!" She pointed at Holly.

"I wouldn't have," Father said, but Holly didn't believe him. He would have listened to Mother the way he always did.

"I was just about to run for you," Holly announced, but Vivian wiped at her tears and shook her head—*"no way."*

Mother looked straight down at Vivian. "I would have left you. Don't make threats you don't intend to deliver on. It makes you look weak."

1997

Four years later, the day after the incident with the journal exercise, Mother brought it back up—both the near miss with the ferry and the trip to Green Acres Mall. Mother had put Holly and Vivian in two separate rooms and used the painful accounts of what happened at the beach and the mall to try to coerce information out of them about the journaling exercise. In case the girls had forgotten the details, Mother had two Polaroid pictures that she kept in her office to remind them.

One picture was of Mother with a less-than-amused expression on her face, standing in front of a washing machine with a giant red bow slung around it. As a promo, Sears had taken a picture of their buyer with a purchase of a new machine. The other was a Polaroid of Mother and Father on the ferry from that awful trip where Vivian had almost been left behind. Mother was in a striped dress looking beautifully relaxed as Father leaned on the rail of the boat in shorts and a linen shirt.

They owned a camera, but for the life of Holly, she couldn't remember who'd taken the picture that day. It'd been years now, but she assumed it must've been Vivian and that she'd snapped the photo on their way to Fire Island—not on the way home, because no one had been relaxed then. Holly often liked to stare out at the water, lost in thought, so she'd probably missed it.

Holly had never really forgiven Vivian for leaving her at the mall, and Vivian was still sore with Holly for not preventing their parents from boarding the ferry without her. Vivian had insisted to this day that she'd been left behind and that she couldn't find them. Holly didn't believe her. She'd remembered that Vivian had wanted to go into another gift shop, and their parents had told her no because they didn't want to miss the ferry and be forced to wait for the next one.

Mother knew these grievances existed between the girls and used them to try to trick each sister into giving up the other one. Their father had exited the house for the duration of their inquest. It was likely too painful for him to watch, but it would be more painful for him if he protested.

"You know Vivian left you in that mall all alone when you were just a little girl to be kidnapped and God knows what else without a care

in the world. She just wanted to go to the arcade. I know you cheated off her, and I'll threaten to ground her for the entire summer if one of you doesn't confess. What do you think that will do to your alliances if I threaten her whole summer when she flaked on you for a video game and a stuffed bear?"

These words would be repeated to Holly over the years. There were some nights she'd recall them in her sleep. It was like her mother's voice was on repeat in her head and never stopped, the aqueous memories that went along with them swishing in and out like a dream.

There were days as an adult when Holly randomly *still* heard her. Holly had felt so awful that day, locked in her mother's office, pitted up against the cushioned chair made to look whimsical with its pea-green paisley pattern and rigid brown feet and handrails. Such a friendly-looking chair, and she'd gripped it for dear life as she fought to keep up her lie.

Vivian had nodded at Holly from the formal living room, where she was being detained until she could be questioned. Her nod had said, *"Stick to the story."*

"You'll be in so much more trouble if you continue to lie and she tells the truth. You'll be grounded, and she'll be allowed to roam free. And you'll be given extra journaling assignments. Just tell me you cheated. Truth is the easiest way here."

Holly remembered grinding her teeth and biting her tongue, hard, until it bled and feeling like she was going to throw up. Her memory of what'd happened with the journals was so much more vivid than that of what happened at Fire Island. But they'd been there so many times, the trips had started to blend together.

The journaling incident was unique, though, memorable, and one where Holly had messed up. But if she buckled now, Vivian would never forgive her. They didn't always see eye to eye, she and Vivian, but this was different. It was mental warfare against their mother.

Later, Vivian would tell Holly that the same tactic was used on her. *"Holly would've left you at the docks, maybe even waved from the ferry. Spineless. And vengeful after the stunt you pulled at the mall. Give her up. You shouldn't protect her. She's a yellowbelly. She'll turn. Doesn't have it in her to hold in a lie and you know it."*

But Holly had held the lie. And so had Vivian. And it was a decision both girls would come to regret, because it'd meant they'd beaten their mother at her own game.

And for that injustice, there would be serious consequences.

The traffic jam wasn't letting up, and Holly couldn't read and play bumper cars anymore, so she pulled over into a drugstore parking lot and did a quick internet search, which showed that any amount of cash was legally allowed to be sent through the mail. Although not advisable, a person could insure up to $50,000. Holly assumed that when Tom had said he sent *"the max allowed,"* that's what he'd meant.

Holly was baffled. Had Tom been the one who was following Vivian, or was it someone associated with Clay?

There were so many new worries that she hadn't had before. Offering these chat sessions to the police would help reveal who Tom was, and hopefully, the rest would follow.

Holly was angry with herself, remembering how Vivian had said Clay was adamant about not reporting the man in their backyard. It was a sensitive time in his case. Sadly, Holly recalled how she'd agreed that Vivian shouldn't report it *for now*. Looking back, her ill advice came from trying to preserve the peace in Vivian and Clay's marriage.

Up until this point, Holly had always been about keeping the peace, taking the path of least resistance. The two people Vivian trusted the most, her husband and her sister, both told her not to report the man who might have done her harm, just one more thing Holly blamed herself for.

Vivian had been in terrible danger. And it was time for Holly to take all this information to the two-bit cops and let them figure out the rest. Sadly, the sunlight, or most likely the stress of the morning, was bringing on another headache. *I have to make it there today.*

She reached into her glove box and realized she'd left the ginger pills at home. *"Shit."* She just couldn't get anything right. But maybe because she'd been too distracted before, it only now occurred to Holly to wonder again why the professor had been in front of Vivian's house that evening. Even if he lived nearby, it was an odd coincidence, given his relationship to her parents.

Holly opened a browser window and searched "missing professor, Long Island, 1990s," and immediately stumbled upon the curious man on the street corner—Dr. Archibald Steiner.

She placed her fingers on her temple, wishing the headache away so she could get on with solving the crime. Holly vaguely recalled how their mother referred to him as Archie, and for some reason, their father hadn't liked it. It wasn't like Mother to be playful at all; maybe that's why Father hadn't seemed to care for him.

"Oh, Archie. Now, there's a man who can wear a tweed jacket, although he wears it more like a taxi driver than a prof."

Holly remembered her parents getting into an argument about this very comment, because Mother was trying to insinuate that Archie looked too rough around the edges to be a teacher, but their father hadn't liked how she'd said he *"can wear a tweed jacket."* Vivian surmised there was hidden meaning there. It could be that Mother's favorite movie was *Taxi Driver*, and that she was a huge fan of Robert DeNiro, who Archie looked nothing like.

Holly couldn't read between the lines, and she still didn't understand why no one had questioned why Mother's favorite movie was about a homicidal taxi driver and an underage prostitute, but she guessed it kind of fit the bill. Mother loved examining the mentally unstable and human sexuality.

Dr. Steiner had been a colleague of her parents, a professor of math or science or something totally unrelated to their department, but occasionally they'd all get together for happy hour and stay out way too late. In the early years, they'd go away to conferences with spas. Holly knew this only because Vivian was left with a babysitter once when she was an infant so they could attend, and she'd been so bad for the sitter, they'd never gone again.

It was the first time Holly had ever heard the term *separation anxiety*.

Holly knew Archie had been at the conference and that there was a story there, one where their parents had gotten too drunk and words were flung around, their parents' likely much more polished than Archie's, but all the hubbub about the man seemed to dissipate completely until years later, when he'd pulled a disappearing act.

Holly had a wild revelation that maybe Archie hadn't been on that street corner just walking his dog. Maybe he'd been checking out the house of the woman who'd gone missing because he knew a little something about that subject.

And maybe he could help Holly, with both locating her sister and getting some more of those magic pills. Upon closer inspection, Archie's ginger pills were a lot higher strength than the kind sold online. Holly didn't trust the online brands because they had a bunch of other ingredients on the label that she didn't recognize. She wanted what Archie had. And it might be fitting to turn to Archie for more than just his pills since Holly's mind kept clawing at her to look at the past for answers to the future.

Bay Shore. The marina. The games Vivian had played with her parents.

The games she'd played with her at the mall.

Their childhood.

The wacky professor who'd been inside their home during that time.

SassyVivi's mascara and leather jacket were also a throwback, making Holly think of young Vivian, pushing her boundaries with their parents.

Had she been doing it with Clay and Tom too?

12

Clay swiped his hand across the wooden top of his desk, his pinkie finger coming away with a fresh coat of dust. Vivian hadn't been there to clean it, and Clay had never taken care of the house himself. He would need to hire a cleaning crew.

He would need to do a lot of things differently without her there.

He sat at his desk, exhausted, throwing his head back into the headrest of his office chair. His case was over, but he'd lost so much in the process. He knew he'd caused Vivian stress before she went missing, but her going missing wasn't his fault, and now he needed to prove that too. He'd pulled her little book of poetry out of his desk drawer, but he couldn't really make sense of it. Well, most of it. There were some clear inferences to her disdain for people near and far, and he could only assume the ones who were near were the neighbors and himself.

Clay should hide the book, but the police weren't banging down his door anymore.

They had warned Clay not to leave town. He'd laughed in Rigby's face—as if that were an option. The senior partner at the firm asked him not to come back to work until his personal life was sorted out, and skipping town now would be the same as admitting he was guilty.

Besides, he wanted to see his little girl again. He'd been promised. As he watched the digital numbers tick forward on the wall clock, he thought of all the things he'd say the next time he saw her. She might be too young to understand, but he'd tell her he hadn't known about her. And that if he had, he would've come for her a long time ago.

He'd tell her that she'd be seeing him more often. Then he'd ask her what her favorite things were—colors, animals, ice cream flavors—and then he'd deliver them in one way or another. He'd buy a shirt or a toy in the color, take her for ice cream, visit the zoo that had her animal of choice. It was his mistake getting involved with Frankie in the first place, but she'd warned him, *"You'll have a hard time forgetting me."* And she hadn't been kidding.

It was a September evening three years ago when he'd met Frankie—a total game changer, the same year he'd left the DA's office to go private and work for Horowitz and Hauser.

Clay had just gotten his first major acquittal in a trial with his new firm. It would've been an excellent time for celebration, but Vivian wasn't interested. He couldn't bear to go home to her. He was supposed to be enjoying this moment, and she would suck the joy, all the color, right out of it.

He was sure her attitude was in reaction to his most recent blunder.

She'd made an appointment at a fertility clinic, but she hadn't checked his schedule first to make sure he was available, and he was due in court that day. He didn't understand what was so hard about rescheduling it, but she took it to heart. Clay also didn't understand why they couldn't try to conceive again instead of going to see a doctor.

They'd created a baby twice; they could do it again.

The miscarriages had been hard on their marriage, and she wouldn't tell him why she didn't want to try again. Ever since he'd missed the doctor's appointment, she'd been rigid toward him.

To make matters worse, he hadn't booked their vacation to the Catskills in time.

"Peter and Eve got Winter Clove," Vivian had whispered breathlessly in regard to their neighbors, who'd actually booked their reservation in a timely manner for the Labor Day weekend getaway. Clay had been working on his case and hadn't booked the resort she wanted soon enough, and they'd missed out. It angered him that she couldn't pick up the phone and book it herself.

She'd explained—Clay was the vacation planner, the reservation maker, the person clearly in charge of this endeavor, and he'd let her down, even though he'd offered to book any other resort in the Catskills that she wanted, but nothing was good enough, because her anger wasn't directed at Winter Clove. She was still making him pay for the missed doctor's appointment. Maybe he'd messed up there, so instead of finding a silver lining, she'd colored it in darker.

She'd explained that none of his alternate choices for a vacation spot compared to Winter Clove, which was the only five-star resort on three hundred sprawling acres. None of Clay's selections included a white Colonial mansion built in the 1800s with a wraparound porch and a red roof cupping the upstairs dormer windows, the floor where Vivian liked to stay.

So they just didn't go anywhere, even though he'd already taken the time off work. It was the most miserable week of his life, when Vivian just sat around sulking about how she wished she were at Winter Clove with her friends.

And no sex either.

If they were going away together, he was guaranteed at least that, but he received nothing but the cold shoulder for missing the reservation window.

He'd tried to focus on the positive following his acquittal, because it had been a beautiful day outside, the sky bright blue, the sun shining. The office had been buzzing his cell all day, and he'd just seen another call from one of the partners. He didn't know what Ari could possibly want, since he'd already talked to him several times that day.

"Eddy here."

"Are you at the bar with Vivian drinking the good stuff yet, superstar?"

"Going out, but not going home. The wife's sick," he lied. It was easier to make up excuses for Vivian than actually admit that she didn't give a shit about his life accomplishments.

"City-bound? Anywhere near Farmingdale, by any chance?"

"Why, Ari? You need me to pick up your dry cleaning again?" Clay joked.

"That was an isolated incident, prick."

Clay laughed. He had a great relationship with the partners at the firm, but that also wouldn't stop him from taking their spot one day.

"Listen," Ari said, "you should go visit a prospective client. He's offering twice your usual retainer after watching what you did with Cohen. He called here specifically asking for you."

"Twice?" Clay's eyes lit up at the price tag. It was like what he'd told Vivian. The Cohen case was just the beginning. "Stellar. Send me his contact info."

"Ah . . . you'll know the one, Nicky Bellini. I'll send the contact to your email."

Clay was surprised Ari would pass this job along. "You want to associate the firm with that crew?"

"It's your call, Clay. You can check it out yourself and see if it's legit. His bottling plant is located in Farmingdale. He said to stop by whenever you have a moment. He'll be working after hours there tonight."

Clay would have to do some poking around to see if he wanted to represent a man rumored to have connections to the Mafia. Nothing could put out his professional sizzle faster than taking on a case he couldn't win or one that could mar his up-and-coming reputation. But a retainer fee that large sounded mighty nice.

"Thanks, Ari. I'll check it out and let you know."

"All right. Be good now," Ari said.

"I'm always good." Clay hung up the phone and smiled. He felt like being anything but well-behaved tonight. With little else to do, he decided it was as good a time as any to check things out.

Clay left Sayville and drove the twenty miles or so west to Farmingdale. He parked in front of a gentlemen's club. The club wasn't his destination, but Bellini's place of business was right next door, and Clay didn't want to just roll up unannounced. There were lots of people on the streets for a Wednesday evening, and it made Clay feel as though he should live closer to a more bustling area. Maybe his life wasn't just a reflection of his colorless wife but the dull town in which he lived.

Sayville was once voted the friendliest city in the entire country. Friendly was great for double-date bonfires at the beach and monthly cards club, but there was no outlet to get laid seven ways till Sunday. Clay's sex life was so nonexistent, even the girl winking at him on the neon sign was a turn-on.

Not that he'd ever strayed before.

He'd been a good husband, and he was almost certain his father had always been faithful to his mother, but his parents' relationship hadn't lacked for anything. They'd still held hands and pecked kisses into their golden years. His mother had given his father three children, not jilted him like Vivian, who'd given up trying to create a family the natural way just because things hadn't gone smoothly in the beginning. Not that he had a good relationship with his sisters, but that wasn't his fault. After their parents had passed away, his sisters up and moved to California, which somehow included disbanding their relationship with him, especially after he wouldn't make the trek out there to visit. He couldn't take the time off work.

As he observed the men in suits drifting into the strip joint, he decided he'd join them. Why the hell not? No one else was interested in going out with him tonight, and it'd been an eternity since he'd admired the curve of large breasts in a tiny top, the firmness of well-conditioned buttocks hanging upside down from a pole, a practiced dancer staring at him with wanting eyes.

He wouldn't touch, but he had a strong desire to look. Winning Cohen's case had somehow piqued his libido.

When Clay exited his car, he was stopped by a beautiful woman with raven hair and a low-cut red dress. She appeared too classy to work at a strip club, her makeup tastefully drawn on around her dark eyes, her dress elegant and perfect on her slight frame.

"Mr. Bellini has been waiting for your arrival," she said.

Clay glanced over his shoulder in surprise.

"He has?" How did they know he was coming? Were they watching him?

"This way." Her plump lips were bright red like her dress, and she was standing, pointing to the brick storefront of the building he already knew was Mr. Bellini's company. Clay wondered why she was so dressed up to escort him inside a bottling factory in the middle of a strip mall.

He took two steps and paused. "I'm not sure I'm ready to meet him yet."

"You're here, aren't you? You're ready." She said it so surely, he believed her.

"Very well," Clay said. *I'd follow you anywhere.*

She beckoned him with a wave of her finger, and he trailed behind her as she led him inside. She wiggled when she walked in her heels, her small ass fluttering like a butterfly.

They didn't speak as they entered the building. It was dark by now, and the workers had all gone home. The bottling plant was shut down. Clay picked up a glass jar from a box—pickles. Mr. Bellini sold pickles.

The woman took the jar from his hand. Their fingers brushed, and Clay had a strong desire to touch the rest of her. He could get lost in those black-brown eyes of hers.

She placed the jar back in the box. "The clientele at Mr. Bellini's are much better and cleaner than the ones you were about to entertain."

Clay had no idea what she was talking about. He nodded, because he never liked not being *in the know*.

"The strip club," she said, answering his questioning eyes.

Clay sucked on his lip. "Oh, no. I was just looking around, wasn't sure where I was."

"Right." She rolled her big eyes. "Well, before I take you in to see Mr. Bellini, I have to make it clear that you can never speak of this place after you leave. I can't promise your safety if you don't agree."

He glanced around at all the bottling machines with their prefab molds and cranks, the whole operation a likely cover for whatever illegal business Bellini was running. He might be using the plant to clean money or hide something else, but Clay was certain it wasn't his primary source of income.

Cold sweat as chilling as the metal in the gleaming factory spiraled down his dress shirt. Clay knew these underground operations existed, but this one still surprised him. He'd expected to see *The Godfather*, twenty-first century: data theft instead of laundered money, tech viruses instead of car bombs, death threats via text messages from gangsters in Gucci shoes.

He shouldn't be here. He should turn around.

"I understand," he said.

Clay wasn't sure why he agreed to follow her. He could've exited the building, climbed into his vehicle, driven back to his quiet neighborhood, convinced his wife to go out for a drink with the neighbors, researched Bellini's pending charges, and reassessed whether he should take this case or not.

Instead, he chose to follow the woman in red.

He followed her all the way to an old-fashioned elevator, rickety and clanking with rusty chains. It took them down to the basement.

When the elevator door opened, vibrant sound exploded in Clay's ears. Men crowded around tables playing poker and blackjack. Others shouted, "Seven, eleven," rolling dice against long, narrow tables. The certain ticking of a roulette wheel was drowned out by people laughing, a few screaming. Ladies in tight dresses perched on men's hips or sat directly on their laps as waitresses in little black outfits served them drinks. There was too much cigarette smoke in the closed-off room, making Clay's eyes water and sting.

Still, he let the mystery woman lead him through the crowd.

Clay noticed men pretending like they weren't watching him discreetly eyeing him as he made his way to the thick wooden bar. There was music playing, jazzy but modern. He could barely hear it over the people.

So many people.

So much noise.

He watched as the men tossed money on the green felt tables—hundreds, thousands—thrown in the center like they were pitching pennies in a fountain. The whole scene buzzed with an energy Clay had been missing all his life.

When he neared the bar, a blonde in a gold sequined dress hip-bumped him. He startled and stared at her, waiting for an apology, but she just smiled, her contact clearly intentional.

"Newbie?" the blonde asked his raven-haired escort.

"Yep, here to see the boss."

"Better get 'im something strong, then." She licked her lips before walking away, her soft pink gloss getting lost on her tongue.

"You like her? That's Carla. You can have her if you agree to go to work for him," the girl in red said.

Clay's lips parted at her comment. By *"have her,"* he was sure she meant he could sleep with her. His pulse raced south of his beltline. Clay could hear the beating of his heart in his ears.

"And what's your name?" Clay asked.

"My name is Francine, but everybody calls me Frankie."

"Frankie?" Clay asked. She nodded and held out her hand to formally introduce herself. He shook it. Her hands were soft, her fingernails painted red to match her dress and lips. Someone was taking care of Frankie. Clay was sure he wouldn't have the pleasure of *having her* anytime soon.

Clay retracted his hand and coughed into it, his lungs struggling against the smoke in the room and the criminality of his surroundings. He'd observed at least twenty counts of illegal gambling, and that was just after one quick scan.

"What'll ya have?" the bartender asked. He was young with slicked-back hair and eyebrows that seemed to stretch across his forehead in a single line.

"Scotch, splash of ginger," Clay said.

The bartender placed a glass of Chivas with a splash in front of Clay. He took a long sip, enjoying the burn as it sizzled down the hatch.

A tall man approached with an entourage of two, but there was no doubt who was in charge. He had shiny hair, a belly hanging over his tailored pants, and skin pocked and ripened like an olive. He stood in front of Clay for a moment without speaking. "So you're the famous lawyer. Case dismissed in three days?"

Clay cleared his throat. "That's me. And you must be Mr. Bellini, I presume?" Clay put out his hand for a shake. The man gripped it and shook it fast.

"Certainly!" Mr. Bellini laughed, and so did the men at his side. They were even taller than Mr. Bellini, six four at least, barrels for chests, one very pale and bald, the other tanned and shifty, like Bellini.

"Call me Nicky—everyone else does." The men laughed again. "Pipe down, Russ." He shoved the bald one in the shoulder.

What were they laughing at? Clay's chest rose and fell and clenched and seized. He didn't know what he was doing there, but Frankie had almost promised he would be harmed if he backed out now.

Clay searched for her then, but she had tactfully slithered away.

"So you've decided to take the job?" Nicky asked.

Clay eyeballed the room. "What were you charged with again?"

"Illegal gambling."

The two men who flanked his sides busted a gut laughing.

Clay took a gander around the room, sucked on his lip, and let out a little laugh too. "What do they have on you?"

"A couple undercovers came in," Nicky said.

Clay glanced over his shoulder instinctively.

"Not here, buddy. My last place," Nicky clarified.

"Ah." Clay sipped his drink, embarrassed for not doing his research first. "Well, if they have proof, what am I supposed to do about that?"

"You got the Jewish guy off. Cohen."

"The Jewish guy was innocent," Clay explained.

"So am I." Nicky smiled, his mouth wide, his teeth gleaming. "Look, I know those cops were ready to put that guy away, and you somehow pulled it together for him. Tells me you're one sharp guy capable of going the extra mile to win the tough cases."

"Right. And thank you." Clay coughed again.

"So does that mean you'll take the case? You do one favor for us and we've got your back for life," Nicky said.

"Is that right?" Clay really liked the sound of what Nicky was offering, and it also explained why they'd singled him out. They didn't just want a lawyer; they wanted *him*. He let his eyes cascade around the room, and he could feel the camaraderie, a sense of belonging somewhere outside the circle of his sad little life at home. His win in the courtroom today wasn't enough. He had no one to share it with. Not to mention, he loved playing cards.

"I'll do my best to represent you, Nicky. This will be a tough case, though. No promises, all right?"

"Fantastic!" Nicky slapped Clay on the back. "Line up the bar. This wise guy's gonna get me off the hook!" The whole place lit up in excitement, and Clay turned three shades of pink as he realized winning for Nicky meant winning for the entire room.

Clay took a shot of whiskey with Nicky and a gang of people he didn't know. The heat spread from his throat down his chest. Sweat broke out across his brow. He needed to use the restroom. He felt as though he'd just signed a deal with the devil.

"Around the corner," a guy yelled.

There was more slapping on his shoulders as he made his way to the men's room. He'd been patted on the back so many times today, he was beginning to feel like a baseball player after the winning game. His wife hadn't cared about his wins, only his losses.

"Hey, pally." One big guy gave him a fresh slap on the shoulder, rocking him backward. These guys knew how to hit.

They probably knew how to kill too. What had he gotten himself into?

When Clay exited the bathroom, Frankie was waiting for him in the hallway.

"Carla's interested in leaving with you." Frankie's dark eyes smoldered through him.

He thought about Frankie's offer. Nothing in this place seemed quite real. It was like that elevator ride had transported him into a different dimension. Something bad was happening to him in this strange place—something bad and something very good. The dark, smoky hallway obscured him, everything else hazy but his desire for Frankie. He'd gone so long without needy hands on his body, steamy breath on his neck, someone to whisper his name, something more than a restless wife offering a pity fuck on bedsheets that were always clean.

"Really?" he breathed out. Frankie nodded, but neither one of them moved.

No man should be deprived like that. He'd done his best to make Vivian happy. Marriage should not be a license to become impotent, a grocery list of boredom wrapped up in a neat, sterile package, all freshly ironed shirts and stocked refrigerators, a life full of triviality and empty calories.

He was still alive. He had needs.

The woman in red moved closer to him, as if trying to hear his answer better, even though he hadn't said a word. Her breath smelled like mint and alcohol, like she'd drunk a ton of liquor, then popped in a stick of gum.

"It's not Carla I want." The words fell out of his mouth in a rasp. He edged closer to her. She trembled and took his hand, leading him somewhere else. It was dark in the area between the restrooms and a storage room in the back that Clay hadn't noticed.

So much anticipation raced down every inch of Clay's body, the hitching of his breath, the feel of Frankie's smooth skin on his palm. He watched the curve of her behind flutter in that beautiful dress as she steered him somewhere he shouldn't be. Clay wasn't a fussy man, but his physical needs were vital, like air or water, and he'd been starved.

Frankie led him around a series of boxes to a table and swiped papers off the surface. The moonlight and a single overhead light provided the only visibility in the room, acting as a spotlight on the curves and crevices of the goddess laid out before him.

She scooted up on the edge of the table and spread her legs. He came undone, wrapping his arms around her waist, running his hands down her back until he reached the perfection at the bottom. He tasted her lips, hungrily devouring the perfume on her neck, finding her breasts in his mouth. Frankie pumped her hips with want, undoing his zipper. Things were happening, and he couldn't stop them.

He didn't want to.

Afterward, he felt fulfilled, like he'd been fed his first hot meal in years. They were quiet and alone, breathing on each other in the dusty box room. His attention was drawn to his wedding ring, glimmering in the night, stunned by his lack of guilt.

"I want to be with you again," she whispered in his ear.

God, how he wanted that too. This place was magic. But it wasn't reality. Clay zipped up his trousers, and he could barely see Frankie in the light, the shadow casting a half glow on her somber smile.

"I guess this would be a bad time to tell you I'm married," he said.

She shrugged. "Everyone here has a wife. I know some people who can make her go away if you want," she whispered and then giggled.

"You're joking, I hope." Although somehow the idea didn't seem all that bad. He asked himself: If he could snap his fingers and make Vivian disappear—poof—would he do it? That's why this place was bad.

Fantasy.

Reality.

The lines were beginning to blur.

"Well, you think about it. Because you'll have a hard time forgetting me," she said.

He took her hand. "I have no doubt." They shuffled through the cardboard boxes and out of the room, into the light. He blinked his way back to the casino. Clay said his goodbyes and kissed Frankie's hand before he climbed aboard the elevator. He drove home wondering what he'd gotten himself into—and when he could go back and do it again.

13

Holly remembered the missed call and grabbed her phone while sitting in the pharmacy parking lot, thinking maybe it was someone with an update on Vivian. But instead she saw a calendar reminder for her therapy appointment. *Damn.* It told her how frazzled she was, because she rarely missed them.

She dialed her therapist. "I have to cancel my appointment."

"I thought you would surely keep this one with your sister missing," Dr. Fineberg said. "How're you doing?"

Holly had an odd relationship with her therapist. Dr. Fineberg was approaching sixty, with a shock of white hair that she likely had no intention of cutting. She sat and listened and rarely offered feedback, but Holly had returned to her month after month because she'd packed in so much of her life with this woman that it'd be exhausting to start over with someone new. Sometimes she felt the same way with her husband.

"Not well, but I just don't have time to talk right now. I'm trying to help the cops find Vivian." Okay, so that was a lie, but Holly liked to think she was part of the investigation. As soon as the traffic let up and she got her evidence in order, she'd get back on the highway and be on her way to the station. They'd surely take her seriously after she told them what she'd found out today.

"Dr. Fineberg, do you think Vivian might be repeating the acting out you've told me she engaged in as a child?"

"It's not uncommon for adults to repeat the coping mechanisms they used as a child. Especially if those methods worked well for them."

Holly hesitated. "Does patient confidentiality apply to criminal cases?" she asked.

"In most instances, yes."

"Okay. My sister's husband was having a physical affair, and I think my sister might've been having an emotional one. Do you think if Vivian's husband found out she was forming a relationship with another man, it would be cause for him to harm her, even though he wasn't faithful himself?"

Silence filled the other end, and she could picture Dr. Fineberg tilting her head the way she did when Holly was on her couch. "Possibly. Men handle infidelity differently than women."

"How so?" Holly asked. She was thumbing through the pages of the chat logs.

"Usually for women, affairs are more emotional. It's about establishing connection. Men often view affairs as more physical, but due to ego, they have a harder time accepting their partner's infidelity. It can make them feel weak and powerless. A man will almost never stay with a woman after she cheats, but a woman will often try to work it out in reverse situations."

Holly's nose twitched at the double standard. It wasn't just a gender bias that occurred in the work world, like when Mark's job took precedence over hers, but with sex as well. Sickening. "So you think, yes, he could've harmed her if he'd found out about this man she'd been just talking to?"

"I don't think yes or no." Here she went—the nebulous answer. "I'm saying if he's an egocentric man who thrives on power, it could have negative results. In some cases violent."

Holly stopped midflip. "He's definitely an egotist. He's a pompous lawyer."

"And how does that make you feel? Remind you of anyone you know?"

Dr. Fineberg was the only one who knew all the dirt of her childhood. "My mother. She got away with so much because she always had a way to validate her own actions, even when they were wrong."

"Precisely."

The one thing she hadn't gotten away with was murder—of a human, at least—but perhaps Clay thought he could. "I'm on my way to the police station."

"Okay. Well, if you have evidence of everything you've told me, I'd say it's worth sharing."

The cars were moving more swiftly now. "Done. I do have to run. Thank you. That was helpful."

After Holly hung up the phone, she started her engine. She felt better after speaking to Dr. Fineberg, like she'd let go of some of what she'd been holding inside. But the shrink term she'd used—*egocentric*—also reminded her of her mother.

It was actually the description their mother had used to describe Vivian when she was younger.

It made Holly wonder who was the egotist in this situation—Clay or Vivian? If Vivian had needed Tom to feed her ego, was that as bad as Clay sleeping with this other woman to feed his? Clay seemed more at fault because he'd acted on his urges, but at a granular level, they were both seeking out things in other people that they couldn't find in each other.

Vivian was reserved, but she did have an ego. And when they were younger, Mother had pushed back every time Vivian had tried to flex that ego. The consequences of that had been devastating for all of them.

❧

1997

After subjecting Holly and Vivian to an inquisition about whether they'd shared their journal entries, Mother was infuriated she couldn't shake a confession out of them. She'd sent them to their rooms without supper. The next morning, she announced that they could emerge, and Holly and Vivian had crept down the stairs, hungry and hopeful for a bowl of cereal.

But instead, they had found a full spread of pancakes, waffles, bacon, and fresh-cut fruit.

Mother was humming a chipper tune like she'd just come home from the theater. "Would you like fresh-squeezed orange juice or milk?" she asked.

Holly and Vivian looked at each other, teenage fingers hanging on to the maple stair railing, afraid to descend the rest of the way. Holly was relieved at her mother's pleasant demeanor, but Vivian frowned. Holly knew it was because she thought there was a catch, but Holly didn't care.

She was just glad no one was yelling at her this morning.

She'd expected a formal grounding, the taking away of their most prized earthly possessions. She was sure her Game Boy would be confiscated, Vivian's boom box placed in quarantine.

Instead—this.

"Juice, please," Holly said.

"Very well, and for you, Vivian?" Mother asked.

"Same," Vivian uttered.

Mother flitted around the kitchen in her day dress and apron like she actually enjoyed it, while they both knew she hated to cook. Father was usually the breakfast maker, but Holly could already see his silhouette on the back porch, sipping his morning coffee. If he was out there, it meant he was at ease, which made Holly relaxed but didn't seem to do much for Vivian.

Holly sat down, and Vivian just stared into open space. It was probably because the last time they were near that table, their mother had thrown papers at them and accused Holly of plagiarism. Why couldn't Vivian just be glad they weren't being punished for cheating? Although it was a lot easier for Holly to be forgiving, since she'd been the one to cheat.

Mother served each of them a generous portion of everything she'd prepared. It looked absolutely delicious. Holly's stomach growled, and she couldn't stop herself from shoving pancakes, loaded with butter and drippy syrup, into her mouth.

"Pace yourself. You don't want to make yourself sick at the beach. You shouldn't eat a ton before you swim," Mother said.

"You're letting us go?" Vivian asked suspiciously.

Mother poured herself a cup of coffee. The pot was almost empty. When she and Father weren't drinking and smoking, they were guzzling black coffee to ward off their cravings. "Yes, you may go to the beach today. Or Summerfest."

Holly swallowed. "After we finish our assignments, you mean?"

Mother cleared her throat and swung around to clean the cutting board full of cantaloupe rinds and strawberry tops. "Not today. I think we could all use a break from journaling."

Vivian coughed, practically hacking up her eggs. She hadn't touched the rest of her plate, picking here or there, but then she never had been a good eater. It was probably one of the reasons Holly had the lion's share of the curves in the family. Mother ate like a bird too.

"Okay, sounds good to me," Holly said. She shot Vivian a wide-eyed look and shrugged. Maybe their little stunt had been a good thing? Maybe their mother had a moment of contrition watching how much her research was hurting them? Or their father had finally stepped in. He'd been plenty upset about Mother's day-drinking. It wasn't likely, but it was possible he'd been able to influence her behavior.

After breakfast, the girls hurried upstairs to change into their bathing suits and cover-ups. Holly grimaced at the noticeable bloat from all the food she'd eaten and wondered if that had been Mother's intention. Had she served an insane amount of breakfast because she knew Holly would then go to put on her bathing suit, examine herself, and feel bad? Would she be watching Holly as she descended the stairs to leave for the beach, studying her? That was what made living with Mother the hardest. Was it their mother making them breakfast or the professor manipulating them like lab rats?

As much as Holly wanted to believe she and Vivian had gotten away with lying about the journals, this entire morning felt like a test.

Holly knew Vivian thought so too.

Vivian teased her usually straight bangs in the mirror and pushed a cherry-flavored Lip Smacker over her mouth. "So what do you think she's up to?"

"Maybe nothing?" Holly shrugged, hoping for the best. She was by far the most positive person in the family.

"Probably something," Vivian argued, meeting Holly's eyes in the mirror. Vivian shared their mother's eyes, and Holly had to catch her breath to make sure it wasn't their mother watching them—listening in.

"We should get out of the house before she changes her mind," Holly said.

On the drive to the beach, they passed the site of Sayville Summerfest. A Ferris wheel with bucket seats in rainbow colors was being erected, along with wooden booths set off by red flags for the carnival games. Through the open station wagon windows, they could hear a Bon Jovi cover band warming up. Their mother may have grown up with cornfields and public swimming pools, but this was how Holly would always remember her summers—lazy beach days, boogie boarding at the beach, and Summerfest, with its local bands, cotton candy, and fried dough with remnants of powdered sugar clinging to her face.

Vivian and Holly had a nice afternoon together, which was odd. Holly thought Vivian would be angry with her for asking to cheat and causing the whole big fight, but they didn't speak of the incident again, and Vivian actually let Holly hang out with her the whole time.

When they decided to go home to change before going out to listen to the bands at Summerfest, their parents were both there, and dinner was prepared.

"You can just grab some before you go back out," their father said, referring to the chicken and veggies in the glass dish on the stove. "Your mother made it. She's on some kind of culinary kick. The original Cynthia Child, Sayville's finest." He laughed warmly. Holly sometimes had fantasies that her parents would divorce, and she would get to pick their father as guardian. "Maybe to make up for yesterday," he said, but that was his biggest fault. That he ultimately let Mother rule with her tyrannical iron fist. Above all, he wanted there to be peace in the house. Peace among the women he loved. It made him the ultimate enabler.

"Okay," Holly said. "Thanks." She kissed his cheek.

Their mother appeared right before they dashed out the door again. "Be home by midnight. Also, your father and I are going out tomorrow night. I have a surprise for you girls. I'll ask that you be home for it. It'll arrive after we leave."

Holly scrunched her brow, but she was too psyched to catch the Hootie & the Blowfish cover band to care, and she knew Vivian was pumped for the girl from their high school performing Alanis Morissette, but it didn't keep her from asking the question. "What kind of surprise, Mom?"

"Oh, you'll see. Don't worry. Go on, have fun." Her black eyebrows peaked, and Holly felt something cold slither down her shoulders.

Vivian didn't speak to Holly all the way to Summerfest, her sun-stroked cheeks pinched in like she was chewing on the insides.

"What do you think it could be?" Holly asked.

"I don't know," Vivian said stiffly.

Despite their nice day at the beach, it felt like Vivian was back to resenting her for being incompetent and screwing up their whole summer because Holly wasn't creative enough to make up a few sentences on her own.

At least Mother had clearly gotten over it. Or so Holly told herself.

Mother's big surprise would always be marked by the sound of insects, needling little arms and legs, flapping wings, odd chirping. It wasn't time for the cicadas to arrive, but it was a muggy, hazy summer night, and as Mother opened their front door, all Holly could hear were the moths buzzing against the sallow porch light. Holly wanted to tell her parents to shut the door, but she was too stunned by her mother's appearance to say anything.

Mother and Father were all dressed up to go out, something they rarely did. Mother had on a burgundy dress Holly had never seen before. It was sleek, silk, and hugged her body in a way that shouldn't be allowed for a woman in her forties. She had a shawl draped around her neck and shoulders, the diamond necklace she wore only for the holidays plunging down her neckline.

Mother was a simple woman, really, with one set of diamond earrings, one necklace, and a tennis bracelet. But the dress was not simple at all, and it confused Holly. Their father had on normal attire for him: tan slacks, a white button-down shirt, and the same navy jacket he always wore with the brass buttons at the cuffs. He'd gelled back his dark hair, and it looked nice.

"We're going to be out late, so don't wait up, but we do have someone coming over to house-sit," she announced.

"House-sit?" Vivian asked.

Mother smiled tightly at their father. "Yes, since we'll be gone so long. It's the surprise."

"Like a babysitter?" Vivian laughed.

"No, you'll see. They should be here any minute."

"Dad?" Holly asked, stumped.

Father shrugged. Vivian had always babysat her in the past, but Holly was at the age now where she'd started sitting for the neighbors here and there, and her parents had most certainly left Holly alone when they'd gone to see Vivian's debate club competitions. Holly already knew how much smarter than her Vivian was. She didn't need to see how much smarter Vivian was than the rest of the county too.

"It will be all right. Your mother's idea," Father said. He had that goofy smile on his face, and Holly could only guess it had something to do with Mother's dress. Most of the time, she wore a teacher's clothing—cardigans and pencil skirts and shirts that buttoned at the neck—most certainly not the "Hot For Teacher" kind, like in the Van Halen video they loved to watch on MTV.

"It's a surprise. See you girls later." Their mother blew them an imaginary kiss that left Holly even more frightened.

They waved goodbye and closed the door, and the yellow glow went away and the insect sound stopped completely, but when Vivian turned to Holly, she was pale and shaking. "What's she up to?"

"I don't know." The house was near spotless, but Holly's first thought was to clean up for their guest. It was what they always did when someone was due to arrive. She began straightening pillows out of habit, or fear, or just to do something with her hands so they wouldn't quake like her sister's.

"What're you doing? Stop that," Vivian said.

But Holly couldn't. It comforted her to fluff the fringe tassels on their velvet pillows.

"Should we leave?" Vivian asked. She dashed to the kitchen, and Holly watched as she searched for the keys to her mother's Volvo wagon. She smacked the wall above the key ring with her palm. "The keys aren't here!" She turned to Holly. "What if we take our bikes? Ride them to

Summerfest? Tell Mom we're too old for house sitters, further protest her bullshit."

"She said it was a surprise. What if it's a magician or something? What if she hired someone to entertain us?" Holly asked. There were lots of performers in town for the festival. Maybe their mother thought it would be fun to hire someone to give them a show while they were out.

"I don't think she hired fucking puppeteers to come in and perform for us, Holly!"

Just then, the doorbell rang. "Crap," Holly said. Too late now. Had she made another mistake? Had they really had time to get away?

Vivian looked at her, deer in headlights.

"Get it," Holly said.

"Why me?" she asked.

Holly couldn't move. She'd reached her special state of immobilization. "Because I can't." She clung to the tassel pillow like the baby blanket her mother had burned. Everything was happening faster than she liked, and she didn't know why this felt like one more thing.

"Ugh, God." Vivian took each step so gingerly in her jean skirt and tank top, she practically waddled to the door. She opened it slowly, and they both gasped out loud when they saw who was on the other side.

"Rico?" Vivian asked, as if there was another smooth-skinned, deliciously sexy, A.C. Slater look-alike who happened to live in the area.

"You sound surprised, Viv." He leaned in the doorway, his black motorcycle jacket pressing into the side, his backpack half obscuring the glow of the porch light.

"Please come in. Where're my manners?" Vivian let out a little laugh, and Holly didn't know how she could turn it on like that.

Rico stepped inside and closed the door, and all Holly could do was clutch her pillow to her chest and stare. It was the first time she'd ever seen Rico in anything besides red lifeguard swim trunks. Somehow he looked even hotter covered up in jeans and a jacket.

"Hi there," he said, waving to her. "I've seen you at the beach. Holly, right?"

Holly opened her mouth, but only a mild croak escaped. Vivian shot her a vicious look that said, *"Get it together."*

"Hi," Holly managed.

Vivian and all her friends had been chatting up Rico at the beach on the regular, and Holly was sure Vivian didn't want her acting like a total spaz in front of him.

"So, ladies, I guess your mother didn't tell you I was coming. I can't believe it." Rico threw his backpack on the ground, and it made a loud *thud*. He smiled wide, and Holly almost peed her pants. He strode in and took off his jacket to reveal a plain white T-shirt and a ripple of biceps that looked much larger close-up. Holly was used to viewing them from afar on his big white chair. He was safer up there.

"She didn't. She likes to surprise us sometimes." Vivian widened her eyes at Holly, and she just realized she was still clutching the sofa throw pillow like a teddy bear. Holly immediately dropped it.

"What do you have in your backpack, bricks?" Holly asked, trying to be normal.

"No, I brought something much better. Refreshments!" Rico started pulling out bottles of beer and one clear bottle of something else. "Can't watch your house if I'm parched."

"Why're you watching it again?" Vivian asked.

"Kidding, right? Your mother asked me to come over because of the escaped convict."

"What escaped convict?" Holly asked.

"Don't you people talk in this house? Or watch the news?" The girls shrugged. "Jeez, I thought my family was messed up." Rico flipped on the TV, and it was true. The first headline that popped up on the news was a clip of Gary Smithers, escapee from the Nassau County Correctional Center, on the loose after killing a guard during a hospital transfer. He was a convicted felon sentenced to life and considered armed and dangerous.

Neither of them had been watching the news, but what was more disturbing was the fact that their mother knew that Gary Smithers had been roaming the streets for a few days and hadn't so much as warned them about him while she let them run around, attending Summerfest, spending long days at the beach. Maybe she was afraid it would ruin her big surprise. Rico thought he'd been hired as their bodyguard, but little did he know he'd been entered into an experiment by the good professor.

Who are you most likely to have sexual fantasies about, in real life or on television, and why?

This was worse than any journal exercise.

Vivian grabbed for a beer. "Thanks for bringing these." She cracked it open and sucked some down.

Holly went for one, too, without asking. Vivian didn't stop her.

Screw it. They were in hell together. Might as well take something to calm the flames. Holly took a sip and tried to hide the sour face that followed. She'd had wine before, but beer was new, and it tasted like gasoline smelled.

How do people drink this stuff?

"Well all right, all right. Atta girl, small pint." Rico pushed on Holly's thigh with his finger, and it made her blush.

"We have snacks," Holly said.

"Okay, I could use some."

Holly got up and ran into the kitchen. She saw the back door that connected to the porch and contemplated running away, because she could feel something dangerous coming by the way Rico had pushed his tanned fingers into the flesh of her thigh. How it'd made her tingle with warmth and quiver in fear. But she couldn't leave Vivian alone drinking with this college-age, nothing-but-trouble, town lifeguard who'd brought his own liquor.

If you were in a romantic setting with the subject in question two and there were no consequences to be had, emotional or physical, would you engage in sexual activity or abstain?

Holly returned with a bowl full of pretzels, and they watched the news and sipped their beers, and for a while everything was okay. Vivian turned on her boom box. Rico was rocking out to "Closer" by Nine Inch Nails. They censored out the explicit sexual lyrics on the radio, but Holly could barely handle Rico screaming them out loud anyway—because they both knew he was thinking about it.

"What's in there?" Vivian asked of the clear bottle with the spouted top made for pouring.

"That, young lady, is grain alcohol. It's pretty strong. I brought it more for me because your mother said she would be late, but I'd never be so rude as to not share." Rico's dimples appeared when he smiled, and Holly was smitten again.

"I'm not scared," Vivian said, and she sounded way too rebellious.

Rico didn't ask Holly if she wanted any but poured them three glasses of the clear stuff and what appeared to be cherry Kool-Aid out of a bottle that he'd pulled from God knows where.

"What else do you have in there? An Orange Julius machine?" Holly asked.

"You're too cute," he told Holly, and she sipped her drink quickly because she wasn't sure if he meant she was cute like a little girl or cute like a girl he'd like to kiss with his cherry-stained lips. She could see Vivian making awful faces as she sipped the drink, and it probably did taste horrible, but Holly was too buzzed to notice. She tried hers, and it was actually a little more tolerable than the beer, but the instant zing it gave her sent her eyeballs rolling to the back of her head.

She needed to get up.

"We're out of pretzels." Rico held up the bowl.

"Oh, I can get more."

Holly swayed to the side as she tried to rise. She giggled. Rico stood up and took her arm to help support her wobbly legs. "I'll help you with the snacks," he whispered. He was so close, she could feel his lips graze her skin. He had on cologne, Cool Water maybe, and his hair product was so thick that she could smell that too. But somehow, she liked it. She liked all Rico's scents.

Vivian was still fighting down the liquid and seemed too distracted to notice the two of them slip away, caught up in another tune from the boom box, "One Headlight," by The Wallflowers. Holly had gotten lost in that beat before, too, but right now she was trying to focus on the inside of the pantry while Rico leaned against the wall. She reached in to grab the chips. "Are these good?" she asked. She couldn't remember at the moment where she'd put the pretzels.

"That's not what I'm hungry for." His lips latched on to hers, and as surprised as she was, the way his lips gently massaged hers made it easy. His kisses grew hungrier, his tongue finding his way inside her mouth, but he was good at this. Soon his hands were roaming over her curves, the ones she'd been trying to hide for the last year. Rico didn't seem to mind them one bit, and she didn't feel like hiding them any longer, not when his touch felt so good. His lips were everywhere and fabulous, her nerve endings tingling on end.

"Holly!" Vivian said. Holly opened her eyes and found her sister leaning on the kitchen table. "Stop."

"Don't be a buzzkill, sis," Rico said, backing away.

"She's only fourteen, Rico," Vivian said.

Rico backed even farther away, bumping his head on the microwave. "She doesn't look like she's fourteen."

"I know," Vivian said, and Holly had never been so mad at her sister in her entire life.

Rico stepped closer to Vivian. "Well, how old are you?"

"Seventeen," she peeped.

They were all drunk at this point, and Holly felt suddenly hot and flushed. At first, she was so angry at Vivian that she could scream, but all she wanted to do now was lie down. She pushed past them and collapsed on the couch.

When she woke up, it was to her mother screaming from the upstairs bedroom. Father was chasing Rico out of the house with a chef's knife like in a sick dream. From upstairs came slapping and ear-piercing squeals. Holly could only assume their mother was beating the shit out of Vivian.

She'd done *it*. Holly knew what'd happened without asking any questions. What she was too inebriated to stop from happening or to do herself.

"It's what you dared us to do," Holly wanted to scream at her mother. Vivian had written that she would *engage*, and their mother had pushed her to do it. If they'd failed her little experiment, she'd have found a way to punish them, but because they'd done exactly what she'd predicted, she'd punished them too.

Not only was Vivian grounded for the rest of the summer, but the girls were kept separate as a joint punishment. Holly was okay with that at first because she'd been a little angry at Vivian for stepping in and treating her like a baby. There was a lot of crying on the upstairs floor in the months that followed, a lot of yelling too. In the fall, Vivian was sent away to a private boarding school while Holly attended their usual private Christian school.

It was how Vivian had gotten a taste for Harvard, where she'd met Clay, and where she'd definitely divided from Holly forever. None of which seemed to be of her choosing in the first place.

14

Clay laid his head down on his desk, sleep a luxury he was no longer afforded since Vivian had gone missing. He was woken up by the giggle of a little girl lost, the clacking of news cameras outside making him think of his wife's high heels, a sound he might never hear again. The pounding of Vivian's heels transformed into crashing waves, rocking the little boat docked on the sound. The one where Frankie probably slept now.

She'd grown up in chaos, the youngest of three, with two older brothers. He knew her childhood hadn't been easy. She might have posed as high-class, but there was hurt draped beneath her jewels. She'd told him her father was locked up, and her oldest brother was in witness relocation—she didn't know where. In exchange, he'd led the Feds to the cartel whose drugs he was transporting on his boat and had given up the names of the others in his family who were involved in the transfer, so he could never see them again.

This had pained Frankie. No wonder she'd been so upset when Ray had almost been pinched for those stupid Oxy prescriptions. She had Clay to thank for his freedom, but he was bothered about Aliza Levine's homicide just before she was going to testify against Ray. Clay hadn't heard much from the club since the trial, and he was afraid to ask questions.

I don't want to know.

Clay had grown up a lot more serenely, but whenever he heard waves, he'd always think of Frankie lying next to him with the sound of lapping water through the window. Almost three years ago now. The last night they'd been together before all this.

There were Christmas lights strung around the tiny inside of the cabin, and they lay naked on the comforter without a care in the world. The boat belonged to Nicky's henchman Russ, but it was open game for anyone in the club. The windows let in a breeze that stroked their skin in a light massage. He felt so sated, he could have stayed like that forever.

"You don't love her. And you say she doesn't love you. So why don't you leave?" Frankie asked in a whisper. Clay's eyes fluttered, but the cadence of the waves was rocking him to sleep. Frankie was the only one who could calm him like that.

"Marriage is tricky. And I'm not allowed to be with you and the club at the same time, right? *There are the wives and there are the girlfriends, and these things are not interchangeable.'* Those are Nicky's rules," he murmured.

Frankie nuzzled into his side, kissing the skin on his neck. "So you just go unloved, then?"

"Well, that's why I have you," he said, even though he knew she was talking more about herself than him. He also knew that Frankie deserved better, and as much time as he tried to carve out for her, it was never enough.

Frankie drew a finger down his chest. "What if she left you first?"

Clay let out a puff of a laugh, his eyes open now. "Who, Vivian? She couldn't survive on her own. She's not exactly your picture of an independent woman."

"She's a leech, then." Her hot breath feathered his shoulder. "You've got your work. What does she have? What drives her?"

He shut his eyelids, searching for an answer to this question. "Books, the library—her one source of authority. She's into words, writing. Find a way to stimulate her literary libido and she'll be in heaven. She likes the ocean too." He chuckled because Vivian would live in one of those houses on stilts in the water if she could. He'd managed to find her a beautiful house as close to the shore as possible.

Somehow, she still wasn't happy.

"I see." Frankie took a nip of his neck in her mouth and bit it softly.

He growled. Frankie reminded him of a playful kitten when she did this. If he had to assign her an animal spirit, *cat* would be it, but she had a killer scratch, too, a mean little streak hidden in there as well. If she gave him an ultimatum, he'd leave Vivian for her. He just didn't want to leave his wife if Nicky wouldn't let him be with Frankie. "You need to talk to your cousin."

"Yeah, I do," she said.

"What if we took off?" A smile suddenly stretched across his face. "We can be anybody we want when we leave this place." The idea of starting over, away from this predictable town—one cutout Victorian after another, nosy neighbors, boring dinners—was beyond attractive.

"You know, my brother is a doctor. He helps me out a lot. I'd be lost without him."

Clay had wondered how Frankie was so well-kept. Then he realized it was her brother supporting her expensive tastes . . . before he came along.

"I'm glad. You deserve to be taken care of." Clay was one wink away from sleep.

"My dad was a doctor, too, before he became a bum and got mixed up with Nicky's dad."

"That's too bad. You've been through it, that's for sure."

"That's okay. He taught me a lot about his work before he quit his psychiatry practice and started up with them. Nicky paid a lot more. When you have to shake someone down, having a man trained in brain mastery is useful."

Frankie's story made him bristle. Vivian's parents had been psychology professors, though never licensed physicians. They'd dealt on the scholastic side, whereas it sounded like Frankie's dad treated actual patients. In any case, the similarities hadn't escaped Clay. He was attracted to Frankie because she was sexy and smart, but he feared it might also be because she reminded him of Vivian before she'd gone cold. And he didn't like that at all. Frankie had always seemed like such a different woman than his wife.

"The guys were into heavier stuff in their younger days . . ." Frankie trailed off.

Clay's eyes blew open for a second. *What kind of heavier stuff?*

"Dad was really passionate about his work. He'd studied human conditioning. Did you know you can make someone crave something just by repeating a behavior that gives them the inference of joy, over and over again? It's addictive, like caffeine or sugar. A child will hear an ice cream truck and feel excitement long before they taste the delicious treat, just from hearing the music."

"Mm," Clay said, drifting off again.

"The most famous example is Pavlov. He wanted to prove that a dog is conditioned to know that when the bell rings, its food is on the way. So he put meat powder beneath the dog's nose every time he rang the bell. Then the dog always associated the bell with food. Simple as that. Humans are the same way. The challenge is figuring out what stirs their appetite."

"He sounds like he's a smart guy, your father."

"He was. He just never used his smarts. A few years practicing and not enough money to pay for our walk-up in Queens, then he teamed up with his brother-in-law, Marco Bellini. Once he crossed that line, nothing was off-limits. Including other women and drugs."

She nudged him, and he opened his eyes again. "I'm sorry. I wish I could relate. I had one of those childhoods straight out of a Norman Rockwell painting. So normal, it hurt your eyes to look."

She laughed. "Then how did you end up here?"

"I don't know," he said honestly, because it was no place he imagined he'd ever be.

"It's because you're one of us, Clay. Just accept it."

"Are you psychoanalyzing me now?"

She didn't answer. Vivian used to do this to him sometimes. He both hated it and loved it. She hadn't done it in a long time, though. She hadn't done anything in a long while that'd made him feel as though she thought about him at all. And that, he decided, was how he'd arrived at this special place with these corrupt people.

"Maybe I am. When I finally answered my father's pleas to visit him in prison, he told me if I was going to run with this crew, I could either be the other woman or I should find a guy on the outside. It's some of the best advice he's ever given me."

"You seem too smart to choose the other woman."

"Well, maybe someday I won't have to do either. When Nicky finally learns to bend his own rules." Frankie traced a pattern on his chest like there were imaginary dots only she could see.

"I wish," Clay said.

"Do you really?" she asked.

"I do. But I can't go up against those guys. You know I don't stand a chance."

They fell asleep together like that, boat rocking, future unclear, but with the promise that there would be a tomorrow, a real future together in some capacity.

There was certainly never a discussion that it was over.

Clay had to find out the hard way when he'd tried to call Frankie a few days later and she was just . . . gone. Her phone number was disconnected, her apartment was empty, and no one at the club seemed to know anything they were willing to tell him. He got into a few heated arguments with Nicky about his cousin before he realized one more might be cause for physical harm.

Nicky had put Clay in a headlock as he delivered the message. "You're married. Time to go home to your wife. The girlfriends are supposed to have an expiration date. You've exceeded yours." Then, strangely, he ended it with, "You're welcome back here when you stop asking questions about her."

Clay needed to find Frankie, but he was locked out of the club, and if they knew where she was, they weren't telling him.

It'd been a wake-up call, though. He'd decided they were probably right. He should try to make things better with Vivian. He should try to be a better man, a better husband.

So that's what he did.

He took his wife on a beach vacation with the neighbors and tried like hell to forget about Frankie, to extricate her from his mind. He tried and failed repeatedly.

"You'll have a hard time forgetting me," Frankie had told him.

She hadn't been kidding.

Clay realized too late that Frankie had been his true love. He should've fought for her, pushed back on Nicky's rules. It was probably what she'd wanted, but of course Frankie wouldn't ask; she was too proud for that. She'd been trying to tell him that the last night they were together. The lesson he hadn't grasped had been wrapped in her father's words.

He'd taken Ray's case a few months ago as a means to get her back.

She'd returned only because of the trial. And that was when he discovered the club had made Frankie take off because she'd gotten pregnant with Giana.

It infuriated him. But it also made him want to start over and do right by Frankie and his child. After the trial, he was going to make a bold move and leave Vivian. He hadn't told Frankie any of this, because he'd given her false hope before, and he didn't expect her to listen this time.

She was too smart for that.

He'd intended to prove it to her instead.

But then Vivian had gone missing—poof, just like that. He wanted her to be found so the media attention would go away and he could be with Frankie and Giana.

He'd sacrificed a lot for Frankie, taking her brother's case, and now she was gone too.

He was all alone—a fear that he'd never thought would come to fruition.

15

Now that her vehicle could actually accelerate, Holly pushed the gas pedal and tried to aggressively maneuver through traffic. She still had a lot to do today before the kids got home, but it wasn't her daily task list that had her in a rush. The window of time to find Vivian alive was closing, and now that she thought she knew who was responsible, she wanted justice.

Mark's number flew across the caller ID screen. "Yes," she answered in a strained whisper. She'd promised she wouldn't dodge his calls anymore, but this was a terrible time. She needed to get to the police station.

"Where the hell are you?" he screamed.

"What? Why? Where am I supposed to be?" Panic filled her chest like a balloon as she grabbed for her planner, thinking she'd missed a dentist appointment or a parent-teacher conference, but when Holly looked, the only thing noted for today was her therapy appointment.

"The school called. Tyler is vomiting. They pulled me out of a meeting, but I can't leave. I have clients in from Dubai. They did not understand when I had to take a call for my child. They asked me where my wife was!"

Oh, crap. The unidentified number she'd passed off as a telemarketer was the school. She scrolled back through the numbers and recognized it immediately. There'd been a voice mail too. She'd been so distracted while driving and reading and absorbing all this life-altering information about her sister. "I missed the call."

"But where were you, Holly?"

"I'll go get him right now, but it will be a half hour."

"Why? Where. Are. You?" Mark asked. She understood why he was confused. They lived only a few miles from the school. "I'm not asking again. I need to get back into my meeting."

"Leaving the Suffolk County courthouse."

"Why in God's name? Investigating again?"

"Yes. I have to go. I'm going to get Tyler." She hung up before letting him respond because she didn't know how to explain herself.

Damn it. The police station would have to wait, but maybe she could call them to come to her. Then again, if her son had the stomach flu or some other vicious virus, that wasn't ideal. Poor Tyler. Beginning of the school year always brought on the bugs.

When Holly arrived at the elementary school, she quickly parked and ran into the nurse's office. Tyler was completely miserable, the color of split pea soup, sitting on the exam table leaning over a garbage can. Mark was right. She needed to get her shit together. If she hadn't been so preoccupied hiding in maintenance closets, she would've been closer to home, able to receive the school call quicker to retrieve her ill son.

"Poor baby." Holly quickly scooted Tyler off the table.

"What took you so long?" he asked.

"I missed the call, Ty. Mom's sorry."

Tomorrow was Saturday, no time for further investigating. It was the beginning of the fall sports season, and Otto had an early hockey game, and Tyler had soccer—if he wasn't still vomiting. She and Mark would divide and conquer, and one kid would undoubtedly be unhappily dragged to another's event, and if they were lucky, maybe they'd reconvene for dinnertime. But Holly would be totally screwed if Tyler was still sick tomorrow. She'd be trapped at home.

But maybe Tyler would be well enough that she could invite over Nadia and Rigby or just one of them. All she needed was one.

Anyone to share her evidence with.

Everyone stared and whispered as the Boswell family entered the ice rink Saturday morning, a place that had practically been their second home since Otto was in second grade. Otto's game was first, bright and early, seven a.m. They had to be there an hour early for warm-ups, and the whole family had come because Tyler was feeling better and wanted to play his soccer game after all. Normally Holly would make him sit it out, but he had no fever this morning, and Mark hadn't protested, so neither had she. Tyler would need to be dropped off near the end of Otto's game, but clearly from their looks of reproach, the other hockey parents didn't think any of them should be there.

News traveled fast in a small town.

Otto's aunt was missing, and there he was in his warm-up gear, doing sprints like it was any other Saturday. It might've been okay for Otto to still show: parents might say that sports would help keep his mind off his aunt. But Holly—how unthinkable for her to be there with her sister still missing.

She rubbed her temples, the glare from the ice worse than those of the other parents. She was getting another headache. "I shouldn't be here," she whispered to Mark.

He put his coffee to his lips, ignoring everyone else but his son. Mark was good at that, not one to be sociable at sporting events. He was there to watch his kids play, and everyone else could piss off. Holly always thought it was because he was a dedicated parent, truly invested in his sons' athletics, but he reminded her of a hockey scout right now, intent on evaluating his son's value. Was Mark only there to determine Otto's scholarship potential? Holly had a bad taste in her mouth when it came to all things Mark at the moment. She looked around the rink. She liked to make her rounds and catch up with the other moms when she went to the games; it was the only real time she had to hang out with other adults. But not today.

"Did you hear me?" she whispered again.

Mark turned his head in Holly's direction but didn't actually look at her. "Nonsense. It does you no good to sit at home and worry."

Holly sighed. She had a lot more to do than sit at home and worry. She had pages of evidence burning a hole in her planner at home on her bedside table. She'd have to stop there before she went to the police station. She couldn't take the planner with her after the stink Mark had made the other night, and if she'd tried to disguise it in another note-book, he'd know and poke at her independent investigation like she was a child on a treasure hunt.

This morning, when Holly had seen the printouts peeking from her planner, she knew she'd waited two days too many to hand them over. By thinking that she was protecting her sister's good name, she'd endangered Vivian even more.

"I want to be the one to run Tyler," Holly said. She needed to get out of there. For more reasons than one.

"Fine," Mark acquiesced, pressing his stainless-steel mug to his lips again. "I thought watching the boys might take your mind off things."

Wrong, wrong, wrong.

Why did she need to barter for time with her husband? All these secrets she had to keep from Mark just to help her sister. The cold stadium seating of the ice rink made her think Vivian was onto something with the special friend she'd kept online. Tom's words nipped at her heart—*"Nothing is sadder than being in a room full of people who make you feel like you're all alone."*

That's exactly how she felt at the moment. It was like the community and her own husband had turned on her in a matter of days. The judgment was unbearable. Sadly, she wished she had a Tom too.

Tyler and a friend were running around the rink somewhere, probably by the video games. Holly caught a pop of his navy-and-gold soccer uniform and knew she'd be able to find him quickly when it was time for his drop-off.

With Mark still staring intently at the rink, Holly slipped out her phone. She had two goals for today: deliver the information on Vivian's Hangouts sessions to the police. And track down Archibald Steiner.

She rubbed her temples, hoping she wasn't going to seize up with a stress headache. That would be ironic. She hoped Dr. Steiner could give her more magic ginger pills to treat the stress headaches.

Her search for his address in the white pages had turned up empty, so she shot Jane from the library a quick message. Jane had been around back in the heyday and had befriended many of the professors, although she didn't drink, so she never participated in the happy hours. But maybe she knew where to find him.

Holly hadn't known she'd missed Otto's goal until Mark snatched her phone from her hands. "You missed it! He just scored." Mark's teeth were yellowed, one of the front ones chipped. He was too cheap to get the tooth fixed. Holly had the strong desire to knock the rest of them out.

Didn't he understand she couldn't *get in the game*? That she had other things on her mind?

Holly glanced up at all the people standing and cheering. The game was tied now. Worst of all, Otto was looking into the stands at them with his hockey stick raised in the air, and she knew when they made eye contact that her son could tell she'd missed his goal—worst feeling in the world.

She shouldn't be there.

"I'm going now." She ripped her phone out of his hands. "I have to stop at the store really quickly after I drop Tyler, but I'll circle back to his soccer game before it's over."

Mark checked his watch. "You could wait until the game's over. There's time."

"I'm leaving now."

"Fine," he said.

She rose from the ice-cold seats and pounded down the bleachers before he could stop her.

Holly made good time and dropped off Tyler. She had approximately an hour to drive home, pick up the printouts at her house, find Dr. Steiner, and then get back to Tyler's soccer game.

On the way, Holly drove by her sister's house. To her amazement, there were no news trucks there this time. Even the media took Saturday morning off, it appeared. Instinctively, she pulled her van to a screeching halt. She peered up the long driveway and noticed Clay's car wasn't parked there either. Clay had been hiding something from her the other day, standing firmly in the doorway, acting strangely when Holly asked about the neighbors. Holly needed to find out what was going on there. She might not get another opportunity like this one—no Clay, no press. Maybe she could find a contact for this Frankie too.

Holly glanced at her watch again, knowing she didn't have time for an extra stop but feeling the urgency to investigate. She ran across the street, even though it was broad daylight and anyone could see her. She crept up the front stairs and knocked on the front door. No one answered, and it was all dark inside.

Vivian's home had an antique feel to it, although her unique adornments were polished and updated. Holly had always loved the birdcage on the front porch. It was once owned by a movie producer who'd used it to hold his cigarettes. Holly opened the little brass birdie door and reached inside, and when her fingers felt the grooved key beneath the faux birch chips, she was elated. Holly quickly unlocked the front door, walked inside, and shut it, her heart like gunfire in her chest.

The house was quiet and still, the espresso hardwood wainscoting she'd loved so much closing in on her from every direction. What was she doing?

It's my sister's house. She took a deep breath.

She should be allowed in there.

Holly ran upstairs to Vivian's bedroom. Everything was so meticulously organized, she realized there couldn't be a thing in there that would lead her to Vivian. Her sister's clothes were hanging neatly, her jewelry arranged in its tiny metal box, sans the tennis bracelet. Holly let out a withered breath. She knew that bracelet she'd found was Vivian's, but it still didn't make her feel better seeing the half-empty box to confirm it.

And it sickened Holly that the contents reminded her so much of her mother—one pair of diamond earrings, a matching necklace—simplistic elegance. Holly's accessories were everywhere, and they were mostly costume jewelry. Mark hated it. She tried to keep her necklaces on the jewelry tree, but they always fell. Her earrings were mostly studs, and they ended up all over the place too.

Holly's next thought was that as much as their mother had tried to present to the public a fabulous, neat life, she'd died heinously, messily, and in vain. Holly placed her hand over her mouth, trying not to imagine Vivian going out the same way.

"Hurry," she whispered out loud. It was weird creeping around in someone else's house, but there was nothing in that room for her to find. She wouldn't go through the drawers, because she was sure if there were something suspicious, Clay would've already found it and hidden it. He was a defense attorney, after all.

The police said they wouldn't officially classify Vivian's disappearance as a missing persons case until forty-eight hours had passed, but Vivian was Clay's wife, so they couldn't just sit on their asses. Clay was a public figure, and the press had leaked the information about his wife and her abandoned car. This only worked to Holly's favor to get the authorities to move faster.

Vivian's laptop had been confiscated by the police, which left Holly wondering if they'd already gotten into her Gmail account and found her Hangouts archives. That made her pause for a second. Even if the police had seen the chats, Holly could give them context—that it wasn't like her sister to be carrying on with someone, that some of Tom's statements were worrying.

Holly was running out of time to get any of that done, though. She ran downstairs and walked into Clay's office.

What're you hiding? Besides your dirty mistress?

The PO Box Vivian had mentioned to Tom added an extra layer of deceit that didn't seem right either.

Holly rifled through the files on Clay's desk. One was labeled with a blue Post-it and marked PERSONAL. Inside was a photo of a blonde woman coughing in a stairwell. It was Aliza Levine, the lead witness in Clay's case who'd been murdered—and he had surveillance pictures of her before they'd even gone to trial. Holly recognized her picture from the news, but this one was dated July, and Holly knew the trial hadn't started until August, right after they'd come back from vacation.

Holly's fingertips lit up with flames, the shock hitting her so hard, she dropped the photograph facedown so she didn't have to look at it anymore.

Clay had been watching her. Or he'd had someone else watch her. And Holly suspected he'd had her killed so he could secure his not-guilty verdict for his client. Did he think he was above the law now and that he could just dispose of people as he pleased?

She shoved the picture behind a legal document also in the file. Then she pulled the legal document out. It was a life insurance policy, but it was dated recently, which Holly found odd. She took a quick picture of it with her phone.

Under a stack of papers, Holly found a little notebook with bumblebees all over the front.

This doesn't look like Clay's.

Inside were words scrambled together, but Holly recognized the handwriting from all those years of journaling—it was her sister's.

Her most recent entry was barely legible.

I Remember You

> I remember you, but you never knew me
> Tiny hands and feet
> I remember you, but you'll never know me
> And we'll never get to see all you could be
> Would you have gotten your dad's dark eyes or
>   my gray and blue?
> I remember you, but you didn't get to stay
> I'll always regret the day
> I didn't stand up for you
> Every September fifteenth, I think of you
> And I still remember you

It was dated early September, nearing the anniversary of whatever traumatic memory was portrayed in her poetry. Vivian had always liked to scribble, mostly poetry, but this little book made Holly uneasy. Holly would never touch a journal again—the thought of it made her nauseous. But Vivian had been journaling or doing something very similar.

The sentiment in the poem seemed hard to miss. She knew Vivian had been in a dark place after her miscarriages, but the last had been ten or so years ago. Obviously she still carried the pain of the aftermath with her.

Then the date in the poem caught her eye again.

Had Vivian lost a third baby and not told Holly? The first miscarriage had occurred in the winter, the second in the summer. It sounded like she'd had a third and not told her. Her poor sister had been grappling with awful things—infertility, her husband's infidelity, the paranoia that people were following her or the actual man who was.

Was Vivian in such a dark place that she took her own life, as the police seemed to suggest? Even Clay had alluded to the fact that she wasn't well. What else could he have meant? Did he think Vivian would waltz back home after some sort of depressive episode? The closet con-versation in the courthouse made it sound like he had no idea where she was, but the other broad, Frankie, was somehow sure Vivian was alive somewhere. Was Clay not frantic because he knew this, too, or because he just didn't care—a weight off his shoulders?

It didn't make sense.

Holly thought about what her parents might say in this scenario. Suicide was an impossibility. Perhaps Vivian had wanted it to look like she was being followed so people wouldn't know she was deeply depressed. Maybe the story she wanted others to believe was that she'd been kidnapped and killed so she could go out peacefully without the shame they'd been taught to feel for choosing to take their own lives. Or maybe Vivian had wanted to carry out the forbidden act, ultimately defy their parents' prin-ciples, and forever sully Clay's reputation for bringing her so much grief.

"Ugh." Holly put her hand over her mouth to stifle the rising sick.

Vivian's little book was shaking in her hands. It was a book of suffering.

"If you don't write it down, it didn't happen," Mother used to say.

Holly still kept her childhood journals in a storage bin in her house. Despite all the trauma they'd caused, she couldn't bear to destroy them. It would be like annihilating her entire childhood. Vivian hadn't felt the same. She'd asked Holly to get rid of them for her when they were clean-ing out their parents' house after they'd died. "Burn them—I don't care!"

Vivian had basically given Holly the same instructions in prepara-tion for their mother's funeral—*"Just cremate her; what does it matter?"* As much as Holly had harbored hard feelings for Mother, too, she was still surprised at Vivian's level of hatred. So Holly had settled on tossing Vivian's journals in an incinerator one day and cremating her mother the next with a small ceremony to follow.

But here Vivian was journaling once again. Why?

Holly really didn't understand the part of Vivian's poem that said she hadn't stood up for her baby. Did she feel guilty? What was that about?

The thing that bothered Holly the most was the handwriting. Vivian had angelic handwriting, perfectly spaced, nice strokes. But it became more erratic the further Holly paged through, so that the final entries were practically chicken scratch. She wondered if it was a sign of Vivian's deteriorating mental state.

Holly looked at her watch again.

She had to run.

She took Vivian's notebook. She didn't understand why Clay had buried it under a stack of papers on his desk in the first place. Was he trying to hide it from the cops?

Maybe he thought it would be embarrassing to admit he had a wife who suffered from depression and anxiety. Lord knew he'd contributed to her breakdown, if that's what'd happened, between the affair and the fact that he'd never been able to accept the fact that Vivian couldn't have his children.

Vivian said that the words had never come out of his mouth, but they both knew he was thinking it, awful creep. Or maybe he was hiding Vivian's notebook to cover up his mistress. Vivian probably wrote about her too.

Holly slunk out of the house onto the front porch, locking the door behind her. As she did, her phone buzzed in her pocket.

Mark: 911 Someone broke into our house, police are there. I have Otto, you have to pick up Tyler right now.

A home invasion? Holly's stomach swirled at the thought. There'd been a rash of break-ins of all sorts in their neighborhood, mostly cars, mainly drug addicts looking for something to trade quickly for a hit.

The sunlight hit her eyes, and she groaned in pain. She'd been so pressed to go to the police, but it turned out they were coming to her. Holly's email pinged, and she saw that she had a reply from Jane, the librarian.

Contact for Dr. Archibald Steiner

She glanced at the address. He lived way up on Broadway, not exactly walking distance from Handsome Avenue. Holly didn't like that at all. Why had he been near Vivian's house the day it was announced she'd gone missing?

She'd find out once she called him. There was a number attached to Jane's message and a little note.

> I'm not sure why you're looking for Archie, but tell him Jane sends her regards. He was a brilliant professor; your mother was always fond of him.

Archie must've been a quirky old bastard if Mom had liked him. So long as he was a quirky old bastard who could tell her where she could get some more of those ginger pills, she didn't care.

Holly carefully planted the key back in the birdcage. She really needed to hurry and pick up Tyler and get home.

"Hello there."

Holly jumped at the voice. She looked over her shoulder and found Eve Carrington staring at her suspiciously.

"Hi, Eve. I was just checking . . ." Her voice trailed off.

"Clay's not here." Eve placed her hands on the hips of her black spandex pants. An athletic trainer, she rarely wore anything else, according to Vivian. Holly had never bought into the wear-your-yoga-pants-everywhere craze that so many other Long Island mommies had adopted. She could hear her mother's criticism of them from the grave—*"Women with curves should opt for A-line, always. Attention seeker. Histrionic personality disorder. Every single one of them."*

Mother would've lost her mind over the sorts of things people posted on social media. Holly and Vivian had exchanged an entire text thread over the summer that had lasted into the next day about that.

"Social media is the impetus of narcissistic personality disorder," Vivian had mimicked.

"Right," Holly said to Eve, anxious to leave. "I see that. You don't have to tell him I was here; it's not urgent. I have to go." She was ready to race down the steps.

"You mean that you broke into his house," Eve said.

Busted. Holly stopped in her tracks and glared at this woman who'd obviously been watching her. Eve had too many sparkles on her lips for an adult, her light-brown hair streaked blonde on the bottom—skunky. As she shifted her weight, Holly noted her muscled legs, the kind that could only be acquired from weekly squats. She wondered what Vivian could possibly have in common with Eve. It was then that Holly remembered the rumor about Vivian and Peter.

"I'm glad I ran into you. You know Viv is missing?" Holly asked, because Eve didn't seem concerned. "There was talk about your husband maybe having a clue, something about Vivian thinking he might have been in her backyard—"

"Oh, no, not that bullshit again!"

Holly looked at her, startled.

Eve flipped her hair. It seemed to sparkle too. "I'm sorry, but your sister was a lunatic."

"Excuse me?" Holly said, taking a step back. Eve's hands were so dark, the spray tanner had stained the inside of her knuckles. *"She's so narcissistic, she paints herself a different color."* Holly's mother's voice was still echoing in her head.

"I told the police. She was losing her mind in the weeks before she went missing. Accusing people of following her, accusing my husband, my *busy* husband"—she paused for effect, which had none on Holly—"who runs multiple oral surgery practices, of following *her* of all people."

"What do you mean, *'her of all people'*?" Holly crossed her arms, offended by this overly glossed, overly siliconed woman Vivian had claimed was one of her friends.

"Really? A mousy librarian? Do you think my husband would've married me if he liked mousy librarians?" She tutted out her chest.

Holly laughed in her face. *"I don't know who would marry you at all,"* she wanted to scream. But instead, she walked away, down the stairs. "I see how concerned you are for your missing friend."

"Friends don't accuse other friends' husbands of stalking them and embarrass them in front of an entire community," Eve shouted at her as she crossed the street.

There were cop cars in the driveway when Holly arrived home with Tyler. A female detective with a cue-ball haircut stood on the porch—Nadia.

Holly staggered out of the car. Tyler followed. "I'm sorry; I'm having a migraine," she said to Nadia. "How much was taken?"

Nadia shot Holly a cursory glance. "Nothing, actually."

"What?" Holly asked.

"Did they take the Xbox?" Tyler asked worriedly. Holly hadn't done a great job in the car comforting her younger son about what'd happened, only telling him that they had insurance for these types of things and that anything taken would be replaced. Not that she should make those types of promises. Mark would have to agree the lost items were worth replacing.

"No, the electronics are all here, by your dad's account," Nadia said. Tyler blew out a sigh of relief, and Nadia remained unfazed.

As Holly walked in the door, she saw that all their drawers had been removed and overturned, the uneasiness twisting her guts like a dishrag. What a mess. She placed her hand over her chest, imagining someone else in her house touching her things. "Wow. What were they looking for?" Holly asked.

"Exactly." Nadia shot her a much longer look than the last. Holly peered down at her hands.

Tyler started to cry. Holly grabbed his shoulder. Otto walked in the living room from the kitchen and took refuge under Holly's other arm. It was good; she needed them to hold her up with her headache and the feelings of nervousness coursing through her veins.

She could hear Mark upstairs talking to someone. Holly and the boys followed Nadia to the master bedroom. Detective Rigby was standing next to Mark with a notepad, likely taking inventory of everything that had been stolen.

All her jewelry was overturned from the box, but nothing seemed to be missing. Mark was palming a gold watch given to him by his grandfather, undoubtedly, the one thing he was sure he'd lost. He looked angry, though, as he bounced it in his hands, and Holly just assumed it was because of the mess and the cost of the broken glass on the front door, where the criminal had gotten in.

"Hi, honey," Holly said.

Mark didn't answer. He only shot daggers at her with his eyes.

"It's awful, isn't it? What did they get? Did the neighbor scare them off before they could take anything?" They lived on a busy street.

Mark's vein was pushed out in his neck, jaw clenched. He nodded at Detective Rigby.

Holly turned in the detective's direction, and it was only then that she noticed her planner was flipped over on the bed, its pages partly ripped out. The detective was eyeing it strangely, and Holly understood why. It wasn't something a common thief would likely go after, unless they were looking for something else. She didn't have to examine the inside to know the computer printouts from the library, her evidence, were gone.

Then she remembered the missing page. The one from Vivian's Google Hangouts that she couldn't account for when she was trying to read in her car after leaving the courthouse.

The missing chat!

It was a loose end, and someone had found the page and probably tipped off the people who'd done this.

16

The house was numbingly quiet when Clay came home from the club, the only place he felt like he belonged, but Nicky hadn't been there today, only his messengers. Ray had confirmed the fact that Clay would not be seeing Frankie and Giana anytime soon. Frankie had reneged on her promise to let him see Giana following a positive verdict in the trial because of Vivian's disappearance, and Nicky wouldn't show his backstabbing face because of it.

Clay's missing wife made him a person of interest and a threat to Nicky's cousin and her child. Nicky wanted him nowhere near Frankie and Giana.

There hadn't been any other information about Vivian, only that Russ swore her disappearance wasn't club related.

Clay had worked so much before that Vivian would often greet him at the door if he made it home early, take his coat for him. The sound of her high heels clicking through the foyer used to fill the downstairs.

Last night he'd woken up twice to the sound of her shoes, only to fall back asleep and wake up to the imagined laughter of a little girl, but that was all a bad dream.

A bad joke, really. And the joke was on him. Both in regard to Vivian and the men at the club he'd been pretending to call his friends for the last three and a half years.

Everything could've been so different if he'd known about Giana in the first place. He could've left Vivian like he'd planned, started over with the new family he'd always wanted. But the club didn't like that idea at all, so they'd made Frankie go away, shamed her for being irresponsible, like it was 1920.

It was so archaic, their Rat Pack rules—*there are the wives and there are the girlfriends*—and now everyone had suffered the consequences because of them, perhaps even Vivian. He wasn't sure anymore.

He was beginning to wonder if the club was somehow connected to his wife's disappearance, even though Russ had made a point of telling him it wasn't. As much as he racked his brain, he couldn't think of a single reason why they'd want to whack his wife.

His whole life had turned into a waking nightmare, like sitting in a dark tomb, waiting for someone to close the lid.

He heard a noise on the front lawn and peeked out the blinds. The press had been gone when he arrived home, and he'd been hopeful they wouldn't come back. The buzz had died down, and there were no new leads in Vivian's case.

But it was wishful thinking. They'd just taken a short intermission. Gone home to see their families to tell them about the man who'd lost his.

At first he saw just one news truck.

Then a second one drove up. And a third. Soon there were just as many as before, set up like an un-welcoming committee.

And—ugh—was that a food truck? Now a line of people was forming up the street.

This place had turned into a zoo.

He phoned the police to call in the spectacle. That food truck couldn't be zoned for residential areas, and he wanted it out of there.

They transferred him to Nadia.

"Please, you gotta get rid of this thing. It's drawing an even bigger crowd," he said. With the exception of his trip to the club, Clay realized he'd become a shut-in, hiding behind his blinds, calling the police to break up the outside commotion. Just last week, he'd headlined the news for a different reason, the successful attorney taking on yet another tough case, and now look what he'd become—a recluse, an enemy of the people he once defended, a suspected murderer.

"What is it you want gone, exactly, Mr. Eddy?" Nadia asked.

He blubbered into the phone, realizing he'd never actually said the words. "A damn food truck, that's what!"

"Done. We're sending a squad car. I was actually just going to call you. Some evidence has surfaced about your wife, and we need you to come down here." If they were asking him to come into the station, it meant they had evidence they couldn't discuss over the phone. His eyelid leaped; his heart thumped.

"I'll be right there." He hung up the phone.

Clay hopped in his car and clicked the button for the garage door, fearful he wouldn't be able to make it out of his spot. He wondered how long he'd have to live like this—afraid to leave his own home to go somewhere as simple as the local deli for fear of being harassed.

Not that he felt like eating. Clay was in a perpetual state of sick. The kind that came with having a missing family member and a daughter you've never known and probably never would. The awful dread of the unknown.

Maybe the detective's new evidence would shed some light on the subject. He was just afraid they would uncover too much, and their light of conviction would shine back on him.

Luckily, the food truck line had been enough to distract the press, and he was able to back out of his driveway.

He flipped on the windshield wiper cleaner, his front view smudged with dirt and grime like the rest of his miserable life. There was no way to wash it off, the thick film that'd grown there. The only thing he could do was cover it with more shit. But pretty soon, he wouldn't be able to see out the front anymore—and he'd crash. It was the trajectory his life was on right now.

He was going to fucking crash and die.

All he wanted at this point was any type of finality to this nightmare.

He wanted so bad for it to all be over, to skip the pain of loss, the turmoil of separation he'd felt when his parents had died in their car crash.

He'd tried to reach out to his sisters to talk to them about Vivian, but they hadn't returned his calls. He shouldn't be surprised. Once they'd taken off for the West Coast, they rarely phoned, and he hadn't made an effort to keep in touch either. They never had forgiven him for not attending either of their children's first birthday parties, but he'd explained he couldn't take that much time off work for a cross-country trip.

Vivian had wanted to go. He should've. He realized now that he might have someone to actually talk to if he had.

Instead, he'd spent years hanging out with gangsters who'd taken him for a ride.

And he'd let himself fall in love with one of their girls. One of their tawdry mistresses who'd split at the first sign of trouble. He could still fight for his daughter when this was all said and done.

First, he had to prove to the world that he had nothing to do with Vivian's disappearance. He'd hired an attorney to represent him, because he wasn't confident enough to represent himself at this point and Ari didn't want the firm involved, which was beyond disappointing. One more person he'd thought was in his corner who really wasn't.

He walked into the station and met his defense attorney, Brent Frazier, a newbie hotshot out of Westchester with hair gelled up in the front like the kids did these days and thick black glasses that Clay figured probably passed for hip.

He'd hired Brent because the kid reminded him of himself at that age—hungry, ready to put in the time, make a name for himself. He'd also graduated top of his class from Harvard Law, like Clay, and had a voice that could command an army.

"Hi, Clay, get any sleep last night?"

Clay shook his head. Every time he closed his eyes, he saw a mash-up of Vivian's and Giana's faces. The lost girls.

Clay and Brent were escorted to the interrogation room. This time, Clay wasn't offered a drink, and the door was slammed behind them.

Brent raised his eyebrow. "You piss them off?"

"No." Clay blew out a hot breath, assuming it was just another bad day at the station with too much work and too little pay. Rigby and Nadia entered the room minutes later and sat. Rigby slapped down a file folder between them and let his long fingers rest on top, keeping the contents concealed.

"New information on my wife?" Clay asked hopefully.

Rigby held a grim expression on his face. "We didn't call you down here to talk about your wife."

"I don't understand." Clay's stomach tightened and curdled.

"We called you down here to talk about your girlfriend." Nadia smiled, but it was tight-lipped.

"Wait a minute," Brent objected. "I'd like to have a few minutes in private with my client."

"It's okay, Brent," Clay said. "Because if I had a girlfriend, that still doesn't make me a murderer." Clay chose his words carefully. He hadn't admitted to having a girlfriend, and he hadn't admitted to not having one either.

"No, but if you had a girlfriend, you might need to earn some extra cash. Because it costs a lot to float two women, doesn't it, Mr. Eddy? Especially if you had a child with that woman."

Clay swallowed hard, and Brent actually whistled out loud. "I have plenty of equity in my house and a healthy bank account, if you looked at my records. No problem paying debts on my end. This is all hearsay anyway," Clay said defensively.

"Is my client being charged with something?" Brent asked. "We were under the impression you had some new information about the location of his wife."

Rigby ignored him. "You have a lot of financial responsibility. It caused you to notch up your wife's insurance policy by another five hundred grand right before she disappeared. Here's the evidence." He drew a piece of paper from the file and smacked it down on the table. It was a photograph of an insurance policy.

His new life insurance policy. He wondered how they'd gotten it.

"Vivian didn't even sign that policy. She went missing before she could."

Rigby watched him. "And what a shame for you, because now you can't collect."

Nadia scowled.

"This is shit. I should sue you for violating my rights. How did you even get that copy?"

"Did you kill your wife, Clay?" Rigby asked.

"No." He blinked at the question. "And you can't charge me over an insurance policy that doesn't even have Vivian's signature on it."

"Did you burn the body? Leave your wife's car at the marina to make it look like she took a dive? We found your charred clothes in the fire pit in the backyard."

Nadia placed the remainders of a red tie in a plastic baggie on the table. The only reason Clay knew it was his was because his gold tie tack had survived the blaze. His mojo had been so thrown off from losing his lucky red tie, he'd had to buy another one before the trial.

"What the hell?" he said, furious. "I didn't burn my own tie. Why would I do that? And why were you on my property without a warrant?"

Brent chimed in. "Unless Vivian's blood is on that tie, you're going to have a hell of a time proving anything in court."

"Any good lawyer like you, Clay, knows if you burn someone's clothing, it will destroy the DNA. I wonder what a jury might have to say about that?" Rigby mused.

"This is bullsh—" Clay said.

Brent held up his hand. "Ask your questions regarding things that actually pertain to my client's missing wife, or I'm going to request we be excused." He was whistling into the air again like this was the most ridiculous thing he'd ever seen.

"Were you aware your wife called your boss the week before her disappearance? When she suspected there was someone in your backyard?"

"No, I was not aware of that," Clay grumbled.

Ari. The bastard had not only refused to defend him but had sold him out? Did he not have a single friend left in this city? But something else bothered him—if Vivian had been looking for him the week before she went missing, and Ari had told her where he was . . .

It was the night he'd met with Frankie and Giana for the first time. His stomach knotted.

"It's interesting," Rigby said. "Vivian wanted to confirm where you were doing business. Ari confirmed it, but he also said he thought she was going to look for you there because she was scared."

There'd been cars zipping in and out of the parking lot at Pickles and one in the back parked with its lights shining right on him. Clay remembered feeling as though he were being watched that night.

"Did your wife see more than a client meeting?" Nadia asked. "Like maybe you meeting with your mistress and child? Did she confront you? Plan to file for divorce? And so you bided your time until the night of the storm—the perfect opportunity to off her."

"No." Clay shook his head. He couldn't believe it. He hadn't known it was Vivian watching him, so why bother to incriminate himself further by admitting he'd noticed a car parked?

"It's funny—there's a security camera attached to the strip club next to Bellini's plant that recorded footage of Vivian's '16 Mercedes pulling into that same parking lot where you were. And we got footage of Vivian's car pulling out of that parking lot too."

He couldn't hide his alarm. She'd seen him. With Frankie and Giana. *Fuck.*

It had probably destroyed her. He'd been so happy to finally meet his little girl.

"Well, that's too bad if she saw me at the club when I said I was at work. She just didn't realize, maybe, that I was conducting business there. I was going to tell her everything after the trial was over. I'd planned a vacation for the two of us, and I was going to come clean. Why would I buy plane tickets for the two of us to get away if I was planning on getting rid of my wife?" Clay felt the heat of the evidence mounting, but it was only circumstantial at best.

It was true. He'd bought the tickets before the case, before Frankie had come back to town, when he thought there might still be a chance to reconcile with Vivian. She'd been so despondent, he thought a vacation might wake her up, shake her out of her funk.

He was also tired of playing cat-and-mouse games with her. He'd work late just to avoid conversation with her, and she'd greet him at the door and then retreat to a quiet corner to watch TV or read, ignoring him. So he'd planned a trip to the Florida Keys after hurricane season was over to see if they could reconnect. It was better than the existence he'd been living, worth a shot.

But when he learned it was Nicky who'd kept Frankie away and that she hadn't left him of her own accord, it changed everything. Even though he still didn't trust Frankie, he understood the power of the club.

Nadia bared her teeth.

Rigby clapped his hands together, making everyone jump. "I'd say planning a vacation would make you look good, like you were trying to be a decent man and a good husband, but given your mistress and child, it's obvious you're none of those things. So this can go one of two ways,

Mr. Eddy. You tell us the truth about what happened to your wife and we lock you in here and we keep you safe. You tell us how you did it, we discuss the best plan of action, and we get you out in as little time as the judicial system allots. Or we let you out and you're responsible for your own safety."

"What the hell is that supposed to mean?" Clay blurted out.

"This story is out there. The press knows about your alleged mistress."

How? he wondered.

Rigby shook his head. "The Gallo trial is over. I don't want to be the bearer of bad news, but these guys tend to dispose of people who attract negative attention and no longer serve a purpose."

Clay blinked at this information, speechless. They were his friends. They wouldn't kill him. Plus, they needed him for future cases.

"You've got nothing," Brent said. "So his wife was in the same parking lot he was. You don't even have them together arguing. There's no body. There's no weapon. There is nothing linking my client to a crime."

"There is one other thing we do have." Rigby paused, eyeing Clay curiously.

Clay knew it.

They'd saved the best for last.

Rigby stood up. "We'll release you, but when you get home, you may want to check your belongings."

"Why's that?" Brent asked for him.

"Because your sister-in-law is here. She's been arrested for a few things, one of them breaking into your house earlier today. I'm assuming you didn't know your sister-in-law was inside your home earlier?"

Clay's eyes bugged out of his head, his ears growing hot with rage. *"No."*

"Concerned neighbor. She phoned it in."

Thanks, Eve.

"Mrs. Boswell took a few things from the house."

Clay rolled his eyes. He knew exactly how the police had gotten the life insurance policy now. It had been sitting on his desk right next to Vivian's poetry notebook, which Holly had probably gotten her hands on too. That nosy bitch likely had better luck interpreting Vivian's crazy ramblings because it was probably written in their journal code or some BS.

"Is that right?" Clay sneered.

"Yes. We need to know if you'd like to press charges against Mrs. Boswell. There was no forced entry, but the items stolen from your desk were on her person."

"Absolutely."

17

When Holly had been asked to sit in the back of the squad car, her children cried. The last thing Mark had said to her before they tucked her head under the door was, "Don't expect me to bail you out."

She'd been sweating in a holding cell ever since, wondering how many crimes she'd committed and if she'd have to do any real time for them. It was her sister's house. It couldn't technically be breaking and entering if it were a family member's home, could it? Vivian wouldn't have minded. She would have understood why Holly did it.

But Vivian wasn't here.

Clay was. And Clay was an attorney. If he were mad enough, he could prosecute her to the highest degree.

Nadia was still barking about withholding evidence, when they couldn't even prove there'd been any—because it had been stolen. A fact Holly still couldn't quite believe. Holly said she needed an attorney present before she'd talk to them. She'd watched enough *Law & Order* to know that's the way it worked, and having Clay as a brother-in-law, he'd always instructed both her and Mark not to talk to law enforcement without him there. Fat chance now.

Finally, the detectives entered the room. They already looked tired by the time they sat down. "We just finished with your brother-in-law. He was made aware you broke into his house."

"Great," Holly said, throwing her hands up in the air. They couldn't let her tell him and explain? That was shit.

"He's pressing charges," Nadia informed her.

"What?" She couldn't believe it.

"Your public defender should be arriving shortly—"

Just then, a stout, square-shaped man entered the room. A smell like that of fried ham filled the air. No way Mark would spring for anything better than a public defender.

"Hi, Ernest Clout, but you can call me Ernie." He shook Holly's hand. His palm was fleshy and damp. "May I have a few moments with my client?"

All hope of being released that day fell apart at hearing Ernie's voice, high and overaccentuated. Ernie reminded Holly of Newman from *Seinfeld*, and Newman almost always lost.

The guard and Nadia left, and Ernie sat down too heavily on a chair that wasn't fit to hold him. He riffled through a file folder busting with too many papers. He didn't look up as he spoke to her. "Hello, Mrs. Boswell; it sounds like you've been charged with breaking and entering, tampering with police evidence, obstruction of justice, and trespassing?"

Holly let out a squeak. Those charges sounded so much worse than the ones she'd imagined.

"Well, is that right?" he asked, still not looking at her.

"Yes," she whispered.

"And you're the sister of the lawyer's missing wife? That's why you did all these things, looking for your sister?"

She took a deep breath. "That's correct."

"Okay, you're a first-timer, and the court will most likely have sympathy for you, given the circumstances. We're going to try to plea you down to just a fine, but someone will still need to post bail. Just let me talk. Not my first rodeo."

"Okay," she said. Maybe Ernie wasn't so bad.

Ernie motioned to the guard outside the window, who escorted the detectives back into the room. They slumped down in the chairs, and Holly wondered if they'd slept at all the night before, if anyone had since Vivian went missing.

"You know why you're here, Mrs. Boswell. We're more interested in learning about what you found on that chat session than condemning you for keeping it from us, not that you won't be held accountable."

"Yes, sir," she said to Rigby.

"So you said you found evidence that your sister was chatting with a man who may have been a threat, and you didn't come to us?" Nadia leaned back in her chair, annoyance on her pinched face.

"Yes, that's correct."

"Why?"

"Because she was having an online affair, and I didn't want it to ruin her reputation or make you fight less to find her."

"We don't judge our victims," Nadia said defensively. "And you think he was a threat? This man?"

"Yes. I'd just finished reading the entries, and I was about to bring them to you, and I just can't believe that—"

"They were stolen from your house," Rigby finished her sentence.

"Yes!" Holly still couldn't process it. She wouldn't mention the missing page, the carelessness that had most likely gotten her there. Holly suspected that she'd dropped it in the courthouse. She thought she had all the printouts with her before the trial, but she couldn't be sure. She'd been in such a rush. Frankie had been behind her when she was running away. If she'd dropped it, Frankie would've been right there to swoop it up.

"Who else knew you had the printouts?" Nadia asked.

"No one." She was in enough trouble with the law. She could not mention how she had been hiding in a closet in the courtroom to obtain confidential information between a lawyer and a client.

"You didn't tell your husband?" she asked.

"No."

Rigby held out a piece of computer paper. "We got the log from the library where you printed out the copies to verify your story."

"Why, you didn't believe me?" she asked.

They didn't answer right away, but their vacant stares told her all she needed to know. They'd suspected Vivian had lost her marbles and thrown herself into the ocean, and now they were assuming Holly might not be that far behind.

"Why in the world would I make it up?"

"Why in the world would you keep it to yourself?" Nadia threw back at her.

"I just told you why."

"This is repetitive." Ernie looked at his watch.

"I'm sorry about your house being broken into, Mrs. Boswell, but our tech team was able to access your sister's email account, and there're no Google Hangouts conversations. They would be attached to her email account, and there's nothing there."

"Then someone must've deleted the Hangouts archive."

"That shouldn't matter." Nadia looked at her with that same tired expression. "We'll subpoena the data from those user accounts, but unless you deleted your sister's chats, why aren't they there?"

"But that doesn't make any sense."

"You're the one who's not making any sense, Mrs. Boswell. You're saying you had evidence about your missing sister, and you didn't hand it over to the detectives working on the case. Did you take pictures of the chat sessions, make additional copies? Like you did with the insurance policy? Most people would have," Rigby said.

Holly grazed her right arm with her fingernails. "I did not. But I never dreamed someone would steal them!"

"You realize you put Vivian in more danger by not coming to us immediately, right?" Nadia asked.

Holly nodded, and the tears finally leaked down her cheeks. Over and over again, she'd failed her sister. Just like that afternoon on the back porch when she couldn't complete the journal assignment and then the evening that followed, when they were staring out their parents' back door. Vivian had wanted to jump on their bikes and ride away, and Holly couldn't do it. And then at the pier in Bay Shore during the storm. She hadn't been able to get there fast enough.

"Our tech team is very efficient, and they're still looking into this, but if your house hadn't been broken into, we wouldn't have any reason to know the chat sessions you're speaking of existed. So if there's something else you need to tell us, do so now."

Holly wiped her face. "They existed! The person she was chatting with was suspicious. Flirty. He talked about going on private hikes and put it in quotation marks like they were going to do far more than hike. It gave me the creeps. He could be an online predator." Holly realized nothing she said held water without those printouts.

This was *really* bad.

How stupid of her not to make copies, but at first she hadn't known they were important, and she'd been trying to hide them from Mark. It was too embarrassing to admit that part, though.

"He lived on a beach. He had a boat and a dog named Bodie. You can search for him that way."

"Is that all you've got? How do you know any of that was even true if he was a possible predator? Most of the time, those people make up their identity when luring their victim," Rigby said.

Holly nodded. "I know, but it could be a lead."

"Let the cops do their jobs, Holly. This is what got you into this mess in the first place," her attorney said.

Shut up, Ernie!

The detectives didn't seem convinced at all. Their stares had turned from rebuke to pity.

"Your leads about the mistress, life insurance policy, and the hidden journal are helpful. We're still exploring those. Is there anything that would make you think Vivian knew about the woman? Or the child?"

"I don't know. I think she might have," Holly said. Vivian knew there was another woman, but Holly still wasn't sure if she knew about the child. Still, wasn't that enough for the cops to prove that Clay might have had a motive?

"What about the PO Box I told you about?" she asked.

Nadia's nose twitched, and she exchanged an unspoken conversation with Rigby.

"The one at the post office in Clay's name?" Holly said.

Rigby cleared his throat. "There's no record at the Sayville Post Office that a PO Box ever existed for Clayton or Vivian Eddy."

"That's impossible."

"I'm sorry, Mrs. Boswell, but maybe you got sucked into some kind of internet black hole. A lot of things you've described from those chat sessions haven't panned out. Like the chat account and the PO Box."

What? But those chat sessions were everything. Holly had become acquainted with her sister in a way she never thought she could by reading those. They were real.

The lawyer was talking about charges and such, and thanks to New York's new speedy arraignment process, they already had a hearing set up for Monday. But Holly was told bail would likely be set at no less than $2,500. Holly had no friends she could call with that kind of money. Vivian was gone, and her parents were dead.

That left Mark.

When she called him, he only repeated the same phrase he'd said as she'd been carted away in the squad car. "Don't expect me to bail you out." The only sentence he'd added to that was, "Your boys will not recover from this."

To which she replied, "Then bail their mother out!"

The line went dead. She only got one call.

She would never know if it was what she'd done by withholding evidence or the amount of money needed to undo what she'd done that led Mark to let her rot in a prison cell for two whole nights. Monday, at the bail hearing, she was released, but it wasn't Mark who'd bailed her out. When she asked the identity of the person who'd posted it, the name couldn't have shocked her more.

Dr. Archibald Steiner.

18

After he'd left the station last night, the media parade had picked up speed with the release of his involvement with Frankie and Giana. He'd stayed away all day doing recon to help clear his name, but as he pulled up his driveway now, he saw that there was a fresh yellow crust on his bedroom windows from where he'd been egged. He'd never be able to get outside in time to scrub it off before it destroyed the paint on the black shutters. The ones he'd picked out with Vivian.

He needed this to end. He needed his life back.

The angry mob of people refused to let Clay pull into his driveway, acting as a human firewall with their microphones and cameras rolling and ready. They were preventing him from getting into his own house until he answered a few questions.

As he pulled up a little farther, he saw another food truck.

A different one this time—Mama's Cuban Kitchen.

Good God, make it stop. Clay hadn't realized how hungry he was until he smelled the deliciousness through the car vent. He'd been on a strictly vodka-and-wine diet. It helped him pass out easier on an empty stomach.

Clay refused to let the press bully him into an interview. What a circus. They should be arrested for harassment.

Every. Last. One. Of. Them.

He tried to weave through them to get up his driveway, but he could still hear their barrage of questions through the rolled-up windows.

"Mr. Eddy, what comment do you have on the allegations about your mistress?"

If Clay had a more experienced lawyer, the press would know that he had no comment.

"Mr. Eddy, did you use your own home or Ms. Gallo's for your affair?"

Ugh. He had the urge to run them all over with his car. Clay revved his engine, thinking about actually doing it, how the camera equipment would break and crunch along with their bones. What difference did it make? His life was total shit anyway, and he was sure Nicky's guys were just waiting to get him alone before they made him their next hit. Might as well get locked up and keep himself safe just like Detective Rigby had suggested.

Clay had to bat away a few reporters to make it into the garage.

He could still hear them through the window. "Attorney Eddy, do you care to comment on—"

No one knew all he'd sacrificed to be with Vivian. She wouldn't try for another baby, she wouldn't adopt, she wouldn't consider surrogacy, and he was just supposed to be okay with that—not having a family. She'd made one appointment at a fertility clinic, but she wouldn't make a second to accommodate his work schedule.

Infertility was something women lamented and blogged about and received undue sympathy for, but what about the men who wanted to become fathers? They were somehow forgotten or dismissed, because if their wife couldn't produce a child for them, they were supposed to support her.

But there were lots of alternate ways to create a family these days, and Vivian had been interested in none of them—at least not enough to do something about it. She'd claimed it was probably better because of the mental abuse from her own childhood, but Clay always pointed out that Holly's children seemed well-adjusted. Clay couldn't say the same for Holly, who always looked like she was two steps away from a panic attack. Always complaining about something Mark had shorted her on when she wasn't moaning about shuttling her children to an activity. She had two healthy, athletic, brilliant boys, and all she did was complain about her life. It drove Clay nuts.

He would love to have her problems.

Vivian had scoffed at his remark about their nephews and said that Holly hadn't received as much abuse from their parents as she had. He never had pried any more out of her on that subject, only that her sister had somehow gotten off easier.

Clay could still hear the ominous sound of cameras clicking outside as he made his way inside his home, feeling the cacophony of watchful eyes on him. He was under siege.

What the hell were they taking pictures of anyway?

He couldn't stay in his house much longer.

The cops weren't on his side, and the press had become a horde of wild animals. Clay leaned on the door that led into the kitchen. Once safely inside, his heart pumped hard in his chest. He'd been afraid to open his own door for fear it might blow up. The cops had made him paranoid.

Clay moved to turn on the kitchen light, but something caught the corner of his peripheral vision.

A figure materialized out of the darkness, and for a second Clay thought he was imagining the shadow, but then it was barreling toward him, full force, and he wasn't moving his arms up fast enough to block it. His hand flicked on the light switch and then—bam—fist to the face.

Clay fell down, his dress shoes sliding out from under him, his wrist bending awkwardly against the baseboard. Fear enveloped him as he floundered on the floor and then—wham—kick to the balls.

"You piece of shit!"

Clay looked up to find Eve, his neighbor, hovering over him with the craziest fucking look in her eyes. Living next to her for years, he'd seen *all* her crazy looks.

"How many were there?" she asked.

He didn't know what she was talking about. He was going to try to get up now.

"Eve, calm down." He was on his feet, holding his crotch, and Eve was so close to him that he could see her tiny nostrils flaring.

"You asshole. How many women were you screwing? Do you know what the neighbors have been saying about my husband, and you're the one who's been messing around?"

Clay raised his arms to surrender. "She was the only one. Got mixed up with her years ago and I didn't know about the kid."

"Liar!"

"Look, Eve, things with Vivian and me weren't good for years—" Kick to the testicles again.

"Stop doing that!" Clay covered himself again and closed his eyes, trying to breathe through the pain. *Fuck, that hurts.* He should've let the cops lock him up. They were right. No one could protect him from all the dangers he'd imposed on himself.

"Frankie took off when she found out she was pregnant. I didn't have any contact with her for a long time."

"So you moved on to me?"

"You approached me, Eve," Clay said defensively, remembering the night after the rumor had spread all over the gym where Clay belonged and Eve worked. People were saying Eve's husband was sleeping with another woman, and it was more than her pride could handle. It made her inflamed, vengeful, even though it was mangled gossip that she'd somewhat started.

The evening of their huge blowout, Vivian had claimed that Eve had shouted at her like a wretched bitch from her back porch, "Get on some meds, Viv, and quit spreading your ridiculous rumors. My husband has no interest in you."

It was all a show, really. Vivian was just asking Eve if Peter had been in the backyard, and for some reason, it'd escalated. But now Clay saw that it was Eve's doing.

"See what you've done," Clay had admonished his wife. He felt sorry about that now, seeing what she'd been up against. Eve was an ego demon.

"And it was only once," Clay said. Eve had kicked his balls into his kidneys with those long-muscled legs of hers, and he was still struggling for breath.

"You didn't exactly protest," she said.

Not true. He'd protested a little. "I'm sorry if I hurt you," he said.

He thought that was a safer response. Eve had come over one night when he was home and Vivian was working, and it had only happened once, at the height of Vivian's crazy accusations. Clay had never felt so disconnected from his wife, and Eve was so close and panting in his ear. *They want to make fools of us? We'll show them.*

He couldn't care less what the townspeople had said about Vivian and Peter, because it was so preposterous, it was almost comical. *"We shouldn't do this,"* he'd said after a few sloppy kisses. He'd watched Eve prance around the beach in her too-short running shorts on more than one occasion, but he'd never act on it.

"She shouldn't run her mouth," Eve had said in between kisses.

Eve backed away from Clay now, and he let out another deep breath. He was actually afraid she might kill him, and now that he had moved, his back was pressed against the counter, the knife block directly behind him.

"Did you tell Vivian about us?" she asked. Her blue eyes were glassy and frightening beneath the dim lighting. And maybe that's what this was about. She was afraid they'd try to blame her—or find her out?

"No, of course not."

Eve had on black yoga pants, but they were rhinestone-studded at the top; she was always too blingy. "I was coming for you once this was all over. Peter and I are getting a divorce." She said it like Clay had just won a prize.

"What? I'm sorry to hear that." Clay was suddenly paranoid that someone had seen Eve sneak into his house with her glimmering attire. He was being closely watched. The last thing he needed was to be seen with another woman. Clay shifted his weight, trying to create some distance between them. "Eve, how did you get in here?"

"Don't worry—no one saw me. Vivian told me where you hide the spare key. I snagged it earlier when there weren't so many people around."

Note to self: move spare key from birdcage. He'd assumed Holly had keyed in from a spare Vivian had given her, but she could've used that spare too. He still needed to deal with his snooping sister-in-law, although a night in jail might've done the trick.

"There are a million people outside. I doubt no one saw you," Clay said.

"Our backyards border each other and are guarded by a fence. They'd need a helicopter to see me."

As if on cue, the sound of a helicopter sounded above. Clay rolled his eyes. The key to the front door opened the back door as well. A convenience that was now proving to be a safety concern.

"I have on all black; it will be dark soon. Don't worry—I won't incriminate you further, as if that's possible." Eve looked like a thief. She did have on all black, as usual, but not in the I'm-about-to-work-out kind of way, more in the I'm-going-to-break-into-your-house-and-steal-all-your-shit kind of way.

An eerie feeling overtook Clay as he wondered how many other times she'd been in their house when he wasn't there.

When Vivian wasn't there either.

It was clear—Eve was a narcissistic sociopath.

The only thing Holly had taken was Viv's scattered journal and a picture of his incomplete life insurance policy. *Bitch.* All he needed was the cops to find a way to tie this whole thing together. He'd looked guilty before, but now thanks to Holly, he looked guilty as sin.

"Did Vivian ever tell you she wrote poetry?" Clay asked.

Eve seemed amused by this question. "What? No, why?"

"Because some of the things she'd written were pretty strange and dark right before she went missing. Do you think she might have suspected us?"

Clay had read one of her poems he couldn't get out of his head. It was short, but it said all he'd needed to know.

> All the girls, are close and far
> The closest ones, smell sick and sweet
> Her skin is glazed, a piece of the sun.
> But everything's dark from where I'm standing.
> The porch is pitch-black. Why won't you fix the
>   light? Is it so I can't see her?

He'd stopped breathing the first time he'd read it. Held his breath for a whole minute before he exhaled.

Eve often smelled like tanning lotion and fruity skin products, and the light on their back porch had been burned out for six months. Their fling had happened shortly before Vivian had gone missing. If she'd found out her so-called friend was sleeping with Clay on top of everything else she was dealing with—the man in their backyard, seeing Clay with Frankie and Giana, the twisted thoughts erupting in her journal from her miscarriages—it could've really made her come undone.

Eve rolled her eyes to the top of her head, and Clay thought it was an excellent time to grab a knife, because while he wasn't sure if Vivian had been mentally ill, he was fairly certain Eve was.

Eve was coming for him?

What the hell was that talk about?

They'd never discussed starting a relationship. They'd had sex once. It was a revenge fuck, quick and awful, and he'd never wanted to see her again, let alone date her. He'd regretted it afterward, mad at himself for pissing in his own pool.

"Maybe. She might have had reason to doubt me, but when I tell you this, I want you to know I only did it for our own good," Eve said.

Uh-oh.

Clay tightened his fingers around the chef knife. Maybe he should flash the lights, invite the press inside so they could save him from his murderous neighbor.

"You're going to hate me." She pinched her face.

Already there.

"What is it, Eve?"

"I treated Vivian horribly right before she went missing, and I didn't really care that she thought Peter was following her. I needed a reason to end our friendship, so I ignored her calls. I threw her out of my house. I was an awful person." Eve was sobbing.

Clay let go of the knife. Anger filled the place where fear lived only moments earlier. "Why?"

"Because I needed a reason to break away from Peter and her. We were going to be together someday, you and me, after the kids graduated, but it was taking too long. If I had to wait another two years until Paige graduated, I was going to lose my mind. Living with Peter is like Groundhog's Day in Pleasantville."

Clay had to digest this information and nodded in agreement, even though he didn't agree with a thing. Was this the plan? Had they discussed this? Eve had said a lot of bizarre things in the heat of passion, but he hadn't really listened. He assumed it'd all been dirty talk, something to get her rocks off and nothing more.

"Eve, did Vivian find out about us before she disappeared?"

"Maybe." Her voice broke, and she looked down at her black sneakers. "She'd come over a night or so after our fight to try to make amends. She grabbed my sweatshirt from the gym and did the strangest thing."

Clay shifted his weight more, and Eve took a step back. "What did she do?" he whispered.

"She put my sweatshirt up to her nose and sniffed it. Then she made the most awful face."

Clay was making the most awful face just thinking about it.

"Peter was disgusted that she would do such a thing, but the way she looked at me, I think she knew." Eve's voice quivered, her guard down.

Clay considered drawing his weapon, but he let her finish, because he wanted to hear the rest. "And?"

"And then she was gone."

Clay thought about the strangeness of Vivian smelling Eve's sweatshirt, and then it all made sense when he thought of her poem, that one verse that circled his brain like a bad rash that wouldn't go away. Clay hadn't been careful to wash Eve's scent off his body that night. Vivian had made the connection.

She likely saw him with Frankie and she'd figured out he'd been messing around with her friend too. But which one had caused her disappearance? He thought of her body again floating in the water, her dark hair fanned out in the waves. It could've been a combination of both.

"I didn't mean for it to go this far, but I was afraid if I didn't tell you, you would hate me," Eve cried.

I do hate you.

He was dumbfounded by how calculated Eve had been in her pursuit to take ownership of him. They'd lived next door to each other for more than a decade. There was subtle flirting, but how she could assume they had anything tangible, he didn't understand. Clay really doubted her mental state. What else was she capable of?

"Eve, did you do something to Vivian?" Clay asked.

His hand was wrapped around the chef's knife again. She had motive, might as well go down with a fight.

"No! God, no. Where is she, Clay? This wasn't part of the plan. Our families were supposed to break up. Then Peyton was supposed to go off to college, and Peter and I were supposed to get divorced. Then you and Vivian were supposed to get divorced, and yeah, it would've sucked for Paige still at home, but then it was supposed to be our turn. My turn."

That was Eve's plan?

That was never his plan.

She'd just wanted to end her marriage and couldn't be alone, so somehow she'd set her sights on him.

Eve neared him, teary streaks making her mascara run, a scarier image than before.

She stroked his cheeks and tried to embrace him. He flinched, his insides recoiling at her touch, his hand still wrapped around the knife. "I don't know where she is. I think she might've known about you and she might've known about Frankie, and I don't know what she would've done if she found out about both at once," he said.

"Since when do you care about Vivian?" There was ugliness in Eve's voice.

Clay pushed Eve away with his free hand. Her back slammed up against the island. "Clay!"

"What is wrong with you? I loved my wife." Clay's heart pulsed heavily in his chest. "You were a mistake and nothing more. Now, get out of my house!"

"Don't do this, Clay," she seethed. Eve was nearing him again, but he wanted her as far away from him as possible. Eve didn't want to be with him. She just didn't want to lose to Vivian or any other woman. And she was acting out because she was separated from Peter, and she felt alone and insecure. "We can be a team," she pleaded.

"Where is Peter, Eve? Go home to Peter," he said.

"Fuck you and fuck Peter!" She wasn't leaving, and he was losing his damn patience.

"Get out or I'm calling the police." He picked up his cell phone.

"You're going to be sorry." She charged him again, and this time, he put his hands up and launched her across the room toward the mudroom. Then he ran across the kitchen, opened the door, and shoved her into the attached garage, then locked the door behind him.

Crazy bitch.

She could get to the backyard through the side door in the garage and slither her way home. Hopefully, she'd slither, because if she were pissed off enough to make herself visible, he was really screwed.

"Clay! Open this door right now," she demanded, banging on the other side. He shut his eyes, willing her away. Willing all of it away. The press and the cameras and the police and the women in his head who had deserted him, and the ones whose sweet voices he still heard when he laid his head down on his pillow. And the crazy ones—Eve and Holly—demanding his attention right now.

"Clay, open this door right now or you'll be sorry!"

Too late. He already was. He was so very, very sorry.

19

Holly was a sweaty mess when she returned home from the police station—free at last—her nerves redirected to her hands mashing through mounds of ground meat like a woman possessed. Her kids had just gotten off the bus, and she watched until they were through the door. It was horrible to live in fear. At first it was fear of what'd happened to her sister, but since their house had been broken into, it was fear for everyone around her too.

Her children stopped in the foyer and gawked at her as if she were an actual escaped felon.

"Hey guys, I'm sorry about the other day. I was looking for Aunt Vivi and got carried away."

They didn't respond, avoiding her gaze—forget a hug. Holly had no idea what Mark had told them, but she guessed it was misinformation to make her look worse than she already did. She and Mark weren't on the same team anymore, and he reminded her every chance he got.

Otto and Tyler nodded, dropping their backpacks on the floor and running toward the basement. "Do your homework first!" she yelled. She loved Mondays because there were no sports practices, which meant her kids would try to get to their video games or outside as quickly as possible. It was also the night she usually cooked dinner, a meal that might provide leftovers for a couple of nights.

She was anxious to get back to their "normal." She didn't really have time to make meatloaf today, but the ground chuck would go bad if she didn't use it, and Mark would bitch about her wasting food. She didn't need one more reason to be on his shit list, even though the list was growing by the day.

The evidence was gone, and the police wouldn't take her seriously now even though she'd just hand delivered vital information, specific names, including Frankie and Giana, which she'd learned from hiding in the courthouse maintenance closet. Someday she hoped to report in the light again. She'd even quickly scrolled through jobs but hadn't had time to really look; she just wanted to convince herself that her vocation hadn't become extinct.

But first—Vivian.

Holly needed to recall everything she remembered from those missing chat sessions, page by page, before the words evaporated from her mind forever.

The silver pan slid into the oven.

She set the timer, washed her hands, then returned to the dining room, which had been transformed into a crime lab. Mark still hadn't spoken to her, and she'd stopped caring what he thought. She wasn't going to hide her blind obsession with finding Vivian any longer.

Holly posted that shit up in the dining room so everyone could see it.

The whiteboard easel her kids had used for art projects had become a smear of words and pictures. Notes about Tom and Vivian's chat sessions that Holly had scribbled down from memory were spread all over the table like a police station breakout room.

She heard her kids approach the island to do their homework and have a premeal snack. They could get it themselves. After surviving her own mother, Holly had promised herself she'd be an attentive parent. It was one of the reasons she'd initially agreed to give up her job, vowing to never place her work before the boys. Her kids were spoiled because of it, but this research was different from her mother's. Her mother's research was only for herself—this was for Vivian.

"Mom. I need help with math," Otto said.

Holly huffed, threw down her papers, and walked over to the island. Tyler set his Star Wars backpack down and looked right at her, his first attempt since she'd come home from the slammer. "Jail is a place bad people go," he said.

Well, that broke her heart.

She took a deep breath, smiled, and said, "Jail can also be a place people go who make bad mistakes trying to help other people out. Like your missing aunt."

Tyler blinked and softened at the mention of Aunt Vivi, but she still didn't think he fully understood.

Holly looked at Otto's math homework, and she didn't understand why the hell they had to change math. What was this Common Core crap? Math had been just fine the way it was. That's all she needed—one more mystery to solve. But her brain liked numbers, and she was able to figure it out quickly. Holly demonstrated how to complete the one lingering question on Otto's homework assignment, and he finished it on his own successfully.

At least she'd helped solve something today. "Very good," she said.

"Can I go out if dinner's not ready?" Otto asked impatiently.

Holly sighed. "Yeah, but take your phone. Don't go past the stop sign." She looked at him sternly. Holly wanted to keep them close with danger lurking near.

"Okay." He shrugged and ran out the front door, slamming it as he left. Holly flinched at the loud sound. *Boys.*

Holly let Tyler play with the neighbors for a bit in the backyard, where she could see him, wondering what they thought of her family now that news of Clay's mistress had been splattered all over the news. Holly was initially angry it'd circulated so soon, not sure if it would help or hurt her case.

She had the full names of the crime family Clay had been involved with, and she'd done some digging of her own.

Francine (Frankie) Gallo was a cousin of Nicky Bellini, the lead crime boss. Ray Gallo was Frankie's brother, the doctor Clay had represented and gotten off in court. There were a lot of news articles about the Gallo family. Both Frankie's father and her oldest brother had gone to prison. Her brother had been charged with drug trafficking and shooting armed guards, but he gave up the family. Holly couldn't determine from her research what'd happened to him, but she was almost sure he must be dead by now for selling them out. Their father was still locked away in Poughkeepsie for embezzlement.

From what Holly could gather, these people didn't have a lot to lose. Their lives were already a wreck. Holly could see what might've drawn Frankie to Clay, who grew up in Fairfield, Connecticut, in a picturesque family, the kind she'd never known.

Holly wondered again how much Vivian had told him . . . the things she might've said about her.

It's the way Clay had looked at her when he'd said it—*"You had the same parents. You understand her demons."* It bothered Holly that he might know something she didn't. There'd been a lot of hushed whispers between her sister and their parents that summer before Vivian was sent to boarding school. Holly had assumed she was excluded from the conversation because she was the youngest, the most protected, but part of her wondered if it was because there were secrets too—things they didn't want her to know.

The next step was to piece together the facts of Vivian's disappearance using bits from her chat sessions and old criminal cases like Vivian's. Holly believed Vivian had left subtle clues of duress behind in her journal, which the cops had kindly returned to her because—they didn't speak poetry. They should've returned it to Clay, but they hadn't protested when she'd asked for it back.

But where was the arrest?

Holly had been arrested for tiptoeing in Clay's house, and she knew he had connections, but she'd handed the police a mistress and a life insurance policy, and she'd expected to see him in handcuffs by now. She would've handed over the picture of Aliza, too, but it wasn't uncommon for defense attorneys to research the witnesses in a trial. He'd wiggle out of it somehow. But with the other evidence, she just needed the police to use the age-old headline and move on with their lives—*Man kills wife to be with lover and collect hefty life insurance policy.*

Holly knew there was more to it, but she'd take whatever she could to put Clay behind bars. The truth was that the only person Clayton Eddy truly loved was himself. Holly didn't believe that he loved this *Frankie*. What kind of name was that anyway?

And secondly, Clay wasn't a poor man. He probably had a few extra million lying around, so he had no need to go through the dirty work of murder to collect more. Why not just divorce Vivian if he wanted to get away from her so badly? Murder seemed an extreme measure with too many risks for someone as calculated and wealthy as Clay—unless he was angry with Vivian.

Unless he killed her in some fit of rage because she'd discovered something about him or his secret life that he didn't want other people to know. Something that would threaten his business.

Before the cheating husband angle had surfaced, the detectives were convinced that Vivian had just lost her damn mind and leaped over the rail into the ocean. Well, if Vivian had gone mad, it was because her husband had driven her to it.

Holly flipped on the television and wasn't stunned to see her sister's face, but it still made her queasy. *Oh, Vivian. She's so beautiful.*

Holly paused the television and stared at her pretty sister. Vivian shied away from public attention and she wouldn't like this. Holly's breath rippled in and out of her mouth in uneven breaths.

It was *the picture*—the one the press had likely pulled from social media as Vivian's "missing person" photo. Strangely, when Holly had watched missing persons shows, she'd puzzled on which one they might use for hers. Mark had never let her pay for professional photographs. Vivian's LinkedIn librarian photo shone across the television, her dark hair cascading over her shoulders like shiny, thick drapes, her wispy bangs angled toward her thin face, stripy eyebrows perfectly arched over blue-gray eyes. She had a slight smile and an inquisitive look that implored Holly to find her. Her sister's absence was consuming her, the emptiness furling in her chest.

Long Island defense attorney Clayton Eddy was having an affair with his client's sister. Did sleeping with the mob get his wife killed?

That headline made Holly blink back tears. It wasn't what she'd expected them to say, but she supposed the affair would make for better headlines. Maybe if the news attracted more attention to the story, Vivian would be found sooner. Holly could only hope.

Along with the breaking news was a photograph of Clay and Frankie, the edgy, dark-haired woman Holly recognized from the trial. They were all dressed up in handsome attire, Clay with a wide smile, dress pants, and a crisp white shirt, Frankie with a closemouthed, sneaky grin and a slinky black dress. It was a bad selfie, really, but the perfect shot for the news to sleaze up the story. Holly wasn't sure if Clay had killed Vivian, but Frankie also had a motive.

Holly froze the picture and walked closer to the screen, focusing on everything around the two lovebirds. She knew this would be one of those photographs that would recirculate on the news a thousand times, but their faces weren't what grabbed Holly's attention.

There were small, round windows in the background behind Clay and Frankie that reminded Holly of something specific. They weren't sitting in a typical house or apartment.

Holly examined it further and noticed white lights strung around a very low ceiling.

The photograph had been taken inside a boat.

Those were cabin windows, and they'd been belowdecks when the photo was taken. Holly wondered whose boat it was. Clay and Viv didn't own a boat, although it could've been Frankie's or one of Clay's friends'.

It was nothing, really, but it niggled at Holly.

If Clay had a boat, he could hide a ton of things on it.

Holly wrote *boat* on the whiteboard. She was sure the police had already checked it out, but they had sorely disappointed Holly before, especially giving Vivian's poetry book back already. The notebook held lots of clues to Vivian's internal thoughts. They just didn't want to take the time to pick them apart because they'd already found their motive—*the mistress.* Holly didn't buy it.

She did a brief internet search.

When she logged on to the website for New York State boat ownership, she discovered that every state, including New York, required that owners register their boats. Mark would absolutely kill her, but when Holly was prompted for payment to find out if Clay's name was on any boat records, she whipped out their credit card and paid the twenty or so dollars. Mark would pay dearly for not bailing her out, Holly had decided, dollar by dollar.

She didn't know if she could ever forgive him for leaving her in jail to suffer. Didn't he think she'd suffered enough with her sister missing?

Holly had figured Mark would take her seriously, since the chat sessions were apparently important enough to steal, but the theft had elicited the opposite reaction. He'd turned further away from her, made her the enemy, blamed her for the home invasion. His communications came only in the form of texts, all of which she'd received after getting her phone back that morning.

Mark still hadn't forgiven her for breaking the law, for *"placing their family at risk,"* as he put it. They were at a domestic stalemate, where each person thought the other was at fault. She wouldn't admit fault under the circumstances, and he wouldn't apologize, so they'd just remain in this awful place until one of them relented.

It was probably what had happened to Vivian and Clay, too, Holly had decided. Perhaps they'd reached a marital impasse and hadn't found a way through it. Clay had apparently found this Frankie instead. It made Holly sad, all the stages in a marriage and how lucky the couples were who could drift through each one and never hit these horrible patches of indifference.

When Holly punched Clay's name into the search window, it came up empty.

Then she ran another one—for Francine Gallo.

And she gasped out loud when the search returned a record. She scribbled down the hull number and the name of the marina where the boat was docked. It had only recently been transferred over to her by a Russell Ambrose.

A quick search on Russell Ambrose pulled up a recent acquittal in the Liebler jewelry robbery, the attorney on the case—you guessed it—Clayton Eddy.

"Son of a gun." Holly had filed that information away in the courthouse bathroom but had never followed up on her mental note. So Clay had gotten this guy off, maybe to repay him for using his boat, and now it'd passed hands to Frankie. Something was up with this boat.

Frankie had said she and her daughter were staying at a marina. It was a detail Holly'd neglected to tell the detectives because she hadn't remembered it until now.

Holly ruffled the untamed blonde tufts on her head. She'd always had thick, unruly hair that never settled right without a curling iron, and right now she looked like a prisoner who'd been left in her cell without a bath. Well, she'd been released but still maintained the look, and she imagined her sister might be in a much worse state, if she was still alive.

She placed her hand over her mouth to stifle whatever was threatening to come up. She needed to find out what had happened to her sister before she could engage in normal life again.

"Mom, I think we have a problem." Tyler was soaking wet and lingering in the opening of the sliding glass door off the back patio.

"What's wrong, Ty?"

"We got out the water hose to up the stakes on the Nerf game and . . ."

"And?" Holly asked.

"And Jace tried to tie something around it to make a launcher, and it cut the hose."

It was only sixty degrees outside, Tyler was shaking, and Mark would flip a shit if the neighbor kid had destroyed the garden hose.

"Seriously, Tyler? Come inside and dry off and tell Jace you're done playing."

Tyler looked over his shoulder and shrugged. Jace had probably already run his little butt home.

"Get upstairs and change while I deal with this."

Tyler skulked his wet body, wrapped in a Star Wars towel, quickly up the stairs.

Holly made her way through the path of destruction to the sodden lawn and shut off the hose. It was cut open in three places. Jace had tried to hold it together with a pair of wire cutters that had sliced right through it. She picked it up, noticing the bruise on her wrist from where Clay had grabbed her the other day. She hadn't mentioned the argument to the cops and thought maybe she should have. Holly needed to do anything she could to perpetuate an arrest so they could put Clay behind bars and squeeze the truth out of him.

She picked up the rubber pieces. *"Damn it."* She wouldn't tell Mark about the hose. It was autumn, and he wouldn't need it again until spring, and he could figure it out later. Who knew what their relationship would look like by then anyway. She'd questioned it in that jail cell last night.

What kind of man leaves his wife in a jail cell?

She wasn't sure if it was the kind of man she wanted to spend the rest of eternity with, that's for sure. Holly coiled the broken hose into its holder and went back inside. She suddenly became fearful of where her older son was and what havoc he might be wreaking at other people's houses in the neighborhood. Punctured holes in water hoses were small problems. They could be patched. Tyler was fine. Jace's ass was grass, but telling his parents what had happened could wait too.

Investigating Vivian's disappearance, however, could not wait.

Holly felt responsible.

She'd known something was wrong in Vivian's home, she'd decided to remain silent, and now she needed to rectify the situation if she was to ever have any inner peace.

Her email dinged. Archibald Steiner had returned her message. Holly had been trying to reach the professor ever since he bailed her out. She didn't understand what would possess him to do that. Holly had called his cell three times, stopped at his house once, and emailed. It was hard to think of the old man in the midst of trying like hell to find her sister, but she made a point to do it every spare chance she got. What Archie had done for her was no small favor.

Dear Mrs. Boswell,

It's been a long time since I had to post bail for someone. I hope you're doing great things with your newfound freedom! Thank you for the notes of kindness and the gift card. It really wasn't necessary. You mentioned wanting to know where the ginger pills came from, and I can help you with that as well. A chat is long overdue; why don't we meet?

Please let me know your earliest convenience. I'm sure your family is still reeling from your missing sister, so no rush. I may be able to add some insight, as I, myself, was once a missing party.

All the best,
Archie

Holly smiled. Archie sounded like he had a sense of humor, this old man. Although she needed to budget her investigative time wisely. Her first priority was checking out Frankie's boat. Archie had said no rush, so she'd circle back after she left the marina. She drafted a quick message back that said she'd stop at his house tomorrow if that was all right, between eleven and two. That should give her enough wiggle room.

She needed to figure out why this man had loaned her $2,500. She'd find a way to pay him back.

Holly walked to the kitchen, a feeling of unsettlement overtaking her as she poured herself a glass of water. She texted her older son and asked him to report back right away and tell her where he was.

Just then, her cell phone lit up.

Otto: I'm at Isaac's.

Isaac was the good neighbor kid up the street.

Holly let out a sigh and texted him back. Be home for dinner in a half hour.

A flood of relief rushed down her bare arms. Her sons were okay, and the hose could lie flat on the ground and dry beneath the sun, and they would all fall asleep in that house and wake up the next morning as a family. But her family wasn't a family without Vivian.

20

Clay had barricaded himself inside his house since Sunday. He'd placed one delivery order yesterday, for nonperishables, frozen pizzas, and a lot more vodka so he didn't have to come out for a while.

He'd drawn the blinds, put on his sweatpants, and settled in for a nice long shitstorm.

This was going to be very bad for him. It would be better if they could stop flashing that damn picture of him and Frankie all over the television.

Where did they get it? Who sold me out at the club?

The picture was almost always followed by the torturous professional photograph of Vivian.

"Who takes out the town librarian?" one reporter had speculated.

"Not me," Clay wanted to cry at the television.

But there was a newscaster on *Real Crime TV* who was already gunning for Clay. Hadley Bleaker's answer to that question had been, *"The same kind of guy who has the soccer mom a town over offed so he can win his trial."*

Now they were blaming him for Aliza Levine's murder? His career was toast. Ari hadn't reached out since the news about Frankie and

Giana had been mass circulated. No one at the club would call him back. His own damn sisters wouldn't even call him back.

He collapsed onto his leather couch in tatters. Things couldn't get any worse.

"A break in the missing attorney's wife case heard first here from his other mistress and neighbor—Eve Carrington."

"What?" Clay actually shook his head at the television in disbelief. He rubbed his eyes, especially the one that had never stopped jumping, but now he thought his ears were going bad too. Surely he couldn't have heard that correctly. Clay's heart did a double thump as he took in Eve's appearance on the flat-screen. She was positioned at a podium before the press. It was very early morning. Too early for a press conference. He had to squint to make sure it was really her on the screen.

Eve didn't look like Eve, though. He'd never seen her in anything except black spandex and tight dresses. Today she had on a full navy-blue suit with a white collared shirt. She must've bought it special for the press conference or it was her funeral suit, because he'd never seen it before. The load of makeup she usually wore was toned down, and her tan skin seemed to take on a lighter glow. It was as if she'd hired a style consultant to make her look demure, if that were possible.

"She never dresses like that. She looks like she could teach Sunday school," he said out loud. He'd taken to talking to himself, since no one else would. His biggest fear since his parents had died in the crash was coming true—to end up all alone.

"My name is Eve Carrington, and I've been having an affair with Attorney Clayton Eddy." The crowd at the press conference let out a stir of disapproval.

Clay gasped. Her wardrobe was the least of his worries. Clay's phone lit up, his call-waiting buzzed, and even though he'd been dying for someone—anyone—to call him, he ignored it so he could better hear the final blow to the one-legged stool he'd been balancing on for the better half of the last week.

"*I'm not proud of what I've done, and I'm only here to provide evidence to help bring Vivian home.*"

Eve broke into hiccupping sobs and had to momentarily excuse herself while she dabbed her eyes with a tissue.

"That's horseshit!" She never gave a damn about Vivian. Eve used to make fun of her behind her back. The situation had just gone from bad to so much worse. If he wasn't an interested party before, he damn sure was now.

"*Clay pursued me hard,*" Eve went on.

"That's a lie!" he shouted.

"*It started when we vacationed together in Montauk. Peter, my husband, and I were having problems, and Clay knew this, so he fed on my insecurities. He told me I was beautiful and that he'd always found me attractive. He told me his wife no longer wanted to sleep with him and it had forced him to look outside his marriage for affection.*" Eve paused for more tears.

"Oh, please! Affection? Affection! I would never in my life use that word." Clay let out a howl.

"*He had this way with words, which I'm sure most lawyers do. And then when false rumors circulated about my own husband and Vivian, Clay said we needed to even the score.*"

What? Those had been Eve's words. He was screaming inside, but he could no longer speak. This couldn't be happening to him. This was a revenge scheme because he'd rejected her.

"*I caved to Clay's advances, but Vivian was my friend, and she'd confided in me. I'm here to tell you what she said about Clayton Eddy. She said he'd been abusive in the past. She said when they fought, he'd gotten in her face and screamed at her, usually after a drink or two.*"

A steady moan of *ohhs* cascaded through the audience.

"*I've wanted to leave my husband for some time, and Clay said I should. When it wasn't moving fast enough*"—pause for more crying—"*he got physical. I have the bruises on my arms from last night to prove it.*"

Eve ran off the stage, covering her sniffling nose and fake cries. The press started firing questions at her from every direction, following her with cameras as her attorney and security guards warded off the reporters.

Clay clicked off the television and stared at it long after it'd faded to black. "This is bullshit." He knew Eve craved attention, but this was a disgusting display. Then he figured out what she was doing. She was protecting herself.

Vivian hadn't been found, and Eve had already implicated herself in the case by admitting to fighting with Vivian before she went missing. And after their argument last night and the news about Frankie and Giana, Eve was airing out her dirt first before he could. She was afraid he would try to turn Vivian's disappearance on her somehow. Not that Clay would've.

He had underestimated Eve. He never thought in a million years she'd trash her own image to upend his. Although the bit about Peter and Vivian circulating in the community had had her completely disturbed. Maybe she didn't think that what she'd done was that far of a stretch, or maybe she wanted everyone to know she hadn't tolerated her husband's behavior, filing for divorce, making her affair public, getting back at Peter—by using Clay.

He should've turned Eve away that night he'd slept with her. He'd known it was a mistake even as it was happening. What the fuck would he do now? He lay down on the couch and put the pillow over his face. What a mess. He lay like that, paralyzed. When he got up, he noticed that none of his phone calls were from his lawyer. When he called Brent for guidance, he got his voice mail.

Clay looked out the window and was disheartened to see that the media parade had continued while he had his hours-long breakdown. As he pulled out of his driveway, he tried to maneuver around the angry mob of people forming a barrier with their microphones and cameras rolling and ready. They were holding him hostage from getting in and out of his own house until he answered a few questions, but he needed his mail.

As he pulled up a little farther, he saw another food truck. A breakfast one this time.

Good God, make it stop.

Clay refused to let the press bully him into an interview, so he drove up alongside his mailbox because he was sure the mail was piled up in there, and it was a federal offense for them to block it. But as he lowered his window, he couldn't miss the new questions about his mistress that had replaced the old.

"*Mr. Eddy, is it true that Eve Carrington was best friends with your wife? Some people are saying there's motive. Comment?*"

"No comment!" he yelled.

"*Mr. Eddy, did you use your own home or your neighbor's for the affair?*"

He tried to ignore them with no success until his fingers hit the package in his mailbox. It was in a manila envelope with no postage stamp, but it was sealed with red lips—Frankie's shade. His body flooded with joy, and he hated that she had so much power over him. He decided not to try to pull back into his driveway, so instead he drove to the stop sign a few car lengths up from the food truck and put his car in "Park." He tore open the envelope. There was a little note inside.

I told you I'd be back for you and to wait for me.

I'm disappointed you couldn't do the same.

Go to our favorite place "in lights," and I'll explain the rest.

Clay felt what was left of his stomach bottom out. By "*disappointed,*" Frankie meant she was livid. She was a controlled woman and rarely lost her cool. Using an emotional word like *disappointed* worried Clay.

He pulled his car onto the main road and then the highway, driving toward the North Shore, where Russ's boat was docked on the sound. He braced himself for what Frankie might say next. She was probably just irate their picture together had been leaked to the press. Maybe she even thought Clay had something to do with it, that he'd cracked under the pressure of the law.

She should know better.

It was time to go to their place "in lights" and clear everything up. Russ's little boat in the marina.

21

The address for the marina from Holly's internet search was located in Port Jefferson on the North Shore, offering boaters quick access to Long Island Sound and the Connecticut shore. Port Jeff had a different ferry, and Holly wondered if it meant anything. It was obvious from the photo blasted all over the news that Clay had used this boat as a little love nest, a meeting place to entertain his lady friends.

Holly stuck out her tongue, repulsed, wondering if she should take this investigation any further. If she could confirm the boat was there and provide the location to the police, it might help find the missing evidence they needed to make an arrest. She couldn't show up at the station with another false lead, though. Those missing chat sessions had put her in a bad place with the authorities. The way the detectives looked at her like she was a complete loon made her furious.

When Holly reached the entrance to the marina, she stopped in her tracks. It was huge, the size of a small amusement park, and U-shaped, with boats stretching as far as the eye could see. She wasn't as familiar with the North Shore as the South, where she'd grown up.

Where to start in this unfamiliar place?

She needed to find something there to prove Clay was responsible for Vivian's disappearance or worse, her death. Even if he hadn't pulled the trigger, Holly was convinced he'd at least been connected to the person who had, and the evidence might very well be on this boat.

Locating Frankie's boat wouldn't be easy, though.

Holly had written down the boat hull number, BCD 43783 0317, and the boat's name: *Proud Mary*, which should've been plastered somewhere on the vessel.

It seemed like enough information to go on when she'd left this morning, but Holly had imagined it as simple as walking up and down the parking lot aisles at the mall, hoping her eyes would grab on to a specific color and model. Instead, all the boats were white and looked very similar. Holly wondered which aisle to stroll down first. There were so many.

She spun around on the damp dock and realized how ill-prepared she was for this undercover job. She and Mark certainly weren't boat people. Boats required money. What she knew of them was limited to an introductory sailing class that Mother had forced them to take one summer to make them more *"cultured."*

Holly stopped and looked down at her Sperry shoes. She'd worn her boat shoes for her marina investigation, and she felt silly about it. She may not be the most prepared detective, but she'd possibly found a clue here, one the cops might not know about it if they hadn't specifically searched for it. It's not like boats popped up on a DMV report, something they'd typically run on a suspect.

Maybe Clay had plans to set sail with his mistress, although now that there were two girlfriends, the second mistress invalidated the first. Holly didn't know at whom to point the finger. She'd had her suspicions about Eve after their run-in on Clay's porch and then later, when she'd ratted Holly out.

Eve was just another victim of Clayton Eddy's. Her problem was, she'd thought she was the only one. But which one got rid of Vivian—Frankie or Eve? Or did Clay have a favorite and orchestrate the murder himself so he could be with his girl of choice?

One thing was for certain, Clayton Eddy was a pig. A pig Holly was about to roast once she pieced this thing together.

She glanced at the row of boats again. What if she found the boat, and there was a person on it? What if that person was Vivian? *Dead.*

A sick feeling washed down Holly's throat, as if the salt from the seawater had found its way inside her vocal cords and stuck there. She swallowed, wishing she'd brought a bottle of water with her.

You're such a wimp, Holly.

She sucked in a breath, channeling her inner Mariska Hargitay. It was as though she'd been priming herself for this moment her whole life; it had been her area of study in school, her chosen vocation that she would soon return to if she survived this.

Suck it up, Boswell. This is for your sister.

She inhaled again, moving forward. Holly had always wanted to be a detective, and outsmarting the police had given her more of a rush than she'd ever admit. But knowing she could fail and quite possibly die in the process of solving this mystery was not part of the dream.

At least in the maintenance closet, she'd been concealed. Even though she'd worn her baseball cap and sunglasses this morning, she could still be easily identified.

Several men had given her questioning stares already, as if they wanted to ask her if she was lost, but she'd ducked them and moved in the opposite direction as soon as they'd shown too much interest. What would she say anyway?

Yes, could you help me find a boat I don't own so I can break in and see if my sister's dead body is inside? Thanks.

She kept moving, her eyes conducting a roving process of elimination as she walked by each dock spot. On the third row, on the far side of the marina, Holly stumbled upon the dame in question, and to her surprise, *Proud Mary* was a lot smaller in comparison to some of the other boats she'd passed on the way. It did have a bottom deck, but the top resembled a little fishing vessel.

Holly double-checked the hull number and could tell right away that the boat was not a new purchase; it was rusted a bit with dings on one side. She peeked in the window, and it was dark inside, no one home. She was sure it would be locked, but she had brought a pocketknife with her just in case, knowing full well she had no idea how to pick a lock.

She looked over her shoulder one more time.

No one there.

Should she do it? The likelihood of getting inside was slim, so why risk someone reporting her? Another arrest meant serious jail time.

Come on, Holly. It's for Vivian!

Holly took a deep breath, mentally preparing herself for the fact that Vivian's body could very well be on the inside if she did pick the lock.

Either her body or pieces of her body. People like Nicky Bellini liked to cut people up, place them in bags, dispose of them in places like junkyards and construction sites and—the ocean.

Holly leaned over the roped railing and held her breath before vomiting. Nothing came out. Just a quick dry heave. She'd never been a good puker. She had a college roommate who could heave and ho like a champ, but it'd always been an awful struggle for Holly.

"Ugh, damn it." This was all too much. She wiped her face and pulled herself together. She needed to do this for Vivian. Holly took one more look over her shoulder before she held her breath and stepped onto the boat. Her legs shook as the boat rocked to and fro. She didn't have the sea legs for this. Her body pitched with the light waves. Holly found the little door to go below deck and pulled on it first.

She almost fell backward when it opened. "Well, holy shit."

Holly couldn't believe it was unlocked.

Her blood was pulsing in her ears. She'd never expected to actually get inside the boat if she found it.

If she was being honest with herself, this was the furthest she thought she'd get. Now, if she climbed down those stairs and someone came in after her, she'd be trapped. What to do?

Crap. Any good detective would keep going. She'd found a secret boat owned by the girlfriend of the lead suspect in the case. If the police had known about it, they would've roped it off or commandeered it for inspection by now, but maybe they hadn't had enough time to run the report. She'd only given up Frankie's name Saturday.

Holly *had* to check it out. She *had* to find Vivian.

It was like Pandora's box, staring into that black hole. Holly had always grouped people into two categories based on their childhood. There were the kids who wanted to shine a light in the dark cave to see what was inside and those who didn't want to know. Holly had always been a light shiner.

There could be a mystery in there.

She proceeded down the stairs.

A damp, musty smell filled her nostrils, like a gym locker room or a basement fruit cellar. She flipped on the light to view the tiny quarters. A bed, a bathroom with a little push-in door, and a small couch and bar area greeted her front view. There were white Christmas lights strung up around the perimeter, which made Holly's heart blip, because it was definitely the boat from the photo featured on the news.

But no body.

If there had been a body sealed up on that tiny boat, Holly knew from watching all her crime investigation shows that there would be a rancid smell to go along with it. But there wasn't anything of substance below deck except a distressed leather couch with a small end table next to it. As Holly neared the table, she saw a white envelope on top with Clay's name scrawled across the middle in neat handwriting.

Someone had left it for him.

Holly kept the hatch open to the upper deck so she could hear anyone approach. A breeze hit the boat, and it made Holly nauseous as it rocked.

228

She had to read what was inside that envelope.

It could be a clue.

Holly carefully opened the white envelope, the size one might use for a greeting card. Inside she found a set of keys and a Polaroid picture wrapped up in a folded piece of paper. Holly unfolded the paper to find a letter, then deliberated on which item to examine first—the letter or the picture. The picture had a Post-it note attached to it that said *check the photograph* and *only shake it once*. That sounded strange.

Holly glanced at her watch and realized she'd been inside the boat for five minutes already. She needed to hurry up. She set the photo and the keys down next to an ashtray with stray cigarette butts, the ends smeared with red lipstick. Now Holly knew what the musty smell was in the cabin—stale, used cigarettes. Frankie's cigarettes.

She picked up the letter. Holly pictured Frankie sitting there on that leather couch, lighting up one cigarette after another, writing this note to her lover.

Her stomach lurched at the thought of the people she'd associated herself with, and she suddenly felt suffocated belowdecks in this stranger's boat. Holly quickly snapped pictures of the letter so she could pick it apart later. She wouldn't make the same mistake she'd made with the chat sessions. Then she grabbed the photograph and examined it.

The corners were fat to the touch. It was a Polaroid, as suspected, but the photo paper was thicker than she remembered. The other unusual thing was that the front of the picture was completely black, like it was overexposed. There was no picture on it at all. She shook it once just as instructed.

It sounded like a thousand tiny pieces of sand were wrestling around inside it. "What in the world?"

She held it up to the small circular window and could see a picture materializing. It was an image of two people on the beach from a distance, a handsome man with jet-black hair slicked back and a woman with short, spiky red hair. Holly didn't recognize either one.

A sound like a cable being retracted through a metal reel zipped from above. *Oh no.*

Holly panicked and shoved the letter and the Polaroid in her purse.

She darted up the stairs of the boat and popped out of the hatch, gasping for air like she'd been trapped below the surface of the ocean, not the deck of a boat. The oxygen tasted good and so did the freedom. She didn't bother looking for the source of the noise she'd just heard. Instead, she just closed the hatch behind her, leaped from the boat—and ran.

22

Clay's feet were like lead balloons, pounding down the dock. As much as he tried to put energy behind his footfalls, he couldn't travel fast enough to the spot where Russ had always docked his boat.

It was possible Russ had strayed from his normal spot on the far end of the marina for a larger parking area to accommodate his new vessel, a recent purchase he'd made with his girlfriend, or so Clay had heard.

It'd been a year since Clay had secured an acquittal for Russ in the case of the Liebler jewelry heist. When Clay had reviewed the surveillance tape of the masked men, the footage was grainy, the thieves' faces unrecognizable, but Clay knew who they were from their build and movements—Russ and Vinny. It should've been a moral dilemma, but because they were members of the club, he had to take the case whether they were guilty or not and represent them to the best of his ability.

Mr. Liebler hadn't done anything wrong, but the State of New York was suspicious that the robbery had been an inside job. And they'd been right. Liebler's wife, Mary, had been seeing Russ behind Liebler's back, and she orchestrated the whole thing. The prosecution had dug this up, and Russ's freedom was in peril, but Clay persuaded the jury to believe it was a legit robbery and that Russ hadn't been involved.

Shortly after the trial, Mary Liebler filed for divorce, taking half of the score from the insurance payout—and half the score from her boyfriend's loot pile.

Russ had even changed the name of his boat for her—*Proud Mary*. And now Clay had to find it in this huge-ass marina, which seemed to have gotten even bigger since the last time he'd been there.

The air was heavy in his lungs as he walked faster, his body spent from lack of sleep and malnourishment. He hadn't seen the inside of a gym in a week, and he couldn't go back to his old one because Eve worked there. If Clay saw her again in the presence of heavy barbells, he made no promises he wouldn't use them to blast her in the skull after all the lies she'd sputtered in front of the cameras.

His scalp heated up just thinking about it, all the ugly ideas that had rolled around in his head about what he'd like to do to Eve after that press conference.

The only bright spot in his miserable life was that there'd been news that Mortimer Levine, Aliza's husband, owed $3 million in back taxes. The cops always looked at the husband first, and he was no exception. Maybe the public would stop thinking that either Clay or Ray Gallo had offed her. They would be whispering that Mort's financial situation may have had something to do with his wife's death.

Clay wasn't so sure it did. If Ray had been convicted, Aliza could have filed a civil suit, and the Levines might have gotten a nice payday. He thought it was unlikely the man would kill his potential cash cow, but if it took the heat off Clay, it didn't much matter to him what people thought. He couldn't have the firm thinking he'd had a witness against his client killed—if the firm ever let him come back.

Speak of the devil, Ari was calling his cell. He was tempted to ignore it. Or to unleash a string of obscenities that would let Ari know how Clay felt about Ari selling him out to the cops. But he needed that job. Needed to get his life back on track.

"Hey, Ari. Couldn't make it this long without me, right?" he joked. He could use some friendly banter right now.

"I'm afraid not." Ari sounded glum.

"What's up?"

"We've changed the code to get into the building, Clay. Some people here feel you're a threat. I'm afraid we're terminating your employment. I'm sorry."

"You can't do that!" He hadn't even been formally charged with anything. He could sue them.

"We're a private firm. We can," his boss said with no mercy. "Our clients have to be able to trust us. Can't have a known philanderer, especially one with girlfriends publicly associated with the mob, connected with the firm," Ari said plainly.

"Allegedly!" Clay screamed into the phone. Apparently, Ari had forgotten the legal process in his desire to protect his business. The most ridiculous part was that Ari had been the one to set him up with Nicky Bellini in the first place.

"Goodbye, Clay. We'll be in touch. I wish you the best." The line went dead.

Clay spit on the ground, the remains of last night's drink heavy on his tongue. It was all a waste. The time he'd put in there, this place, the people he'd invested in. They'd all turned against him. His whole life here a total wash.

He needed a do-over.

Once he was allowed to leave his neighborhood and this blasted state, he was going to get the hell out of New York and start over somewhere no one knew him, put all of this behind him. He'd take Frankie and Giana with him. They could rebuild as a new family in a different town. It would suck to start from the bottom again at a new law firm, but he'd do it to escape this pity of an existence.

Clay stopped to grab one of the railings, huffing over the side. One more night with his lips wrapped around the bottle and he might not wake back up. Vivian's mother had drunk herself to death, and Vivian rarely drank at all. Clay had always tried to be mindful about his alcohol consumption around her, but she wasn't there to keep him in check. He caught a glimpse of himself in the water, and even his reflection looked ragged and bloated.

He hoped Frankie would have mercy on him after all he'd been through. Russ's boat stirred up some strong memories of the two of them, and the idea of climbing belowdecks made him woozy with the feels. Frankie had most likely been angry with Clay because of the leaked picture, but once he explained he had nothing to do with its release, he was confident he could repair things between them.

He hoped Giana was inside the boat too.

Their little family didn't have to hide anymore.

Maybe they were even meeting today at the marina so they could sail away together.

Clay had dreams of fake passports and bags of cash, his beautiful girlfriend and adorable daughter waiting for him in the confines of the boat. If they weren't sailing away, maybe Russ was steering them to a train station or an airport or whatever other zany scheme Frankie had cooked up, because she was good at taking off and hiding when she wanted to.

He knew. He'd looked for her everywhere the first time. He didn't think he'd have to look any further.

Once he got to Russ's old parking spot, there she was—the same old boat. *Proud Mary* looked exactly like he remembered. Clay didn't care about the outside of the boat, though, because he knew there was something special waiting for him inside. Tears pooled in the corners of his eyes. All his pain had been for this moment.

It was always her.

It was always them. Clay would finally get his do-over. And he'd get it right this time.

Clay pulled the boat door open and climbed down the steps, his legs still heavy, his breath labored.

When he got belowdecks, the first thing that hit his nose was Frankie's cigarette smoke. It was odd, because she'd always hid the habit from him before, but he'd caught her smokes on her a few times. She'd been defensive about it. *"I only smoke when I drink."* But he knew she was just trying to hide her less polished qualities from him, self-conscious because he'd married a fellow Harvard grad, and he'd always gathered she'd never felt like she measured up because of it.

"Hello!" he shouted into the tiny space, but he already knew with one glance that it was empty.

There was a single white envelope with his name across the front lying on the end table.

His heart burned with horror and regret, because he knew what that meant.

"No, no, no!"

He could barely walk over to the table, but he needed to read what was inside that envelope.

Clay sank into their old couch, the one they used to sit on with the windows cracked, spilling their dreams into the ocean bay. He'd never opened up to any woman like he had to her. Frankie could pull information out of him that he didn't know existed, the deep-down stuff he didn't tell anyone else.

And now she'd do it on the written page; he was sure of it.

Clay opened the envelope, but there was nothing inside. On the table, next to the envelope, was a set of keys and a note to *check the photograph* and *only shake it once.*

"What the hell?" There was no photograph. Only keys. Clay was sure the photo had to have been proof of Vivian's murder—her body or an unmarked grave. That's how the club usually used their "special" pictures. It was evidence they wanted to flash in someone's face that instantly disappeared so it couldn't be used against them later. Clay thought of old Mafia movies he'd watched where packages showed up with body parts inside—this was the modern-day version of that.

But what was their motive for harming Vivian?

Clay couldn't accept another person disappearing on him. The boat rocked, and Clay's sorrow quickly turned to fear.

It wasn't like Frankie to leave a note like this with nothing attached. Someone must've beaten him to the boat. It was unlocked so he could get in and retrieve the keys, but that also meant another person could get in too. Someone else must have the evidence of Vivian's demise, and they were probably going to use it against him.

Right now.

Clay ran to the top deck, envelope still clenched in hand. The morning sun was bright, and he put his hand over his eyes, shielding them, scanning the dock for signs of an intruder, but there wasn't one.

"Son of a bitch!" He fell to his knees on the deck and pounded it with his fist.

Is Frankie playing some kind of sick joke on me?

"You all right over there, brother?" The voice to the left came out of nowhere. Clay turned slowly. A man on a neighboring vessel was reeling a rope into a pulley. He must've been entertained watching Clay have a complete adult tantrum on the deck of Russ's boat.

Clay stood up promptly. "Uh . . . hello." He smoothed his hands on his khaki shorts and tried to collect himself. "You didn't happen to see anyone else on this boat today, did you?"

He wanted to know how long ago Frankie had been there.

"Yeah. And I don't know why you let your girlfriend wear that shit." The man spit a gigantic wad of tobacco into the ocean. His barbed-wire tattoo slithered like a snake in the sunlight.

"What're you talking about?" Clay asked.

"There was a lady with a Mets hat here earlier." He spit again. It wasn't until then that Clay noticed the man was wearing a Yankees T-shirt. Must be a diehard.

Frankie wasn't a sports fan and would never wear a baseball cap. But Clay knew who was. The only woman who could've possibly climbed inside this boat who might own a Mets cap had two sons of her own who were big-time into baseball. It was fall now, but they both played spring ball.

Holly.

He thought she'd learned her lesson after she broke into his house and spent the weekend at the station. He didn't know why he kept underestimating her. Why he just assumed she'd stay her same annoying self, subdued and under Mark's watchful eye.

And then there was Eve's announcement.

Holly, just like everyone else, was probably sure he'd had something to do with Vivian's death now, but it just wasn't true. What he didn't understand was how she knew about Russ's boat. She was probably on her way to the police station right now to report what she'd found. He couldn't let her take him down.

Not the freaking Boswells of all people.

Mark had once tried to barter with Clay over the cost of an old entertainment center Clay had listed on Craigslist, and ever since then, Clay had decided he didn't like him. Mark was cheap, and Clay didn't like Holly because she'd married him knowing this and because she was so comfortably seated in Vivian's shadow.

"Vivian got the looks. Vivian got the brains," Holly would gripe. Her compliments were all to make up for the fact that Holly had the one thing Vivian never could—two beautiful children. And it annoyed the piss out of Clay.

"Did the woman have curly hair?" Clay asked, because he had to make sure before he put an end to her one-party search, indefinitely.

"Sure did. Looked funny under that hat too." The man scratched his armpit and kept reeling.

"Thanks!" Clay hopped off the boat and was running down the dock. Holly, that nosy bitch, had beaten him to the punch. Clay didn't know how she'd discovered Russ's boat or what she'd done with the things Frankie had left for him in that envelope, but he was going to find out.

23

Holly's head was swimming with stress when she made it back to her van. She was about to read Frankie's letter, but then she remembered the meeting she had with the old professor.

Her phone started ringing. She knew it was bad news before she even answered it. Thanks to Bluetooth, *Detective Rigby* blew across the monitor on the van's dash. Had someone reported her already?

The boat had been unlocked, and Holly wondered if that was still considered breaking and entering. She wasn't sure, but she'd stolen something, and the detectives had promised her she'd serve prison time if she were brought up on the same charges again. She had to pick up the call, though, because—*Vivian.*

"Hello," Holly answered.

"Mrs. Boswell. I'm glad we caught you."

Did they catch me? Her throat went dry.

"We found an article of clothing that may have belonged to Vivian and wanted to know if you could identify it."

So it wasn't about the boat. But it was about Vivian. "What is it? And where did you find it?" Her voice trembled. She was afraid to ask.

"It's a gray leather jacket. It had a credit card zipped in the pocket with Vivian's name on it."

"Oh God." Her parched throat closed. She took a sip of water. She kept bottles in the car to dilute the alcohol smell on any given day.

"It was discovered by a couple walking on the North Shore, actually. Poquott Beach."

That was close to Port Jefferson, where Holly was now, on the other side of the island from Bay Shore—nowhere near where Vivian's car had been found. But it was near Frankie's boat. Holly gasped. "She did have a gray leather jacket."

"That's what we gathered from a social media search and a recent receipt from Saks. Just wanted to double-check. Forensics thinks it's unlikely with the water patterns that it could've floated over there."

Because it came from Frankie's boat! But Holly couldn't tell the detective that she knew where the boat was, because then they'd ask how she knew. It would be one more important piece of information that she'd withheld from them.

"It's unlikely we'll be able to pull DNA off the jacket, because it was submerged in water, but the water in the sound is different from ocean water, so it's possible."

Holly thought she understood what Rigby meant. Long Island Sound was an estuary, where fresh and salt water mixed. Salt water might erode DNA, but maybe they could pull something off the jacket if it were floating in mostly fresh water.

"We're more curious why it's over here and may move our search to follow the jacket if we can prove it's Vivian's," Rigby said.

"Okay. Let me know what you find." Holly was trying to find a creative way to tell them Frankie's boat was nearby, but she was coming up empty. Also, alarm bells were going off in her head that this jacket was a diversion of some sort. How odd for it to turn up now, days later. Holly hung up with the detective and sped off, watching the Port Jeff ferry chuff away.

Wrong ferry, her insides screamed.

Wrong side of the island.

Vivian hadn't disappeared into the sound. Holly had heard from her last in Bay Shore. She'd gone missing from there. Something was wrong with her jacket showing up at Poquott Beach.

Holly drove to Archibald Steiner's house, more confused than when she'd left that morning. The professor's house also sounded like a fabulous place to hide and gave her an alibi if she were questioned later about who'd broken into Frankie's boat. But she also needed to read that damn letter. Maybe she could park in front of Archie's house and read it before she stepped inside, to see if the letter contained any clues related to Vivian. But if it mentioned something horrible, something that alluded to Vivian's death, Holly would be immobilized and crumble.

She wanted to read it, and she was terrified to read it.

When she pulled up to Archie's house, he was sitting outside on his porch, drinking a glass of something. He waved at her, so she couldn't just sit there and read as she'd anticipated. But she also reminded herself that if something happened to the very important piece of paper in her purse, she'd at least been smart enough to take a picture of it this time with her phone . . . in case it evaporated into thin air or was stolen from her nightstand.

She didn't plan on staying at Archie's long. She just wanted the answer to one small mystery in her life—why had this man gifted her $2,500?

Mark hadn't seemed to care much about why the random ex-colleague of her parents had bailed Holly out, only that he hadn't had to pay for it. *Probably some do-gooder with more money than he could spend.*

Holly had chuckled at that. She hadn't mentioned to Mark that Professor Steiner was hardly known as the town do-gooder, having abandoned his wife and three children for months without a trace. Meanwhile, laundry wasn't getting done at home, and she was doing the bare minimum in helping with her boys' homework. She just couldn't concentrate on anything else until they found Vivian, and if Mark couldn't pick up the slack, things would just have to be not perfect for now.

Holly waved as she approached Professor Steiner's mint-green Colonial with black shutters. He appeared to be sitting on a rocker. The wraparound porch was encircled in a beautiful white railing. Lovely manicured bushes and flowers led to the porch.

Holly climbed the steps. "Dr. Steiner?"

He twisted his lips in amusement. "Please call me Archie." He extended his hand. His handshake was firm, gracious. He had a head full of white wavy hair that bobbed around. "Have a seat, my dear."

Harley—she thought she remembered the dog's name—had been sitting on the floor and immediately shot up on his back legs to greet her. She rubbed the space on his head between his pointed ears and sat in a matching white rocker next to Archie. Harley nestled at her feet as the sun warmed her face, making her feel at ease for the first time in days. She couldn't remember the last time she'd sat on a front porch to talk to anyone, especially with an animal at her toes. She'd always loved dogs, but Mark said they were too expensive and dirty, the same excuse her parents had given her growing up. Maybe she'd stop at the shelter and pick one up tonight.

Take that, Mark.

"I have to say, a simple thank-you would've done, but the gift card you left was a nice touch too." Archie smiled and shook his head, his nose waggling along with it.

Holly could feel her cheeks warming up. "You're a hard man to track down," she said.

He nodded with a wry smile. "Drink? I got everything," he said, rattling the ice cubes around in his glass.

"Yes. Dealer's choice," she said. Her brain was fried. Choosing a drink seemed taxing at the moment, and it suddenly occurred to her that the last time she'd had a drink was the morning after Vivian went missing. She'd had the shakes the first night in jail, but that wouldn't stop her now. "It doesn't matter what."

Archie laughed heartily and went inside, returning moments later with a glass of something ruby-colored. Holly sipped greedily at the cranberry and vodka, a small slice of heaven. She knew why he'd chosen that drink. It was her mother's favorite. "Thank you."

"You're welcome."

"And I don't know how to thank you for the bail money. I mean . . . I only saw you that once on the street corner. As grateful as I am, I don't understand why you paid it."

"Yes, that's a more complicated answer. First, let's talk about your sister. Any leads?"

Holly was surprised Archie wanted to talk about Vivian. *So he wasn't in front of Vivian's house that day by accident?*

"They think they may have found an article of her clothing. But it was on the North Shore." She shook her head. "That's not where Vivian called me from. She called me from Bay Shore. South Shore." The placement felt wrong. "But they won't know if it's hers until they run some tests. And there's something else . . ." The letter was burning a hole in her pocket.

"Doing more of your own investigative work?" He raised his frosted eyebrows. "I only have so much in my savings, kid."

She laughed. "Hey, if I get myself in another jam, I deserve to stay there!"

"Right, well, I guess your husband thought you did the first time too."

Holly rolled her eyes. She guessed the whole town had heard that she'd spent a couple of nights in lockup. One of the reasons she hadn't agreed to run the kids to sports practice today was because she was too embarrassed. "So why the interest in my sister?"

Archie was long in the torso and leaned way back in his chair, stretching. "You know I knew your mother?"

"Yes. You worked at the university together?"

He nodded.

"How did you know I was in jail, by the way?" she asked.

He smiled that toothy grin again. "I stopped by the library. Jane told me you were looking for me and then mentioned you'd been arrested."

Holly put her hands on her cheeks to cool them. "Oh, I was going to ask you where you got your ginger pills. I've had migraines my whole life, and I've never found anything that worked so well and quickly."

Archie's smile slipped off his face. He reached for something out of the same old leather satchel he had on him the day she saw him in front of Vivian's house. She wondered if he always kept it on him. He pulled out another pill bottle, nondescript and amber with a white lid, and shook it. "I get them compounded at the pharmacy. Need a script for them, but they're harmless."

Holly's heart quickened at the word *compounded*. "Is there anything else in them?"

"Nah, it's just a higher concentration of ginger, less of whatever additives they put in the other stuff."

That's what she'd gathered from her online research. "Is that legal?" It didn't sound legal.

"Sure, people get all kinds of things compounded. It's just ginger, Holly; let your hair down a little." He laughed, and it turned into a raspy cough.

Archie handed her the bottle, and she took it. "Well, I don't want to take yours. You've given me enough."

"I have plenty. Keep it!" He didn't look like he was going to take no for an answer, so she put the bottle in her purse.

"So you knew my parents," she said. "And you took an interest in Viv's case?"

"I knew your mother," he corrected, pointing his finger at her.

"But you worked with my father, too, right?"

"I did, but he didn't like me."

"Why?" Holly asked.

"Because your mother did." He laughed again, and Holly shot him a half smile, remembering the comment about Archie and his tweed jacket and how much her father had disliked it. She tried to picture her mother flirting with Archie and couldn't fathom it. Archie was an r-dropper, a true Long Islander. When he said *"ginger,"* it sounded like *"ginga,"* and there's no way Mother could've liked talking to him.

Although maybe she just liked looking at him.

"Okay," she said, still trying to figure out the connection.

Archie leaned in, elbows on knees, as if he were waiting for Holly to catch up. "You hear about me? I'm the one who went missing years ago. You might've been too young—"

"I remember," she said quickly, looking down. She knew it was the stunt that had taken him down.

Archie sighed. "Yeah, well, no one can forget—that's the problem."

"Why not move and start over, then?" She immediately put her hand over her mouth. "I'm sorry; that was rude."

"No, it's a totally reasonable question. My kids all settled around here. I wanted to be near them. Not that they come by to see me. Still haven't forgiven me for my time away."

"Still?" Holly asked, dumbfounded that anyone could hold a grudge for that long. Then she remembered her own mother and shrugged off the thought. If her mother were still alive, sadly, Holly wasn't sure she'd talk to her either.

"Oh yeah. I missed my only daughter's wedding. And forgiveness is a gift I have yet to receive."

Holly winced. She didn't want to tell him that she sided with the daughter on that one.

"My boys will occasionally come to see me, and if I'm really lucky, I'll get a sighting of my grandchildren." He laughed, but it wasn't funny at all. Holly suddenly felt bad for this old man. He'd made one mistake and had spent his whole life paying for it. Holly knew exactly what that felt like. Her whole life, both hers and that of her sister, could've been different if she only hadn't cheated on that one journal entry. Vivian would've finished out school in Sayville, not met Clay, likely not gone to Harvard. She might be here right now.

"So you disappeared without a trace?" Holly asked, still trying to figure out why he had been outside her sister's house the day after she went missing and how this related to her being bailed out.

Archie leaned back in his chair, stretching his torso. "Yes."

"How did you do it?" Holly asked. "Disappear, that is?"

Archie took a deep breath. "Well, back then, it actually wasn't that hard. There wasn't social media. There weren't cameras in every corner of earth and space. The world was a different place." Archie said this as if he missed the old world. "So I planned for a few months. Packed up what I needed on my back, just enough cash in my pocket to get to Grand Cayman, no credit cards, and I left. I felt bad about my kids, although they were mostly grown by then. I left the note so they wouldn't think I was dead and to see if my wife would bother to find me." Archie had a great storytelling voice. "The note was in all numbers, nonsensical to most, but at least they'd know I wasn't murdered."

Holly cringed at the word. It was what people might assume when someone went missing without a note—like her sister.

"It took your wife a while to find you, right?" Holly asked. "To decode your numbers to longitude and latitude."

"That's right. Although I didn't know my wife would enlist the whole damn country to help her and draw a media bonanza while she was at it. I was almost retired by then, ya see. I'd given her everything she'd ever wanted or needed over the years, but she'd never been happy with me. She stayed in the marriage for the kids, but the last birdie was about to leave the nest, and I felt a divorce coming. After all my years of hard work, providing for my family, I finally had the time to spend with her, and she decided it was then that she didn't want to be with me anymore."

"Well, she must've loved you enough to find you," Holly said, thinking of her own marriage and how similar it sounded to Archie's. Would she even still be with Mark if it wasn't for the kids? Holly had been thinking of her own possible exit strategy only two nights earlier, locked in a jail cell because her husband was so terribly unforgiving. Was anyone truly happy? It made Holly wonder.

"You're wrong, my dear." He wrinkled his old brow.

"Well, no one goes to that much trouble to find someone if they don't care," Holly argued.

"They do if finding that person turns into an instant payment."

"What do you mean?"

"If Louise had found me, she could've divorced me and taken half of everything I'd worked so hard to save. Which was fine—she could have it; I'd made enough." Archie motioned around him. "But if they found me dead, she made out even better with a fat life insurance policy. The only problem with either of those scenarios was that if they didn't have a body, there was no payout."

"And going missing was your only way to give her the screw?" Holly made a fist and effectively twisted it in the air.

Archie laughed. "Yes, so being that they couldn't find me, she couldn't divorce me, and she couldn't cash in the life insurance policy, either, because there was no body. So she couldn't collect."

"Well, that's too bad if those were your wife's intentions."

"So now that that's out of the way . . ." He blew out an exaggerated breath.

Holly didn't want to laugh, because it didn't seem right with her sister missing. It didn't seem right to have happy feelings with her gone, but Archie was a character. It was the first time she'd felt the pressure lift even an inch since Vivian's frantic phone call.

"Why don't you tell me what you found along with that life insurance policy when you broke into your sister's house."

Holly shook her head, pushing a curl out of her eye. "Just Vivian's poetry. It seemed to get sadder and more erratic as time went on." Her voice wavered. "How did you know I found the life insurance policy there?" She was sure Clay knew it'd been her who'd given up the policy to the police, but something about it being public information made her jittery.

"The news broke the day after I bailed you out that Clay had recently upped the policy. It didn't take a rocket scientist to figure out that's what you'd found when you'd broken in. Good job. At least your stint in the slammer wasn't for naught." He laughed. "Just poetry or anything else?"

"Well, not at her house, but there is something else. The cops won't acknowledge it, but my sister was chatting with a man online before she disappeared. I printed out the chat sessions, and then someone broke into my house and stole them. When the police checked out Vivian's email account where the chat sessions were accessed, the chat history had disappeared. Someone must've deleted it."

Archie perked up and sat straight in his chair. "Holy smokes. Did you get any clues as to where the guy was located from reading them?"

Holly's nervousness abated just hearing Archie take interest in the chat sessions. Her husband had dismissed them because the cops had. Mark said if it were a solid lead, they would've followed it. Such a lazy answer.

"He lives on or near an island with a dog and a boat." Holly shrugged.

"That's it?" Archie asked.

Just as quickly as her hopes had been lifted, they deflated. "Yeah. I think he may be a librarian. How many islands can possibly have a library?" she asked hopefully.

Archie shrugged. "Lots, kid."

"Oh . . . well, he seemed really into her, telling her their connection was kismet, that the only thing he looked forward to every week was their chat sessions."

Archie cleared his throat. "I'm glad I wasn't a part of internet dating. Sounds strange."

"Agreed," Holly said. "Vivian also called me the night she disappeared and said someone else was there. Archie, you've been following the story. Tell me, what do you think happened to her? Do you think Vivian could still be alive?" Her voice broke. If Archie was some sort of expert in disappearing, maybe he'd seen or heard something that could help her.

Archie pointed at her again. "Here are my thoughts . . ." The sun had dipped between the clouds, as if to give Vivian a moment of silence. They sat there enjoying the day for just a minute before he spoke again. Archie shut his eyes, and Holly sipped her drink. She wondered if he'd fallen asleep, but then he said, "I hate to say it, but her husband has a mess of a life, mixed up with this crime family and their women. Men like that don't like it when you turn the tables on them. Maybe her husband found out she was talking to this guy, and he took her out. Had a little life insurance paper drawn up so he'd profit from it."

Holly gulped, remembering the way Clay had handled her that night at his house. "He's never shown signs of violence like this in the past," she said. *But he sure has in the present.*

He shrugged. "I'm not saying it was him, but he knows people."

Holly swallowed again; she didn't like these answers. "What's the alternative?" she asked, because there needed to be one. "And why take her out before she signed the papers?"

"Something went wrong, I think. But if your sister was unhappy, she had the best setup in the world for running away without anyone coming to look for her."

Holly jerked up. "What do you mean?"

"I remember the news saying she'd reported a man in her backyard, the same one she mentioned to you. Was there really a man?" Archie gave her a smart look.

"It's interesting that you ask that, because no one else saw this man. She was the only one," Holly said.

"It works for her either way; don't you see? The first time I heard it, I thought, *oh, that was the mob tailing her*. But maybe that's just what she wanted us to believe. Her husband told her not to report it so it wouldn't hinder his case. Selfish bastard."

"Yeah," Holly agreed, even though she'd given Vivian the same poor advice.

"But Vivian knew he would do that, didn't she? If he was embroiled in this scandalous case going to trial, she knew he wouldn't want her to report anything." Archie gazed at Holly with raised, frosted eyebrows, obviously waiting for her to get it.

Holly considered what he was saying. Vivian couldn't have planned something like this, even if it was to get away from her corrupt husband. Not without telling Holly, at least. But then she remembered something Vivian had said to her a long time ago. *"You know that if I really wanted to, I could hide and you'd never find me."* She closed her eyes at the chilling recollection.

"That doesn't sound like something Vivian would do," she said.

"Does whispering sweet nothings over the internet to a man she's never met sound like her?" Archie asked.

"Well, they weren't exactly doing that, but no." But neither had the leather jacket and the thick slab of mascara she'd been wearing the last time Holly saw her.

"People can turn into surprising creatures under the wrong circumstances. Maybe she found out about her husband's affair, and things got ugly. Maybe that crew he ran with saw her as a threat to the Gallo trial, a threat to one of their own, and she knew it. So she left behind a few things in her absence, like the phone call to you and the chat sessions. Clues to where she'd gone. The chat sessions must've been important, or they wouldn't have gotten stolen."

Holly's thoughts exactly. "But she didn't leave me the chats; I found them."

"She probably anticipated that."

Holly shook her head. "You're reaching."

"Am I? I was a statistician; my assumptions are usually based on calculated thoughts and facts."

"Vivian was smart, but she wasn't running scared," Holly said. "That desperation in her voice . . . it was . . . something new."

"Maybe new to you. She could've been struggling for a while. You mentioned the book of distressed poetry. Your mother was big into journaling. Used to hide hers in a fake book. A hollowed-out *Oxford English Dictionary*, of all dreaded things."

At Archie's wry look, Holly smiled, because she shared his hatred for the dictionary, always had. However, she'd never known her mother to journal, not in the traditional way people keep a diary anyway.

"Right," she said, but it was the mention of the poetry, the struggles, that had her thinking now. Had Vivian known she was close to death, or had she suspected it was coming?

Clay used to work for the DA. He probably had his hands shoved in the right pockets on the police force in the event Vivian had tried to come forward about his illegal dealings with Bellini's men.

Could Vivian have left behind clues to her own murder?

Holly got a chill and wrapped her arms around herself. "I was thinking of asking the cops to dig deeper for the chat sessions. I know the chats existed. I saw them with my own two eyes."

"You sure you want to do that? If theory number two is correct, maybe your sister was cutting ties with this life. And if she was in trouble and successful at cutting those ties, maybe you should let her go."

It didn't add up. If Vivian had been leaving willingly, she wouldn't have called Holly in a panic. "What?" Holly's head was spinning. He couldn't be serious. "I can't just give up on finding my sister!" Her pulse accelerated at the thought of letting Vivian slip away.

Just like when she'd watched Vivian leave for boarding school after what'd happened in their home that awful summer night.

Just like at Bay Shore Marina.

Archie looked at her seriously. "Well, then you have to figure out what clues to her whereabouts were in those chat sessions. Nobody else saw them, right? If they were stolen, I'm convinced there's something important in there."

"But that's just alternative ending number two." Holly's voice wobbled. "And you're leaning toward number one, aren't you?" Her chest burned. Vivian was dead, and it was all her fault. She hadn't saved her in time, and she'd lost the evidence to find her, and how could she ever live with herself?

"I'm not sure. I think you need to examine all your facts. You could always come back and talk to me when you figure out more, ya know? I'm pretty good at cracking codes."

"I will, thank you," Holly responded, but absolutely nothing made sense today.

Holly's palm was sweating on her purse. She could barely wait to get home and read the letter and search her whiteboard for more clues. Archie was right. The police hadn't taken the chat sessions seriously. There had to be more there.

He watched her carefully. "You need to go home and start researching. Come back when you've got something new for me." His half smile returned; Archie was enjoying her company.

"Are you kicking me out?" she asked playfully.

"You've got work to do, my dear."

"This is true. But what about the bail?"

"We can talk more about that later. It's not important why I bailed you out, only that you use your freedom to find the answers you're looking for."

She stood, feeling suddenly motivated to take this thing head-on. "Thanks, I'll be back," she said.

"I'm counting on it," he said.

24

My dearest Clay,

This will be the last time you hear from me, and I think you'll want to listen to what I have to say.

What a mess you've made of everything.

Destroying all my hard work with your lies, ruining my careful plans like a backhanded compliment.

I'd gotten rid of her for you just like you wanted, but you managed to screw it up anyway.

You always underestimated your wife, Clay, but I didn't.

I studied her closely, and so did my helpers. Your wife needed to feel heard, needed something to long for.

I know how to dangle the carrot, to feed that longing.

You told me hers was books. Did you know, Clay, there's a man who's a sucker for the ocean who loves reading too? He understood what made your wife tick, saw why you had loved her, gave her what you stopped giving, what she needed to feel whole.

How perfect for her to find what she needed, right?

All I needed was you. For you to wait for me. Until the time was right for us.

I even found a way to accept the fact that you were married. I created an acceptable spot for your wife in our lives, a temporary placeholder.

And that was okay because I had all the best parts.

I was the only one who shared your bed.

And your heart.

Or so I thought.

Until you went and upset the order of things. You know how I like balance, and there can be only one wife in our world.

The symmetry of two halves makes a whole, but splitting things into threes doesn't divide evenly. Why did you do that, Clay? She was your wife's friend, your next-door neighbor. You've proved to me now that I was just another placeholder, someone to pass the time, not someone to spend a lifetime with.

You betrayed me after everything I did for you. Things I've never done for anyone. The trouble I went through to make your wife disappear. I even left you the Polaroid to prove it.

The blood on my hands from my brother's trial will never wash off. And if there's anything I've learned from all of this, it's that you'll always put your own needs first. Before mine and before our daughter's. I can't have you in her life.

Please know, the only reason you're still breathing is because of our little girl. I know what it's like to have a father who's dead to this world. But please understand that your life continues only under the provision that you stay in the club, work for them. Burn this letter. If it resurfaces, I can't guarantee your safety. You know too much, and you also know what I'm capable of. Turning in this letter or moving out of state will be like cutting your own throat.

There's no proper way to make you understand how I've suffered, but watching what happens next will be the best revenge of all.

Deepest regards,

~ F

P.S. The boat is in my name, but it's yours now, keys enclosed. Russ's gift for all your hard work on his case and a gift to make up for selling our picture to the news. Too bad you'll never be able to go anywhere on it.

"Oh my God." Holly took a picture of Frankie's letter again with her phone. Then she took the printout and pinned it up on her war room board until she could make sense of it. The letter filled in so many blanks.

Vivian *had* been lured away, but not by Tom, entirely. Frankie had a hand in it. Or she'd paid some man who lived by the ocean to have a hand in it, but if her end goal was to lure Vivian away so she could kill her, why not just finish the job here, more simply?

Maybe she had. Holly thought again of Vivian's jacket.

She was sure now that the men Frankie ran with had killed poor Aliza Levine. It's what Frankie had meant when she said *the blood on my hands from my brother's trial will never wash off*. She'd made the message subtle, though, so even though she might not be able to wash it off, the statement didn't provide tangible evidence the police could use against her.

She hadn't admitted to anything.

Holly understood the Polaroid picture now too.

That photo of the woman was Vivian—maybe her last.

Holly could see it now. Sure, Vivian's hair had been cut and dyed, and she had sunglasses on, but it was her—Holly could picture it in her head. Vivian hadn't smiled like that often, but the smile that had been plastered on her face in that photo would be sealed in Holly's mind forever.

Mother had stolen Vivian's happiness along with her childhood after treating both her daughters like guinea pigs in her science experiments. Vivian had been desperate to prove their mother wrong, but in doing so, she'd lost a part of herself in that upstairs bedroom. Even after all her time away from the family, she hadn't come back from boarding school the same.

Vivian hadn't really wanted to sleep with Rico—not like that. She'd either felt like she had to in order to prove their mother wrong or— Holly didn't like to remember Rico's hands on her, his insistent kiss— she'd been pressured into it. Holly had never given much thought to what that actual experience had been like for her, if maybe she'd felt trapped once the bedroom door had shut. Perhaps Vivian had had a moment of alcohol-induced bravado on the way up the stairs but then changed her mind. They'd never talked about the incident, so Holly had no idea how Vivian felt about it.

Whatever had transpired between that night and her graduation from boarding school had deadened something inside Vivian. But in that Polaroid, for the first time since before Vivian had left for her senior year in high school, Holly had seen happiness in her sister.

The old Vivian. The daring, sharp-mouthed girl who'd challenged their parents and tried to save her little sister.

This made Holly more upset than almost everything else that'd happened, because it was all a ruse. A cruel joke. If her sister had found out that they'd fooled her, that her relationship with this man was based on lies, she might've not needed Frankie to off her. She might've done it herself.

This—what she'd just read—was something that might send Holly over the edge too. Which edge, though? The finding of the leather jacket made sense now. Frankie was trying to frame Clay for Vivian's demise by throwing the jacket in an area near his mistress's boat. The police would move their investigation to search the waters in Long Island Sound, but they wouldn't find anything, because Vivian didn't disappear into the sound; she'd disappeared from Bay Shore Marina. Frankie was using the jacket to move the scene of the crime away from the real crime scene and closer to Clay. Cunning little bitch.

It made Holly wonder when the Polaroid was taken. Frankie had wanted it to look like it was snapped after Vivian had disappeared. Holly wished she could take another look at the photo just to make sure it was her sister and not an optical illusion, but the image had vanished. She still had it in her purse, and it looked like the same overexposed image as when she'd discovered it, but when she shook it again, nothing appeared.

Holly swallowed, thinking about the type of people she was dealing with—the ones who'd also probably been crawling around in her bedroom stealing evidence. Who else would break into a home and steal only the contents of her day planner? They were the kind of people who made photographs and secret chat sessions and wives disappear. Vivian. Aliza Levine.

Vivian hadn't just been lured away.

She'd been tricked into leaving town for a fictitious man, a carefully crafted love interest, all so Frankie could dispose of her. Holly wondered if the man was even real or if Frankie had been the one sending the chat messages. *Poor Vivian.*

She blinked back tears.

Everything looked a little clearer after reading that letter, but she didn't think she wanted to see the whole truth now. It supported the first alternative to Archie's theory. Vivian was dead, and Frankie or her cousin's men were responsible for it. Holly gulped at the air, the dread of the letter fully settling in, gripping Holly tightly, like a fatal diagnosis for which there was no cure.

"Pull it together." She exhaled a shaky breath. Nothing would ever be normal again since these mobsters had gotten ahold of her family.

Holly clenched her fists. Mark was an only child, her parents were dead, and Frankie had taken Vivian too. She'd had to destroy what little family Holly had left. It was all such a tragedy. Holly wiped at her face again.

She had a greater desire than ever to find out what had happened to Vivian now. Maybe there was some evidence buried along with her sister that could further incriminate Frankie—the real murderer here. Because even if she hadn't pulled the trigger with her dainty little hands, she'd planned the whole thing with her evil mind, and she should pay.

The other line of that letter that had Holly reeling was that Frankie said she'd given Clay everything he'd ever wanted by getting rid of Vivian. Had Clay been in on it? Holly couldn't believe it was true because of how poorly everything had turned out for him.

The way Frankie had worded the letter sounded like she'd manipulated Clay too.

At least Clay would pay the ultimate price for bringing this on her sister and their family. He'd gotten greedy. Not only had he strayed in his marriage, he'd cheated on Frankie with Eve. According to Frankie's letter, he'd earned himself a life sentence working for the Mafia because of it—either that or sudden death.

Holly could take the letter to the police, but it was the same as slitting Clay's throat and possibly her own. She shivered. The letter had made it clear that Clay would be killed if Frankie's letter surfaced—and

Holly would surely be next on the list if anyone discovered she'd delivered the evidence.

And what about her boys?

Holly had never healed from her childhood wounds. Her mother's psychobabble remained a constant echo in her head; even the obituary exercise was enough to damage anyone. Holly's therapist had said that the obit exercise was one of the most warped things she'd ever heard of, and that was saying a lot, considering she'd been in practice for more than thirty years.

Dr. Fineberg attributed the exercise to Mother's own need for self-gratification. She'd wanted her children to recognize all she'd done, and she wanted to see it in writing. Holly's whole goal in life was to get her children through their formative years without any lasting bumps and bruises, although they'd surely felt some the last few days. Those were the kind that didn't leave physical marks that could be seen with the naked eye, but they were sometimes the most damaging.

It wouldn't be worth the trouble to turn over the letter and Polaroid to the police. There wasn't anything on the damn Polaroid anyway. Once again, Holly had no concrete proof of something she'd seen because the evidence had disappeared.

She sighed.

She could persuade the police to try to recover the image, but if they came up empty, they would think she was certifiably nuts again. Missing papers, vanishing photographs.

Archie's words from earlier came back to her. Since the chat session printouts had been stolen, they had to contain something important. Maybe Frankie hadn't anticipated anyone would find them so quickly, but she'd done a super job of deleting the content, both from Vivian's online account and from Holly's bedroom.

Holly was still grappling with the fact that Vivian had been tricked into actually listening to this man—Tom—and taking off for this island. But from reading the chat sessions, she also understood how it'd happened. Tom had seemed so real, so sincere. He was the person *Dateline* was talking about when they said the internet was dangerous.

And that Polaroid picture had said a thousand unspoken words too. The woman in that picture was in love with the man with the wet black hair standing behind her on the beach. Was it the last one Vivian had taken before Tom slit her neck?

A knock at her front door startled her.

Holly didn't know who it could be. She wondered if maybe her neighbor Mrs. Billings had locked herself out again. Since she'd turned eighty, it had been happening more and more, and Holly had a spare key to her house.

Holly flung open the door and almost threw up on the doorstep. She sucked in a huge, audible breath and must've looked like she was scared to death, because she was.

"Hello, Holly." It was Clay, and he sounded like a serial killer. "I'm sorry I haven't been in touch. I've been a bit preoccupied, as you can imagine."

She couldn't breathe. Her first thought was, *He's so sweaty.*

It wasn't a little spray around the hairline after a summer stroll; it was massive perspiration, the kind that occurred after a long sprint. His T-shirt and khaki shorts were soaked through, too, his face puffy and wet.

"Aren't you going to invite me in?" he asked with a wicked grin.

"No," she said. "Why don't you run to one of your girlfriends if you need somewhere to go?"

He rolled his eyes. "Now, Holly . . . I apologize. I've been dealing with a lot, but I need to talk to you."

"Well, that's too bad," she said without a lick of sympathy. "I needed to talk to you once, too, and you would've slammed the door in my face if the press wasn't standing right there. You brought this on yourself. I know what you did, and you can go to hell!" She tried to close the door.

Clay shoved his foot inside, and she jumped backward. "This won't take long."

Shit.

This man was a murderer. She needed to run or scream or call the police, but she was too stunned to move.

"I need to head to the store. I scheduled a curbside order at the grocery store, and I don't want to miss my time slot. I was just heading out the door." Maybe if she walked outside, that would save her. She lived on a very busy street. If Clay tried something, she could scream. Mrs. Billings wouldn't hear her, but someone else would.

"It's a good day for running, isn't it? The guy at the marina saw you running there today," Clay said.

Holly's throat closed shut. "You must be mistaken." Fear was making her words unsteady.

"I'm not mistaken." He had that same smile on his face that showed no teeth, reminding Holly of Patrick Bateman in *American Psycho*. Clay had been in her family for years, yet she felt like she was looking at a terrifying stranger for the first time.

"We don't own a boat." She found her voice. It became firmer, but her heart was beating so fast, she thought it might explode.

"I know that. I just want what you took from the boat you visited today. I came here to get what's mine, and then I'll leave you and the boys alone." His voice was dark and quiet.

She hated how he threw the boys in there, his own nephews. "What're you talking about? I wasn't at any marina. You need to go!"

Clay kicked the door with full force, and it blew back this time. She tried to scream, but he charged inside and moved behind her. Then he put his hand over her mouth and bent her forward before shutting the door behind him with his other hand and locking it. "Give me what you stole from me, you nosy little bitch."

Holly couldn't breathe. She'd taken a breath before he'd put his hand over her mouth, but she was beginning to feel woozy. Tears pricked at the corners of her eyes, and she wanted to fight back, but she'd turned to Jell-O in his arms. She'd never been a fighter. Not this kind, anyway.

Vivian was the fighter.

And now Vivian was dead. And she was next.

Clay bent her harder until she was almost touching the floor. Her mouth was pressed open from trying to scream, and his hand was slick and salty. He pushed her to the ground. When she was on her knees, he unleashed his sweaty palm from her mouth. "Where is it?" he yelled.

"What?" she asked, because she wasn't sure what he was looking for. She'd taken all the evidence and didn't think there were any cameras on that boat . . . but there might've been.

"Whatever was in this envelope." He slapped her in the face with it, and she realized her tragic mistake. She'd left the envelope. How could she have been so stupid? She had been in such a hurry to get out of the claustrophobic space that she'd left behind the damn empty envelope with his name on it.

She gulped for air and tried to steady her heartbeat. She imagined Clay reaching in and pulling out her heart until it stopped. But she could not die. Even though she loved her sister, she was a mother, and she needed to stay alive for her boys. If she left Mark to raise them, they'd become rigid assholes like him.

"I don't know what you're talking about," she said weakly.

Clay walked toward the dining room, leaving her in a pile of fear. She wanted to run for the door—*but God no, please don't go in the dining room! He'll see the war room.*

He turned back around and dragged Holly across the floor. "I don't want to hurt you. I just want what's mine!" He sure sounded like he wanted to hurt her.

"Ouch, Clay, stop it. Seriously, we're family." Holly was surprised at the way her body involuntarily shook as he pulled her along the fake hardwood. Even though she was the freeze-up queen, she'd always imagined being able to defend herself if she were attacked, but she'd been wrong. Holly had gone limp, just like always, and her sister wasn't there to help her.

Clay let out a hack of a laugh. "I realize you didn't grow up with a normal family, but this ain't it, sweetheart."

She watched as he eyed her laundry room with reproach, articles of clothing vomiting into the hallway. Then his eyes found the dining room, and his mouth dropped open in utter disgust. "Well, you've been busy."

He let her go, and she fell on her face as he examined her handiwork. The whiteboard had a corkboard attached to the bottom of it with his picture pinned up, along with lines drawn to Vivian's photo and then to Eve's and Frankie's.

"I was trying to find Vivian, no thanks to you!"

He laughed out loud, and he couldn't seem to stop himself. He'd totally lost it, and she just wanted him out of her house.

Clay plucked a tack out of the corkboard. The papers came apart and flew all over the place. "Are you fucking serious?"

Holly flinched. "I was just trying to find her." She stood now, balancing herself against a chair, terrified and embarrassed that the very man she'd been studying was standing in her research room staring at all his very personal information displayed for the world to see.

He picked up the boat registry off the dining room table.

"This says the boat is registered to Frankie." Clay looked at her.

Holly nodded. *Did he not know that?*

"Ha! That would explain why she left me the keys. I assume the rest of the information is in the letter you stole. Give it to me and I'll leave you alone," he said.

She shook her head. She knew she was being unreasonable here, arguing with her attacker, but he didn't deserve resolution. He deserved to sit up wondering what had happened to his life every night, as Holly had the last few. They always said during a robbery to just give up the goods, spare your life, but she didn't want to oblige, especially after he'd just roughed her up. *Asshole.* Holly had no idea what her sister had been dealing with. Holly would've believed in a virtual man far, far away, too—anything to get away from this one.

"It's not yours!" he screamed at the top of his lungs, and she slumped behind the chair. This wasn't worth it. She needed to stay alive for her boys, even though she was *so* close to figuring out the mystery. She had pictures of it all, she reminded herself. Holly stood up.

"This is my life you're playing with!" He began savagely ripping down pieces of her work, including the photo she'd snapped of Frankie's letter from the boat.

Holly prayed he didn't notice that particular one.

He didn't.

But then he darted to the kitchen table, where her purse was located.

"Wait!" She made a run for it.

Her phone, the letter, and the darkened photograph were all in there. Clay beat her to it, snatching her purse away by the strap.

"Is this where it is?" He held it above her head, reminding her of Mark, and then took her shoulders and pushed her into a kitchen chair so hard, it hurt her backside, reminding her nothing of her husband.

"Ow." She sniffled.

"You think that hurt? You just wait." He pounded his fist on the table inches from her face. She jerked in the air but remained seated. "Quit fucking with my life, Little Orphan Annie." She tried not to purse her lips, sure he'd said that because of her hair and her dead parents.

Clay took her purse and dumped it out on the nearby counter. The contents fell out, including the letter and the photograph. He snatched the photo. "Only shake once?" he asked, confirming he'd seen the Post-it note she'd left behind with the envelope.

She nodded.

"Are we done here?" Clay sifted through the other items, quickly grabbing the folded letter addressed to him and heading for the door.

She should let him go. She was out of the danger zone, but she had questions. And he was the only one who had the answers. "Maybe you can just tell me. Did you have Vivian killed, Clay? I miss my sister, you son of a bitch!"

He stopped in his tracks, almost tripping over the carpet as he turned around to face her. "If I had, wouldn't I have to kill you, too, then?" His voice was cold.

There it was: the threat she'd been waiting for. Danger prickled her already brush-burned arms and legs.

She didn't answer him. Her hands were still balled into fists, but she wouldn't move from the kitchen table. She could feel the blood leave her face, but she refused to look away from him. All her life, she'd chosen to look away—from the mental tortures of her childhood, hoping they'd disappear as time went by. She told herself she'd fix her fractured marriage later, too, when she had more time to focus on it, but she knew it was beyond repair. It was time to look the ugly in the face. And he was standing right there.

"I assume you won't be mentioning this incident to the police or your husband?" he asked.

"You wish," she seethed.

"I heard you've been having trouble with the law lately." He leaned closer to the door. She would need a drink after this.

"It's been handled," she lied.

"No, it actually hasn't. You have a record now, and you won't breathe a word about any of this or I'll have to tell them that not only have you broken into my house but that you also broke into Frankie's boat. Your fingerprints are likely everywhere." His words had an extra bite that felt like a smack. "And there were witnesses who saw you and no doubt cameras at the marina. I'm sure Mark wouldn't like it if I turned you in. Especially since he didn't care to bail you out the first time." He let out a ripple of laughter again.

She pulled a face. "Get out."

"I'm not a killer, Holly, and for that you should be grateful. But I know killers. And if you so much as sniff your backward-ass body in my direction again, it will be your last breath. Do you understand me?" He was standing by her front door, glaring at her now, dangerous.

"Yes," she said. And she did. She got it. Clay slammed the door behind him.

She was no detective. She should go straight to the police and tell them what'd happened, but then she'd have to admit what she'd done to get the information, and Clay would press charges, and she really would go to jail this time.

And Mark wouldn't bail her out and neither would Archie.

It wouldn't be worth it, either, because the letter and the picture didn't say anything of substance. But they'd said everything to Holly. And if she got locked up, who would bring justice to Vivian?

Frankie was clever, but she wouldn't outsmart Holly. Holly grabbed a glass of water and rinsed her mouth out in the sink to rid herself of the taste of Clay's sweaty flesh. Then she reached below the sink, pulled out her hidden flask, and took the largest swig of clear liquid she'd ever taken in her life.

25

The numbing aftermath of being dragged along her foyer by her brother-in-law lasted until she heard the echo of Mark's screams when he came home and found her drunk. Holly was a high-functioning alcoholic, though, and she'd cleaned up the mess Clay had made of the war room. She knew she didn't smell of alcohol, because it was vodka she'd drunk, and she hadn't spilled any.

But still, somehow Mark knew right away.

His yells sent the boys, freshly home from practices, running upstairs. "So this is what's going to become of you? One hard bump in the road and you're going to turn into your mother?"

Holly couldn't look at him or respond. She was so tired, and the marks on her skin were turning purple from where Clay had grabbed her, and she couldn't tell her own husband about it. She didn't feel comfortable confiding in Mark, and she feared Clay's threats that he'd press charges against her for breaking and entering if she did. Worst of all, they could take her boys away from her, and Mark would let them. He would say she was unfit to care for them, especially now that he'd caught her drinking.

Holly tried to explain that she'd had a hard day and that she'd just had a drink to quiet her nerves, and what was the harm in that? But the truth was that she'd drained the whole flask again. She wouldn't have to drink if she didn't live with a man who referred to her sister vanishing into thin air as *"one hard bump in the road."*

This was more than a fucking bump.

This was a crater that she would never climb out of. The only thought that had repeated in her head after she'd drunk the alcohol was that she needed more for next time. And then he said *it*. And she'd never be able to look at him the same.

"Look at you. You're just like your mother! Is that what you want for your kids, for them to find you the same way you found her?"

Holly just stared at him and blinked until he finally left the room. Never before was it so apparent how Mark used every sneaky way he could to control her. He'd never even met her mother. He only knew how deeply her death had wounded Holly. In her determination to face the ugly, she'd discovered that Mark might be the most hideous. Clay's physical offense was harsh, but Mark's verbal abuse over all these years was no doubt more damaging.

All her life, people had tried to control her. Holly saw the parallels now, the vicious cycle for both her and her sister. Their parents had used them for their work and made it look like a favor. It was how they'd expressed their love.

They'd manipulated their children into being the people they wanted them to be. And Holly and Vivian had gone on to marry manipulative men just like their parents, men content to keep them under a perfection microscope and doing their bidding.

Maybe Vivian had finally broken free. Holly might be next.

She was damn sure she wasn't going to die at the bottom of a bottle like her mother.

Holly's mother had been found dead by their father, hunched over her research, which was in disarray on her desk. The documents had been crusted with coffee and booze and vomit. The paper she'd been working on hadn't been going well—a spin-off of Elizabeth Loftus's memory research known as the Lost in the Mall technique, which suggested that memory implantation was possible if repeated to the person enough times that it became their truth. Loftus claimed a person could be convinced that they'd been lost in a shopping mall as a child.

No one needed to convince Holly. Memories of her hide-and-seek mishap at Green Acres came flooding back now, the edges blurry, like a bad photo.

Loftus had been a psychologist at the University of Washington in the nineties, but by the time her experiment had garnered academic attention, it was the early to mid-2000s. Holly was out of college, Vivian newly married. Her study was controversial, but Mother had jumped right on her bandwagon. Mother had been interested in the concept of memory implantation long before the study was published, intrigued by a Canadian neurosurgeon's earlier work that suggested the temporal lobe, a part of the brain responsible for memory, could be influenced to alter memories, if not in whole, then in part.

Loftus's study had given Mother's ideas impetus. She'd believed in Loftus's research so firmly that she'd convinced her university to provide a grant to perform a similar study. Mother's chosen scenario was Lost at the Beach, a sequel of sorts to the original study, which had somewhat recently come under fire for its ethical problems.

The university agreed to run the trial, but Mother's research project was flawed. Part of the inclusion criteria was that all the participants had to have been to the beach at least once in their youth. The study investigated two theories: that damaging events that occurred in a participant's childhood could be altered to make them forget—a bad day at the beach that they came to remember as neutral or even pleasant—or that partially new memories could be implanted. Mother had asked each subject for a photograph from a youthful visit to the beach, then repeatedly exposed them to a fabricated event that had occurred to them during the same period.

She'd blamed her failure on the participants being too old to have their memories altered, but the end result was that neither component of the trial had succeeded. Even till her death, Mother hadn't let go of her theories.

Thinking about it now reminded Holly of the time Vivian had almost been left at Fire Island when they were little. It also made Holly think of the location they'd taken the ferry from that day.

The location, Bay Shore, meant something; she was sure of it. Why had Vivian gone there during the storm?

Holly thought about what Vivian had said to her on the ferry ride home the day she was almost left behind.

Holly had slung her arm around her sister that day. Their parents had looked picturesque, Mother in a striped linen dress, flat sandals, brimmed hat, and sunglasses to hide the cruelty on her face, dark hair flapping behind her like an opaque flag. They'd seemed unbothered by the trauma they'd just caused their older daughter, but Holly could see that Vivian was still scared, and Holly was trying to comfort her.

"Someday I'm going to leave and never come back," Vivian had said.

"I hope you do," Holly had said, but she knew her sister was just upset. They were too young to go anywhere on their own.

"You know they don't log passengers on the ferry?"

"What do you mean?" Holly asked.

"At an airport, you have to show a ticket in your name. A bus too. Not on this boat. You could just pay and ride, and no one would ever know you were aboard."

Holly had thought about this and had immediately decided her sister had been planning to run away. And that she'd thought far enough ahead to plan how to do it undetected. These were the days before security cameras were everywhere. It made Holly shudder to think that even if there were cameras now, it might be easy to evade them on a ferry. She didn't know why she was thinking about this. But it mattered, didn't it? All of it. That day on Fire Island. The way their mother had reacted.

The study. Mother had become obsessed with the Lost at the Beach study, which kept failing to meet its clinical endpoint, to the extent that the university had threatened her employment if she didn't shut it down.

She'd drunk herself to death first instead.

Cirrhosis of the liver, so severe that when she died, her liver had actually burst from years of scarring that'd led to infection. The disease had caused the alcohol that she had inhaled for years to become poisonous, spreading to her blood and oozing out of her body from her mouth, a mixture of brown, foul-smelling bile and fat.

Toxic.

So when Mark said those horrible words—that Holly had become just like her mother—he'd known what he was suggesting.

And one thing was for sure: she would never forgive him for it.

When Father had found Mother, and Vivian and Holly arrived on the scene, he wouldn't let them upstairs, but they'd both insisted. Holly wasn't sure now why she'd been so eager to see the body, but if there was any moment in time she could take back, the one thing in the world she could unsee, that would be number one on her list. She hadn't wanted to see her mother for the reason most people might've assumed, that she needed closure.

No, it was to make sure the witch was really dead.

Holly hadn't believed it until she saw it with her own two eyes. Her mother, reduced to a pile of her own mess before her sixtieth birthday.

"She missed the obituary date I chose by twenty years," Vivian had said with no inflection in her voice.

"Twenty-two for me," Holly whispered, and it was the first time either of them had conferred on their answers for the obituary journal assignment.

In the true order of things, Father had died six months later of a massive heart attack. Out of the two parents, he'd been an adequate nurturer, although Vivian and Holly both knew he could've done a better job protecting them from *her*.

Neither of her parents was any type of model anyone should follow. Dr. Fineberg had confirmed these thoughts. *"Find your allies in life and keep them close. Let all the rest fall by the wayside. Don't waste your energy on people who drain yours."*

It was some of the best advice she'd gained from therapy. And Vivian, despite their differences and the periods of distance between them, had been an ally. Holly owed it to her sister to figure out what had happened and preserve her memory. But she needed help. When she searched her brain, she thought of one person—Archie.

He'd told her to come back when she had more information, and she did.

He didn't owe her a thing. In fact, she owed him for bailing her out. She couldn't go to the police now, because Clay would clobber her with criminal charges. And there was only a small chance they'd take her word that the gray leather jacket was a false lead.

While the detectives were wasting their time swimming around in the sound, Holly had to use her resources to find Vivian. She remembered what Archie had said about her mother's dictionary, and she wanted to check it out. She'd kept one bin with her own journals dating back to elementary school. It seemed a waste to throw away all that hard work, even though she'd hated writing every single word. She'd packed the dictionary in the bin at the time only because she thought it was an awful shame to throw it out, a hardback, in good condition. She'd wait until Mark and the kids were out of the house tomorrow to dig it up.

Another half of a week gone already, and her sister hadn't been found. With an empty house, it was time to investigate the dreaded bin. Holly walked down the unfinished basement steps and moved quickly toward the far corner, the one she never visited. She swatted away cobwebs as she pulled down the Rubbermaid bin, the feel of the dry residue on the top scratching against her fingertips and chilling her to the bone. She carried it upstairs, because she couldn't see anything in her dungeon of a basement.

When Holly opened the lid, even though it was plastic, it creaked like she was unfastening a lid to a coffin. That's how it kind of felt too. Her belly rumbled with unsettlement. It wasn't a box she'd ever really intended to reopen.

She reached her hand inside and palmed a stack of lined books held together with shoestring. The mere touch of the journals brought horrible feelings to the surface, reliving those awful moments at the kitchen table in the winter, the back porch in the summer, when their mother would breathe over them to *write*.

Her hands shook.

She wished she had more vodka, and that's why it was good that she'd drained the flask. She'd have just a sip to quiet her hands—but it wouldn't be enough—and then she'd have more.

Holly dropped the stack of journals, wiping a tear from her face, mad at herself that they could evoke such strong emotions. She didn't want to give her mother the power to make her weep from the grave.

Then she saw it, the dictionary Archie had mentioned. Maybe Mother did have an entry or two about herself jammed in between the pages. Holly had concluded later in life that she really knew nothing about her mother.

Her curiosity was getting the best of her, and she picked up the dictionary. It was featherlight, too light to be a real book packed with pages and not nearly heavy enough to contain every word in the English language.

It was a false book, and something was rattling around inside it.

Holly hadn't noticed it years ago when she was trying to clean out their parents' big, old house, shoving things in boxes and dumpsters, hoping the memories would be disposed of with them.

She had to really use her hand muscles to pry open the dictionary cover. It snapped off with a *pop*. There was a bit of dust that tickled her nose as she waved it away to see a small journal inside—her mother's journal.

How in the world did Archie know about it?

Holly picked up the tiny, nondescript black notebook and opened it to find her mother's equally tiny handwriting. Holly's memory was jogged, and she did recall seeing her mother write in this book, but she'd assumed it was an address book or a calendar planner. Holly breezed through the dated entries and noted they were all from the nineties.

She was most curious about the last summer they were all home, and she found herself on an entry dated September 1997, right around the time Vivian would've been sent off to boarding school after her July stunt with Rico. If Holly closed her eyes, she could still see the baseball-size welt around her sister's eye from where Mother had smacked her. It was the one and only time she'd ever gotten physical with either one of them.

Rico had not only left their house in a hurry after that, but his whole family had actually moved. Mother had learned that his father's business did the landscaping for the university where she worked, and she'd pulled some strings to get them to cancel his contract, which was Rico's father's largest account.

When Vivian heard the awful news, she'd protested, but their mother had defended herself, saying, *"Can't have that sleaze around me pruning the bushes while I'm walking to work. Lots of businesses require landscaping. He'll find work elsewhere."*

Holly despised her mother by that point. They both did.

She read an entry close to the end of the journal to get some clarity, but she read it through parted fingers because it was hard to "hear" her mother's voice in her head again, even through scattered words on a paper.

September 22, 1997

Dear daughter,

I know you think I've failed you because of what has happened, but what you have to realize is that you've failed yourself. Your decisions were yours and yours alone to make. Even though I placed the land mines in your way, you didn't need to step on them with such enthusiastic recklessness, jumping on every trigger until you could feel them all exploding at your feet.

You took no precautions in your pursuit to prove me wrong, and as a result, you endangered yourself and compromised your future. Someday you'll see that this was the only way to ensure you reach the greatness you were destined for, by ridding you of your mistake.

It was a giant mistake, and we'll all move on from this.

Well, a very small mistake. The only thing that made it large was the fact that it had its own heartbeat.

I've learned my lesson here as well. Studies are for work and not home. I'll no longer journal about them either.

Until we meet again, Professor Cynthia Forester

26

Holly crouched on the floor between the fireplace and the sofa, the bin resting between her legs like she'd just given birth to a hideous beast. The lie her family had been covering up all these years, the big secret they'd been keeping from her was larger than she could've ever anticipated. Holly felt dizzy after reading her mother's journal entry, which read more like a letter to Vivian than anything else.

A tear trailed down her cheek, but she couldn't feel anything at this point. Her truths were tangled, and she needed to at least get them right in her head.

Her sister. Who was she? Who had she been? She'd changed so much from her junior summer to who she'd become. Holly remembered the day she'd left for private school to start her senior year of high school.

Holly would've thought she'd be devastated, leaving the friends she'd grown up with, going somewhere new, but she was strangely quiet, waiting at the bottom of the steps with her floral suitcases and taped boxes, her nineties bangs in full bloom to hide any emotion in her eyes. They'd been kept separate the rest of the summer, and Holly had been bowled over with feelings of sadness that her older sister was leaving and she didn't know when she'd see her again.

"There'll be a fall break," she'd said to Holly. Vivian didn't seem to be having the same feelings of grief. She'd pushed a curl out of Holly's eye. "Don't let them mess with you while I'm gone."

That was the worst of it, Holly's biggest concern—that Vivian was leaving her to fend for herself. Holly feared their parents had messed with Vivian in ways Holly wasn't aware of. Vivian had been keeping something from her that day, her aloofness a cover for everything she couldn't tell her.

Vivian hadn't been sent to boarding school because she'd slept with Rico. She'd been sent away because she'd slept with Rico and had gotten pregnant, and their mother had made her get an abortion against her wishes.

"Oh God, Vivian." Why hadn't she told her? What a huge secret to keep all to herself.

Holly remembered the hushed arguments between her mother and Vivian that usually ended in crying and screaming. She'd always assumed it was because of what'd happened with Rico. It was, but for an entirely different reason than Holly had thought.

Father had gotten into it, too, with Vivian and Mother one night, and Holly had peeked her head out of her bedroom door to see what they were yelling about, because Father rarely raised his voice. They'd caught Holly right away, and everyone had gone immediately silent.

"Go back to bed; this doesn't concern you!" Mother had crowed. Holly had quickly shut her door.

Holly was sure up until the day her mother died that she had never blamed herself for what had happened with Vivian and Rico. The story she'd told was that Vivian was sent away for bad behavior. There was no mention of the fact that she'd left her teenage daughters alone with an older boy, one she knew they both found attractive. Maybe she thought there was safety in numbers and that Vivian wouldn't do anything with Holly there, but just like her memory project, Mother's experiment was tragically flawed.

She hadn't accounted for the fact that Rico might bring alcohol.

Or that Vivian and Rico would disappear upstairs.

Or that Rico wouldn't wear a condom if they did.

Holly shivered at the fact that it could've been her. It was funny how her memory of the incident had changed now that she'd read her mother's journal entry. Rico had wanted Holly first, and Vivian had stepped in. Holly had been annoyed with Vivian for treating her like a little kid. But now she saw it for what it really was. One of them had to prove their mother wrong, and it couldn't have been Holly; she was too young.

Vivian wasn't treating her like a baby. She was protecting her.

All the pain Vivian had lived with over the years could've been Holly's. And that child was the only one Vivian could've ever had. Later in life, she was unsuccessful bringing a pregnancy to term. Holly was furious that her entire family had kept this giant secret from her, making her feel more alienated than she ever had before.

Holly the outsider.

Then again, maybe it was the thing that had kept her alive, because they were all gone, and she was still here. Holly swallowed a lump in her throat at the morbid thought. She clicked the top of the bin shut and held on to Mother's little black book.

She'd failed Vivian in more ways than she could've ever dreamed that summer, and she wouldn't fail her again now. Holly had to find out what had happened to her sister.

She'd save her this time, or at least the memory of her.

Vivian hadn't taken her own life. Something or someone had taken her, and Holly was going to prove it.

She pushed herself off the floor and took a deep breath. She'd written down as much as she could remember from the chat sessions; she just didn't know what to make of them.

Upstairs, Holly grabbed a pen, not a pencil. A pencil was too reminiscent of the past. A pencil left room for error. She needed to get this right. Then she walked into the dining room and looked at her clues. What writing exercise might her mother have used to try to solve this? She thought about the most painful facts her sister had uncovered. Her mother's awful voice echoed in her head:

Journal about what the two women, Frankie and Eve, meant to Vivian, particularly the illegitimate child.

Holly wrote the answer from Vivian's point of view, finally putting her old journaling skills to good use.

I knew he hadn't been faithful for a long time, but what I didn't realize was that his affairs would be so deeply personal. First, the neighbor who I'd imagined was my friend all these years, a woman who lived next door, one we'd dined and vacationed with.

You made fun of her, my dear. You said Eve was brainless and shallow and wore too much makeup and too little clothes. So I know that she could not be the reason I am not here. You would not ruin your self-important image and threaten your beloved business and sacrifice all you had for a woman you could not hold a conversation with. That is not your way, Clay. You're way too intellectual for that.

No, it's the other one. She's the threat. The cunning little dark-haired girl. The one who gave you the child I couldn't. That's the heartbreaker. The killer. It's her.

Holly's hand cramped up, and she threw the pen across the room. "Go to hell!" she shouted at her dead mother. Somehow, this was all her fault. If they'd only had normal childhoods, maybe they would have married nice men and led average lives. But Dr. Cynthia Forester had just helped Holly from the grave. Her damn writing exercise had worked. The boat and the jacket had been huge, but Holly needed to be sure.

Whatever had happened to Vivian, it led back to Frankie.

Holly took her mother's journal as well as Vivian's poetry book. She'd written down what she remembered of the chat sessions and brought those notes with her, too, along with a printout of Frankie's letter. Her head felt like a freshly rung cymbal after reading her mother's little black book. She took a ginger pill and washed it down with a left-over bottled water once she was in her minivan. It would taste better if she could gulp it down with vodka, but she had to drive.

She didn't know where to go, how to find Frankie. But Archie, the statistician, might.

The thought of seeing him again made her heart lighten a bit. She still couldn't believe he'd managed to make her laugh yesterday. And he'd led her to her mother's hidden journal. He was helping her. But why?

It was early Wednesday morning and Archie wasn't on the porch, but his car was parked in the driveway, an old Cadillac sedan. Holly smirked because she could picture him rolling around town in it.

When she knocked on the door, he cracked it open with a coffee in his hand.

"Holly, my dear! I knew you'd be back." Archie's winning smile was pressed across his face. Why had Louise wanted to divorce him? Perhaps she'd grown weary of his humor after so many years of marriage. Holly didn't think she could ever tire of it after the humorless marriage she'd endured for so long.

"Hi, Archie. I'm sorry it's so early. I needed someone to talk to about Vivian's case. Do you have a minute? I wanted to pick your brain."

"Well, I don't know how much is left to pick, but you can try." He let out a dry laugh that turned into a cough. "Please come in."

She walked into Archie's home and was pleasantly surprised that it was clean and tidy just like the outside. A large grandfather clock stood tall and straight in the foyer, just like Archie. The hardwood was a shiny cherry. There were a few family pictures on the walls, mostly very old photos, some of him and his ex-wife, most of his children as little kids, which Holly thought was heartbreaking. His foyer was like a time capsule of the era before he'd gone missing.

"Coffee?" he asked.

"That sounds perfect."

They sat at his kitchen counter. Archie was so tall, he just sort of leaned on the stool with one hip. Holly wondered if it was bothering him and if Archie had anyone at all to help take care of him at his age. He poured her coffee into a large stoneware mug. "Cream or sugar, sugar?"

She smiled. "Black, thank you." Holly hopped up on the stool with her papers. She placed her fingers around the mug, enjoying the burn on her hands.

"So tell me, kid, what did you find?" he asked.

Holly tried to think of the best way to convey the information. "Have you ever felt like you're the only person on the planet who could figure out a giant puzzle?"

"Actually, I do. It was my job for years." The reverent statistician showed Holly his toothy grin. She'd done her research on the old man, and he'd been so good at his job at the university that the government had contracted him out to help crack code.

"Well, I've never had the opportunity to feel like that, and it's weird, but it's almost like Vivian left this behind for me to figure out."

Archie leaned forward. "Why do you say that?" He took a slug of his coffee.

"There're things only I would know."

She thought about those things again. She hadn't been able to stop. The location of Vivian's disappearance. How Vivian had almost been lost near that same spot years ago. Her mother's study on being lost. The chat session on getting lost with a man she barely knew. Holly couldn't put her finger on it, but she knew there was a connection somewhere. "And she called *me* when she was in trouble instead of the police. Maybe it was because I was the only one she could trust. Here's what I remember from the chat sessions that were stolen."

She passed the re-created chat sessions across the counter to Archie.

"They're not exact, but I did my best from memory," Holly said.

She thought of Loftus's study and her own memory, and she wondered how much her mother had messed with theirs, even on their little excursions. Mother had been interested in the topic of memory implantation long before her university study, and Loftus's work provided validation for her ideas. For as many failed studies as Mother had, she'd had twice as many successful ones. Holly and Vivian had been her favorite subjects.

"Okay." Archie took the papers, and she could tell he was reading because he moved his lips as he did.

Holly took out a pen she'd packed and began writing again. She hated journaling to find the answer, but it'd worked earlier. And journaling was the common thread, the pain, that connected her to her sister. She'd shut down that part of herself, but in reopening it, she was gaining the clues she needed to find Vivian.

She wrote: *Green Acres Mall (1991). Subject: Holly, left alone, eight years old.*

Subject unharmed.

Result: Holly angry with her sister, felt betrayed.

"It sounds like she was very much into this Tom, and you think he was luring her?" Archie asked.

"I do." Holly looked up. "I also think Clay's mistress, Frankie Gallo, set it up. I have evidence of that. I'll show you that next."

Archie lifted his eyes slowly from the papers. "*Whoa.* Not good, kid. Not good. Your poor sister."

"I know." Holly shook her head, still wondering why Vivian hadn't confided in her. She never had, really, and after she'd been sent away for school, their divide had only grown. Holly wondered if it was because Vivian blamed Holly for what'd happened with Rico.

Archie raised his frosted eyebrows and breezed through the papers, still moving his lips, still reading. "Well, all this tells me is that she trusted this man, and she likely tried to go wherever he is, but there's no clues as to where that might be. He lives on a boat near the ocean."

Holly knew it wasn't much to go on, but thinking back to her mother's and Loftus's studies made Holly reflect on Green Acres. Could Vivian be playing hide-and-seek again? And the ferry. Vivian had told Holly once that if she wanted to, she could leave on a ferry and never come back. Coincidence?

Come out, come out, wherever you are, Vivian.

Vivian had left Holly some clues at the mall. She'd told Holly she was interested in going to the arcade. Then she'd smartly figured out a way to get there and even managed to bring home a prize. Even though Vivian had been chastised for her little stunt, she was clever and sneaky. Holly wondered if Vivian had done the same thing here.

Holly looked at Archie hopefully, nodding. "And?"

Archie looked up at her with a snarky grin. "And there are four gigantic oceans that cover seventy-one percent of the Earth's surface, and Vivian could've traveled to any one of them." Archie threw up his hands dramatically, and Holly couldn't hide her disappointment. The corners of her mouth fell into a frown, but it did make her feel better just talking this over with someone.

"I need more to go on, or you need to shake down your brother-in-law or this Frankie if they were in on it."

"Frankie took off with the kid. Clay's kid," Holly explained.

"Yeah, heard about that on the news. Real winner, that one."

Holly looked down at her wrists and palmed the bruises. She didn't want to cry on this man's shoulder about what Clay had done to her, but she could sure use a good cry. It was better to keep the real victim at the top of Archie's mind, though, so he could help find Vivian. "What you didn't hear on the news is that Vivian and Clay couldn't have children. I think Vivian might've found out about the little girl right before she went missing."

Holly thought about the PO Box. Vivian hadn't put it all together at first, but she at least knew there was another woman at that point. If Vivian knew about Clay's mistress, chances were she might know about their little girl too. Finding the PO Box had occurred the week before the storm. "It's the only reason I think she might've jumped. It wouldn't have been the mistress, or mistresses, for that matter. It would've been the child."

Of course, there was no evidence of the PO Box—just like the chat sessions, it'd vanished into thin air. These details were the only things that made Holly pause. Frankie's people could make Holly disappear without a trace too. She needed to stay alive for her boys, but she owed it to her sister to find out the truth.

Holly clenched her teeth, thinking of the information she'd just learned about her sister from her mother's journal. She instinctively pulled out the black book, wondering if she should show it to Archie. She didn't know if it was even relevant.

"Wow. So you did find your mother's dictionary?" Archie straightened in his chair, pointing to the book.

Holly was more than surprised he recognized it. "Yes. You seem to have been closer to my mother than I realized."

He paused midstep. "So you did read it?"

"Just a little. I'm not sure I want to read the rest." She squirmed at the memory of her mother's later entries and Vivian's final poetry entry too. They were eerily similar. Both about Vivian's lost babies. She had to hold on to Archie's countertop as the powerful short verses flowed through her head. Now she knew exactly what Vivian's poem written in erratic handwriting was all about, and it was devastatingly sad.

I Remember You

> I remember you, but you never knew me
> Tiny hands and feet
> I remember you, but you'll never know me
> And we'll never get to see all you could be
> Would you have gotten your dad's dark eyes or
>   my gray and blue?
> I remember you, but you didn't get to stay
> I'll always regret the day
> I didn't stand up for you
> Every September fifteenth, I think of you
> And I still remember you

"Guess we can both use some of this." Archie pulled out a giant pitcher of something red with ice cubes and fruit floating inside it. This man was full of comical surprises. "I don't expect anything from you after all this time. I know a get-out-of-jail-free card is hardly a consolation for any of it. Just remember we were all different people back then and try not to judge me too harshly."

He poured himself a glass, and Holly had no idea what he was talking about, but she was pleasantly distracted by the sting of the alcohol rising up to greet her nose. *Birds of a feather,* he and her mother. But what had he meant by *"we were all different people"*?

"You want a glass?" Archie asked.

"Definitely." Holly let him pour, but she had a sudden urge to stand, so she strolled around Archie's kitchen. She'd felt the energy in the room shift since she pulled out the black book, and Holly couldn't figure out why. He obviously thought he had a part in Mother's journal, and that confused Holly. Why would her mother include him in it? Had she done a study on Archie? The tousled hairs on the back of her head stood on end.

She picked up a framed picture of a woman standing in front of a garden.

"That's my mother. She was nothing like yours." Archie laughed.

Holly laughed too. "No one quite was." The lady in the photograph had curly hair and a big smile. It was black and white, but Holly could clearly make out Archie as a little boy holding her hand. His mother was holding the watering can with the other hand, and two smaller girls were on either side, helping her.

"She was a strong lady. Holocaust survivor. I think you got her hair."

Holly set the picture back down. "That's amazing. You mean my hair reminds you of hers?" she clarified. She thought of how unremarkable her own mother's life was. A terrible mother, a subpar wife, a decent professor, but in her pursuit to leave her mark on the world, she'd caused more harm than good.

"No, I mean because technically, she's your grandmother," Archie said.

It took a minute for the words to sink in. Her grandmother's hair? Archie's mother. Archie was saying he was her . . . "You think you're my—" She couldn't finish the sentence.

"Well, yeah, I'm pretty sure. You don't have to say the word, haven't acted like one so I don't deserve the title. You look surprised. You said you read the journal." Archie appeared nervous now. He chugged down some ruby liquid. "Isn't it in there?"

She stared at the man. It made so much sense and no sense at the same time.

The realizations of all her mother's evils, all the harms she'd caused others, were never-ending and life-shattering. That's why her father had despised Archie so much. Had he known? Or just thought Mother was infatuated with him?

"How do you know?" she asked.

"I don't for sure. But I always suspected. You look just like my mother, first off. I'll show you a picture from when she was around your age if you want," he said.

"I don't." Holly didn't want to see it. She couldn't see any more today.

"Okay." He put his hands up in defense.

She couldn't be mad at Archie, though. It was *her*—Cynthia Forester—she did all of this.

"I'm sorry she got to you too," were the words that rolled out of her mouth. She knew they weren't the right ones. "Archie, I don't know what to say about this."

"She insisted you weren't mine. I should've pushed for a test. I've made a lot of mistakes, kid." His hand shook a bit as he drank. When he pulled his glass away, his eyes were serious, but his lips were painted a rouge color, and all Holly could think in that moment was that she wanted to get back to the place where she could laugh with this man, because she hadn't laughed with anyone in ages.

She remembered Dr. Fineberg's words—*"Find your allies in life and keep them close. Let all the rest fall by the wayside."* Holly didn't have many allies, but Archie was one of them.

"Haven't we all made mistakes?" she said, and she hoped it was acknowledgment that she wasn't perfect either. And unlike her mother, Holly didn't expect everyone in her life to be flawless.

She needed to think about this new information. But for now, she was happy her immediate family wasn't all gone or perished. There was one person left. She didn't know him, but maybe she could get to know him. "We'll get back to the family stuff once I've processed my other family stuff. Deal?" she asked.

"Fair enough," he said quickly, sucking down more of his drink. He seemed relieved to move on from the conversation.

"This question is going to sound odd, but do you think my mother could've implanted memories in our heads? Mine and Vivian's?"

"Oh, I know she tried. It was something she'd been working on even before the Loftus trial. And your mother was never much concerned about professional ethics when it came to her studies."

Holly inhaled sharply and placed her cup down, the blood draining from her face. How much of her life was real? How many of her childhood memories were false?

"She was a crazy old bird. If I would've known you were mine for sure, I would've fought for you, but she insisted, and I mean insisted, you were not. You girls also seemed happy, and I didn't want to break up a family," Archie prattled on. He thought this was about him. It wasn't. Although she could've used rescuing long ago.

Holly shook her head. "Give me a second." She had been inundated with information faster than she could manage it today. But the fuzzy memories—the one at the mall and the one at Fire Island the day Vivian was almost left there—something was off about them. The one at Fire Island felt real until they were boarding the ferry, when Vivian was nowhere to be found. How had her sister just disappeared from her side and Holly hadn't noticed? Holly could still feel the fear of that moment, but the picture was blurry, like a television that'd lost its signal.

The soft wisp of the words *partial memory* filled Holly's mind. Vivian had insisted that she'd been almost left on the island that day. Had Mother only implanted that?

"Archie, the memories in the implantation study. Did they . . . look different to the patient? Colors and such?" Holly couldn't explain it well. There was no way to crack open someone's brain and take a snapshot of their thoughts, but she hoped he understood what she was trying to say.

"Yeah, sure. She'd studied Wade, too, who had made people believe they'd ridden in a hot-air balloon when they hadn't by showing them pictures of the balloons. Fifty percent of participants believed they'd taken a balloon ride when they really hadn't."

"That's right," Holly said in a low voice, remembering that study. Her mother had been obsessed with it too. More so than Loftus's, but luckily, Holly was out of the nuthouse by then.

"Were there any physical elements that she showed you from the memories you suspect weren't real, like toys or anything?" Archie asked.

Holly sucked in a breath and held it there, remembering the teddy bear with the dress from the mall, the one that had sat on the top of her dresser until she'd left for college, and the bottle of sand from their trip to Fire Island beside it. Almost every time their mother had mentioned the incidents, and she'd done it many times to try to turn Holly and Vivian on each other by reminding them of the way they'd each betrayed the other, she'd taken the items and placed them in front of her. Holly hadn't recalled it until the very moment Archie had mentioned it, but Mother always had props with her.

A picture is worth a thousand lies.

Mother rarely took pictures, but she did have photographs of herself in that striped linen dress with the hat and her father standing on the ferry next to her clothed in resort casual apparel. She'd said it was from the same day they'd taken that fateful trip to Fire Island when Vivian was almost left behind, and perhaps it was, but Holly hadn't recalled anyone taking a picture that day. It could've been a half-truth, one she'd used to cement the false half. That's why the first part of the memory was clear but the second half, where Vivian had been almost left, was fuzzy.

Wade's study wasn't published until 2002, but the clinical trials to prove her theories were done before that. It made sense that Mother would want to test them out herself, especially since it was a theory she'd believed in all along.

"The pictures aren't clear because they're not your own," Archie said.

"They weren't real," Holly said out loud. "Archie, the false memories she implanted were horrid. They made my sister and me fight. Why would she do that?" she whispered.

Archie sighed. "Oh boy. I should've gotten you out of that house long ago. I suspected things weren't right, but from the outside looking in . . ."

She didn't blame him; she just wanted answers. "Archie, the memories?"

"Okay. This is all I know from our talks. One wartime study she talked about used soldiers and POWs. They tortured them into believing their brothers in arms gave them up so that they'd relinquish sensitive information to the government."

Holly placed her hand over her face. "No."

"I'm sorry. I'm sorry for whatever happened in that house and for not being there to help." His words were genuine, but they did not erase the grim fact that Holly was now certain their mother had implanted memories in their brains, and she'd done it so she could cause a rift between them. That way, she could use the rift to extract information from them, get them to turn on each other when she needed them to. It was like one giant science experiment, one that had spanned years. Mother must've loved watching her theories come to life, but this wasn't an ethical psychological study—it was child abuse.

Of course, Vivian and Holly had believed what she'd told them; she was their mother. Dr. Forester had become distraught when her Lost at the Beach study hadn't panned out, but that's because she hadn't had years to gain her subjects' trust and pound memories into their heads. Mother couldn't admit the fact that she'd performed this very study on her own children and it had worked. That would be highly unethical. The whole world would see her for the sick exploiter she truly was. However, it probably goaded her that she'd been successful in proving her theory under her own roof and couldn't share the information or make it work in the one area that would bring her clinical fame.

"Please sit, dear. My sangria is strong. I used red wine, and your cheeks are just as pink."

Sangria? "What did you say?" Holly whispered.

"Sangria?" he said uneasily, watching her fall apart. He pointed to the pitcher.

Sometimes the missing bits and pieces of Vivian's chat sessions came to her at the oddest times. A song or something on TV would trigger a word, and she'd remember a verse or phrase. Today she was especially intuitive to all senses and thoughts. "It's not all sangria sunsets and rosy beaches," Holly said out loud.

Archie laughed. "No, it ain't, kid. And I'm sorry if I have anything to do with that. Planning a trip to the Caribbean or the North Atlantic?" he asked.

Holly walked back over to the kitchen counter, wondering why he'd say that. "No, never been to either. Why?"

"Oh, well, as you may know, I've hopped to just about every island in my time away, and I can tell you, the only place I've ever seen with 'rosy' beaches is Bermuda."

Holly's body flooded with exaltation. "I'll have another glass of sangria now, please."

27

The plan was created two glasses of sangria later. Holly was sitting at Archie's kitchen counter, astonished by the obvious yet not-so-obvious discoveries. First, Archie Steiner might be her father. She'd think about what that meant at a different time. Most women would be angry, but for now she'd blame her mother—the real culprit here. The more important subject was Vivian. If Holly had thought the line in the chats about the rosy beaches had meant something, she would've researched it days ago, but she was so poorly traveled, she didn't realize pink beaches were rare.

Something else she blamed on Mark.

"You need to go to Bermuda and find your sister, kid."

"I know, but . . . I can't afford to go to Bermuda. And it's the beginning of the school year. And Mark . . ." She shook her head.

"I'll pay your way. I got more money than I can spend, and no one who wants to spend it with me." Archie smiled when he said this, but Holly found his comment incredibly depressing. She still couldn't believe none of his children had forgiven him for what he'd done after all these years. Was Archie just living in his little time capsule with Harley, hoping someone might pop in one day? It was heartbreaking. Holly's parents were warped humans, but she missed her father so badly some nights, she still cried.

Archie's children would be sorry later. Especially his daughter.

"Come on, they're practically giving away trips to Bermuda these days. It's hurricane season." Archie made expressive motions with his hands, as if a hurricane were going to spiral out of them. "You know . . . the Bermuda Triangle." Then he proceeded to make a triangle with his fingers. "Great deals this time of year."

Holly sucked in a deep breath. "Triangle. His little patch of triangle."

Archie put his expressive hand up to his ear. "What now?"

"He'd mentioned he lived on a little patch of triangle." She couldn't help but smile. "And a song. Are there songs about Bermuda?" She hadn't been sure that Tom was definitely in Bermuda until she'd just remembered the other two things. Now she was certain. She'd cracked the damn puzzle with the help of this stranger, this genius man—her father—and it was a beautiful thing.

"Well, of course—the Beach Boys had a song. There's a whole tune about the Bermuda Triangle. You're catching up a little late again, dear. The locale is Bermuda, and you need to go!"

The Bermuda Triangle, which could be perceived as a *dangerous location*—another thing mentioned in the chats.

"Oh my." Holly didn't want to laugh or feel joy, but she was full of a revived energy, giddy almost. Archie threw back his head in a hoarse laugh, and they were both excited—because they may have just solved the damn puzzle to Vivian's disappearance.

The *where* anyway. Vivian had told Holly she'd leave one day and never come back. That memory was one her mother had implanted, though. Holly still couldn't wrap her mind around it entirely. However, it was an implanted memory they both shared, *so it was real to them*.

She thought again about the way Mother had used the picture taken on the ferry to firmly implant that memory, one of her own creation. She'd also had a picture of herself and Father with a wrapped red bow around their brand-new washer from Sears—a picture-worthy event in their home. She'd used that photo as well when speaking of the day at Green Acres Mall, but Holly hadn't attributed it to anything special.

To Holly, it had just been another old photograph. But now she was sure that with the exception of the actual purchase of the washing machine, the event had been fabricated, because the entire memory was watery. She'd always thought it was because of her young age. But the memory wasn't watery because Holly had been eight years old at the time—it was watery because the memory had been implanted.

It was all so difficult to absorb. First, the disappearing photograph of her sister, and now, realizing the photos she'd viewed growing up were false was beyond jarring. She saw again why she'd initially grabbed on to Mark, a pillar of stability in her otherwise wobbly existence.

Holly also remembered what Vivian had said to her on the ferry—the thing she was probably counting on Holly to recall if she ever wanted to find her. *"They don't log passengers on the ferry."*

Holly thought she knew *why* their mother had implanted that false memory too.

She was probably testing Vivian to see if she'd actually run away, pushing those industry vs. inferiority, oppositional defiant disorder boundaries Mother was so intent on studying over time.

Vivian never had tried to run away on the ferry, but perhaps this information had helped her later in life when she'd needed to. The ferry had been docked at Bay Shore that night when Holly found Vivian's abandoned car. At the time, to Holly, it was just a large, tethered white object bobbing and swaying to the wind and the water. She'd thought nothing of it, but now it meant more.

Holly inhaled and exhaled sharply at all the information she'd just uncovered. She really did need to go back into journalism when this was all over. She was too good at uncovering clues not to.

"Well, are you going to go, kid?" Archie asked.

"Bermuda Triangle? Are you trying to get rid of me, Archie?" she joked.

"Of course not. You're my favorite visitor," Archie said, and Holly got the impression that she was his only visitor. She wanted to find a way to have a relationship with Archie after all this mess. A relationship with her father—the parent who'd cared enough to apologize for his mistakes.

Maybe someone had or had not been following Vivian the night she disappeared, but Holly was convinced the ferry had something to do with it. Vivian may have been lured by Tom's chats, but maybe Frankie's people had never intended for her to make it as far as she had. Perhaps they were setting her up to make it look like she'd run away, but something went wrong.

What was it?

Did Vivian assume Holly would think to look on the ferry, their old stomping grounds? The storm had been too volatile, her mind on Vivian's empty car, not a boat. Maybe Vivian would assume that the next day, Holly would think about Bay Shore and the ferry. But again, she hadn't done that either.

She didn't know why she hadn't figured it out sooner, and she was angry with herself and ready to solve this mystery now, however it might end. She smiled at Archie. "You probably have better things to do than solve my assorted puzzles."

"Not true. I haven't had a good one in a very long time. Now that we've figured it out, what are we going to do, Miss Holly, about getting you to that island? Time's a-ticking." He slapped the bare spot on his wrist, his imaginary watch.

Holly bit her lip. She wished like hell she would've discovered all this sooner. The clues were coming together too late, and now she feared *she* was too late to save her sister.

Holly knew she needed to get there.

To the island.

It seemed like such an impossibility. There was school, and to say she was on Mark's naughty list was an understatement. She couldn't even imagine saying the words, *I think Vivian might be in Bermuda. Can I buy a plane ticket and go check it out?*

He'd lock her up. Or he'd tell her to take her idea to the cops, but she couldn't do that, because she'd gained Clay's letter illegally, and to bring up one piece of evidence meant that she'd have to disclose all the rest.

She couldn't very well show up and ask them to fund a search to Bermuda. They were already paying for a bogus search in Long Island Sound. And she couldn't utter that her tip for Vivian's location had come from an implanted memory from her childhood, because they'd look at her like an alien and laugh her right out of the station.

"You cannot pay for me to go to Bermuda," Holly said.

"My debt to you can hardly ever be repaid at this point," he said sadly.

Holly cocked her head to the side with a sympathetic grin. Archie had made huge mistakes in his life, and she wasn't happy he'd withheld his suspicion that he was her father, but she understood the cunning mind of her mother. If the evil professor had wanted to convince Archie that Holly wasn't his daughter, she could have. Hell, she could've even implanted that truth in his head, for all Holly knew.

"You're getting good at this investigation stuff, kid. Had a few learning curves, but you're on your way now." Archie gave her a playful punch on the shoulder.

"Thanks, and I think you're right. I do need to get to Bermuda."

Archie nodded vigorously. "I appreciate you giving me leniency on the paternity stuff, but you should really read your mother's journal for the whole story. If not, that's okay too. Just promise to visit me one last time either way when you get back from the island."

"Okay, but Mark will never let me go to Bermuda," she said. Who was she kidding?

"What if you disguise it as a couple's getaway?" he asked.

"Ha! We don't do couple's getaways. And especially to somewhere lavish like Bermuda." She remembered how Mark had balked when she'd suggested going to Saratoga Springs for a few days. If he wouldn't consent to a spa a few hours away, a tropical island was out of the question.

Archie sighed. "You deserve better than a cheapskate warden for a husband."

Her eyes shot open in surprise.

"We have to get you there!" he said.

"Mark's impossible. He hasn't forgiven me for getting arrested, and he went ballistic on me because I'd been drinking the other day. If he catches me again, I swear he'll send me straight to rehab." She picked up her empty glass.

Archie's eyes lit up like light bulbs. He poured Holly some more sangria.

"Oh, I shouldn't," she said.

"No, you should. It's your ticket to Bermuda."

"What're you talking about?" Holly asked.

"Go home tipsy. When you get there, get stinking drunk. When Mark comes home, tell him you have a problem, and there's a place upstate you want to go, but they're cash only. They're the best, though, and you need help. You want to do it for your family."

Holly started sipping hard at the sangria, her body buzzing with possibility. "That's brilliant," she whispered.

"He can't say no. It will also feed his ego that he was right all along. That you have a problem, and this is why you've been acting like this."

I do have a problem, she thought as she gulped down the delicious wine. The problem was that she could drink the whole pitcher without blinking.

"The cash part will be hard," Holly said.

"Do you guys not have it? I just said cash because he'll be able to track credit card charges."

"We have it, but getting him to relinquish it is another story. Tighter than I-495 at rush hour."

"Ha. Well, I say it's worth a try. You need me to drive you home? If you had to leave your car because you were too drunk to drive, that would up the ante. Also, I don't want you to die on your way home. I just got to know the only daughter who will speak to me. And I sorta like you."

Holly blushed, her eyes growing a little wet. She wiped at them, because she kind of liked him too. Now she understood why her mother had taken a liking to him. He was just sarcastic enough to appeal to her cold demeanor, but he was sweet too. "I'm going to get going."

"Sure you're okay to drive?" he asked again.

Holly walked an imaginary line on Archie's floor with ease. It was the test she'd used in college to determine if she should drive or walk. "I'm good. I gotta get home. I've got some drinking to do."

"Atta girl. Alka Seltzer for that kind of headache, though. Ginger just won't do."

28

The only fun part of this plan was picking out the type of alcoholic beverage when Holly got home and giving herself the permission to drink as much of it as she'd like. But not enough so that she couldn't carry out the rest of her plan. Holly's mouth watered on the drive, but she promised herself it would be her last bender.

She *did* have a problem.

And that was one of the uglies she'd faced through all of this. As much as she'd harped on Mark for not letting her have a drink, she realized now it was with good reason. It still didn't excuse the other ways he'd tried to control her—restricting her alcohol consumption was just one of them. She'd chosen Mark as a spouse for the wrong reasons. She'd chosen him because he expressed love the same way her parents had—through control and manipulation.

And that was not healthy. It would not be a part of the way she chose to receive or express love in the future. It wasn't just for her own mental well-being but for that of her boys.

The kids were due home from school, and she'd do her best to hide the fact that she'd downed two bottles of wine from their dining room wine rack, a selection reserved for dinner guests, which usually meant just the holidays. Mark would be pissed she'd dipped into the expensive bottles, but if this were going to be her last hurrah, she was going to drink the good stuff. Wine seemed like the most logical choice after Archie's sangria to minimize a hangover. She had a lot planned for tomorrow, and it would be a small miracle if she pulled it all off. She needed a level head.

When the kids came home, Holly had a nice dinner prepared—a lasagna, fresh bread, and a salad, something that would feed them for a few days. Mark wasn't much of a cook. Her boys didn't say anything as she fought the tears back while dishing out their portions.

This would be the hardest part of it.

Leaving her boys and not knowing if she'd make it back in one piece.

Holly had never spent more than a long weekend away from them since they were born. She'd been the one who kept all their schedules straight. Otto wasn't doing well in math; Mark would let it slip, and she knew that, but if she didn't do this right now, there'd be a lot more missed homework and failed tests, because Holly wouldn't be able to concentrate on anything else until she saw this through.

If she flew down to Bermuda and searched for Vivian and found nothing, at least she'd know she tried. She'd take that little bit of closure, come back, and try to work on her own family, which had fallen by the wayside ever since she'd received Vivian's frantic phone call.

She'd blamed Mark for a lot of the demise of their marriage, but when she sat back and looked at her own behavior, she realized that although he was mostly wrong, she wasn't 100 percent right either. She'd made mistakes, kept things from Mark. She'd gone on alcohol binges. She needed to reevaluate her marriage with a fresh lens when she came back and figure out if it was worth salvaging.

If Mark would even let her come back after he found out about this, that was.

Once the kids were finished with their meals and their homework, Holly kissed each one on the cheek and told them that she had to go on a little trip and that she loved them. She also made another promise she didn't know if she could keep—that she'd be back. She excused them and told them she had to talk to their father.

Mark came into the kitchen shortly afterward to find her teetering over a crystal goblet of cabernet.

"What the hell, Holly?" he asked, much quieter than the night before.

"I can't do this anymore, Mark," she said in her best fake attempt at desperation.

He looked up, alarmed. "I know I've been hard on you with Vivian gone. I'm sorry, Holls. I don't know how to make it better, and I just want my wife back." The look on his face made her take pause. "The kids want their mom back too."

Holly almost felt bad for lying, but if he wanted his wife back so badly, he'd have bailed her out of jail. She would've let the words fly, but even in her inebriated state, she knew she needed something from him, so she held it in.

"I know . . . but . . ." She sighed and stifled a fake cry. "I need help. I've been drinking every day." This was not in any way true. "I think you're right." Then she gulped down the words that were the hardest in the world to say. "I think I *am* turning into my mother."

Gah. She'd needed ten bottles to get those words out. Especially after the journal entry she'd read earlier. She was *nothing* like that evil bitch. What she'd done to them with the journal exercise and Rico was bad enough, but at least they'd known she was studying them then. It was all the times she was performing experiments on them when they weren't aware that really rocked Holly's world.

She planned on reading the rest of her mother's journal on the plane ride, but she was also afraid to find out any more. Dr. Forester had planted in their brains that Vivian would run off someday from Bay Shore Marina. Vivian actually doing it was beyond frightening.

"Oh, no, Holly. I shouldn't have said that. I didn't mean it." Mark placed his hands on her shoulders. They were warm and consoling, and she wanted to let him wrap the rest of himself around her, because she needed that, but she couldn't fall into this old familiar trap. She needed to step out of her comfort zone to get this done. Vivian had done it for her when she'd climbed the steps to the master bedroom with Rico.

"The stress of Vivian missing has been just too much . . ." More tears came. These were real.

Holly started bawling in a way she never had before, crying for all the things she'd held in the last week. She cried for her sister, and she cried for her sister's unborn baby who she'd never gotten to meet because their mother had taken that chance away from both of them, and she cried for Archie, her father, who was so fantastic but had no visitors.

Mark came over to her side of the kitchen counter and hugged her, and she let him, and it wasn't like her to turn into a soggy mess, especially a drunken soggy mess, but she decided she needed to for her own mental health, and she thought it might actually help her cause here.

"We'll get you some help, honey. I'm sorry I haven't been better at this. I've never been good at things I can't fix."

And there it was—the sum of all the reasons Mark had been such a colossal asshole boiled down into one simple phrase. If he couldn't fix the problem, he didn't want to be a part of it. Let the fixers (the police) do the fixing, he likely assumed. It was maddening. Especially when the problem involved a family member.

"I found a rehab place upstate. They only accept cash, but they're the best, and I like what the program offers. It's only two weeks."

Holly handed him a slip of paper with the name and number of a real rehab facility. It wasn't odd for rehab facilities to be located in rural areas, as she'd learned from researching, so he shouldn't suspect anything. She held her breath while he scrunched his forehead.

"Cash only? No points?" he grumbled.

Holly gutted him with her eyes but didn't say a word. *Credit card points?* Mark was hardwired to think cheap. He knew no other language. *Breathe.*

Mark made eye contact with her and realized his blunder. "Right, I'll withdraw the money in the morning if this is the right place for you. How much?" he asked, wincing.

She whipped out an envelope. "Seven thousand." His eyes practically fell out of his head. "I went to the bank already. To get into the program, I need to leave tonight. Their spots fill up quickly."

Mark looked at her as if she were out of her mind. "Holly, that's a lot of money."

She started crying again. It wasn't hard to make the tears come; they'd been dying to spring loose for days.

"But I guess it's all right."

What a jerk. When she'd gone to the bank, she learned they had more than $100,000 in their savings account. "I can't drive you to upstate New York tonight, though. The kids have homework; tomorrow I'm busy with—"

"I'm getting an Uber, Mark, right now. This can't wait. It's bad. I've driven drunk with them in the car." It was a lie that was hard to tell, but she needed to pull out the big guns to make this happen.

After her false confession, Mark arranged for the Uber himself. The last thing she told him was that there was to be no family contact of any sort for the first week and to please respect their process.

Holly was amazed somehow that she'd made it onto the plane without anyone stopping her.

After she'd gotten in the Uber, she asked the driver to pull over and said she'd be taking the train the rest of the way but that he could keep his fare. The driver did, but Holly was worried somehow that Mark would find out, so she threw in an extra twenty dollars and told him not to talk if he was contacted.

Once the cabin door to the plane shut, Holly exhaled. She was on her way. She waited until the plane took off before she opened her mother's little black book. Her first course of action was to honor Archie's wishes, so she scanned each page until she found one with his name on it.

Henry is growing weary of Archie's not-so-subtle woos for my attention at happy hour, and I know what he thinks, but the fact is, it doesn't matter.

Nature vs. Nurture, Gesell, 1992.

Who she's raised by will determine who she'll be, not some mishap of a night after the end of spring term party. She was named right by when she was born, and she'll be raised right by Henry and me, and none of the rest matters.

It's been psychologically proven.

He needs to give up on the paternity test.

It didn't say much, but it was enough. "Wow." Holly wiped a tear from her eye, and the lady sitting next to her asked if she needed a tissue.

"No, thanks. I'm actually reading something about my father." She liked saying the words out loud. She had a father. And he was still alive. "These are happy tears."

The lady smiled uneasily and then went back to her own book. Holly felt a little traitorous toward her father, the one who'd raised her, but she'd never fit in with that family. She didn't look like them, and she didn't act like them.

It was about more than keeping her real father from her; it was about making her feel like an outsider her whole life because she didn't love introspection like they did. Now she knew why. It's because she favored her other father—her biological one. And Holly intended to try to have a relationship with him when she got back. He may not have been there for the first thirty-five years of her life, but he had helped her through the hardest week of those thirty-six when no one else would, and that had to count for something.

Holly scanned the pages for any other hints at the memory implantation study. She didn't find anything on the mall, but she did find references to the beach. Of course she did. That's what her mother's study was about—lost at the beach.

I don't understand why it's not working. It was the details that captured both Vivian and Holly, their father's sandal getting caught in the slot of wood and his almost falling. The real fear Holly expressed for leaving her sister. The urgent stress of Vivian, sure we wouldn't leave and then realizing we would and running for the ferry. The chuffing ferry, its engine starting, people boarding. People staring.

The picture of my striped dress, my hat.

They saw those things with their own two eyes. I had to buy the colored bottled sand at a gift shop on Fire Island myself, but that was easy. The picture was easy too.

I don't understand why it's not working with the participants in the study.

Holly gulped loudly, and the woman beside her looked at her strangely again. "It's a touching memoir," she explained.

The woman smiled with tight lips and went back to her reading. Yes, Holly was acting very strange, because her life had been very strange. Strange and false. How much of it, she'd never know for sure. She couldn't find anything in the journal about Green Acres, but she didn't have to. She knew it was implanted.

When the plane touched down at the Bermuda L.F. Wade International Airport, which consisted of one strip of land surrounded by clear water that shimmered with the brilliance of neon-blue Christmas lights, Holly checked her phone immediately.

Why leave the airport when Mark was just going to make her fly straight home once he figured out her lie? But she had no messages. Holly couldn't believe he'd honored his part of the deal so far. She was sure his neuroses would have him calling the facility to verify she'd made it, to make sure his cash was going to good use, but she must've done such a good job of convincing him that he hadn't. Archie had helped her so much with the plan, and she owed that man her life.

Holly exhaled. She may have just pulled off the first part of this thing. As for the rest, who knew.

After she'd collected her luggage and stepped onto the curb to hail a cab, Holly glanced at her surroundings. It was nighttime, but that didn't stop the lights from shimmering off the breathtaking water. "Well, this is fucking beautiful, isn't it?"

"First time here?" the cab driver asked with a British accent.

Holly hadn't noticed that his window was rolled down. "Yes, I'm sorry for my potty mouth." He gave her an interesting look, and she was sure it had more to do with the fact that she'd used the word *potty* than the fact that she'd sworn. Holly needed to remind herself that this wasn't a trip to Splish Splash and that she was on an actual adult trip.

"Need a ride somewhere?" he asked.

"Yes." She gave the cabdriver the address for the bed-and-breakfast she'd found online, close to Horseshoe Bay, on the east side of the island, where the pink beaches were located. She hadn't had much trouble buying an airline ticket with cash, but most of the chain hotels required a credit card.

When Holly arrived at her little room, with its white beadboard bed and pictures of sailboats above it, she immediately lay down. She was mentally and physically exhausted from executing her escape plan, and she hadn't planned to fall asleep right away. There was too much to do, but she set an alarm on her phone for bright and early just in case.

A siren blared in her ear. She blinked and was somehow in a different universe.

Did yesterday really happen?

Holly opened the window to the waves rushing in and out on the beach, and she was out of her mind in awe at the beauty before her. She'd learned from the cabdriver that the east side of the island had pink beaches because of the tiny red organisms that live and grow off the coral reefs there.

It looked otherworldly, like someone had taken a container of blush makeup and spread it miles long, making it appear luminescent next to the crisp blue waves. "You've got to be kidding me."

The smell of the ocean was intoxicating, too, and even though she was there for a very specific reason other than vacation, Holly closed her eyes and inhaled the ocean breeze and let the sun warm her face for just a moment.

Why hadn't she and Mark ever been to a place like this?

Why hadn't she known places like this existed, just a few hours away, via a direct flight?

Screw money. Why did Mark care so much about saving all of it? This island was why they made money. Money should be spent on places just like this.

The wild thoughts were unending and Holly's brief therapy as she stood there with her eyes shut. Forget Dr. Fineberg. She needed more island time in her life. Holly had initially been worried that she had only two weeks to find Vivian, but as she stood in front of that window, a week there, with no children or house obligations, seemed like a lifetime. Her body was physically sore from the stress of yesterday, but the urgency to find Vivian returned.

She glanced at her watch—8:45 a.m.

Time moved slowly here. Gloriously slow.

But Holly had a job to do.

She thought it would be hard to locate Vivian or her abettor, Tom, but Bermuda was a small island, and if Tom's boat was docked near one of the pink beaches, that narrowed it down even further. From her online research, she'd learned there was in fact only one marina close to the pink beaches, and that was Peppercorn Marina.

Holly closed the windows to her room and changed out of her jeans and T-shirt and into a fresh pair of yellow shorts she hadn't worn in ages and a tank top, then ventured out. It wouldn't be her first marina bust, but it could be her last if this Tom character was really there—and a murderer.

When Holly arrived at the marina, she walked around aimlessly. She wanted to carry the investigative intensity she'd had in Long Island, but the place was just too damn beautiful to be stressed.

She should be nervous.

The only person who knew Holly was there was Archie. She'd called him from the airport and told him that if she didn't come back in a week to let Mark know where she'd gone.

Her expectation was that she'd find nothing.

That whatever had been done to Vivian had already been covered up or hadn't made it past Bay Shore Marina in New York.

As she walked around, a familiar hankering started in her mouth and ended with her holding her hands steady so they wouldn't tremble. She needed a drink. She licked her lips. *No.*

She would not have a drink. Holly was determined to use this trip for its intended purpose—to get sober. Then it wouldn't be a total lie to her family. Not to mention, it was completely necessary if she were to go home and start over like she wanted to and restart her career.

As she fought the cravings, Holly thought about what kinds of questions she might ask the workers to identify Tom. She needed to ask clever questions. Questions Archie might ask. She channeled her inner Archie: *Use the information you've got. The answer is likely right in front of you*. What else did Tom have besides a boat that was unique? What might identify him?

"Can I help you?" an older man asked. He was wearing a white polo shirt with a name tag—Calvin.

"Yes . . ." Holly fretted. "Is your marina dog friendly?" she asked.

"Sure. We don't have a problem with dogs. But the marina is full if you're looking for space. Sorry. Not a lot of marinas down here."

"That's what I hear." Holly tried not to smile. But she'd never been in a place so gorgeous. "My friend has a boat here. His dog's name is Bodie. I'm looking for him; you wouldn't happen to know—"

"Oh, you mean Tommy?"

Holly couldn't have hid the expression of surprise on her face if she'd tried. "Yep." A familiar feeling of shock ripped through her body, the same as it had in Port Jefferson when she'd found Clay's unlocked boat. The fear came back again too. She'd never intended to climb into that boat, just like she'd never expected to really find Tom.

Then again, she'd flown all the way down here. It wasn't for nothing.

"Sure, straight back that way, last boat on the right, the *Second Wind*."

Holly smiled at the name. "Thanks."

She had to remind herself that she didn't want to like Tom, and he wasn't the man she'd read about in the chat but a perverse internet stalker. But if any part of his story were true, he *had* come down there for a second chance. She could at least like the name of his boat, *Second Wind*.

That's why Vivian had wanted to escape there, too, but nothing was as it seemed.

A breeze from the ocean touched Holly's skin and made the flesh rise and dimple. She was definitely over her head on this one. She should call Rigby and Nadia and fill them in and have them send help.

Holly wasn't equipped to deal with this guy alone.

When she'd actually made it inside Clay's boat, she'd been only miles away from home. A quick distress call to the police or Mark and she would've had a fighting chance, but not here.

A seagull zipped by, making her heart race, and she was probably in danger, but still she kept walking toward the boat.

Walking toward the man who took her sister.

She'd been hiding from the truth her whole life, and it was time to face it. Time to face a guy named *Tommy*. So he did use his real name.

As she walked down the dock, she thought of many things, the most profound being her sons swaddled in their blankets when she'd brought them home from the hospital and how their love had saved her life.

When Holly reached the end of the dock, she almost fell over the side into the brilliant blue water. She could see the name on the side— *Second Wind*—and on the upper deck, a floppy-eared dog sunbathing.

Holy crap, Bodie?

But where is Tom? And more important, where is Vivian?

Holly stood there and gaped at the boat and the dog for a while.

Holly began to panic and pace. What was the best, next logical step? She wanted to call Archie again and ask him, but she hadn't had time to change her roaming plan to include international coverage before she left, and if she did it now, Mark would become suspicious.

She walked over to a bench that wasn't that far from the boat. She could still see the *Second Wind*, but she didn't think anyone from the top deck could see her. Holly was suddenly weary again. Maybe from her plane ride yesterday, but perhaps more so from all the discoveries in the journal and now the shock of actually finding what she suspected was Tom's boat.

She tried to calm her breathing as her heart beat faster and faster.

Maybe I should regroup, hatch a solid plan, come back tomorrow?

The chill of the breeze feathered the hair on her arms. She knew she wouldn't be able to rest if she didn't solve this right now.

There was no way she could leave the dock without knowing if her sister was on that boat. She'd sit there until someone retrieved Bodie. They couldn't leave the dog up there all day—Holly would wait.

Two minutes passed; she checked her watch. She bit the side of her cheek. *Just one drink.*

She resisted the urge to go somewhere and get one of those delicious cocktails with the little umbrellas she always saw people post on social media. She'd never had one, and she wanted one.

Don't give in.

She fought it with all her might. If she got up and left, she could miss the owner. Worse yet, if she left that spot, the boat could sail away—with her sister on it—forever.

Holly got up and paced again, making sure her flip-flops didn't get caught in the wide-planked wooden dock, an awful feeling settling over her as she was reminded of her mother's fake memory, and her father tripping, and how that part in particular had bothered her—her father almost falling. Father's concern for Vivian. It was all a lie. She had no way of discerning the real memories from the fake ones.

She was looking forward to getting to know her biological father. A real family. Not the one that was designed by her mother.

As she waited for someone to retrieve the dog, Holly decided to dip back into her mother's journal, although she wasn't sure why. Every time she read something, it was like ripping open a fresh wound. And sure enough, there was one more entry that would. It was dated shortly after Vivian had left for boarding school.

9-27-97

I know she blames me for what happened, but honestly, the OB-GYN said the cervix might be fine. Just because the man who performed her procedure wasn't world renowned doesn't mean he wasn't properly trained.

Henry claims he wasn't. Henry likened the place we took Vivian to a chop shop, but what does he know about women's health?

If Vivian hadn't been in so much pain after the procedure, we would've never taken her to the doctor. I should've given her more time to heal. Now there's a chance others will find out, blame me for any problems she has in the future, but I was only doing what was best.

Holly wiped away tears. Their mother was the reason Vivian couldn't have children. No wonder Vivian had held such vitriol toward her after her death. No wonder she'd asked for her journals to be burned, as well as Mother's body. It wasn't just because of what they'd endured as children but because Mother had prevented her from having children of her own.

Holly walked closer to the *Second Wind*.

The dog was gone. *No.* How had she missed it? Where had Bodie gone? She was about to turn back around when she felt it.

Her neck was hot.

Because there were fingers on it.

They were lightly gripping her flesh, damp with perspiration.

Her heart was erupting in her chest, so loud. She imagined she would hear it until it stopped beating.

Holly was frozen, even though her mind was telling her to move. She wanted to swat at the person gripping her body. Breath wouldn't come.

She thought of Clay's hand pressed over her mouth, dragging her across her kitchen floor.

She'd wanted to fight him, but she'd clammed up like a fly in a Venus flytrap.

This hand had long fingernails. "Hey," the voice whispered in her ear. "Come out, come out, wherever you are, Holly."

29

"Shh . . . don't scream," the voice said. The woman placed her hand over Holly's mouth. But she'd know that voice anywhere.

Vivian.

Holly tried not to tremble as she turned around on the dock. The wind picked up her hair, and a funnel cloud swirled in Holly's chest. Her sandal slid on the wood, and she almost tumbled when she saw *her*.

Vivian was standing right in front of her. Alive.

"Vivian?"

Holly smiled. It couldn't be, but there she was—her sister. Vivian had a mess of short red locks, her haircut almost entirely bangs with shorter sides. It was just like Vivian. She'd cut off all her hair and had kept the bangs.

Holly gasped and fell into her arms. Vivian was warm from the sun and smelled like toasted coconut.

"I'm so sorry, Holly. I wanted to tell you, but when you found my chat sessions, it messed everything up. When we went in to delete the records, it showed that there was activity."

"Oh my God, *Vivian*. I'm just glad you're alive," Holly said. They hugged and cried until the clouds rolled over the sun, making it appear as though the large ball of gas was bobbing on the sea. Holly could hardly believe it was really her.

Am I dreaming? Holly needed someone to pinch her. There were levels of surprise, and this one stunned her from the inside out—a radiation of shock and joy making it hard to speak. All she could do was cry and stare at an undead Vivian. She stroked her sister's face. "It's really you."

It didn't look like her—the hair, the tanned skin, the smile. Vivian looked so happy.

"Come with me," Vivian said. "I'll tell you everything." Vivian grabbed Holly's hand and gave her an equally exasperated, exhilarated look. Holly never thought she'd ever see her again. A familiar dare flitted across her sister's face. "Let's go!"

Vivian pulled her down the dock, and Holly had to fight to keep up, the fantastical island landscape zipping by her like a movie reel from the past when they used to run down the beach at Fire Island chasing crabs, untethered to the pressures of the real world. It was early morning and Vivian's flowing linen swimsuit cover-up flapped in the breeze. Holly followed her, a giggle escaping her lips because she was running—with her sister.

And she was alive. *Alive!*

Archie's alternative theory number two was actually correct. Brilliant man.

Holly's mission there wouldn't be about discovering Vivian's murderer and bringing the killer to justice but about discovering she was never murdered in the first place. Holly's bare legs buzzed with adrenaline. The sea air rolled off the water in her side view, and nothing else mattered in that moment but now—the fact that everything would be okay because she'd found her. She'd found Vivian.

They ran away from the boat and finally settled on a couple of raised sand dunes that looked like they'd been man-made.

"Remind you of Sunken Forest?" Vivian asked while Holly caught her breath. Vivian was referencing the rare ecological sunken forest between the sand dunes on Fire Island where they used to play. But

Vivian wasn't talking about the actual forest. She was speaking of the mystical feeling that accompanied their summer explorations there— as if they were caught between two portals, the forest bordering on a magical plane only they could touch. That's what Bermuda felt like right now. They were also in that freaky triangle people talked about, so maybe that had something to do with it as well.

"Yes, it does. But tell me everything." Holly was breathless, even though she'd had time to recover from their run. Her jitters from the actual discovery made her heart pump faster, her body tingle all over, especially the places where the sand touched.

Vivian flipped her bangs out of her eyes and took a deep breath. She'd been cheerful, almost playful up until this point, but Holly knew this would be hard for her to explain, because Holly was a little bit mad at her. Even if Vivian was running from something, how could she not have told her? Leave her to believe she'd died? Vanished?

Vivian straightened her back against the dune. "That night of the storm, when I called you, I was followed on the docks. I'd driven to Bay Shore. I was going to leave for Bermuda in the morning and meet Tom. The storm was the perfect alibi to get lost. I'd planned a much cleaner, staged suicide mission, with a note and all. I even had it drafted in my head. In the note, there would be clues for you that I hadn't really died, but others would think that I had. I figured you would know in your heart it wasn't true even without the clues, because of Mrs. Burgess." Vivian let out a stifled breath, and Holly made an *ugh* sound.

"I knew once they investigated Clay, you'd understand why I left, and I hoped you'd be okay with it and understand I needed to leave. Disappear."

"What was it going to say?" Holly couldn't have been more intrigued. "The note?"

She cleared her throat. "Holly, this part is for you. Mother always told us we were quitters and that if we couldn't succeed, we should just give up. Well, I've lost here, and now it's my turn to forfeit the game." Vivian twisted her lips at her.

"She would never—"

"Well, that was the point. Foresters don't quit. And neither did you in finding me. I'm impressed." Vivian continued. "But I never got a chance to write it. I was going to camp out near the Bay Shore ferry, never go home that night, have my car discovered in the morning. But I'd been followed. I never wrote the note. The person didn't find me, because I snuck onto the ferry before you arrived."

"Damn it." She'd been right. If only Holly had known about the false memories, maybe she could've figured it out sooner. "But how? That storm was so bad. You're lucky you didn't go under." Holly still fought the shiver when she remembered how cold that water was when it'd washed down her sweatshirt.

"I had to go. Tom used to work in import/export; that's how he got into trouble with the Feds. Tom's family had asked him to smuggle something illegally. Drugs. Tom's family is mixed up in all kinds of crime, and when I found out Clay was having an affair—"

"With Frankie Gallo." Holly finished her sentence, and Vivian looked at her, stunned.

"You have done your homework. And Tom is Frankie's brother. He still talked to Frankie, his baby sister. The only one from the family who hadn't abandoned him," Vivian continued.

"What?" Holly gripped the sand, surprised at this piece of information and mad at herself for not figuring it out when she'd charted out Frankie's family tree.

Tomaso Gallo. Tom. She'd drawn a line after his name that simply said *missing*. She'd assumed he was dead, said to be in witness relocation, but more likely killed by the family he'd betrayed.

"The cops didn't even find me hiding that night, which surprised me. I thought my whole plan was shot."

"Sounds about right on the cops. But why the running part?" She was mad at herself for not thinking of the boat. The large vessel had always been docked in the same place, but it wasn't operable that late at night, and it hadn't crossed her mind as a viable hiding place.

How had she gotten aboard? So many questions to save for later. She was sure Tom had given her the answers.

"They were going to kill me, Holly. They just needed to make it look like I did it on my own so the murder wouldn't get pegged on them or Clay. See, they wanted to keep Clay as their lawyer so he could get them out of their legal jams, but Frankie found me to be a nuisance. Wanted me out of the way."

Holly squinted at the sun reflecting off the water, one of the most beautiful things she'd ever seen amid the horror of this shocking news. "How did you know?"

"Frankie used Tom to lure me to the marina with the weak promise that my life would be spared if all went well, but she was just using him. She never intended for me to make it out of New York. She was setting up a fake suicide for me so it wouldn't link back to her. But nobody would believe it without a body."

"Wow." It was all Holly could say. She knew Frankie was manipulative, but she never dreamed she'd also manipulated the man Vivian had been chatting with, and that it was her own brother. The letter had stated as much, now that she thought about it, but she'd just assumed Tom was in on it too. If Frankie was the only family member Tom kept in contact with, he likely would be loyal to her.

"Tom and I . . . you found the chats." Vivian blushed. "We fell in love. A kind I haven't known before."

Holly raised her eyebrows at her sister and gave her a brilliant smile.

"Frankie hadn't anticipated that. When I got away, I think for almost a day, she was toying with the idea of letting Tom 'keep' me. There was a lot of fighting over the phone. Frankie thought Tom was in Galveston, Texas, but he'd departed more than a month ago from his post in witness relocation to here, because he thought she might be up to something all along. He sent Frankie a picture of us for proof that I'd made it, but he'd said it was sent from Texas."

"So he knew?"

"He had an idea, but he didn't *know*. He wanted to think the best of his sister." Vivian pushed a curl off Holly's face and let out a long breath. How could any of this be real?

"When Tom saw that you found the chat sessions, it was a loose end, one that could take Frankie down. She blamed Tom and said he had to kill me now because he hadn't deleted the chats quickly enough. But Tom had already sacrificed a lot for Frankie."

Holly nodded because she had a much better understanding of the Gallo family now.

"He knew Frankie would turn on him if it meant her own head. She has no idea where we are. We think. We might set sail again soon to make sure. I was waiting to see if you found me first. I didn't think you'd do it."

Holly exhaled, glad she'd caught her in time. If they'd sailed to another location, she wouldn't have been able to handle just missing Vivian at the boat docks—again.

"I was going to send you something, but Tom was convinced you wouldn't keep it a secret if you found out. Keeping secrets was never your strong suit."

Holly met her eyes, and she wanted to be furious with Vivian, but she was absolutely right. Holly was terrible at keeping secrets.

Vivian patted her shoulder. "I don't even know if I could've kept a secret that big. I knew it was wrong not telling you, but I hoped you'd figure it out because of the location," Vivian explained. "So, sorry I couldn't write the note or send word like I'd intended. Tom said it would kill us."

Holly thought about the secrets they shared again. "Vivian, I found Mother's journal when I was looking for you, to search for clues. And . . ." She didn't know how to tell her their childhood was a sham.

"Oh, I've read it. I found it during one of my college summers, but I didn't know what it meant until much later. Couldn't stand the entries about me." She shook her head. "You've had it all these years, Holly. I assumed you'd read it long ago and it was just something we didn't talk about."

Holly shook her head, astounded. "You knew?"

"About the studies, you mean? The memories? The ones she devised to make us hate each other?" Vivian looked away into the ocean and threw a piece of driftwood. "You didn't suspect it when she was going apeshit over her beach study? I knew it was because she'd probably done it to us first!" Vivian exhaled hard.

Holly shook her head. She felt so naive. She should've caught on sooner.

"She messed with us good. It's horrible that you didn't know. It probably made it harder for you to put two and two together that I hadn't killed myself."

"I knew that part," Holly said. "I just wasn't sure you weren't murdered."

Vivian put her arm around her shoulder. "I was going to tell you as soon as Tom said it was safe, but he knows Frankie is still out there looking for us. She sees me as a major threat. And I think she still wants to prove that I killed myself, plant my body, so the blame is off her family. She doesn't know who she's up against."

Holly smiled. This was true. "The Gallos have nothing on the Foresters when it comes to mind games."

"That's right," Vivian said.

Holly's smile faltered when she thought of the worst of the mind games. "I wish I would've known about the baby. In high school."

Vivian's hand slipped off Holly's shoulder, and Holly stared at her feet planted firmly in the sand, wondering if her sister had blamed her for it because Rico had wanted her first.

"I'm sorry. It was too hard to talk about. She wouldn't let me." The weight of the last sentence was heavier than the others. If their mother said it wasn't permissible, it wasn't.

Holly also understood how difficult the actual ordeal must've been. If Holly had her reproductive organs shredded when she was seventeen, she'd probably feel the same way. Holly would never want to talk about it again either.

They really had been playing a game of hide-and-seek their whole lives, each sister hiding parts of themselves they didn't want the other to know. Vivian had no idea how much Holly hated Mark.

"How did you get all the way down here?" Holly asked.

Vivian sighed. "When the ferry took off the next morning, I was already on board, a stowaway, and Tom had mapped a way for me to get down to Bermuda entirely by ship, passing cash to the captains he knew."

Holly still had qualms about Tom because he had played such a vital role in luring her sister. He'd sent her money and given her information to make her disappear. And he was related to Frankie. He had bad blood. "And you're sure about this Tom? He's one of them. A Gallo," Holly said.

"Yes." Vivian sounded angry that Holly doubted him. "We're Foresters, and we're nothing like *them*."

This was true. The waves were crashing into the shore now, catching up to their little stretch of beach. "Tom had really begun to turn on Frankie when they set up a PO Box to trap me," Vivian said.

"They set it up?" Holly was rocking back and forth on the sand. She couldn't make her nerves settle down.

Vivian grabbed her knee to steady her rocking. "Surprised you knew about it, but I shouldn't be. Super Sleuth."

She grinned at Vivian's old nickname for her when she used to work at the paper. Holly thought about Delilah Ramirez and how far she'd grown since investigating that case. After she was sure she was "dried out," Holly would be applying for jobs when she got home.

"They knew I was going to the post office that day to collect Tom's package. But it was a setup too."

"What do you mean?" Holly asked. And how could Vivian trust Tom if he'd set her up?

"Well, the club has a guy who works at the post office. They love to recruit civil servants and turn them dirty. Police. Post office. DMV. You name it. Everyone's on the take."

"So shady," Holly said.

"Right. Tom had sent me cash to help me get away undetected, but when I looked up my PO Box, I found Clay's, too, which was a plant. There were two boxes, and my name was on Clay's as well. Of course I was going to look inside."

Holly nodded.

How could you not look inside?

Especially since she'd already suspected him of cheating.

"Well, when I opened Clay's box, I found his next meeting spot with his mistress. Only when I arrived at their meeting spot to spy on Clay . . ." Vivian pawed and punched the sand. "It wasn't just Clay and Frankie; it was his little girl there too. That was it. I was ready then. To get out of there, away from those people, to start over. It's exactly what they wanted. Clay looked so happy with them. Frankie had wanted me to see this, I think. I fell right into her trap. I was ready to take a chance on Tom."

Holly shook her head in disbelief. "A divorce would have been so much easier."

Vivian laughed. "If only it were that simple. As long as I existed, Frankie couldn't claim Clay. It was a rule the club had. And the club wouldn't give up Clay because they need him in court. Frankie had to make me go away permanently." The ocean tickled their toes. "Let's talk more on the boat; you can meet Tom."

Vivian pulled her little sister off the sand. They were both smiling, so much joy in a reunion Holly thought she'd never have. A seagull stretched its wings into the cherry-and-orange-streaked sky, and they both stood there and watched it.

"Okay, but if Frankie's still looking for you, how are you so sure she won't come here? She has to know Tom's not in Texas anymore." Holly's stomach pitted with unease.

"Because we tied up the loose ends. The chat session with the clues to our location is no longer accessible."

The chat session with the clues.

They were walking back the way they'd come when Holly stopped dead in her tracks. "Vivian, I printed those chat sessions out and someone stole them."

"You what?" Vivian asked, eyes wide.

Those chat sessions had existed to Vivian on the internet, a private escape, but Holly had exposed her clandestine world. And now she had exposed *them*.

The right wing of the seagull hitched just a touch at loud sounds like firecrackers exploding, one after the other. But they weren't firecrackers.

They were gunshots.

Holly swiveled her head at the noise and could see a sign in the distance for Cox Bay Beach, but the shot had come from the north, closer to the marina where Tom's boat was docked.

Holly felt her nerve endings prickle with alarm. Fear was etched on Vivian's features, the gleam from the ocean and the blasting sun casting a stark look of terror on her sister's face. "*Tom!* We have to go!"

They ran back to the boat to find Frankie on the top deck with a gun pointing at a man's head that Holly presumed was Tom's. There didn't appear to be anyone else around except for a little girl with pigtails wailing as she tried to call a wild Bodie closer to her and away from the arguing adults. There was a second or two in which the sisters had a chance to run the other way, but Vivian was staring at Frankie with a fire Holly had never seen before.

Vivian obviously wasn't leaving Tom, so that meant Holly wasn't going anywhere either. Holly wouldn't leave her sister behind when she needed her. Not again.

"Vivian, no! Run!" Tom called.

Horror stretched across Holly's face, paralyzing her. She knew she should run. She had kids waiting for her at home.

"There she is!" Frankie said. She pointed the gun at Vivian now. "So nice of you to join the party."

"How did you find us?" Vivian asked.

That was not the question Holly'd thought to ask. She was more concerned with the gun. Spikes of hot waves streamed from Holly's head to her toes. Tom had his hands up, and Holly was shocked by how handsome he was—more than six feet tall; broad, tanned shoulders; black hair almost as long as Vivian's. "Go, Vivian, take Holly!" he shouted.

Yes, let's go. Let's run this time, Vivian. Let's get away while we still can.

"The chat sessions. You didn't think I could figure it out?" Frankie asked.

Vivian stared at Holly as if she'd hand delivered them to Frankie. Holly's mouth dropped open. This was all her fault.

Vivian and Tom knew that Holly had discovered the chat sessions, but maybe they thought they'd deleted everything before anyone else could get to them. But they obviously hadn't contemplated the possibility that the contents had been printed out and stolen. *Shit.*

"I'm not leaving you. She won't kill you with her daughter right there." Vivian sounded like her confident self and directed her attention at the little girl, Giana.

However, Holly wasn't nearly as sure Frankie wouldn't murder Vivian with her little girl there.

Yet, Holly was cemented to the wooden planks. She stared at Giana, trying to clutch the dog for dear life, but Bodie was more concerned with protecting his owner.

"Get this mutt to calm down or I'm going to shoot it," Frankie said.

"No, don't shoot puppy." It was the saddest whimper Holly had ever heard. She wanted to go to little Giana. Holly wanted to make her stop crying.

"Run, Vivian!" Tom called again.

"I just want her." Frankie stabbed the gun in the air at Vivian again. "She better not run, because if she runs, you're dead. And so is your goddamn dog." Frankie kicked at the dog. When Tom tried to come to its rescue, she pointed the gun at him.

What kind of sister put a gun to her brother's head? Maybe the Gallos would win the award for the most dysfunctional family in a match—Forester vs. Gallo—but Vivian's bravery amazed Holly. Vivian and Tom were living this sexy outlaw life, and Holly was just trying not to die.

"I'll come up; you can have me, just take the gun away from his head," Vivian said.

What? No. Holly knew why Frankie wanted Vivian dead. If Vivian ever went back to New York to tell her side of the story, she'd bring the Gallos and Bellinis down with her, not just Frankie and Tom. They'd all been in on it.

And in their world, snitches got taken out. In any case, Vivian was a loose end, one Frankie had intended to get rid of a week ago, so she'd come here today to finish what she'd started. Just like Vivian had said on the beach, Frankie needed a body to prove her suicide theory and take the suspicion off everyone else, including Clay.

None of it mattered. All that mattered was that Vivian survive this, even if Frankie didn't.

Bodie was still jumping about, nipping at the elbow of Frankie's leather jacket. She swatted him with her hand, making the bloodhound angrier.

"Bodie, down!" Vivian called. The dog listened and sat. And now Vivian was walking slowly up the dock to her new boyfriend and dog—her new life. One Holly knew little about, but here Vivian was risking her life for it, and Holly was standing there watching. She should do something. But what? Frankie had a gun, and Holly was sure she knew how to use it.

"I'm coming up there," Vivian shouted. She turned and looked at her sister. "Holly, stay here." Then she mouthed, *"Go."* But Holly wouldn't. She couldn't leave her.

"No!" Tom and Holly cried at the same time. They made eye contact, Holly and Tom, and in that moment, Holly saw the admirable man she'd wanted to see in those chats. Tom *did* love her sister after all.

Frankie dangled handcuffs, and she instructed Vivian to turn around. Tom still had his hands up. Vivian turned and put her hands behind her back.

No. Holly didn't buy it. Vivian wouldn't just give up.

"Why don't you just shoot me if that's what you intend to do?"

Tom looked at Vivian, bewildered, and Holly could hardly hold back the shriek threatening to burst from her throat.

"Because I need your body in New York, not here. So it's believable that you died in that storm. Otherwise the club won't be happy having someone on the outside who knows so much."

"Won't the timing be off?" Vivian asked.

What? Why was Vivian asking her these awful questions? *Wait. She's distracting her.* She would never give up. Foresters didn't quit.

"Ha-ha," Frankie laughed. "You underestimate me. I'll make sure you're long decomposed before your body is discovered."

The little girl, Giana, cried louder.

But Holly saw something then. Just as Frankie was about to clamp the handcuffs around Vivian's wrists, Vivian and Tom exchanged a nod. Vivian was a good deal taller than Frankie, but she suddenly ducked her head and kicked Frankie's leg.

Holly knew very little about sailing despite growing up near the ocean, but she watched in amazement as Tom pushed the boom, the large beam that was constructed to hold sails, in Frankie's direction. The entire sail crashed into Frankie's body at the precise time she fired the gun, causing it to blast into her chest as the beam knocked her into the ocean.

Holly would never forget Giana's scream as she watched her mother go overboard or how that sparkly blue water turned from effervescent blue to a bright scarlet, blood spreading into the water like someone had dropped a bucket of red food coloring over the side, the most bizarre distribution of colors and horror Holly had ever seen.

Giana cried and tried to go to her mother, and Vivian had to run full speed to catch her before she fell overboard.

When Holly left Bermuda, her mind was easy and her heart was full. As angry as she had been with Mark when she'd left, he hadn't called her once, respecting her time away. She'd had to stay at least a full week for her rehab story to be believable, and until the police had tied up their brief investigation of Frankie's "accidental" self-inflicted death. Her family would be alerted, and Holly suspected they'd figure out who was truly responsible.

Holly didn't think it mattered much. The Bellinis had already ousted Tom from the family. Holly didn't think they'd go after him given the circumstances. The question was if they knew Vivian was alive and with Tom when Frankie was murdered and if Vivian was on their target list now too.

There was a lot of turmoil that came with the trip, but Holly would also remember Bermuda as the place where she went to heal. A place where she was awarded a few days with her sister and her new family.

"Are you going to take care of her now?" Holly had asked of Giana.

They'd watched as the little girl scooped sand into a bucket, wonder in her two-and-a-half-year-old eyes that had just witnessed her mother's passing, distracted for a moment with her new toy. Her innocence had pained Holly, especially when Giana had asked if Mommy was done swimming. It was devastating, and it would be trying for Vivian to attempt to parent through this kind of trauma, but hopefully it'd happened early enough in her childhood that she'd recover. If anyone knew about surviving psychological damage, it was them.

"Yes. She's Tom's biological niece. I'll have her call me Aunt Vivi and do my best to raise her." Holly was saddened by this, because her boys had called her sister Aunt Vivi, too, and now they wouldn't get to see her again. But this little girl needed her more.

"She's also Clay's daughter. Will you ever let him see her?"

Vivian sniffled up some tears and looked away. "He'll be too angry now. And his connection to the club—there's too much danger to all of us, Giana included. But maybe one day." She shook her head. "This wasn't how I expected it to end. Clay broke my heart, but I don't think he had any idea what Frankie was up to. I thought I'd be with Tom and he'd have the family he wanted. He deserved that much." She looked over at Giana. "I have to protect her now."

"You'll be a wonderful mother. And she's lucky she'll have you." Holly hugged her sister. "Don't worry. I won't tell a soul. I'll keep your secret, I promise."

Vivian looked at her with a devilish smile. "You better."

They ate fresh cracked crab in the moonlight and snorkeled in the water. Holly fell in love with the island life under the moonlit sky beneath the sangria sunset while lazing on the rosy beaches. She sat with seashells littering the sand like salmon-colored cornflakes all around her, pieces of coral and soft earth settling beneath bare toes as the cold ocean pushed between them.

The sea could cure all.

It had, she was sure of it. And she would never take another drink.

She made promises to herself, and that was one of them. There was one thing the sea couldn't cure, she'd decided—her marriage.

Seeing her sister happy with someone else made Holly want that too. Something real.

Holly could deal with a broken family, as long as it was a genuine one.

30

One Week Later

The movers had done an excellent job of placing the glassware in the boxes. They'd be stacked and stored in a storage unit until Clay could find a place for them. They certainly wouldn't fit in the tiny apartment above Pickles. Nicky had offered it to Clay at a special rate, but he was sure it was probably so they could keep him under their watch. Maybe over time, if he was a good boy, Nicky would loosen the leash.

One thing was for sure. They owned him now.

His life was no longer his. When he'd inquired about Frankie, they told him she was gone for good this time and that she wasn't coming back. The finality in their statement made him certain that she wasn't returning to New York. It didn't mean he couldn't try to find out where she'd gone, though.

Clay couldn't stay in Sayville anymore, in the house he'd purchased for the family that'd never been, with the wife who was no longer there. And he certainly couldn't live next door to the Carringtons anymore. No one in the town wanted him there. It was time to go.

Peter and Eve had somehow reconciled and withdrawn their divorce documents before they were finalized. They blamed Clay for all their troubles. Clay didn't understand how Peter could stay married to Eve, but she had somehow managed to convince everyone, including Peter, that she'd been victimized by Clay and was only one of many women who had been.

Peyton and Paige, the Carringtons' daughters, shouted obscenities at Clay as he walked by. He'd been run out of his own home and his own town. But he couldn't leave New York per the club's rules.

And the detectives had told him he needed to stick around. The police were selling the public on the fact that Vivian's life was so dreadful with Clay that she'd jumped into the ocean willingly instead of continuing her marriage with him. And it didn't help matters that he now had a boat registered in his girlfriend's name in close proximity to where his wife's jacket had been discovered. A jacket that had Vivian's DNA on it.

Frankie. That boat wasn't a gift. It was a curse. But what the boat and the jacket didn't have was any concrete evidence linking Clay to a murder—so for now, he was free.

As ready as he was to leave his neighborhood, it pained him to see the sign in the yard. FOR RENT. The Realtor had told him she could lease it in less than a week. He couldn't even sell the damn house, because Vivian's name was on the deed. According to New York State law, a missing person couldn't be declared legally dead for at least ten years, typically twenty. It was one more thing to tie him to this place, this eternal hell.

When he'd gone outside to do the required yard work for the Realtor, he'd swept up a bunch of cigarette butts under the large tree that separated his yard from the Carringtons'. All the butts had lipstick marks on the tips, and Clay knew that shade of red.

Eve wouldn't go anywhere near cigarettes. Those were Frankie's smokes.

His hand had wavered on the dustpan as he threw them into the garbage can. Frankie had been watching them. It hadn't all been in Vivian's head. Maybe she'd hired men to watch Vivian, too, first from their house and then in Bay Shore. They were all attempts to lure Vivian away. And kill her.

The "disappearing Polaroid" was a popular device at the club used for two things—proof of life or proof of death. Clay cringed. Even without seeing the picture, he knew which one Frankie had left him—proof of death.

The lengths Frankie and the others had gone to in order to make his wife disappear without a trace left Clay unnerved. He'd been completely unaware of the evil people he'd been dealing with over the years, and now he was stuck with them indefinitely. Until Frankie decided to lift the family curse, he was stuck there, right where she wanted him.

He might never know the true extent of what Frankie had done to his wife, but he was sorry for all of it.

Whatever he'd dished out in pain to his wife, he'd gotten back tenfold. And his little girl was lost forever.

Every time he thought of her, his emotions spun out of control. He hadn't really known Giana, but he'd wanted to badly. Every shred of redemption for a better life could be found in those innocent hazel eyes.

Just then his phone buzzed. A new text message from an unknown number.

It was lyrics to Vivian's favorite Van Morrison song, "Sweet Thing," that she used to sing when they rode the ferry, because the song itself was about blue skies and ferry boats. It felt like an intentional jab. But who was it from?

His phone nearly fell out of his palm, which had grown sweaty with perspiration from cleaning. It was a private moment only they'd shared, one only she knew. Vivian had loved classic rock, old soul that she'd been, and she'd loved the poetry of song lyrics too.

Clay could still remember her singing this one out loud on the ferry in their early days of dating. He wondered what it meant. Who'd sent this to him? Was Frankie still torturing him? Or was it . . . Vivian?

31

Holly came home to a house that sparkled with a gleam that hadn't existed since the first week she and Mark had moved into the neighborhood, pre-children. The laundry was all cleaned, dried, folded, and put away.

The kitchen and the floors were spotless, and there was a sign hanging over the breakfast bar that read, WELCOME HOME, MOM! Holly was truly amazed.

She couldn't believe it.

She'd been embarrassed that her children thought she was sick, but Mark had explained that Mommy wasn't feeling well after they couldn't find her sister, and she just needed to go somewhere and rest. Strangely, Mark had been more right than he could have ever known.

When Mark asked why she looked so tan, Holly had to grit her teeth through the lie that the clinic made them do a lot of meditation walks, and most of the group therapies were held outside. Even though she resented him, she hated lying to him.

Although Holly believed she had gone to rehab, just not the kind he thought.

She'd rehabbed her mind and her soul, and even though it took temporarily losing her sister to realize her marriage was in shambles, it had served its purpose to help her realize it was time to call it quits.

Maybe she could even find her own "Tom" one day, but for now she needed to work on herself. And she needed to get back to work. Return to the thing that fueled her, ignited her with passion. She could be a mother and a journalist—she just might need to leave Mark to do it.

At first Holly felt guilty that Mark had gone through the trouble of thoroughly cleaning the house for her return, but then she'd learned that Sue had used her freshly repaired eyes and her flexible water-aerobic limbs to do it for him. He'd been much too busy with work, you see, and could he have the remaining cash back that she'd promised?

No. She told him that he couldn't.

Because she didn't have access to the checkbook, and the attorney didn't accept credit cards for the retainer fee to file for divorce.

Mark didn't seem totally surprised, although he blamed the facility she'd gone to, calling it *"New Age hippie therapy"*—and insisted Holly's newfound "sobriety" wasn't what was healthiest for the family.

And it *"wasn't what he'd paid for."*

She knew the boys would suffer fallout from a divorce, but in all she'd learned, it was more important for them to have a healthy upbringing, and she couldn't do that with Mark by her side. She'd based their relationship off false pretenses, beliefs that had been pounded into her head by sick people.

Mark claimed Holly should keep him around for safety if she thought Clay's men were still a threat, but Holly didn't think that they were—anymore.

Frankie was out of the picture. Tom was her only surviving brother, and their father wasn't getting out of prison anytime soon. Vivian had felt certain that the Bellinis wouldn't see any upside to coming after them.

Vivian had hugged her sister goodbye on their last day on the beach. Holly didn't know if she'd ever see her again, but they'd promised to keep in touch.

"I'll send you strange cryptic postcards from all the places we travel to," Vivian had said.

"I'm counting on it!" Holly replied. Vivian reminded Holly that she wasn't in trouble, just "missing," and she hadn't committed a crime. Who knew, in years to come, maybe she would even return to the States. Holly had watched as the three of them—Vivian, Tom, and Giana—sailed away, a piece of Holly's heart along with them.

It was a shame Clay would never be reunited with his psychopathic mistress. Giana was better off with Vivian as her new mommy, as cruel as it sounded. Vivian would make a wonderful mother, something she'd been dreaming of for years.

And Clay would receive his punishment in spades, according to the letter Frankie had left for him on the boat—a life sentence working for the club, chained in a town that hated him for life, his wife presumably dead by suicide, his mistress and child—dead. Did he have any idea what happened to them? Did he even care? Not Holly's problem.

Cynthia Forester was probably rolling in her grave that the public believed her daughter had taken her own life, but Holly had officially stopped worrying about anything her mother would have thought or said.

Holly was unpacking her suitcase when she got the text message from Archie.

Archie: Did you make it back? Were the sunsets as nice as he made them out to be?

Holly: Hi! YES, and even better!

Archie: Nice. Now you see why I stayed down there longer than I intended

She smiled because she totally got it. Holly had been allotted two weeks. She'd debated about whether she should take both of them even though she'd solved her puzzle early, but she just couldn't stay away from the boys that long. It was like time stood still on that island, as if the outside world hadn't existed, a parallel realm. Almost like her fuzzy memories, only the ones in Bermuda were real. But when Holly came back, everything had changed, as if she'd entered a true portal to an alternate dimension and she'd come out the other side, emerging as her true self.

Archie had agreed to go with Holly for a walk along the docks. Harley was rubbing his pointy German shepherd ears at Holly's side. Holly thought it was only right he come along. The Port Jefferson ferry was getting ready to take off, and Holly was holding on to an old man's unsteady hand as they walked to the end of the pier. She'd told him all about where Vivian was and how they were the only ones who had this information and to keep it to himself. Deep down inside she knew Vivian would be okay with this alliance. Holly couldn't be happier that she had a secret to share—with her father.

He would never take the place of her other one, but her mother had been wrong about the nature vs. nurture stuff, because Archie being her biological father explained so many of her life's mysteries.

It explained why she hated journaling but had enjoyed the hell out of analysis and math—just like her dad.

Her curly hair, just like Archie's mother's in the picture, made sense now too. Her mother had cursed at it, and now she imagined it was her cursing at Archie for passing it down to Holly. Good thing Mark hadn't let her buy the 23andMe kit when it came out, because she would've really been thrown for a loop. And now she had no need for tests.

She looked at Archie, the kind man with the worn face and coif of wavy white hair who'd helped her find her lost sister.

"Can I do it?" she asked.

"I don't know, kid, can you?" he asked, and his mud-brown eyes were earnest. They'd decided the location should be on the North Shore, just on the off chance that the paper documents should ever resurface. No one knew them on this side of Long Island.

"It's time."

"I think so too. Do it."

Holly had her childhood journals with her, every painful word, including the dreaded journals from that summer before Vivian had been sent away. Vivian's journals had been burned long ago, but Holly added her mother's little black book to the top of the stack under the shoestring pack and weighed it down with a giant stone. She waved it over her head and threw it—into the sound.

ACKNOWLEDGMENTS

Firstly, a very special thank-you to my parents for being nothing like the ones in this book. Dad, I appreciate your reading my work to make sure my male voice was on point. Mom, thanks for reading the many versions of this complicated tale. And to my own older sister—I thought of you often while writing this story. If you ever went missing, I'd come looking for you!

This manuscript has gone through many revisions, and my agent, Ella Marie Shupe, has seen them all. She signed me for the original version of this novel, and I'm tremendously grateful for her patience in helping to shape this story and seeing it through to publication.

To my developmental editor, Caitlin Alexander, who took the time to flesh out all my wild characters: Your suggested changes added an extra layer to this story that wouldn't exist otherwise. Thank you to Liz Pearsons, senior editor, who chose to give this story a place in the literary world. To Sarah Shaw and the whole team at Amazon Publishing for supporting the marketing efforts on this book and to fellow Thomas & Mercer author Kristin Wright for fact-checking my courtroom scene. And to my neighbor Jerry Schirato for checking that courtroom scene again—you earned that bottle of bourbon. Lawyers are good friends to have when writing thrillers.

This novel could not have been completed without my Mindful Writers group led by authors Kathleen Shoop and Larry Schardt. Thank you for giving me the time and space to create my stories during your writing retreats.

Other first readers include: Lisa Coulson, Nick DiAlesandro, Virginia DiAlesandro, Vickie Reinard, Natalie Schirato, Janice Sniezek, and the North Pittsburgh Critique Group: Dana Faletti, Nancy Hammer, Carolyn Menke, and Kim Pierson.

Thank you so much to my friend Jennifer Monasterio, whose hometown, Sayville, was the setting for this novel. Your answers to my research questions made this book possible, and I'm glad Harley made the book too. I owe you for lots—add this book to the list!

To my husband, Justin, thanks for all the delicious meals and for understanding when I needed to pull my own disappearing act for a while to write this novel. And to my children, Jackson and Charlotte, who hopefully learned a lot about making dreams come true by watching their mother reach hers, I love you to the moon and back.

ABOUT THE AUTHOR

Photo © 2019 Lisa Schmidt, Moments Kept Photography

Cara Reinard is an author of women's fiction and novels of domestic suspense, including *Sweet Water*. She has been employed in the pharmaceutical industry for seventeen years, and while Cara loves science, writing is her passion. She currently lives in the Pittsburgh area with her husband, two children, and Bernese mountain dog. For more information, visit www.carareinard.com.